The Day I Found You

The Day
I Found You

Pedro Chagas Freitas

Translated from the Portuguese
by Daniel Hahn

A Oneworld Book

First published in North America, Great Britain and Australia
by Oneworld Publications, 2018
Originally published in Portuguese as *Prometo Falhar* by Marcador, 2014

ISBN 978-1-78607-251-1
eISBN 978-1-78607-204-7

This publication was funded by the Direção-Geral do Livro,
dos Arquivos e das Bibliotecas.

REPÚBLICA
PORTUGUESA

CULTURA
DIREÇÃO-GERAL DO LIVRO, DOS ARQUIVOS E
DAS BIBLIOTECAS

Typeset by Fakenahm Prepress Solutions, Fakenham, Norfolk, NR21 8NL
Printed and bound in Great Britain by Clays Ltd, Elcograf S.p.A.

Oneworld Publications
10 Bloomsbury Street
London WC1B 3SR
England

Stay up to date with the latest books,
special offers, and exclusive content from
Oneworld with our newsletter

Sign up on our website
oneworld-publications.com

MIX
Paper from
responsible sources
FSC® C018072

To Bárbara.
To Benjamim.
Because everything.

A Note to the Reader

With more than 1.3 million followers, Pedro Chagas Freitas is something of a Facebook sensation. One day, he asked his fans to suggest sentences to him, and in return pledged to use those sentences to create a story. It was through this challenge that *The Day I Found You* came into being – an unforgettable book that promises fundamentally to change the way we write and read about love.

It is not just the story behind the book that is original; *The Day I Found You* also has a unique and experimental style. The author chose not to follow grammatical rules, as he is a keen inventor of new things, whether it be unusual sentence structures or the radical use of a punctuation mark in a text, a new children's game or a concept for a television programme. In fact, Pedro Chagas Freitas truly believes that a life without creation would not be a life worth living. And so for him, every day is about discovering something new; a value that shines through very clearly in this remarkable book.

I started loving you the day I left you.

Those were his words, ten years later, when he happened to bump into her in the café. She smiled, she said 'hello, I love you' to him but her lips said only 'hi, you OK?' They talked for hours, until he, for it was always him who became shameless however ashamed he was for what he had done (how could I have left you? how could I have been such an idiot not to realise you were everything I wanted?), until he told her just as natural as anything that he wanted to take her to bed. She first considered slapping him and then loving him all evening and all night long, and then she considered running away from that place and then loving him all evening and all night long, and finally she decided to say nothing at all and, slowly, keeping her tears hidden in her eyes, she walked away from him just as a decade earlier he had walked away from her. It was not a revenge, nor even a punishment – she merely understood that she was so lost in what she felt that she needed to go far away in order to come back into herself. She thought this was probably what had happened to him on that distant day when he had left her, alone and flooded with pain, on the floor, never to return.

Of all the things I love it's you I fall in love with most.

Those were her words, a few minutes later, when he followed her, stubbornly, down to the bottom of the road during rush hour. They were standing facing each other, with everybody walking past not realising that in this very place the future of the world was being decided. He said: 'I married another woman so that I could love you in peace.' She said: 'I married another man so there would be a noise to silence you in me.' In truth neither one of them said any of these things because neither one was a poet. But this was what his words ('I love you like a madman') and her words ('I love you like a madwoman') were really saying. The road stopped, then, confronted with their embrace. There is no memory for anyone, on any day, who thought that their embrace was an embrace of betrayal between two married people. Everyone understood, right there, that the only betrayal would be not embracing that embrace, however much there may have been documents proving the contrary. They never married, never divorced. They didn't want to waste time on unnecessary papers. The only papers they signed, every day, were the ones with the poems that they left for each other, religiously, in the most secluded and secret places in the house. They were not great works, and they always ended without any possible variation, always in the same way: 'I love you'. They never received the praise of a literary critic, at which they were distinctly irritated. They learned, years later, that the whole of society had renounced them. They called them the runaways, even. And they, at that moment, agreed entirely. Both knew that they had run away for ten years. And it had been too long.

I do.

Those were his words when she, at the registry office as it needed to be, asked him if he agreed to never marry him.

I used to be nearly a millionaire, did you know that?,
when I had your grandmother in my life,

the most beautiful woman in the world, no one should doubt that, did I ever tell you I'm certain God only took her away because He was jealous?,

and our house, a whole life ahead of us, so many dreams

and I believed one day I'd get to the Moon, mind you, and I wasn't far off, if you want to know the truth, but I'll tell you that story tomorrow, not today,

and I worked in the finance department and people needed me, they came knocking on my door, they asked me to bring the tax form, such and such a document, and sometimes I'd bring it, and sometimes I wouldn't, I never crossed a line,

except at the wheel, I'll admit, I got up to 120 on that straight stretch of road with the petrol pump on, in my Mini, don't tell your father as I drummed it into his head to go slowly, it's our secret, OK?, cross your fingers and promise, go on,

then Afonso was born, a gorgeous young lad, my boy, when I first held him in my arms I believed in eternal life, mind you, I thought something like that could never end, and perhaps it never did end, it's the things all around that changed,

fifty years working, I was never late once, I was the first in and the last to leave, if you could check with one of those computing things you'd see that I missed work twice in two years, one time when I had a car accident, no big deal, a scratch, the other because I forgot to change my watch to summertime and then I was too ashamed to arrive late, where's shame to be found nowadays?, we've gained so much, cell phones, the internet, and we've lost shame, but who is it that has won?,

my father died on me,

death enters our eyes like an invisible powder, you can understand that already, a person has someone else and then he doesn't, the drama of life is having lives installed in ours, we're a merging of various pieces and losing someone is like an amputation, can you imagine finding yourself suddenly missing a hand?, it hurts more than being left suddenly without your Chocapic cereal, just to give you an idea,

and even then I didn't stop going in to work, I buried my father and went back to finance, I believed in the richness of service, in responsibility, I was an exemplary professional, an exemplary head of the family,

when your father was born I felt like a king, and isn't that how all fathers should feel?,

and this house so full of life, the sounds, the smells,

your grandmother was the best cook in the world, no one should doubt that, did I ever tell you I'm certain God only took her away so He could eat well?,

and you see that chest of drawers next to you?, I bought it for her as a surprise, I'd just received my holiday bonus and I wanted to be happy,

and I still do, you know?, the worst thing of all is that we never stop wanting to be happy and there are more and more things we find ourselves without, but I'm not going to talk about sad things, if you want sad you've only got to look at the face on that teacher of yours, to hell with any woman who doesn't laugh, isn't that right?, but don't go telling your father I said that, OK?, there's that pedagogy thing nowadays says you can't say things like that, what do they know about bringing up children anyway?,

your father was taught by me and just look at the man he became, nothing but mumbo-jumbo all this pedagogy, what's important is to love, and I love you very much, Dioguinho, have just one more little spoonful and I'll tell you some more stuff, OK?,

and so I brought the chest of drawers and the whole house was full and she was pleased with me, Afonso and your father helped me to set it up, three really wonderful hours, make the most of them whenever you can, you promise?,

which is all just to say that I used to be nearly a millionaire, all you need is a full house for you to want for nothing, that's just what a millionaire is,

a millionaire's someone who has everything he wants, isn't that right?,

and I did have, when I close my eyes I still do, but sometimes we do have to open them, like now,

my job, my wife,

the best wife in the world, no one should doubt that, did I ever tell you I'm certain God only took her away so He'd have somebody to marry?,

your father's arrived, and I was just about to tell you about what came after I was nearly a millionaire and now you're already going, there's some meeting and he's got to go, I understand, but it's not easy, don't tell him, there's a meeting at seven and he's still going to leave you at some friend's place on the way,

I never left him with anyone, there were so many times I took him with me to the department and he adored it, he'd play around with the computer, he asked me what money was and what was it for, between you and me I'd have liked him still to have those doubts today, maybe staying here with us a little longer, me, you and him at this table, the hearth lit, it would be good to ask him about life, what he does, what he feels, what he dreams of,

but I know nothing about what your father wants, I even suspect I don't know anything about what he is, so many years have passed since I last told him I love him,

I love you, son, do you love me back?,

and he's gone now and you've gone now, and the whole house, so quiet, the chest of drawers gathering dust, even the chest of drawers misses you, my princess, my queen, where did we go wrong to end up like this?, you dead and me alone, so which of us died first then?,

and I just keep going, I have Dioguinho here sometimes, did you see him leaving a moment ago, he's a man now, isn't he?, Carlinha hasn't been in weeks, she's already in third grade, can you believe it?, but time doesn't exist, they tell me, and I believe it, I have to believe it to keep on going, you know that,

you were the best person in the world, no one should doubt that, did I ever tell you I'm certain God only took you away in order that He might be a better creature?,

I used to be nearly a millionaire and time began to take it all from me, first you,

I love you, my wife, do you love me back?,

then the boys, their time, at least, then they reformed me and killed me a little, and mind you, they're now taking a few euro from me at the end of the month, I don't know if I'm going to be able to pay for the medication, you never got to end up as an old woman, such luck, life isn't measured in days, I know that now, life is measured in chemists' shops,

there's a government that wants to lower the deficit,

and you don't want to know what that means and nor do I, it basically means taking from the poor to give to the rich, and this coming from me who doesn't understand anything and who's just an old reactionary, bad people don't change, do they?,

and so lowering this deficit they take what I had left, I don't want to ask Afonso for money, or Carlos, God preserve me with some dignity yet, I'll figure things out as best I can, if there isn't enough for me to eat steak I'll eat soup, as I heard a lady say the other day on TV, I don't even like steak all that much, except yours, of course,

I used to be nearly a millionaire and now I'm nearly dead, it hurts a lot but it's bearable,

what scares me most are the secrets in the darkness, which is why I go out to put an end to the silence,

out on the street there's noise enough to cry without anybody noticing, will you come walk with me?,

you are the best companion in the world, no one should doubt that, did I ever tell you I'm certain God only took you away in order to have somebody to walk with?

Why should I love you,

you ask,

and I speak to you in the noise of the wind in the window when you hold me tight, your head in the mystery that is between arms and shoulders, I hide my fingers in your hair and I hear you breathing, people like us don't look for explanations but survivals.

We should learn to love slowly,

you venture,

and yet I have already placed my lips on yours, your scent is unbearable if I cannot touch you, we would be whole if there were only words, and the most absurd thing is that we don't even need to talk, people like us don't look for eternity but for feelings,

Every moment deserves an orgasm,

I make this up,

trying to prove to you that poems are made of flesh, never of lines of verse, strangely you do not reply and you allow yourself to be looked at, I spend more than an hour just seeing you and it's everything, I ask you to assume every kind of position, there must be some angle or other that isn't entirely yours and your almost-heaven smile, but I don't find it, people like us don't look for skin but the knife,

There's a certain dignity in the way we abandon ourselves,

I say goodbye,

I dress slowly while I love you at last, life doesn't feel sorry for any more than we have, we could try the possibility of a routine, and who knows, perhaps the calm adrenaline of a family, a morning kiss and another at night, a bed not only for sex, even talking that has some objective that isn't pure pleasure, but I don't know if it's love that turns me on, people like us don't look for peace but for fear,

Tomorrow or some other day or how about never,

you declare,

and I understand then that you have given me the most profound declaration of love, tomorrow or some other day or never, and I consent with no hesitation, people like us don't look for promises but still they never fail each other.

There was once a boy who dreamed too much, and one day he dreamed there was a special sheet of paper, so special that it made everything that was written on it come to life and be real, the boy loved the idea and went off to tell his parents

'you're crazy'

but the boy was a boy who dreamed too much and he didn't give up on dreaming, and instead of giving up on the idea he made the idea grow, that's the advantage of being a boy and dreaming, when if you're a boy who dreams and instead of stopping at the dream you make the dream expand, you dream even bigger, bigger still

'and what if instead of a sheet of paper it was a whole notebook?'

and the boy ran off to the bookstore, asked for two sheets of the cheapest paper they had, dreams don't need to be expensive and the boy knew it, after all the best toys he had weren't toys at all, a ball made of rags, a screw that to him is the Eiffel Tower, a block of wood that he's transformed into a car

'vroooom'

him and the blank page, that first experience of magic, here he can invent anything he wants because he has invented the magic sheet of paper, just write it down and it happens, he doesn't know many letters or many words, he's only lately started school, he writes what he knows and what it is he wants deep down

'dad'

then he looks at it and likes it, he rubs out one mark or another, he makes it just right so it all works out perfectly, so the magic happens the way it should, he looks again, it's perfect now, just one word and maybe the magic will happen

'mum'

now tear out the page and the magic will happen, now is when he's going to test out his invention

'dad'
'mum'

and they arrived, the boy tore out the sheet, he read the words several times, and they appeared, perhaps concerned about him, perhaps not knowing what has happened, but the truth is that it happened, the boy explains to his parents once again that he'd invented the magic sheet of paper first and then the magic notebook after that, his parents take a deep breath first and then reprimand him

'don't scare us like that again'

the boy didn't understand, what's wrong with dreaming?, and he went on with his invention that would change the world, simply write and the world would change, imagine what could be done with that, he thought of a thousand and one things to write, a thousand and one things to invent, but he understood then that he didn't know how to write and he needed to know how to write for the sheet of paper to do its job, he could cry and be like all those other boys who don't get what they want and they cry and then stop, but this boy was different like that and when he had a dream he didn't cry but did

'please teach me writing till the cartoons start'

his older sister laughed but she didn't refuse, and at the end of the day, when they returned from school, off the two of them went to the bedroom, nobody knew what they were up to, they said they had work to do and they did, but the boy alone was fighting for his dream, his sister liked playing teacher and taught him everything, all the letters, and twenty or thirty days later the boy who just wanted to dream already had all the tools to create his dream

'there was once'

that's how it started because it seemed to him that was how dreams always started, and he went on writing, line by line, invention by invention, and bit by bit he began to understand that his notebook was even more magical than the one he had invented, you didn't even need to tear the sheet out for it to exist, he went on writing and as he wrote he felt everything happening, the prince who wanted to fly, the princess who wanted to be saved, the boy wrote and all of it happened, he saw it right there, in front of him, inside him, even inside him, every emotion, he laughed, smiled, even cried, would you believe it

'how can you say it doesn't exist if it makes me cry?'

and many years later when there were hundreds of adults and children from a primary school sitting in front of him, he was introducing one more of his books, and he decided to offer each of them a special gift

'it's a notebook with superpowers'

and he handed them a heap of blank sheets of paper just like the one that changed his life

'whatever you write on it really happens'

and everybody laughed except the children, who started trying it out at once.

You are in apartment 4B and I don't know what I'm doing with these nerves,

to hell with love, dammit,

it's so much easier not loving but what the hell are we doing here if we don't love?,

I brought my best shirt, I asked my mother to iron it, I really do like my mother so much, that might be the first secret I tell you, keep it well, and we haven't even spoken for more than two minutes yet, would you believe it, and the second secret is that I love you, or something of that kind,

and I don't yet know what love is really, I'm quite sure that nobody knows, but this seems like the thing we see in books, it really does,

and I ring the doorbell and there's your voice,

oh hell, how can a voice mess with so many different parts of your body?,

come up, and I come up, there's an elevator on the left but I've got more than enough suffocation on the inside already, I take the stairs and that way I have time to think about you,

and I'm not even with you yet and already we're alone together,

and I count the steps and my hands sweat,

you promise that when I kiss you you'll show me what to do with my tongue?,

in English class the teacher saw me looking at you and she smiled, I hope she didn't say anything to you, I want you to learn that I love you from my own mouth,

I'm a serious kind of man, take note of that,

and I arrive up here, I give my hair a quick tidy, I hope you like the Ronaldo style I did just for you, the gel's only the Miniprice own brand but it's the thought that counts, I've brought you a photo of you that I've printed off your Facebook profile,

who's that dude who's always around drooling over you anyway?,

and I look at my reflection in the glass and I prepare myself for the most important moment in my life,

every time I meet you it's the most important moment in my life, did you know that?,

you left the door ajar and that might be a sign, I read somewhere yesterday that to love is to keep a door always ajar, now we'll find out if that's true, literature has a solution for everything, I know that line is nothing special but at least it's mine,

do what you like with it, but with me just put your arms round me, please,

and I go in and you aren't there to receive me, you must be in the living room, most likely, I look around and search for signs of your existence, I would have bet that painting was done by you, only yesterday your mother told me you're very talented, and she's right,

and I swear even if you told me Sporting was your favourite team I'd say you're still perfect,

the living room is large and you're on the sofa, I can tell by your hair resting on the cushion, and the television is on,

do you want to watch that movie with me for the rest of your life?,

and I'm already standing in front of you and I see you're

sleeping, I love your hair but right now you might move it aside a little so I can see your face, just a minute ago you spoke to me and now you're asleep already, or did the stairs take longer than they seemed to?, I don't know what to do, I stand there looking at you and loving you all alone,

standing there looking at you and loving you even all alone is always the right decision,

I still entertain the possibility of saying something but I give up, I'll let you sleep and come back later, I'll write you a note,

I was here and I'll be here always, how does that sound?,

and I sneak out, I look back at you one last time over my shoulder, you're still on the sofa,

you're as beautiful as a title-winning goal, how's that for a declaration of love?,

and you don't even know that I existed here, that I consumed you here, me and you in the intimate moment of your sleep,

we still haven't even kissed and we've already slept together, would you believe it,

and I close the door gently so as not to wake you, down I go in the elevator, despite everything I'm already breathing easier,

a second looking at you and my lungs open up completely,

I press zero and when I look at your door I see a number and a letter that get me thinking,

apartment 3B,

and maybe there's still time to go back up, you're in apartment 4B and with all these nerves I don't know what I'm doing,

to hell with love, dammit.

Just because I'm vaccinated against dengue doesn't mean I'm going to offer myself up to the mosquitoes,

you say so many things that are entirely your own and it's just my fucking luck to have you here, I've loved you even before knowing how and maybe that's the only way to love, I don't know, I'm just saying, before you I thought about the impossibility of a mouth like that,

the first time we slept together we forgot to sleep,

the door to the veranda of my minuscule apartment open, and hellish winter out there and a happy hell in here,

you had a laughing skull printed on your knickers, either that or it was my happy body that was laughing and the skull was as dead as any other,

we were forbidden but we loved each other like God, till death do us part, it's quite clear, the problem is that there were several deaths to experience and that's why here we are,

how many times is it possible to love you for the first time?,

because I want one more, just this one, today we came to a hotel to die better,

I want one of these beds at home,

and you lie down,

and I like it when you play at being grown-ups with me, you invent expressions nobody really says, talk to me about the most trivial things in the world, how that girl with a blog has gone to Brazil, there's a sale at Zara,

and the poem is in the voice, not the verse,

we hugged for a time on the escalator, I can assure you there was an adolescent couple who envied our irresponsibility,

when I embrace you I hope for an embrace, and for it to be you,

our boredom thrills me, your hands on the hair of my chest,

being happy is so simple, isn't it?,

I'm looking at you as I see you, your lips are like clouds when I look at you over my glasses and over a handful of words,

this morning I remembered the times I made you cry, and I cried,

I'm so little for your size, I write some crap that only I understand, and it's inexplicable that you should be mine,

one day I will be a candidate for the Nobel with your skin,

touching you made me a writer, and oh man how lucky,

I write in order to love you better, I think I've already written that before but here it is again, the most ironic thing is that while I'm writing you miss me,

maybe you also write in order to know that you love me, who knows?, but it's truer than true that I mostly write to take you to bed, or didn't you think so?,

I could invent a Bible just for my faith in you, but you don't deliver me from evil, amen,

just because I'm vaccinated against dengue doesn't mean I'm going to offer myself up to the mosquitoes,

you say again,

have I told you I know your crooked teeth by heart when you smile?,

we have only this night for loving each other tonight,

why did I need you in order to be able to live like this?,

we need to make a choice between loving and writing, and I choose you,

perhaps one day I'll know which side you're on.

You're wearing the blue watch I gave you for your birthday and the promise of a kiss, it's all I need to do to open up your arms and invite you under the sheets,

there's such cold in me when you're not around,

I've closed the windows and my eyes and there's no way of getting to sleep, hearing the whole city filled with people and none of them is you,

God happens through difference,

and through the way when you arrive you smile at me and apologise for being late again, with the office and those meetings, it's nearly ten seconds before I wordlessly say come over here and embrace you inside,

there is one life only and you are so unending in me.

We meet as ever in the centre of the abyss, your thick veins, I call you to that space in me where even the skin dares not reach, and love happens,

and I really do feel like just staying still, just listening to our breathing as it calms, my mouth dry but I can't risk missing a second too far from your lips, I have to preserve the moment, each one, whisper in your ear just how deeply I love you, rest my head on your chest and hope that there is never again an afterwards,

but in a few moments you're already gone, you realise the time and the bed is empty again, you say sorry, you slip your body, how I need your body, beneath your clothes, you kiss me gently without telling me you love me, and you leave the bedroom, your phone already in your hand and you answering,

I am, yes,

and by the way you talk it might be your wife asking if you're running late.

and I love you so much but today I've got to take the car to the mechanic, the wheels are making a funny noise, it's probably nothing but it's best just to check, tomorrow I promise we'll see, how about if we eat at that new restaurant by the roundabout, and then I'll take you to the movies, oh boy won't I take you there,

and I love you so much but today I've got to watch the kid doing his practice, the coach called and told me we've got a real ace, our boy's playing like a grown-up, would you believe it, when I arrive back with him see if you can have that food he loves ready, the little bastard deserves it, oh boy does he deserve it,

and I love you so much but today I've got to work late at the office, there's that foreign guy's project to complete, everything here is desperately stressed, I don't know if I can take it, I'll call soon to find out how you're doing, with the kid and everything at home, right now I've got to go show these people what hard work looks like, oh boy do I have to show them,

and I love you so much but tonight I've got to get to bed early, tomorrow's that important meeting I told you about, if we manage to hook this client we'll be so pleased, that house, the new car, who knows?, I just have to try and persuade him, I've got everything all ready in my head and nothing can go wrong, we're going to be rich, mark my words, oh boy won't we be,

and I love you so much but you're not there today, I arrived at the time we'd arranged to take you to dinner but you weren't there, and the kid wasn't either, he must be at practice, OK let me just call, no one's answering, neither you nor him, you're probably planning something, you've always been like that, full of surprises, any second now you'll come through that door and tell me you love me, oh boy won't you tell me,

and I love you so much but today I've got to sign this piece of paper, I look at you and say sorry, I promise there will be no more mechanics or practices or foreign clients or meetings coming between us, I assure you that I want you above anything, I look you in the eye one more time and I try to soothe what is hurting in you, but you just tell me to sign and I sign, hands trembling and I've even shed a tear on them, when our son learns about it he is going to cry like a little kid all over again, our ace, you could at least stay for our ace, or at least for me, to keep me alive, God protect me from not having you with me, I'm an impossibility if I don't have you to like, oh boy aren't I,

and I love you so much but today I've got nothing to do, the house is dark, an empty silence and nothing to do, just wait for you to forget me and go back to loving me, and I love you so much, oh boy don't I love you?

'A tightrope is the only thing that ties you to life.'

'But it hurts. It trembles.'

'And yet hold on. And yet cling on. Make yourself want more of that thing for ever. It's only what slips through your fingers that really proves that you have fingers at all. Only when you're facing near-death that you value life.'

'Do you like trembling?'

'I need to tremble. I need to feel the tightrope wobbling, my legs wobbling, my body wobbling. It's only what takes me out of myself that feeds me. An orgasm makes me tremble, a euphoria makes me tremble.'

'A pain, too.'

'I need to understand what I am, even if it hurts. Only someone who trembles can understand what he is. Other people aren't really able to be: they just are. And they never tremble. I feel so sorry for anybody who's never trembled. What are they doing here? Only things that have made me tremble have ever been unforgettable.'

'Life is there to have unforgettable moments.'

'Never forget that. Life's only there if something in you is trembling. It's only what makes you tremble that stops you forgetting.'

'I make you tremble.'

'Always.'

'And when I stop?'

'We'll have to find other paths. Other ways.'

'Other people?'

'If we must. People keep you attentive, keep you alert, keep you connected. When a person you love makes you disconnect, they're no longer a person you should love. Love demands maximum vigilance, you must be a soldier on the battlefield, your whole body awaiting an attack, a stray bullet. And if there's one area in which love is unbeatable it's in the quantity of stray bullets it releases. Sometimes you get hit and you don't even notice. And then love no longer exists, just a pain spreading through the middle of your chest, a pain that consumes you, tears you to pieces, brings you down. You think it's love and it's nothing but a wound. There are wounds that resemble love.'

'A moment of distraction and love is over.'

'A moment of distraction and life is over.'

'That's what I said.'

What changed without you was mostly the size of things,

of this bed, for example, which was ridiculously small when we loved each other,

how many times did we decide to buy a bigger one, we'd open some catalogue or other, but then we'd forget about it because there was this one and our bodies right here and maybe that was enough for us to be happy, wasn't it?,

the sweat and the tumbles, the whispered words, our breathing lost but not as lost as the rest of us,

I'm not wearing any panties today,

remember when you used to say that to me, your total smile and me at your feet, a bed isn't enough space when you want somebody like that, and now it's so big it's unbearable,

did I ever tell you that when your well-bred father admitted to me that you were the result of a quickie that I replied he had to be entirely mistaken because, like they say, haste is the enemy of perfection?, I'm such a fool, aren't I?, I was just lucky you still loved me all that time,

houses aren't measured in metres, but in silences,

the huge living room, the same four or five pieces of furniture, the TV, the sofa, and so much space to fill, not to mention the size of the pain I'm feeling, of course,

you made me addicted to violence, that's what it is,

and now everything's too calm, and all I wanted was a banal story, the family everybody wants and a more-or-less life to be getting on with, but you showed me where orgasm starts and now we see how little are the banal things I can manage without you,

looking is the beginning of terror, I know that now,

even your cruelty fascinates me, the way you slyly show me your body and you thrill me, what would I have gained in peace and lost in life if it hadn't been for that street on that day?,

you were in the most beautiful dress in the history of fashion and I'm telling you this as someone who didn't even see what you were wearing, because above it your eyes and face were happening and one really must prioritise and I did,

faces exist for hands,

or at least yours did for mine, I barely knew you and I was already risking everything with my right hand fitting perfectly on to your skin, thumb touching your lips, closed eyes seeing live for the first time which part of me happiness comes from,

if butterflies live such a short time why is it that the one that flies in you is still holding out?,

to hell with the Animal Protection Society and all the

other associations, I'm going to stop feeding it and let it end up however it may, between awareness and madness I prefer whichever one brings you back, or rather the one that doesn't bring you back at all, and until then I'll wear a shawl or two and a piece of cloth over my chest,

I've always heard you have to cover the dead as a matter of respect.

You're the woman of my life but the body has needs, you know?,

time exists, and the skin sags, and excitement must be fed with whatever escapes from my love for you, I don't tell you because I know you'd be hurt,

somebody invented exclusivity in love,

and when I seek out other bodies maybe I'm even paying tribute to you and maybe I'm even being a son-of-a-bitch traitor, just another husband being unfaithful to his wife, or to be more accurate I'm being both at the same time, as I love you like a madman and I also betray you like a madman,

whoever said that liking someone this much had to make sense was a fool,

I'm as perfect as I am imperfect when I don't stop belonging to you when I belong to other women,

but I swear to God I love you to the very depths of my days.

You are the woman of my life but you are too beautiful for me to be able to confess to you,

you stroke my hair when I lie with you on the sofa, run your hand through it,

have I already said that God invented your hand to use as a mould for making all the others?,

and over my skin and the world calms, there isn't work happening, or meetings, or even guilt, just look, even that stops happening when you touch me like that, you're so beautiful that it's you who calms the betrayal that pains me in you,

no truth has the right to end with a moment like that, I tell you that I am crazying you, I invent the verb to crazy so as to love you better and so for a few seconds, with that smile you give me, you grant my conscience a little reprieve,

but I swear to God I love you to the very depths of my days.

You are the woman of my life but I am weak in all my life,

and I know that deep down you don't deserve a man like this, those other women,

how many were there after all?,

in between us and you believing in a perfect love, you may not believe it but I do, I love you with all the innocence in the world and the treacherous body isn't what's going to change that,

where have you ever known the concrete to have anything to say about the divine?,

and I continue to respect you more than myself,

morals were invented by somebody who didn't know the dimensions of love,

I make you happy and that's enough for me,

but I swear to God I love you to the very depths of my days.

You are the woman of my life and you had no right to mess with my things,

we always respect privacy and that was the only reason I was careless, the cell phone put down and forgotten about, and your curiosity, all that's left are the tears that stop me from breathing,

I ask your forgiveness, I kneel just like in the movies, but you don't address a single word to me, you gather up half a dozen things and you leave,

your eyes on the floor and a pain interrupting my life,

and I sit at the window to smoke my first cigarette without you, I see you leave,

so many minutes in the stationary car,

you're trying to find the strength that I didn't have to confess my humanity to you,

but I swear to God I love you to the very depths of my days.

So many homeless people,

and yet the deficit is down and the economy's growing,

today I fell asleep thinking about a new book, a novel with people who don't exist and who are already beginning to populate me, it may well be a pathology but I make art of it,

we have to make the most of what we've got, right?,

but I ended up falling asleep thinking about the good fortune of being able to fall asleep thinking about a book and not about being hungry, or about how I'm going to eat the next day, or even my kids' torn clothes and worn-out shoes,

what the hell is the point of a book if you haven't got a piece of bread?,

and literature isn't much when faced with life, I do very little to change the world, I just sit in this comfortable chair, facing the sea,

you have to look at reality from a distance for it not to hurt, isn't that right?,

and I write words that sometimes I don't know where they're heading, like these, for example, where deep down all I want to do is clear my conscience of not doing more for those who are worth as much as I am but who haven't found the same space, the same path,

sometimes a comma is enough to change a life, isn't it?,

people write because they're cowards, there are so many useful things to be doing out there, help a little old man over the crossing,

yesterday this brat wanted to give up his seat for me on

the bus and I told him to go to hell and I wasn't far from giving him a smack across the gob,

where have you ever seen a child giving up his seat for another, right?,

or cleaning the beaches, or the ocean, working like billy-o, as my grandfather used to say,

how many houses did you help to be born?, and myself none at all,

I'm so useless, I should be helping the world to grow, I dunno, but I'm a coward and I write some bits of rubbish or other, I came to believe that I was making a difference, I imagined a woman on the edge of the abyss and a few words from me pulling her back up,

the best literature is the kind that saves lives but it's only the stuff that kills that wins prizes, have you thought about that?,

and I'm so incapable of having courage, of yelling out, of devoting myself to activities that are happy, dancing, singing, telling jokes, even making a child,

I'll always be the son, never the father, isn't that so?,

and the worst is that I never stop writing the same book, one comma more or less, one pronoun more or less, with more or less style, I hang around writing only one book and it's the only thing that satisfies me,

how do you fall asleep with a whole book to write and only one life to live?,

and in spite of it all how do they do it, those people out there?,

my God, living is so badly paid,

we need to turn soup into a banquet, perhaps, how I'd like to be out there, yelling at the bastards that there was no way, that there's no country without people, or numbers without anyone to count them, but instead I write and that's where I get my satisfaction,

I'm weak and I hope my weakness makes someone else strong, isn't that right?,

there's a woman in trouble down there and it's time to take off my glasses, what you don't see you only feel, I'm really sorry,

there are more and more people wrecked on the streets,

and yet the deficit is down and the economy's growing.

He came down the bannister so as to love more quickly,

will you play with me, will you please?, the whole nursery available and his eyes on the way she picked up the Lego, he wanted to play with her, he doesn't know why, he can't guess why, but something draws the little boy to the little girl,

there's always something that draws us towards the smallest things in the world, and they are the things that make us great, isn't that right?,

the teacher smiles, she would quite like never to forget this image, his tenderness as he takes her hand, love is beautiful from the moment it begins, a vast house to be built in blocks of every colour, every size, she looks at him fearfully, then gives a little smile, hands him another piece,

here, it's for you,

and manages to produce the purest declaration of love a human being is capable of,

here, it's for you,

he accepts and builds, even if the two of them are building already,

will you play with me, will you please?,

and she said no, and she did.

He came down the bannister so as to love more quickly,

read with me, will you please?, a desperate happy request, only a child can manage a state of happy desperation, they're the first letters they write and they should be, if they knew how to draw an 'l', for example, I love you, but they aren't, they still aren't, soon enough perhaps, for now they are simpler words, him beside her, he doesn't grab her hand and doesn't show her the path of the 'a' because he can't do it, the teacher says he can't, but they've already looked at each other seven or eight times in the last few minutes, nothing was left unsaid, it never is,

do you want to come with me to the end of the ABC?,

read with me, will you please?,

and she said no, and she did.

He came down the bannister so as to love more quickly,

discover with me, will you please?, they touched gently in the hallway, her left arm against his right arm, or maybe it was the other way around, his left arm against her right arm, no one knows who touched whom, only that the two of them felt the touch as though they were suddenly discovering the beginning of their skin, two or three millimetres, half a second, no more, and the veins dilated more than ever, the high school can't imagine it but two people have just been born here, there are parts of the body that appear from nothing, absurd mental stimuli, a philosophical conclusion only within the reach of geniuses, or of fools,

the direction life travels is from me to you,

nobody says it but they both hear it, many people spend years waiting for a revelation like it, the hallway is full, the groups, pimples, nerves, panics, inventions, distresses, the absurd fear of a life ahead,

discover with me, will you please?,

and she said no, and she did.

He came down the bannister so as to love more quickly,

live with me, will you please?, they're grown-ups and they want to be big, to love like grown-ups, a house, just a room for starters, it could even be in a university hall of residence, the parents won't find out, and to hell with it if they do, they've spent their whole lives waiting to wake up together and fall asleep together and it's time, no one's going to stop them, he'll get himself a job, something part time at McDonald's or whatever's suitable, she's already asked the friend of a friend of the owner of a perfume store to arrange a shift for her, soon they'll be together whenever they are at home,

when you wake up wake me up so I can watch you waking up, OK?,

they know that living like this is transient, that feeling like this is transient, but they also know that living like this is eternal, that feeling like this is eternal, they are young and irresponsible and they don't know what the future has in store for them, no one does, but each has the other in store for them and after all that's a good start,

live with me, will you please?,

and she said no, and she did.

He came down the bannister so as to love more quickly,

marry me, will you please?, it wasn't the most romantic setting, an office in the centre of town, and her not knowing how to answer, a government secretary can't simply embrace one of the heads of the creative department just like that, there are already colleagues with sidelong glances, she has to disguise her happiness, and he who will once again forego the elevator so as to reach her more quickly felt a tightening in his chest, the sweat running but that didn't matter, he looked at her lips waiting for them to move, an inexplicable tension in the air, someone has already got a coffee and sat down, all they need is the popcorn or with a bit of luck not even that because the new machine is ready to use now,

all you have to do is sign and love me for ever, it's only the signing bit that's new, right?,

two or three people cover their mouths so their laughter can't be heard, their jealousy, she doesn't cover anything but nor does she answer, she smiles like she can't stop smiling when he says these things, and the truth is he's the only person who says these things, or it's only him from whom she can hear these things, which might seem the same but it isn't,

marry me, will you please?,

and she said no, and she did.

He came down the bannister so as to love more quickly,

die with me, will you please?, the hospital elevator smells of loss, he rejected it as he has always rejected elevators, even the stairs, he had to reach her more quickly and his old age would not prevent his courage,

before you were ill my back was giving me pain and now it's only you who's giving me pain, thank you,

the white bed, white skin, some white liquid going into her veins, such big tears to cry and a smile coming out,

you have all the episodes of the soap recorded for you to watch, when will you drop everything and come away?,

she stretches out her lips as best she can, she still can, when she sees him she really can, she even says a few words, she still believes in the possibility of for ever, he closes his eyes to swallow his tears, takes a deep breath, thinks she can't see but she sees everything, an insoluble knife piercing the breast, to love is to have the certainty of one day taking an insoluble knife to the breast, and not much more, and yet everything,

    die with me, will you please?,

    and she said no, and she did.

    He came down the bannister so as to love more quickly,

    (…)

    but there was no bannister.

'I like your clothes. But I'm sure I'm going to like your skin even more.'

She had just seen him for the first time and already she had loved him for ever. Love is so easy when nobody complicates it.

'Give me five minutes to have known you for years.'

The problem with people is that they think that for something to have meaning it has to be difficult, that to be true it has to be protracted, and that was probably how he looked at her, his eyes moving in search of the world, an inveterate worldomaniac, incapable of being alive without loving.

'I don't know you from anywhere but I'm yours for ever.'

All declarations of love are premature, and this was no exception, he still wasn't talking but there was the body, the gestures, the way he moved while waiting for afterwards to happen, you don't need a name to love someone.

'I'd like to get to know you better and I can't think of a better place to do that than my body.'

A lot might have been lacking from what they said but there was no lack of urgency, they didn't have time to know who they were but they had time to know what they wanted, around them people danced, people drank, people sang, lights flashing, the music loud, heavy beats, her looking at him and him looking at her, there are too many meanings when you look in that way.

'I've travelled the world but I've never seen anywhere more beautiful than the coastline of your shoulders.'

The bathrooms were also made for loving, the washbasin is the right height, the wall is comfortable, the graffiti might even be exciting, all you need is people who love each other for a space to be made for loving.

'I want to marry you and maybe this is the moment for you to tell me your name.'

Two strangers joined together in matrimony, there will be difficult discoveries, there are so many things he won't like about her, there are so many things she won't like about him, there will be arguments, difficulties, bills to pay, frequent tears, but they will always return to the territory of those shoulders, names will be forgotten, papers torn while the bodies last, love requires two strangers united by what makes them love, and courage.

'We were so happy that night, and we still are.'

Love is so easy to understand.

And so I started loving you for your feet, I was working in the shoe shop in the shopping centre,

or the mall, I dunno what the right term is for it,

and you arrived, your smile, you were in a hurry but you wanted the perfect shoe, I immediately liked that way you had of showing that you were demanding but doing it with the least possible effort,

life is too small for us to waste energy on something that doesn't involve love,

you had the most beautiful feet in the world and I felt like a king serving you, a shoe shop really can be a kingdom when I'm at your feet,

it didn't take long for you to find what you wanted, some green shoes that weren't too flashy and which only served to make you more impossible, and you left,

were you aware that I felt the space between me and the world growing as you went?,

I waited for you to come back another day but it took you four or five weeks, your feet once again, my happiness once again, but it wasn't long before I understood that your feet were no longer enough for me, I wanted more of you, to climb up you,

how do we invite God to be our lover?,

I could even have asked you out, for a drink, talked to you about myself and about loving you already, but I preferred to change stores and in less than a week I was already at Andreia's boutique ready to wait for you, there were no clothes that weren't made with your body in mind, you came at least once a week, here you opened up more and I was now allowed to look at your body,

not that I wasn't still in love with your feet, you do understand, don't you?,

you particularly liked short dresses, not too short,

I'm young enough to be beautiful but not to be a hooker, you said many times to Andreia and such envy I felt towards her,

one day I'm going to have my own store just to be able to call you by your first name,

I was addicted to you, to your feet, to the way the clothes touched and loved your body, but I only started loving your face slowly, I was moving up your outside and I just needed to improve what was seeing you,

I could even have asked you out, for a drink, talked to you about myself and about loving you already, but I preferred to change stores and in less than a week I was already at the make-up store on the first floor ready to wait for you,

as you can imagine it was no picnic, far from it, a man doing make-up isn't easy to take even nowadays, but a quick course at the job centre, a couple of friendly words here and there, and I'd done it,

and your face was a kind of eternity, and I only say a kind because I don't believe eternity is really that unending,

you would come on special occasions,

I only don't do my own make-up when there's an important event, a party or something, you'd explain, which meant you did exactly the opposite to everyone else, you put on your make-up to go to the bathroom, to your parents' house, but never for a party, it was here that I really started to touch you, look at the goosebumps I'm getting just from the memory, see?,

your skin didn't exist however much I touched it, if I had any doubts that you came from a cloud they'd be finished here, at the moment when for the first time your cheekbones, your forehead, an unforgivable light filling the store, not to mention your lips, you always chose the most discreet lipstick, and when you left I'm sure even the food court stopped to look at you, it was my good fortune to be able to appreciate your lips from the outside but there was an urgency in me to know them from within,

it was a complicated mission but I got there, people saw me as the crazy employee and they were right, I was well aware of how hard it would be to move again to some other store but I had to try, I convinced Dona Laura that I was an expert in candies and actually I was,

I knew exactly the curve of your lower lip, the precise angle at which the upper one met it, if that isn't understanding candies I don't know what is,

you went to the store whenever you wanted to spoil yourself, and therefore every day, you liked those cola bottle candies, before you'd even paid for them you already had two or three in your mouth, it wasn't elegant but it was you,

elegance is the moment when you happen, that's all,

and I felt an unacceptable covetousness and slowly I did feel that the inside of your mouth is the best thing in the world but maybe the inside of your clothes is the best best thing in the world,

I'm sorry about the repetitive nature of the phrases I use

but writing a state that surpasses happiness is difficult because of seeming like nobody has never felt it before me,

as I was telling you I wanted more than the inside of your mouth, I wanted the inside of your clothes and I had to take some steps towards that,

I could even have asked you out, for a drink, talked to you about myself and about loving you already, but I preferred to change job and in less than a week I was already at the health club in the centre of town ready to wait for you,

I don't believe anyone has ever got through the massage course as quickly as I did it, they were two intense weeks but I made it to the end, I took the tests in a single day, I got home and didn't know where to put my arms,

or maybe I really did, I just had to put them on you and I would be ready for another three or four more of the same courses in a row,

more than anything you liked to have happiness across your back, you'd been faithful to Marisa for more than five years, every week there you were for her to free you from the weight of the days,

a successful executive like you finds it so hard to impose your authority, don't you?,

I'm really not sure how I managed to persuade her to take the day off on the day you were coming, I probably even had to go out with her just to be able to touch you, but when at last the skin of your lower back was in my hands I felt ready to die right there,

I don't know if I really did die, honestly, maybe it's from heaven or hell that I'm talking to you now,

at last I had the inside of your clothes, your feet, all of

your outside, your face, your lips, the inside of your lips, I couldn't ask life for any more and yet I couldn't stop asking, I'm human and I wanted more,

that was when I decided to ask you out, for a drink, talked to you about myself and about loving you already, I could even change stores

but don't think for a moment I was going to work in a sex shop.

Death is behind your kiss,

　　and I'm not interested in anything that can't kill me.

　　I don't want paths without stones, people without problems, let alone glory without tears. I don't want the tedium of just keeping on going, the obligation to bear up, to maintain a routine just for the sake of it. I don't want the on we go, the that's life, the it's got to be, nothing that doesn't make me moan. I don't want a dish that's always healthy, the pristine salad, the chaste bed, the virgin sex. I don't want sun all day long, straight lines without a single curve, I don't want smooth black or immaculate white, I don't want a perfect poem or undamaged spelling. I don't want to learn only from a teacher, the little pat on the back, the come on it'll pass soon enough, the micro-satisfactions, the tiny euphorias. I don't want lips without a tongue, a tongue without pleasure, running away from whatever provokes fear, even growing accustomed to whatever causes me pain. I want what doesn't fit into the usual, what isn't understood in manuals, what doesn't happen in screenplays. I want the exquisite wrinkle, the untended hand, the risky road, the rain, the wind, the ingrown nail, the animal in the moment. I even want to try what no one else has done before, to look at the unforgivable, spend the possibilities like a madman. Above all I want you to frighten me, the secret abyss, the inside of your legs, how the sweat runs down the middle of your chest, and the impossible way you express yourself when you come.

　　They told me your kiss killed and I paid no notice,

　　is there any way to get out of you alive?

Three years have gone by and I'm fed up with you,

with the way you exempt yourself from being romantic, with how you give up on an I love you when you go to bed, even the empty contents of our conversations when we sit down at the table and share the silence,

when love is born it is for everyone and you should know that.

Three years have gone by and I'm fed up with me,

with not being able to do what I want without your being there, with not being able to say no when you ask me to forgive you, with still believing that one day you'll go back to being the man who won me once, still hoping that one of these mornings you'll wake me up with a kiss and an embrace and tell me that life exists because I exist,

when love is born it is for everyone and you should know that.

Three years have gone by and I'm fed up of trying,

of working like a madwoman, of arriving home and having to cook, and look after the kids, and do the laundry, the washing-up, and going to bed without you there, your head somewhere else,

where have we ended up?, where have we allowed ourselves to end up?,

it's no use to me, this more or less, it never has been, do you hear me?, this more or less is no use to me, it never has been, when love is born it is for everyone and you should know that.

Three years have gone by and I'm fed up of running away,
it's time to do, to act, which is why I left early, took the kids and here I am, my mother understands me and receives me calmly, my father understands me and receives me calmly, there's an unconditional love between us, we'll be happy here, the kids will miss you but there will always be weekends, I know you're a good father, I know you'll understand, you'll cry but not as much as me, but you'll understand that it had to be, there are moments when it has to be,
when love is born it is for everyone and you should know that.

Three years have gone by and I'm fed up of not loving you,
what are they, these days when you aren't here?, what is this thing I have in the middle of my chest when I understand the absolute uselessness of my arms if they can't embrace you?,
and I try other people, I swear I try, I pretend that I'll bear it, that it's all no more than a ludicrous dependency that will pass, I busy myself with hiding the tears when I go out at night,
what's the point of music if not to define you?,
and I imagine where you are and who you're with, yesterday you called me because of the kids and the tears fell, I don't know if you noticed and actually I don't give a damn whether you noticed or not, I just hope you come to fetch

them early and that you apologise one more time, this time I'll accept your apology and say yes, let's try one more time, let's try every other time,

what the hell is the point of pride if I can't hold on tight to you?,

I'm a young woman and I miss our routine, our empty spaces and our silences,

when love is born it is for everyone and you should know that.

I've not yet learned how to describe the noise of the wind, for example, I've heard it as though God were within it, and within me, I've heard it as the voice of pain teaching me the seriousness of life, it's shown me that even happiness can be heard, that there are as many ways of being alive as there are ways of hearing the wind, of looking at the wind, perhaps,

living is unbearable and, fuck, it's so good.

I've not yet discovered how many tears can fit on a face, I'd bet on it being three thousand, a couple more at most, there are many reasons to cry and they aren't all good ones, fortunately, what would have become of me if I wasn't acquainted with the moment of crying, the way it dilates existence, the feeling of encountering the beginning of myself, the millimetre where the emotions begin?, I hope for at least another million tears before my life ends, and that's an optimistic hope, of course,

living is unbearable and, fuck, it's so good.

I've not yet tried nam tok moo, a combination of grilled pork with mint, lemon juice, chilli, spring onion, fish sauce and roasted rice, I've not yet tried shepherd's pie, the pieces of lamb covered in mashed potato, the things we learn about from Google, or Massaman curry, touches of pepper and sweetness, with coconut milk and a lot of curry powder, let alone Kālua pork, goi cuon, suckling pig, fettuccine Alfredo, so many things, so many things, to die is for your mouth to abandon so many pleasures to come, I would have liked to taste the creativity of all mankind, but I'll have only some five or six thousand chances left, I've got to make the most of them, that's for sure,

living is unbearable and, fuck, it's so good.

I've not yet driven at three hundred miles an hour, I'm not even sure I want to, I'll decide sometime, I've not yet tried all the positions in the Kama Sutra, and I'm getting too old for some of them, fortunately I know doctors and they can help me out if something goes wrong, I've not yet told my father a million times that I adore him, but I'm getting close and to tell the truth a million is too little for something as infinite as that, I've not yet hugged my mother and kissed her forehead till my lips dried out and my arms tired out, it could happen right now, when I finish this piece of writing, I've not yet written my masterpiece and I've only got seven hundred thousand million phrases, give or take a little, to try it, and a few more, probably, I'm sure I'll die with my pen in my hand, or a computer on my lap, my last line will be something like 'Please excuse some small things, but do read it, and above all love it', I've not yet smeared myself in chocolate, I've not yet rolled in the sand after coming out of the sea enough times, I've not yet been to the moon, or to Mars, or even to China, and who knows where the most aliens are, right?, I've not yet played football in the Alvalade stadium, nor at the Don Afonso Henriques, nor Luz, nor Dragão, I've not been up onstage at the Coliseu, I tell a lie, I did go up once, but it was when I was doing a report and that doesn't count, I've never sold three hundred or four hundred or five hundred thousand copies, I've not yet saved enough lives, I've not yet annoyed my niece nearly as much as I'd like, I've not yet invented words that give me satisfaction, I've not even thrown cakes in the face of my best friend, I've not yet seen my students win the Nobel, I've never yet fancied dancing on top of a bar, really dancing, I've not shut those bastards up one more time who tell me I'm not able to do what I've just done, who even yesterday were telling me I wasn't going to make it to today, I've not yet shown my children that their father only can because he does, because he cries, he takes risks, he exposes himself, because he doesn't want just to stand still nor could he bear it, I've not yet squeezed my cats till I can feel them in the centre of my bones, not yet, not yet, please not yet, I'm not yet ready to die, I never will be, just another minute, so those after all will be my last words, 'Not yet', with an exclamation mark, 'Not yet!', I hate exclamation marks and when I use my first it'll be my last, 'Not yet!', and it's so little, it should be more, more desperate, more urgent, more absolute, 'NOT YET!', it's not enough but it's what there is, no language is ready for death, there aren't the resources for it, the worst thing isn't the dead languages, it's languages in death, incompetent, incapable, like me, not yet, please, but it has to be, I acknowledge that, but I will never accept, never, I will never accept, when I do they will be indebted to me, I'll be a believer for ever, let that be written down, and now it is, that justice is demanding payment and it is pitiless,

living is unbearable and, fuck, it's so good.

I most importantly don't yet know the colour of your panties today, and that's the thing that I struggle with the most, I confess,

now I know, amazing,
and now I don't know again
(or, oh, I've forgotten),
may the floor enjoy them, lucky thing,
living is unbearable and – oh, fuck it – it is so good.

The first time I saw you was on the street with the shoe shop, you were impeccable but you dropped a poem,

nobody's perfect, not even you, I would have liked to grab it right there and return it to you, but I didn't have the courage and I ended up keeping it for myself, there are poems that need to be kept from the world, everyone knows that or if they don't know it they should,

even if poetry dies there will still be poems,

lunatics laugh at things that make other people cry, even call them crazy,

which is just to say that I'm crazy about you, and that I've followed you ever since that day, I had an appointment at the dentist but I don't think it's important to waste my time on trivialities if there's a poem to return and I don't know how to do it,

between dental health and poetry there's an entire shipwreck, verses are useless and only a fool doesn't know that they're the most important thing in the world,

after you, of course,

you went to the supermarket, you bought two cartons of milk, a bag of sugar and half a dozen oranges, then you went into an office building,

the way you walk proves to me beyond all doubt that God doesn't teach us to live but He might well teach us to walk,

I waited for you at the door, four or five hours, you came out with a man I was afraid was your husband but then I saw he wasn't, he went one way and you the other, and I went to you, I confess, with no hesitation but a kind of elation,

excuse the rhyme, it was unintentional,

lunatics make little planes out of the bits of green paper that other people see as a reason to kill if necessary, even if not necessary, and they call them crazy,

which is just to say that I'm crazy about you, and that all those days I loved you without your knowing, before too long I knew your routines exactly, where you went, what you did, who you went with, you were a free woman and I might have been a hero if I'd said something to you,

forgive me for your being too amazing for me to dare to touch you, yes?,

one day you didn't arrive at the stop at seven-thirty in the morning, the bus came and you weren't there, you were always there on Mondays, at that time, you were normally in your blue sweater, the brown leather jacket, the tight jeans,

you make jeans into a gala evening dress and at the same time a sensual miniskirt, let me tell you that right now,

and I could tell you much more, praise you as best I can, tell you my foolish words, but the truth is I'm too busy trying to learn about you,

where are you, as I need to love urgently?,

I looked for you everywhere but nothing, in the office nobody knows anything,

she left yesterday and didn't come back, we've already called her and no answer, nobody's heard from her and there are a lot of reports to write, it's just so irresponsible, isn't it?,

your neighbours didn't see you go out,

last time I saw her was last night and she seemed strange, I must admit,

but you're not home as I've already looked through the window, I walked along the sill and nearly fell,

you're totally worth a fall from the second floor, even I who am an electrician and don't understand the first thing about economics know that,

I've been to the hospitals already and no sign of you there, just as well, let me take a deep breath now,

where are you, as I need a reason to live?,

after all you'd gone off to some island in the middle of the Pacific and hadn't even said, isn't it useful having friends in the travel agents' and you being the most unforgettable woman in the world?,

and I don't know if you're coming back, actually, perhaps it's time to give up, I don't have you here to look at and I don't know if it's possible to continue to be in love with someone who doesn't know me, what do you reckon?,

lunatics look at impossibility and see all the reasons to keep going while other people see all the reasons to give up, and they call them crazy,

which is just to say that I'm crazy about you, and that my plane arrives there about ten,

will you be waiting for me in your Levi's jeans?,

and she waited,

for a lunatic, a lunatic and a half, or maybe two,

and they lived crazy for ever, and probably happy, too,

you may now kiss the bride, if you wish,

he did, he kissed her, he embraced her,

and gave her the poem at last.

COMPLAINT FORM
Use a ballpoint pen and write in capital letters.

IDENTIFICATION OF THE PRODUCT SUPPLIER/
SERVICE PROVIDER
AGAINST WHOM THE COMPLAINT IS FILED:
(details obscured for legal reasons)

IDENTIFICATION OF THE COMPLAINANT:
(details obscured for legal reasons)

CAUSE OF COMPLAINT:
WITH THE SIMPLE AIM OF PURCHASING A SIM CARD,
THE COMPLAINANT MADE FOR THIS STORE, TOOK
A TICKET AND AWAITED HIS TURN. MORE THAN
FORTY-FIVE MINUTES LATER, HIGHLY IRRITATED AT
THE INEXPLICABLE WAIT, HE WAS FINALLY CALLED.
HE WOULD HAVE BEHAVED QUITE AGGRESSIVELY
TOWARDS THE EMPLOYEE WHO SERVED HIM
WERE IT NOT FOR HIS NOTICING THAT SHE WAS
THE MOST BEAUTIFUL WOMAN IN THE WORLD,
WHICH, THOUGH IT MAY NOT SEEM SO, CAN
STOP A LOT OF GOOD PEOPLE FROM REVOLTING
AGAINST ANYTHING, ESPECIALLY WHEN IN LOVE,
IMMEDIATELY, WITH THE WOMAN AGAINST WHOM
THEY NEED TO PROTEST – AND WHO, AS MAY HAVE
BEEN REPORTED ABOVE, IS THE MOST BEAUTIFUL

WOMAN IN THE WORLD. THE COMPLAINANT THEREFORE INTENDS THAT WITHOUT FURTHER DELAY THIS STORE PROCEED ACCORDING TO THE ESTABLISHED PROCEDURES, GIVEN THAT, AS WE ALL KNOW (OR AT LEAST THE COMPLAINANT KNOWS CLEARLY) SUCH A GREAT BEAUTY IS INTOLERABLE AND ILLEGAL – AND SHOULD BE CONFINED TO SPACES WHERE SHE CANNOT INEXPLICABLY FASCINATE ALL THOSE WHO SURROUND HER. IT IS THEREFORE DEMANDED, WITHOUT FURTHER DELAY, THAT THE EMPLOYEE IN QUESTION, WHO IDENTIFIED HERSELF MERELY AS 'BÁRBARA TEIXEIRA' (THEREBY OMITTING TO MENTION – INEXPLICABLY AND WITH EVIDENT MISCONDUCT – THAT HER FULL NAME IS 'THE WOMAN OF MY LIFE'), SHOULD BE KEPT SOMEWHERE MORE RESERVED AND NEVER IN A PUBLIC-FACING ROLE. IN ADDITION, IT IS A PRESSING CONCERN THAT THE SAME EMPLOYEE SHOULD – FOR THE VIOLENT WAY IN WHICH THE TOUCH OF HER HAND, INADVERTENTLY, LEFT MINE IN AN UNRECOVERABLE STATE OF HAPPINESS FOR EVER – BE CONDEMNED TO SUPPLY THE COMPLAINANT WITH A BROAD SMILE EACH TIME HE (ME) COMES INTO THE STORE – AND, CONSIDER YOURSELVES HENCEFORTH NOTIFIED, MY CELL PHONE IS PRETTY OLD AND HAS BEEN HAVING MORE AND MORE PROBLEMS – AS WELL AS TO ENSURE THAT IT WILL ALWAYS BE SHE WHO ATTENDS TO THE COMPLAINANT, AND SUPPLY HIM WITH HER TELEPHONE NUMBER SO THAT A DINNER, A LUNCH,

OR A SIMPLE COFFEE À DEUX SHOULD, IN THE INTERESTS OF SOME RESTORATION OF JUSTICE, TAKE PLACE AS RAPIDLY AS POSSIBLE. WE AWAIT THEREFORE, FOR ALL THE REASONS EXHAUSTIVELY LAID OUT (AND EVEN MORE EXHAUSTIVELY FELT), THE APPROPRIATE ACTION OF THE COMPETENT AUTHORITY, CONSCIOUS OF THE GRAVITY OF THE SITUATION HEREIN RECOUNTED, AND WITH THE CERTAINTY THAT I ALREADY LOVE HER UNDER PROTEST, MAY GOD AND THE LAW BE MY AID.

I like to love with my fingers,
to find the centimetre where the orgasm is born
in you, understand the extent of how you are startled,
and bring my ear to your mouth to hear the voice of God.

and I like to love with my eyes,
to waste the possibility of sleeping and watch you fall asleep,
the dark night and the silence of an embrace,
and if you want me to tell you
I only chose you by mistake, I wanted the love of books
and I became a writer, whole days waiting for your body
for the metaphors to happen.

and I like to love with my tears,
to practise the abyss, the narrow breadth of your lips,
the sense of too much sea in your tongue,
even the way you move up my sex
with the extremity of your ragged breathing,
and above all to surrender myself to the punishment of the
        emotion
of loving you even after the pleasure has ended,
the little death is over
and all life about to start again.

and I like to love with what remains of me,
and all I know is that what remains for me is to love you.

Don't worry, son, I'll sort it out,

a father is, at the very worst, a hero, a superman, and I'm here for whatever you need, I've already got you on my lap, you're crying but these things pass, a kiss here, a hug there, your mother, just let me give her a quick hug with you on my lap, she'll be breastfeeding you soon and you'll be fine, you're so beautiful, you know that?, people say you've got my eyes and I like that, of course, but what I want is for you to have yours, for you to see everything and to see only good things, I have to go now because the nurse wants to take you off to your crib, it's not the kind of thing one should say but you're the most beautiful baby of all, to hell with half-hearted language, because I love my son completely,

don't worry, son, I'll sort it out,

it hurts a lot but that's the way it's got to be, you'll love learning to read, when you know how to write do you promise to write that you adore me?, one day you could even be a writer like your uncle, you have so many things to learn, doing sums and knowing the names of rivers, we knew all that stuff in my day, the rivers, the seasons, the district capitals, I don't know any of it now but you'll like it, there now, there now, don't cry so, I can't bear it, it hurts so much when good things are hurting so badly, please don't cling on to my neck like that, look at all those children, and the teacher seems nice, she'll help you, I promise, and now that I look more closely I can see you're clearly the smartest kid in the class, I know it's not the kind of thing one should say but I've said it, to hell with half-hearted language, because I love my son completely,

don't worry, son, I'll sort it out,

of course I'll sign, I do like your wife, you've chosen well, you clever little swine, in that respect you've taken after your father since your mother is still unquestionably the most alluring woman in the neighbourhood, and I'm sure you'll be happy, there must be something that can make me happier than seeing you happy but honestly I've not found it yet, I trust you completely, the lady from the bank is an old acquaintance of mine, Dona Emília, who worked with me in the shoe store, a saint, and the house is a wonder, space for a family and in no time at all I want grandchildren jumping around, oh but I do, here's my signature, forty years' savings couldn't be put to better use than this, I'm so proud of myself and of you, my big boy starting a new life, it's hard to lose you but deep down I'm winning you again in another way, you're a good pal, my big lad, I know it's not the kind of thing one should say but when I look at the two of you I can clearly see that you're the best-looking couple that has ever asked for a loan in this bank, to hell with half-hearted language, because I love my son completely,

don't worry, son, I'll sort it out,

it's just a tiny little pain, don't worry about it, an old carcass doesn't split, the doctor said it'll pass soon enough and that I'm fine, you didn't need to come with me, you have your own life, I really don't like messing up your plans, shouldn't we be talking about the current Sporting line-up instead?, that new reinforcement of their defence doesn't look like it's up to much, does it?, I'd love to go with you to the stadium tomorrow but I'm still having trouble walking, no it's not too bad, don't give me that look, there's nothing in the world that can make a man cry like the pitiful expression on his son's face, don't look at me like that, love, come and give me a hug and tell me about your life, is it true what your mother told me, that you're already shift foreman in your factory?, I always knew you'd go far, before you know it you'll be ordering that whole rabble around, dammit, it was just a slip, sorry, I'm fine, really I am, I'll be back on my feet in a moment, let me just find something to hold on to, what could hurt more than needing to be carried by one's own child to get to bed?, I'm better here, just let me rest a bit and I'll go to the living room with you, turn on the TV and put on the recording of that programme you were on the other day, I know it's not the kind of thing one should say but you were by far the best participant that competition has ever had, to hell with half-hearted language, because I love my son completely,

don't worry, son, I'll sort it out,

you have your mother's mouth, that's the truth and I can't deny it, but your eyes are mine, can there ever be a happier tear than the one that falls when you see your own eyes in the eyes of your son?, I have you in my arms and I'm so happy, I only wish my old man were still here, I'm sure he'd say that before you know it you'll be picking up girls in high school and that you'll be the best student in the class, then he'd tell you about the new Sporting reinforcement, when I leave here I'm going straight to the stadium to make you a member, if we can get you his number wouldn't that be the best, I know it's not the kind of thing one should say but you are by far the most beautiful Sporting supporter of all, to hell with half-hearted language, because I love my son completely.

I claim the indignation of the marvellous, the trees turned over with the strength of the wind, the old lady in the window happy with life down there, that smile of hers that's so childlike,

the ingenuousness and the emotional understanding,

the boats docking with their men with long beards and a lot of life,

the stories they'll have to tell you, isn't that right?,

and the peace of your kiss as you lie on top of me.

I claim the engineering of flight, to understand how planes rise into the air carrying so many people who don't know how to fly, to understand how love began,

who was the first person to love and how did they know how good it was?,

to discover where the sea ends and where the waves come from, to cry when my father asks me for a hug, and I give it and only receive,

who invented magical creatures like parents?,

spending the evening tasting chocolates,

and the riot of your sweat as you lie on top of me.

I claim also the formula of the poem, which is at the origin of a finished verse,

from what territory are geniuses born?,

it's the genius and not Jesus who's at God's right hand, or otherwise Jesus is a genius himself, what the hell do I know?,

I'd like to unveil whatever it is that the look in a cat's eyes is hiding,

how many masterpieces would you find there?,

the substance of art is tears and everything else they bring with them, up to happiness, of course,

but I want to lay out the possibility of everyone being Picasso and just not knowing it, no one is immune to fascination, I'm sure of that,

and I claim at last the canonisation of pleasure,

and your unbuttoned shirt as you lie on top of me.

I claim above all the useless object of temptation, which makes me cry when I fall in love, the exemplary ergonomics of your body on mine,

who has understood that there are new meanings for living?,

I refuse to think when there are your lips, the twenty years forever of my loving you, the cocaine of your fingers on my skin,

whoever invented drugs didn't know about love, that seems quite clear to me,

and the indecision over whether I should love you for ever or for ever as you lie on top of me.

What noise does the rain make when I embrace you like this?,

there's a piece to write, a writer's drama is that there's always something to write, and that's also his good fortune, I'm not making sense but you know,

yesterday your hair smelled of an embrace,

I remember a nose never being so happy, the things I write, my God, I could expound on the crisis, the markets and rise of the credit rating or whatever, but I prefer to devote myself to the mixing of the raindrops on the window with the light thread of sweat that runs down the middle of your chest,

when you sleep God wakes up to watch you sleeping,

the Catholics don't know it but the real miracle is loving you, suddenly you turned this way, there's so much that needs writing and all I can write is you,

what a wretch are you who makes me happy?,

perhaps there was a need to explain the existence of sovereign debt, to slag off two or three politicians, or even more or all of them, I'm well aware how they deserve it, but when I come back all I write is the poem you show me,

all those who love are poets,

at least those who love like this, with their verses constantly interrupted, everything to say and so few words to show for it,

how many dictionaries does your body demand?,

and that's not even mentioning your voice, the disgraceful way you tell me you love me and I believe you, it's already nine at night and I have to file a piece at ten, stop looking at me, and you stop, you turn to face the other way but it won't come, I begin some line or other about something, I think this time it was about sport, would you believe, but then your back,

your back is enough to create a genius,

before you know it the deadline has passed but to hell with it, let me in an instant write the desire for my tongue on you, the absolute importance of your hands, or even the calm of being in your arms when it hurts, it's five minutes to ten and I've already got an email from the editor, now's the time, I'm going to write about a solution to the sadness in the country, knock out two or three banalities, quote a few famous authors so everyone will respect me, and then it's done, wait a moment I'll be right back, here goes, a line is done, now another, but there you still are and when I realise where I am I've already written four or five lines about how much I miss you when you're not there, the absurd vastness of the sofa without you, I look at my watch and it's ten,

what do I do to write something not you?,

I press the send button and it's all gone, an entire column about you, I hope they don't find it strange, after all it's the first time I've devoted a whole one to you, today at least, of course, I have an idea that yesterday and the day before it was the same,

will I have to wait too long before you'll give me my congratulatory hug?

I like it when you're a man, you know?,

the way you show me the extent of your strength and hold me tight and small when I'm hurting,

there's so much to hurt about, isn't there?,

the rain and the homeless man with no way of escaping it, the people forgotten in the corner of the bus,

what is all this crap they've invented in the world?,

and then I get home, the whole day on my shoulders, and there's your strength, and you tell me it'll all pass, and it does, when you ask me to let myself be protected,

love might well just be somebody asking us to let ourselves be protected, and then really protecting us.

I like it when you're a man, you know?,

the way after the calm you manage to awaken all the fire I have in me, you don't need much, you talk to me about the space between poetry and your loving me, you tell me the story of the invention of our kiss,

it takes so little to love someone, doesn't it?,

and after the storm comes the storm, love comes not from opposing poles but from the same pole in different places,

I'm so addicted to your skin,

we mingle smells and movements, we know it's only pleasure and that it's going to be so short-lived, which is why we insist,

love might well just be the frequent occurrence of pleasure, and its respective insistence.

I like it when you're a man, you know?,

the way you bravely shrink and show me how big you are, a vast giant who is hurting,

there are so many people who aren't big enough to be small, have you noticed that?,

sometimes there are unsustainable roofs within us, days that ask us to give up, and that's when you lie down and give over to the hope that someone is coming to fetch you,

the world needs periodic givings-up to keep going, that's what you taught me,

you're as much of a coward as a hero and that's how I love you, the little boy who makes himself big to be able to defend me,

I so like the heroism of your fragility,

when we lie down and hold each other in our neediness we know that something is passing through us that has no solution, the ill that we suffer has no cure, and still we cure each other,

love might well just be the impossibility of curing an ill, and then obviously curing it.

An orgasm is a perfect trap,

I use anonymous hands on my body, there's one on top of me now but there's so much missing, an unbearable abyss between each man's body and you, strangers' hands to stop me remembering you,

what country am I from when I feel like this?,

every place recognises you, at midday on the dot I open my legs to you for whoever it might be, this guy's tall and strong, if the soul were reasonable he'd be so much better than you, but the thing is I'm stupid and I still want you, because all beds are a preamble to you, and your mouth is an ancient gesture,

and now I remember what I didn't experience with you,

missing somebody is made up of learnings, of noises that are there to prevent hearing,

either the whole day exists for living or the whole day exists for dying, letting the hours go by, remembering to forget you for good, I need to not need you if I'm to be happy,

everyone who isn't you is just Joe,

we've got to forget about what doesn't fulfil us, I get by without knowing whom I love when I love only you, I call the surrounding world Joe and I use whatever I can, the skin, the flesh, even the potential words,

how many men will I have to sacrifice to keep going and not forget you?,

I tell him give it to me hard, I close my eyes and try to go towards the geography of pleasure, but when they leave I'm left behind and there's the literature of the empty bed, I take two or three letters you wrote me once and finally I strip down so that you can touch me,

whenever I read you I must be absolutely naked,

one more Joe who's left, there was the orgasm and I moaned as best I could, two or three seconds oblivious to you, I swear, probably that's as much as I can aspire to, I've got to be realistic,

I'd like to be the woman who bears it and I'm just the woman who puts up with it,

and I say goodbye to him, a cold see you later and a cigarette, window open, the doorbell ringing, must be another Joe, no doubt, I open the downstairs door without asking who it is,

exactly what fragility does giving-up come from?,

I have no interest in the mystery of death, only of your life in me, the door's already open, I don't look and just let him come, hands first, then the kiss, finally the words,

hi, I'm Joe,

and that's all I need to know it's you, I don't ask anything or want to know anything, there's the chance for a few minutes of just us and I'm ready to make the most of it, show me patiently what you learned far away from me, give me bliss first and silence afterwards, but most of all promise me that you'll never promise me anything again,

and keep it, please.

Two kilos of rice, four of frozen onions, a large carton of milk and a love for ever after,

a shopping list stuck to the fridge, the stove on, pans on the fire, a house as normal as every other and then us,

there ought to be a limit to being somebody's just so we could exceed it as we ought to, right?,

I like holding you tight as we invent a possible fiction, when the rim of the kitchen counter is enough to love you, I lean you against it and tell you I love you, and the worst thing of all is I really do,

have you any idea just how rare our routine is?,

nobody believes that anyone can love twenty-four hours a day for their whole life and nor do we, it seems ridiculous to call the exact time we spend together twenty-four hours, let's call it life and leave it at that,

words are simple after all, and no love ever died from want of words, only from want of love,

and I don't know if I'm saying the right words to you but I love you like a poet, write that, please.

Give me a wet kiss at the door to the supermarket and make me happy,

as adolescent as only you can be, your request, your piercing laugh, the cashier not knowing whether to laugh or cry and your legs around my waist,

I don't know whether to call them lips, those things that make me feel like that, it's not the best way to live, probably, but it's certainly the only possible way, and for me that's enough for everything to be right,

I like it when happiness can be measured, your hand where the flesh rises,

what damned bliss are you?,

if God existed you would make Him sin, now come with me and take a bath, wash my back and rub my skin, I don't know if it's romantic but it makes me cry, you make me not know what I want the whole time and that's my desire,

how many imbalances does a happiness require?,

and at the end of the day or night there we'll be in our normal house, on the usual sofa, your head in my common lap, your hair in my banal hands, and anyone who saw us would think we're just any old couple, and we are, but don't tell anyone that's exactly why nothing compares to us,

the only poverty is having just one single reality to live, and it's just as well we're aware of that, isn't it?,

and I don't know if I'm saying the right words to you but I love you like a poet, write that, please.

If you knew that I don't fear perfection,

because as luck would have it I fear only what's within my reach, like that strange thing your hair does when you arrive at work in the morning, your purse slung over your shoulder and in such a hurry to start answering those emails, the first one is always from me and you've never noticed, tomorrow I'll try sending you the first and also the last, I'll send you one just after you've left and another just after you've arrived the following day, maybe that way you'll notice it's not by chance,

everything you want with such force is by chance, maybe that's it,

I've wanted you since I first saw you and even then you couldn't see me,

if you knew that I've never taken the paving stones' name in vain, let that be quite clear,

but the truth is I envy them, your ordered steps along what isn't me,

where do you go when I don't see you?,

it's hard to bear the existence of your life beyond my loving you, you can call me possessive, jealous, whatever, call me anything you like so long as you call me yours,

all my freedom for one kiss, deal?,

today I invite you for a coffee, it's a good start and always a chance to look further inside you, when I look at you for more than five straight seconds I'm happy for ever, I swear,

if you knew I bought a new suit just to look at you better,

the lady in the store thought it strange, she looked contemptuously at me,

when have you ever seen a badly dressed man in love?,

but she did end up serving me, she chose me a grey one with little blue stripes, I hope you like it, I spent my holiday allowance on it, if the boss knew he'd cut me off completely once and for all, I think he's got a little crush on you, as I saw him look you up and down at the Christmas dinner, if he hits on you just tell me and I'll thump him and I'll quit on the spot, I couldn't care less about the salary but no longer seeing you would be the harder price to pay, maybe you'd figure out some way to see me and everything would turn out fine, you're just coming out and here's the invitation, I'm begging you on my knees to accept, however much I look like your answer doesn't matter,

the drama of the body is in knowing how to lie,

if you knew that what I do for you is not really crying, rather it's dying,

there's no way for you to love me and it'd be best to give up, throw in the towel and go in search of some potential happiness,

who knows, maybe there's a woman hiding you?,

and I go to bed every day with that wish, I convince myself that tomorrow I'll stop trying, but then tomorrow comes and your steps on the pavement, I see them from up here from the window as I drink my coffee on the building's patio, exactly three hundred and seventy-three steps from when you come out of the metro till you reach the entrance to the factory, I counted them yesterday and confirmed it today,

that's the irony of madness, that it knows how to count,

and once again I'm yours any time you want, even my snot is trembling, just so you know, it's not at all romantic but it's the truth,

when I go to the ophthalmologist and he asks me what I see I'll show him a photo of you and then leave, I promise you,

if you knew I love you,

maybe it would be different, maybe you'd lie down with me at night and you'd let me watch you fall asleep, touch your hair all the way to the depth of your tears, bring your head to my fearful shoulders and wait for happiness to arrive at last,

if you knew I love you,

but you do.

Assuage my hunger just so you know I'm insatiable,

I'd so like to tell you like this just how I love you, but there's bashfulness, there's fear, there's shame, all those things,

how many 'No's can a person really bear?,

and when I'm with you we spend the time talking about your sister and about her boyfriend, a complete loser, I have to tell you,

do morons always get the best women or is that just my impression?,

or about one of your classes, 8B, that's doing your head in, some kid called Diogo, really rude,

if there's someone making things bad for you just tell me where he lives and I'll deal with it, OK?,

and when it's time for silence I'd like to take you up in my arms, tell you the story of the unfortunate boy who was only friends with the girl he loved so he could at least be near her for a while, learn about her life, about what's happening, it's a kind of betrayal, I know that, but I don't think it's possible to bear your existence without being able to have you, and he's you and I'm me, what do you do when there's so much to lose and everything to win?,

I just wanted someone who understood me, don't you see?,

and your question deserved to have me say I'm here, and I understand you completely, I know you get afraid of the dark when it's thundering, I know your left leg hurts when the weather changes, that your favourite animal is a cat, your favourite colour is blue, I know you liked living in New York but you don't know why, I know your perfect man is tall and dark but that the only time you ever loved anyone he was short and chubby and even a bit blondish, I know you brush your teeth with your left hand even though you're not left-handed, I know that sometimes you call your mother for her to put you to sleep,

what is it that's so perfect about parents' voices?,

I know you hate driving, and only I know that you found it hard getting your licence so late but it had to be so,

better to be your driver than nothing at all, right?,

people do the strangest things for love and getting a driving licence isn't even one of them, after all it has other uses and even if I only drive for you, don't tell anyone but when I'm not I go by taxi or subway or bus, driving is an act that requires you, just like all the others for that matter,

but enough about me, let's continue with you, your need for an it's all fine when something's hurting, your unlikely need for a goal from your team, I was never a Sporting fan before I met you, you should know that, and only I know how I managed to get such a low membership number just to persuade you I'd been a member since I was little,

not many things justify a swindle as well as love, and there's me seeming like I don't think I love you,

I'm not satisfied with your friendship,

that's the most I can say, for a moment I fear you misunderstand and that I no longer want you here, in the most intimate space of my fragility, but when you touch my ear lightly with your left hand,

when you're in love you're like when you're brushing your teeth, that's curious, and you ask me to make you forget time and I know it was worth it, and it will be,

this, the only thing I know,

I think it was yesterday or the day before that I remembered to love you,

you said to me, and I said nothing because my lips would not speak, truly, and also because I didn't know how to answer you,

when you asked me to make you forget time and I obeyed, you know?, and I think I went too far,

what day is it today anyway?,

the morons always get the best women, and that's my good fortune,

thank God.

'I live in a country where poverty is legalised,'

and Guilherme (a fictional name for someone who should be a work of fiction) pulls his right eye, rubbing the wet skin again and again, the wrinkles showing that it's not only on the inside that time passes. He's seventy-one, his whole working life behind him, and now all that's left to him is the same old falling-down house in the same old run-down neighbourhood.

'I live in a country where poverty isn't a crime,'

his hand still in his tears, people looking at him again fearfully.

'A poor man scares people, did you know that?'

he asks me, blue eyes wide like someone apologising for the smell of somebody who hasn't known what hot water is in years, hands moving as though in a search for a reason for life.

'Sometimes, as a matter of respect, I give up on holding out my hand and asking, I know people have their problems and don't want anything to do with me. Nowadays I go through the trash cans and I haven't even done too badly,'

he tells me, and he manages to smile the bravest smile there is, and this time it's my tears that want to come out; I soldier on, ask him what he used to do, what brought him there, to that piece of nothing in such a big life that has gone.

'I worked on the building sites, I had a grocery store, then I even opened a restaurant, believe it or not. But then came that crisis thing and I had to go back to the hard labour. But nobody wanted me. I was already too old to work, and still too young to stop working,' he pauses a moment, or two, then goes on, his tears have stopped but his head hasn't.

'I was too old to live and too young to die,'

the lives of all the old people in this country, and of so many old people in this world, defined in a single phrase, I want to hug him, tell him to come home with me, that I'll do whatever I can and more, so that he lacks for nothing, but I don't say a word: I know the one thing he is not lacking is the pride that's left to a man who no longer has anything.

"There've been people who wanted to help me, to give me a life far from here, where there was good water to drink and good food to eat. But I don't want it. I've worked for too long to agree to die on charity,'

the expression sticks in my head, and he explains it, maybe there's another tear about to come.

'Living off charity doesn't exist, you know that? Living off charity doesn't exist. Anyone round here living off charity is dying on charity, and I've worked so much, so much, you know? I don't want what I don't deserve, I've never wanted what I didn't deserve. I just want what they said I'd have, but here in this country, I might have said this to you already, poverty isn't a crime, it's like the politicians who're in power now have legalised it,'

and he shows me a newspaper as worn as the skin on his arms, the news of some state budget that's been passed covering the entire front page.

'What they want is for the mob to be afraid of ending up like me. Nothing scares people more than poverty, I may have said that already. Poverty isn't the end but it's an ending that moves, we end gradually on the inside, taken away bit by bit; it starts with your pride, then it takes your self-confidence, until, if we don't keep alert, we're left with nothing, all we can do is to beg and put ourselves in the hands of those who put us here. But I won't let those people take me. They don't get to take me,'

the words waved like a flag, white for peace and never for surrender, more and more people around us, night falling and, in the distance, in the sky, the promise of rain coming soon.

'What they want is for us to take shelter from the rain, you understand? They want us to be afraid of getting wet and to take shelter from the rain, and so for this, for this to happen, we'll do anything they want. What they want is for us all to be little sheep, and they say go and we go, and they tell us to stay and we stay. We're all just as we are now, right this moment, with the rain about to fall and each of us having to choose whether we take shelter or allow ourselves to stay,'

until the rain really does start, people running, the surrounding cafés filling up, the shop awnings all occupied, me and Guilherme alone in the middle of the street.

'See how they all run away? That's what they do,'

the newspaper shaken again, the wet pages coming apart.

'They threaten that there's rain coming, they make it really rain, and people run away, that way it's easier to pretend you can take it; people prefer to be reserved, hidden from what will get them wet. But look: my grandmother, God keep her, always said to me that he who goes out in the rain gets wet, and I prefer to get completely soaked rather than just slightly wet, know what I mean? If you're going to get wet anyway, might as well have a good wash, that's what she used to tell me,' the street deserted now, him and me both soaked, and for a moment even his wrinkles seem to disappear beneath the rain.

'All waters heal. It won't happen in my lifetime but I'm sure one day people will understand that all waters heal, and then the revolution will come. The revolution will come. I'm going to die, you should know this, sir, with hope for the revolution, and that's not such a bad way to die after all, is it?',

he smiles, his lost life in those lost teeth, he runs his hand over my shoulder, a friendly pat on the back, and continues on his way, the rain and his silhouette, the night closing in, and a final refusal when I ask him if he wants me to go with him or to take him somewhere:

'Let it be. I'll stay here where it's raining.'

And he stays. And he stays.

God wears a bikini and flip-flops,

I wrote yesterday on the way here to the beach, I wanted to pay tribute to you, a poem after my fashion, I don't know any better, I'm sorry, my father always said that he who gives of what he has is not obliged to do any more, it's a crappy line but it works for me just now,

lines are worth the aim they achieve, that's the truth,

you leave my certainties in rubble,

and that's true, too, when I see you in that body and in that bikini, you're coming over with so many girlfriends and it seems intolerable for me to believe that one day you might be mine, and that's why I believe, I stare at you exhaustively, I confess, and there might be a thousand police officers and only your brown skin turns me in, the way the sun beats down on your back draws me in so badly it hurts,

give me hope and I'll build a house,

the water is incomplete when you're not there, and I fear that ninety percent of the people are only here to see you, at least ninety percent of me is, the rest stands still when it sees you and it's as though I'm living in parts when I have you there in front of me, either you love indisputably or you love under protest,

my heart's for sale as long as you don't want it for free,

I'm so mediocre when I speak to you, aren't I?, it's you who makes me like this,

how many dummies can just one love produce?,

you should know I'm the best student in the class, I got the

Year Four prize in middle school, and at secondary everyone
wanted to sit next to me during the tests, take this and use it
so that you'll like me, if you can, and also if you can't, please,
better to be desperate than to have no hope for you,

when I saw you six months ago I didn't know how to
swim and now I'm the lifeguard on your beach,

how about that for a proof of love?,

one day I write you a message,

Guedes, who plays at Benfica and who wants to take you
to bed, if he tries to force anything you'll let me know, OK?,
when have you ever heard of someone being taken to bed
who can only be taken to heaven, God that's so tacky, OK, do
forgive me that one,

but one day, as I was saying, I'll write you a message on
Facebook because Guedes got me your link in exchange for
helping him pass Portuguese,

you don't want one of those cheats to love, you promise?,

God wears a bikini and flip-flops,

it'll start like that and then there will be all the words that
are above here after that,

take my whole life and enjoy it,

and me too, thank you.

Your body is visible from my window, it's about ten o'clock, you have your dinner and then you sit there, in that armchair in the corner of the living room, you smoke a cigarette, sometimes two, you look out at the immense space of the city, the still lights, the empty places, and I imagine that you're looking at me, these are the moments I feel moved, the smoke in the air of your living room and me smoking with you, and I can see no greater intimacy than a cigarette à deux in the deepest silence of the night.

Your life is visible from my desk, just a little but it'll do, you only have to go to fetch something from the staple drawer and I can see how weary your expression is, maybe you don't really like filing documents, organising envelopes and receipts, and I like to stop what I'm doing so that I cannot like it with you, I close my eyes and try to sense what's changed in you since last night, to sense if you've slept well or not, what colour the lipstick is that you're wearing today, how many times you look at the photograph of your daughter, and I can see no greater intimacy than us looking together at what you love most.

Your solitude is visible from my table, you have lunch with yourself and I go along too, the corner table whenever you can, a salad or the catch of the day, I don't know if I've told you this already but you seriously don't need to diet, if I could only draw your body I'd be a complete man, all day long watching you, but I'm no artist and I just love you, the corner table far from the window, you're probably scared of people or you're hurt by nobody, and so am I, you should know, I ask for what you ask for and follow you along in no hurry and I can see no greater intimacy than our having lunch à deux, each of us in the secret of their corner.

Your freedom is visible from my bicycle, you run in the late afternoon in the most dangerous park in the city and I protect you in order to protect myself from your ending, I keep an eye on you at a safe distance, the river all the way down there, those low lifes look at you and I tremble, one day this will go badly, I cycle past them and act like I'm a really bad guy, me who's never hit anybody and who was the laughing stock at school, for you I could become a hero and if necessary I really am, today you stopped earlier than usual and you're bent double, I don't know what's going on and I'm alarmed, you're not the kind of woman to stop in the middle of whatever's hurting you, now you've sat down and closed your eyes suddenly, your body switched off and I can't take it any more, I stop my bicycle and grab on to you hard, fortunately it's just a faint and you wake, me with you in my arms and your eyes opening, and I can see no greater intimacy than you opening your eyes and meeting mine.

Your hand is visible from my side of the bed, it's resting on my chest and life may be no more than this, you sleeping with your hand resting on my bare chest, my breathing and your hand rising with it, yesterday you smoked your cigarette on this side, I told you about how I smoked with you, I showed you the angle I loved you from, but the day is happening and the light is coming and there's work, you thank me, you apologise for having been weak and you leave, you mention the possibility that you might call again, you say you don't know what it is that connects us but that you're going to try to find out, I let you go and I smoke a cigarette at the window, the whole city in a search for who knows what, and I can see no greater intimacy than the chance to be here smoking the happiest cigarette in the world.

'I promise to fail.'

It was the only promise he ever made, a whole philosophy in four words, he didn't believe in the possibility of perfection, he didn't even do whatever he could to try and reach it, since if it doesn't exist why go looking for it?, and he let himself go on living for what he had ahead of him, all the options, all the doors, there was always an ideal time for happiness and it was always now, love only exists when one gives up on being perfect.

'I want it so much, but never mind.'

The abominable fear that people have, the abominable capacity for being satisfied with half of something that could be whole, she was afraid, so afraid, afraid of getting it wrong, of not getting it done, afraid of not taking the right step in the right direction, still less at the right time, and when the embrace happened it was two bodies that combined, yes, but much more than that they were two different worlds that didn't know how to connect, love only exists when two different worlds unite without the faintest idea of how they should be uniting.

'The one mistake people make is seeking what doesn't exist.'

And he insisted, he hugged her after sex and explained what life contains, the urgency of skin, forgetting the possibility of a perfect couple so as to savour the perfection of a possible couple, him and her, imperfect like themselves alone, him with wrinkles all over his face, age spread all over the design of his body, her tired of struggling, tired of fearing, her children, her life, an indelible story behind her, him and her with everything to get wrong and it was only this that separated them, just a wish but for different journeys, love only exists when two people meet in the middle of two different journeys.

'I promise to fail.'

I promise to love you to the limit, to kiss you to the final frontier, to run when walking would have been enough, to jump when running would have been enough, to fly when jumping would have been enough. I promise to embrace you with the inside of my bones, to run all over your flesh with total hunger, and go in search of an orgasm every day, at every moment, to find happiness in the sweet absurdity that we knew we were destined for. I promise to fail. With no hesitations. I promise to be human, to be incoherent from time to time, to say the wrong word from time to time, the wrong phrase, even the wrong text altogether, act from time to time without thinking, what the hell is the point of thinking if I love you this senselessly? I promise to understand, I promise to want, I promise to believe. I promise to insist, I promise to fight, to discover, learn, teach. Which is all to say that I promise to fail. And God help you if you don't promise me the same.

'You were the most beautiful way for me to make mistakes.'

And she felt her breathing falter, she hesitated as she had never hesitated before, she wanted to think about it all, lay each of the possibilities on the dishes of the scales, but when she realised, she did not say 'I want it so much, but never mind', when she realised she was thinking about how come she'd stopped thinking, one or two seconds of herself, love only exists when it offers at least one or two seconds of ourselves.

'If you fail again I promise to love you for ever.'

And she failed.

I don't ask much of life, I never have, my body in a fit state to seek you out and anything else is extra. We might also have the possibility of a weekend à deux, just the occasional one, me and you without the world bothering us, someplace that could really be just some place. Next we'd spend the days pretending that there existed something beyond the need for us. I could even get a job, work from nine to five, smile at my colleagues when they told a joke, mutter insults at my boss between my teeth because he didn't appreciate all my abilities, just to be able to get home, with night falling by now, and say to you, 'I love you and I've already forgotten everything I've lived through today' and then you could say, 'How was the day, my love?' and I'd answer like every other head of a family that it hadn't been easy but things are moving along, until having said two or three things of no consequence whatsoever it would be time for the hug and then the kiss and then the body and then the pleasure and then we'd stretch out on some surface where there was room for what we wanted. There would be more moaning than in the past, the neighbours would lodge a complaint with the doorman, the doorman would call up, he'd say, not quite knowing how, that we were bothering people with our noise, I'd say no doorman was going to stop me from loving, and we'd go back to the moaning just to show that when you love someone not even the decibels can be measured.

'Only what exceeds all limits can change the world, did you know that?' you'd ask, cigarette in your mouth, your body naked, the window open and the neighbours opposite, as always, in love with the perfect arithmetic of your body, and me responding as best I could, telling you I hadn't believed there were limits since I'd found the inside of your lips, you'd say at once, in that way you have, innocent little girl and at the same time untameable little slut, that you loved the way I used letters to open your legs, and without my noticing I was inside you once again, your wet thighs on my hips and all the orgasms possible once again.

'Everybody knows the size of an orgasm,' you'd say, without my understanding why or what for, and you'd continue your lecture on the idea that in reality pleasure only exists so that mankind can exist, and that pleasure comes before life, for the simple and elemental reason that it's only this and what results from it that makes birth exist; I'd still be stretched out on the bed, watching your silhouette in the window and under the light coming in through the glass, imagining what the world would be if it weren't for the impotence of not loving you like this, of not needing you like this, I'd also think that none of this would have a future, that we would have no future, we were two lunatics playing bodies, two children playing orgasms, such irresponsibility, such inability to create a future, while you had no idea what I was thinking or imagining and just wanted to convey an idea, which you thought unchangeable and unassailable, according to which love consists in the possibility of finding all the passions in just one body, concentrating all the sexes in just one sex, and you'd conclude that no, you couldn't do it, that you were sorry but there was no way you could love only one body just like you couldn't love only one life, and that this was why you invented people in you, you were girl and adult, rebel and conformist, you were everything you could be, this and its opposite, so that you could resist, not that you were a traitor or an infidel, not because you didn't like me to the depth of your skin and the start of your bones, but just because you had this strange obsession with insisting on being happy.

Then you stubbed out your cigarette, the light of the moon when you turned made me believe that if God existed He would be something like what I saw in you, you gave me a goodbye kiss, you said it was impossible to give me what I deserved, and when you were getting ready to slam the door and leave I simply said that if you couldn't give me what I deserved then I had every right to demand that you give me what I didn't deserve.

I don't ask much of life, I may have said this to you before, just my body in a fit state to love you and your body even if it's old beneath a moon that is only ours.

We were so small and already we were loving a love that was so great.

When we began to love, I would wait for you outside the school, I'd stop my Yamaha next to the pavement, rev the engine two or three times and everybody would stop to look at me, I can't pretend I didn't enjoy it, I did, but what I wanted was for you to hear me, for you to see me and perhaps come running into my arms, and if it was worth having a bike, I alone knew what I'd had to do to buy it, and it was just to make you look at me.

We were so young and already we were loving a love that was so ancient.

At first you didn't notice, I'd be there ten, fifteen, twenty minutes, until it stopped being cool just standing in front of a secondary school, till everyone stopped seeing me as a threatening kind of guy and started seeing me as just some fool who came to a school gate to rev the engine of his bike, and then I'd have to leave, many times, without seeing your eyes on mine or on my bike, without seeing your smile, without the day being worth it. On those days I'd take other routes and wait for you to come out, I'd see you with your girlfriends, they all knew they were friends with the most beautiful girl (you do know that's you, right?) the world has ever known, and I'd think that one day it would be me, me and you, arm in arm, without needing bikes or revs, what a waste it would be to have my hands occupied by a set of handlebars when there was such a thing as your skin to touch before time passed, me and you and the absence of a bike, that's what the perfect world would be like however much just watching you smile may already have been good enough.

We were so naïve and already we knew everything.

Of course we grew up, you grew up and stopped being the most beautiful girl the world has ever known only to become the most beautiful woman the world has ever known, I grew up and stopped having a bike and started to have a car, but deep down we remained the same people, we didn't change even a bit, you kept on studying and I kept on working like a dog just to be able to watch you coming out of school and then university, and I had to, oh didn't I just have to, work up the courage to tell you one day that I loved you like a car needs an engine, like a bike needs an exhaust, like wheels need the road, whatever, some metaphor (that's what you say, right?) or other, forgive me, all I can remember are things from the garage, I just want you to understand, right away, that if I didn't embrace you and tell you I loved you it was only because saying a whole life is still really hard, but I was sure that one day, yes, one day I'd be able to, you just had to wait a little, just a little, OK?

We were so ignorant and already we understood the meaning of life.

You bring me all the wisdom of the world, that should be

quite clear, it happened that day I saw you with that guy you probably met at university, and if I'd been asked on that day to explain what jealousy was I'd have replied 'the thing that kills', and if death does exist it mustn't hurt as much as this, you on his shoulders, your smile and giving up for a moment, but he who loves never gives up, I read that once in a book, one of the books I started reading as soon as I realised that if I wanted to win you I'd have to say the right words and not the wrong ones, deep down the difference between being happy and not being happy is the choice of words, the happiest man, I learned in an instant, is always the one who says things better.

/

We were so incomplete and already we lacked for nothing.

When you hugged me for the first time, you didn't see this but it's true, I dropped the piece of paper I had in my hand and which I'd prepared with such care to give you, I'm no longer sure what I'd written there but it was some way of telling you I loved you in a poetic way, I think it even rhymed, would you believe it, but when you hugged me for the first time, we were alone in the middle of a street full of people, I dropped the bit of paper and told you I loved you, I didn't use poems or verses or rhyme, I said 'I love you' and your eyes opened and closed, then you looked up at the sky, I don't know if you said thank you but I did, and you hugged me again and in my ear I heard somebody say 'me too' and I wanted to believe, as I still want to believe, that it was you, because if it wasn't then that explains that love compensates for blindness by an excess of hearing, and now I'm even trying to make jokes, see what you've done to me, a man practises to be a poet and the best he can manage is to be ridiculous, and maybe they're exactly the same thing now I think about it.

We were so transient and nothing could part us.

Life's a bitch, you know?, it forces us to do what we don't want to, to say what we don't want to, and there are the bills, the jobs, the duties, the weight of days marking time, age which never stops, and when we encounter something that isn't as perfect as us we can't take the pressure, I took the easy way out and was proud, you took the easy way out and were proud, and by the time we realised what was what we were just another more-or-less couple in a more-or-less house with a more-or-less life, and nothing that we were deserved something so insignificant. That was when I decided to leave, I took my dreams and off I went, you stayed, I know you cried as I did, I know you believed that however much it hurt it was the right thing to do, and how the hell do we learn even to allow for the possibility of something that hurts so badly happening to be the right thing? What hurts is never the right thing, that's the only certain truth, and the years passed and there were men and women between us, even wrinkles and children, and when I thought about the value of life I tried just to assess you in full, to understand where you were and what you were doing, until I was bald from it all and old from it all and I took my ancient Yamaha and went to the school gate where everybody looked at me and said I was cool, an old guy who still looked good and kind of cool, but what I wanted was for you to appear again, I thought you wouldn't come, but when I heard one of the girls, she was definitely the hottest, saying 'here comes the teacher' I realised that you were approaching and you were wearing the same clothes (how did you manage to keep yourself so elegant?) and the same certainty that you were, you still are, the most beautiful girl in the world who then became the most beautiful woman who then became the most beautiful old lady in the world, and when you got on to my bike and I did a couple of really big revs so that everybody would notice us leave I realised (did you realise this, too?) that we had never stopped being what we loved.

We were so old and we still had our whole lives ahead of us.

You are all good,

    I tell you, nice and loud, people around us laugh, and you definitely don't like it,

    who would like a construction worker standing on top of some scaffolding with words like that?,

    but the truth is that I love you and what I said to you is so complete it hurts, you're all good because nothing in you could do me harm, I'm not even talking about your body, I'm not all that into bodies however I might seem, what I like are people and to feel like I exist when I look at someone, and as I said everything about you would do me good, everything in you is good,

    you don't need some intellectual to define what love is, you know?,

    You are all good,

    I've known you since childhood, the smartest kid in the class and me too, and then life happens, and my father, I love you so much, God keep you, a stupid accident,

    as though there could be any death that wasn't stupid, right?,

    but like I was saying, life happened to me and to you, too, I learned that you studied journalism, then I started seeing you on TV, I felt like the victor in your victory, would you believe it, I still feel it today when I see you on, I chose this company so I could have you every day, it's the only having-you that's possible, the only having-you that exists, I'm only a construction worker but I love you so much, you don't need some intellectual to define what love is, you know?,

You are all good,

it's not Pessoa or Hesse or Neruda, still less Herberto or Beckett, I've read them all beginning to end and it tastes so good, at night I sit on the sofa, I turn off the TV and devote myself to you, I find you in every page,

because I want to be intelligent and cultured so I feel capable of you,

and I know it won't happen, that day won't come, but every day I'm readying myself for it,

love is being tirelessly prepared for what we know will never happen,

that's not one I read in a book, or maybe it is, I don't know any more, I've read so many of those things, that's another thing you already know, I'm sure, I want to be more intelligent and cultured to be capable of loving you as I know it'll never be time for me to love you, let me tell you with no exaggeration that all I'd need would be a word from you to be happy for ever, it's bad poetry but it's you,

you don't need some intellectual to define what love is, you know?,

You are all good,

if I could change anything about you it would only be your husband, God forgive me, I do deeply want you to be happy and I would do nothing to part you from someone you love, but if I could change anything about you it would only be your husband, he doesn't deserve you but then nobody deserves you, I have to be honest here, today you showed up in your blue trousers, they aren't the ones that suit you best but they do suit you enough to die for,

now I'm a whole heap of banalities and I even know the colour of your wardrobe,

tomorrow you'll probably be in the black dress, they're saying it's going to rain and when it does you always prefer dark colours, must be a way of fitting into the weather, or whatever, I'd bet that tomorrow you'll be wearing the black dress, you won't have it on in front of the cameras, there you'll wear clothes you've borrowed and it all suits you so well, but I know I'm a simple construction worker on some scaffolding watching you go by,

what do I know about poetry if I've never seen any poem but you?,

you don't need some intellectual to define what love is, you know?,

You are all good,

and she stopped and answered, nobody laughed and he came down, she smiled, showed him an old photograph, a scratched, tatty notebook, someone heard her saying she missed talking to someone intelligent, no idea if that's just a rumour or the truth, what's for sure is that since they'd seen a pig riding a bicycle on YouTube nothing else would ever come as a surprise again to those people on the scaffolding,

you don't need some intellectual to define what love is, they knew that now.

My God, but moving house is complicated, even if it's for the best,

this one seemed good, but for the location, I'm far away from everything that matters to me, I like to go out in the morning and have the city right there to hand, the place where I earn my living, the perfect space for a little lunch or a tea or even dinner, being able to take a couple of steps and meet Zé Faria there for some idle chat, this one's out of the question, it's obvious, if I'm not going to be demanding about the place I live what am I going to be demanding about, the place I die, isn't that right?,

maybe this one, everything's nearby, perfect location, no doubt about it, let's see, well, just as I expected, the comfort falls short of what's desired, I try to picture myself waking up here and falling asleep here and I don't like it, it doesn't seem very well lit either, it's not like I'm after luxury but I don't want discomfort either, just what has to be, and what doesn't, I still have plenty of others to look at, I don't need to stick with this one, long live freedom of choice, if I'm not going to be demanding about the place I live what am I going to be demanding about, the place I die, isn't that right?,

it's only by a hair's breadth that this isn't the one, fuck, I really did feel comfortable, perfect location, right at the entrance to the city, Fonseca's café right next door, Guidinha's restaurant, I really was just about to go for this one, but the neighbourhood, ugh, I didn't like what I saw round here, strange people and I don't like strange people, or at least not these strange people, I always end up fearing for my safety, call me a scaredy-cat but that's the way I am, I've got to feel safe and I don't here, you never know who's going to be just ahead, it's true, only the other day I heard someone talking about how murderers don't look like murderers and thieves don't look like thieves, but I have to disagree, I know one or two thieves and they look exactly like thieves, entirely like thieves, or it's that I know they are and so that's how I see them, in any case it's a shame, this place had everything but the neighbourhood I want, I've got to keep looking and not complain, keep on going till that possible perfection appears, if I'm not going to be demanding about the place I live what am I going to be demanding about, the place I die, isn't that right?,

it's just me and my obsession with being strange, I know, there was nothing missing here and I could easily find what I wanted, but your eyes need to be fed, too, and they live, right?, and I do so like living with my eyes, if it's not beautiful it won't make me happy, and this place isn't, it's too grey, too dark, I like light, joy, I'm a kid, deep down, and on the surface too, I'm a kid and I like playing and I like serious things but also hot ones when they're in a good mood, it makes me sad but that's how it's got to be, on to the next one as this one won't do either, I'm sorry, if I'm not going to be demanding about the place I live what am I going to be demanding about, the place I die, isn't that right?,

ah *sim*, yes, wonderful, this place is perfect, the ideal location, not too near or far, near excitement and far from danger, I once read that in a pamphlet from a rally and it became my life philosophy, the neighbourhood is charming, the lady next door is really lovely, reminds me of my mother years ago, we're going to be good friends, I'm sure about that, the space is so full of colour, everything telling me that I'm alive, and I am, I'm happy here, I'm going to be happy here, I've found it at last, *sim*, if I'm not going to be demanding about the place I live what am I going to be demanding about, the place I die, isn't that right?,

and I could bunk up right away, start enjoying the new house and everything it has to offer me, but it's already dinner time and the association stops dishing out soup by the church at ten, let me just sort out my card to reserve the place, just to be on the safe side, and oh, I hope I don't get there too late and someone steals my place,

My God, but moving house is complicated, even if it's for the best.

You told me that all you need is love and new shoes to be the happiest woman in the world and here I am, it's a small shoe shop and I haven't the faintest idea what to choose, maybe the lady serving me could help out, I tell her your name and she laughs, most likely your name isn't relevant to this business of buying shoes, but the truth is I do so like saying your name that I never miss an opportunity,

Bárbara,

I say, and she laughs, and I'm so happy I say it again to say sorry for having said it,

Bárbara,

just once more, this time I don't say it but think it, she's not laughing any more and just waiting for me to tell her what I want, probably boots, or otherwise sandals, I haven't the faintest idea, I attempt an explanation for what I mean but I'm not convincing,

but what do you want specifically?

she asks, I answer with the truth, why the hell would I say anything else when the truth is so beautiful?, what I want is to make her happy, see the look in her eyes when I get it right, when I say the words she wants, when I make the movements she desires, or hug her when she most needs it, or comfort her when everything seems to be weighing her down,

what I want is to make her happy,

I say unafraid to the lady in the shop,

what would you recommend?,

and she smiles again, women in shoe shops have a

very particular kind of condescension about them, she says she likes my answer but that it doesn't help her much, such blasphemy, so many blasphemies, could there ever be anything more useful than making you happy?, I keep walking round the shop in search of something, a sign, something that says yes to me, that model, that colour, that material, so many ways to make you happy and here I am desperate at not finding one, now the lady wants to know what you're like, what you like, if you're tall or short, what kind of clothes you wear, and before I've even realised it I'm already showing her my phone with the photo of you at your brother's birthday party, she sees how you're dressed and I love you, so simple, she immediately congratulates me because you're so beautiful and I even feel jealous of her, only I should see you like this being so beautiful it makes me shiver, I miss you so much when she says this that I call you, I don't say where I am, I just say I love and I need you, I hang up and I'm not satisfied, I send you a text message, too,

I go through life in search of you and it's just as well I find you every day,

and I don't know where those words came from, not being a poet and never having written in my life, the lady in the shop has some options, four or five, I look at each one doubtfully, I want to find out where you are, in which one you are, but none of them persuades me of your happiness, and ever since I met you objects have served to persuade me of your happiness, for a moment I want to choose one of them but I'm interrupted by the sound of the cell phone, and your message in reply,

come on, then, here I am,

and I go, I apologise to the lady in the shop but I've got to go, I'll come back tomorrow and I'll lead you by the hand, after all I too only need love and shoes to be happy, why shouldn't we have it all at the same time?

The morning is a sinuous knife without your hand resting on its shoulder,

that's how I'd start a piece of writing about the different parts of the day, later I'd talk about the sickness of a whole afternoon to be able to feel the burden of silence, and when I reached night-time I wouldn't even have to write anything, two or three tears and a knot in the throat would be enough, there isn't supposed to be night if I cannot sleep with you, that seems obvious,

Because I need your skin to knock myself down, and to bear it,

that's how I'd start a piece of writing on civil engineering, then I would theorise on the pernicious effects of the wind on the window when I stretch out on the sofa waiting for you to arrive, and you don't, as well as on the importance of having strong foundations to hang on to you and to love you against the wall, the best house is a house which was constructed to survive the natural disaster that is love, what kind of crappy colleges don't teach you that?,

Lies console me, and I know now that your sweat was drops of venom,

that's how I'd start a piece of writing on the exaggerated importance of being true, I would look at the need to invent excuses to stay alive, nobody in a perfect mental state can tolerate life, the secret of happiness is the secret of just the right dose of madness, there must be someone who has the courage to accept that secret, and I do, and missing you even more,

I like to lick you and watch you melting with love,

that's how I'd start a piece of writing about chemical processes, I'd tackle the photosynthesis of your embrace, carbon dioxide, water, glucose and an orgasm, and that's it, like the way butterflies live so little and yet manage to be eternal, more or less like the invincible volatility of your hand in mine, anyone who doesn't believe in supernatural forces doesn't love, and I don't believe in them, let there be no doubt,

There is only midday when you arrive,

that's how I'd start a piece of writing about time, it would remind me of our lunch in bed, of course, we called it wasting time but it does in fact taste good, bodies combined in surrender to the urgency of food, I could just as well write about the midnight of your sex on mine, the two a.m. of your sex on mine, anyway, we know all times are sexually active, and completely passive, it just depends on whether you're here or not, take this other responsibility and do with it what you can,

There's a mousetrap and God when your eyes blind mine,

that's how I'd start a piece of writing about ophthalmology, and I wouldn't be able to write another word, I'd be incapable of seeing a single letter, only your body and the lack of your voice, I'd have to be quiet before it was too late, and fuck, it would be,

Daily I discover the existence of unpopulated laughs, sharp little laughs, and nothing more,

that's how I'd start a piece of writing about joy, I'd dismember the ridiculous existence of other laughs that are not yours, only what you have inside you should happen, laughter and tears are exactly the same if they don't come from you, or at worst from beside you, do you see now?,

I feel a pigeon crap on my head when I surrender to another kiss,

that's how I'd start a piece of writing about the flight of birds, the scale of what is moving isn't worth jack shit if you aren't moved by me, I'm just trying to be the best so you will love me more, or so that you will love me at all, what the hell would one single man want with a Nobel, that's what I don't understand, do you?,

I could even run the risk of being prime minister or president of the republic, how very revolting that would be, just so I might bear the strange violence of your side of the bed lying empty,

that's how I'd start a piece of writing about politics, anybody who doesn't have someone to love tends to find the most unlikely occupations, I surrender myself deep down to what entertains me the most and distances me from you, I could be a politician, mayor or clown, you never know maybe even a poet, and that's not bad at all, even if you can't live on it,

I want now, and also later,

that's how I'd start a piece of writing about love, but that's enough of writing to you now, forgive me, I prefer to love you, it's lucky that I have you here reading and that you like what I've written so far, the only unforgivable spelling mistake would be your not liking it, to hell with critics and masterpieces, if it's able to love you then it is art, you don't get any simpler than that,

this is how I'd end a piece of writing about nothing at all, and about everything else, too, and there you have it.

I need to return to you obsessively,

I can hold out for two or three minutes, sometime four or five when I manage to sleep a little, read a book that carries me away, and then I'm back, at last, at the strange need to find you,

there's a voraciousness of affection in me,

it unsettles me that you can exist somewhere where I am not, can your skin do it?, mine surrenders, it throws in the towel and laments, is it possible to have whiny skin?,

I have to learn to prostitute the letters,

everything I write and read brings you, yesterday I read the directions for some medication or other and I invented a poem, it was more or less about the contraindications of your body, the adverse effects of your sweat on the skin, and in the end I just felt like taking all the medication so that something of you could love me,

there's a wound to protect in me,

your gaze is definitive, and everything else passes and even then it doesn't stop hurting, the restaurant of Dona Laura who asked about you yesterday, how's the girl doing?, and I smiled, you're so many people's girl and I wanted you all for myself, there could be love without selfishness, perhaps, but I don't know it and I hate anyone who does, and Dona Laura too,

I need to get myself a name for your lips,

and for you, too, by the way, I thought of calling you water because you enter me and leave me through every pore, then I remembered to call you air because despite being invisible you sustain me, and I ended up calling you mine because you were all I needed,

there's some lack dissolved in my blood,

I like to see a thin glimpse of God at the moment you wake up, your eyes gradually showing me the extent of the clouds, I could just be moved by it but that would be too superficial,

I have to believe that the destruction of the void is the primary aim,

deep down you exist to dissolve entirely, and only you can manage the unbearable wretchedness of all this, there's an installation of pornography and of prayer when you take a kiss and add to it the inside of your thigh,

I need to feel the first shiver of death, and the last of you,

give me each day what's unforgettable so that I can forget about you, I'm such a fool that I thought you wouldn't die,

and I was right,

you could even go and take your body with you beneath the earth,

but don't think I'm going to let you rest in peace.

Dear mother,

Dear father:

Time passes over the tears I shed, I no longer even have the scars from the hurt I once suffered. And yet memory. That bitch memory.

No one deserves a happy memory.

And I was. We were. We were happy. The house filled with our joy inside it. The yard, grandad telling stories a thousand and two times that he'd already told a thousand and one times before, grandma always busy with setting the table, uncles and aunts saying that life comes at a cost. And it does come at a cost, father. It does, mother.

No one deserves an empty house.

And the smells. The smells don't go away. The smells are the best way of making yourself suffer. The smell of the kitchen where life was once. A dream once. Me as a boy in the kitchen full of grandad, grandma, uncles and aunts. Me as a boy dreaming of being big, big like my uncles – 'one day I'm going to be rich and I'm going to buy loads of stuff'. Me as a boy wanting to grow up.

No one deserves a body that grows up.

And the loss. All the fucking loss. Grandma with a cancer inside her. Grandad giving up more with each day that his Maria was being taken away from him. The uncles and aunts and their wrinkles. All of them going with each day I grew up. And everything dies when our dreams die.

Nobody deserves to outlast their dreams.

And there's no grandma now and there's no grandad. There's the smell of the hot kitchen with my dreams inside it. The smell of the bedroom where I hid, under the bed, to hear the grown-ups talk. The new words, big words, bad words. That tight hug from uncle André – 'you're becoming quite the strapping lad, my boy' – around my childhood back. The empty house with what I am inside it.

Nobody deserves to survive what he kills.

And to have a father and a mother. Only when the house empties do you learn what a father is worth, what a mother is worth. And it doesn't matter what had been, what was yet to be. It doesn't matter what words we said one day, the mistakes that one day we didn't avoid making. Father's thick voice doesn't matter either – 'you must be a serious man' – nor does mother's unspoken pain. It doesn't matter what was lost when you have a father and a mother to hold. Here we still are, mother. Here we still are, father.

Nobody knows what loss means as long as they still have a mother and a father to hug.

And as long as I have your shoulders to rest upon, no tears will die alone.

'You could have fucked with everything but the illusion.'

On the esplanade where we met, the end of the world at the end of an afternoon like the end of the afternoon when life started to make sense.

'The end of an illusion, it's the biggest sonofabitch in the world.'

And the city seems to shut itself off with each step I take. Your words are no longer there. Your hands are no longer there, the wrinkly skin – 'they're the hands of my soul; inside I'm an adorable little old lady' – of your hands. And time. Time is like a penitence I must pay.

Each minute without you I live through the whole life I had with you.

The esplanade without your body, the esplanade without your voice. The cruelty of a happy world. How is it possible to be happy after love like this?

'When your illusions are fucked, everything is fucked.'

I told you I could bear it. I told you that the meaning of life was to be found in keeping going. I believed it. I even believed that keeping-going really existed. And it does. Everything I do is exactly that, just that. Desperately that. Going on. Without you, I go on. I go on, myself.

Losing you changed everything even if everything remains the same.

I already can't say how long it's been since I died. How long with that empty esplanade. How long your back – 'grab me like that, squeeze me like that, I like feeling your chest behind me, your sex growing in your trousers' – the distance from your back on the esplanade in which everything was done and everything was undone. I already can't say where the desire for one more day is to be found.

'Don't think my hating you means I don't love you.'

The illusion. That bitch illusion. I let it fall. I let it slip. I let life take care of us. And laziness. That bitch laziness. I let it advance on us, and conquer, one day at a time, a few inches of land. I let the house where two people loved each other become the house where two people lived.

Houses are not for living in; houses are for loving in.

Ours is still here. Really ours even if all that remains is one lost man. Your wardrobe intact, your fingerprints on the glass as proof you still exist. The mirror in which you looked at yourself after you came – 'I like knowing what an orgasm looks like, what an orgasm does to my skin' – and the message I wrote with tears and the lipstick you forgot on the bedside table: 'There's always time for one more illusion.'

Come back now or die for ever.

And if it's already too late, forget about your watch and go.

An embrace from you always arrives on time.

Silence, there's going to be love.

All loves begin like this. In the silence of a look, in the silence of one hand depending on the other, another vagrant hand wandering the night-time city of your body, in the silence of lips chewed, changed, massaged, embraced, and embraced again. All loves are an extended silence.

It's essential to tell politics to go fuck itself. It's essential to understand that only what's politically incorrect can bring happiness. It's essential to refuse what is sold to you and buy only what is not for sale.

Nothing worthwhile has a price.

It's essential to love silence. Reject anyone who rejects it. Demand that they respect it as God is respected.

And only those who do not love fear silence.

It's essential to demand silence. Keep words for after the orgasm, for after the sin.

All sin forgets your words.

And no word is so great that it can be said to unite us.

Silence is essential between two people who want to speak to each other. Silence is essential for love to be heard.

And 'I love you' is a word that is only said like this:

Sssshhh.

The great advantage of life is that it teaches us to cry again. Life is infantilising. It becomes greater as it makes us smaller. It grows outside whatever is lost inside. We spend our childhood wanting to grow, our adolescence wanting to grow. And then we understand that the only people who want to grow are those who still feel small. An adult feels small but thinks the opposite. He feels small and wants to get smaller. Go back to a time when there were dreams.

Where are dreams lost?

All dreams are lost. Even those that you will gain, and you will gain many, they'll all be lost. Because they've already stopped being dreams. You dreamed this, you got this. And that's that. There it went, the dream. The secret is managing to generate new dreams. Dreams that can occupy the white space left by the dream you have lost.

Even if it was gained.

Even if it was gained.

It wanted to be like you.

And I wanted to be like you. I wanted to look ahead and see that the path doesn't end, the path as far as the eye could see.

Does yours not go as far as the eye can see?

Mine makes me unable to see. I see less every day. And every day I see more behind me. Growing up is seeing better behind you with each passing day and being unable to see ahead. Growing up is an illness of the eyes. You get less and less able to see what's behind you. As if you were walking backwards.

Is growing old walking backwards?

Yes. You're walking in the opposite direction to the way you're looking. You're looking forward and dreaming only backwards.

Is dreaming backwards dangerous?

Dreaming backwards can kill. You have to be a child. You have to look at a wrinkle as though you're looking at an Action Man or a Barbie. Take it out of the box, be fascinated by it, investigate it, understand that it's nothing but folded skin: fascinating folded skin. Learning to grow old is learning to play. Being old is learning everything all over again. The world changed when you changed. The world grew old when you grew old. What used to be a banality is now an impossibility. You want to play football and you can't, you want to dance all night and you can't. And your life is many hours of your day of this: you want to and you can't. The world has changed for you. You need to learn everything all over again. What to do, how to do it. You have to invent yourself so as not to be completely wiped out. There's no sadder moment than the one when you desire something and your body prevents you from having something. The body is a bastard. Cover your ears now, please.

I've covered them.

Now listen carefully: the body's a son of a bitch. Never pay it any attention. If the body gives you orders, tell it to fuck off. The body's only good for offering you false hope. It makes you believe yourself capable of everything, feeding you with feelings. And then taking them away. One by one, slowly, to increase the pain. You just need to be able to discover new feelings.

Like a child?

Like a child. However few toys a child has, he will always have all the toys in the world. A child who makes a pair of socks a plane, a chicken bone the Eiffel Tower, a torn jersey a set of football gear. Growing old is transforming a body unable to have the expected feelings into an amusement park to be explored.

I've got to go. My teacher's already called me.

Go. Learn. But not too much. Knowing too much always goes wrong. Limit yourself to illusions.

I like you.

And I you. That's what you must never lose. The capacity to like.

One day I'm going to be big.

One day I'm going to be small again. I promise.

Once you are resigned, there's nothing left for you but to be buried.

Worse than the illnesses, worse than the economic crisis, worse than the defeats that happen every day, the world's great drama is resignation. Complete and utter (and sad, so sad) resignation. Resignation is the absence of dreams, the absence of goals, the absence of plans, the absence of desires: the absence of revolution. And there is less and less revolution in the world. If there's no revolution you can be anything, but you definitely can't be happy.

The problem with the world isn't massification; it's mass *equivocation*.

The equivocating of the masses. The world's problem is linguistic. The problems of the world are not convulsions, but conjunctions. The diabolical obsession with the yet, with the though, with the however. And yet is a fucker. Although is a fucker. However is a fucker. Ninety-eight percent of people say 'and yet' whenever they speak; and the other two percent are happy. However many difficulties they have (and they have so, so many), however much it may sometimes seem that it won't be possible to get there (and there are so, so many times). However much everything might be telling them 'and yet', there are still always people who don't resign themselves.

The big secret to being alive, obvious as it may seem, is not to die till you're buried.

Up till that point, you have an obligation to dream, to plan, to believe. Up till then you have an obligation to try. That at least: try. It's never too late to try. If you're eighty years old and still want to feel the best orgasm of your life: go on – try. If you're ninety years old and you still want to write the book of your life: go on – try. If you're a hundred years old and you still want to find a woman to love: go on – try. Perhaps you won't succeed, most probably. But only what's improbable is worth it. Even happiness, if it's foreseeable, is a sadness.

Believing in the improbable is, probably, the best decision you can make in your life.

And seeing. Risking seeing. Really seeing. Seeing what only you can see. You see things that nobody else sees; I see things that nobody else sees. Everybody sees things that nobody else sees. And it's from these sights I have and you have that the evolution of the world is made. The world only advances when these sights are transformed into implementations: into real acts, into palpable matter. Believe in what you see, and take a chance on what you see being the only kind of altruism the world gives you to implement. Bet on what is yours alone. That's the only way you can bet on everything that is ours.

The blindest person is not one who cannot see; nor even one who doesn't want to see. The blindest person is the one who only sees.

Maybe using pen names is the only acceptable madness.

And there's no name for something that has no definition. I go by what I think, by what I feel – and not by what others call me. But even what they call me does make me. Perhaps if I were Carlos I wouldn't love the same people, perhaps if I were Fernando I wouldn't wish for my wishes, I wouldn't know the same things I know.

Perhaps your name is your inside skin.

And we have several names on our skin. But when we are in pain we hurt with the right name. If I am to hurt I will always be Pedro. I will embrace the names I love with all my letters, I won't allow any reserve to keep me away from the words that define me. Until the time comes for running away. And I can be a fearful man in my own recklessness, a vagrant woman in my reason. When the time comes for running away all people are inside me. And it's only like this that I can escape from what, even if I'm not, only I can be.

Perhaps being many people is the sole allowed form of solitude.

The nights pass and the days pass, and through them people pass, I pass among the people who wander past and who wander past me, without knowing what I'm writing, why I'm writing, for whom I'm writing. And I write. I'm always me, that bastard Pedro, as I write Daniel, and Miguel, and Joana, and Maria. And everything Pedro writes is, even if it's not, what only Pedro can be.

Perhaps making things up is the sole practicable kind of truth.

There are people who don't understand what writing is. I don't understand what writing is. And that's why I write.

Perhaps writing is the only possible victory.

The drama of loving is not having substitutes.

And everything else tastes like shit. Because there was your embrace, because your smell exists. I loved you for ever even though I have already stopped loving you. I have kept within me the evening of our body for the first time (your panting showing me what language is spoken in heaven, your mouth showing me the size of a kiss), and from that evening I was an orphan of a body whenever it was not your body. And when the day came to say goodbye I knew that the day of for ever had arrived.

The drama of loving is not accepting death.

There is one woman too many whenever I love a body that is not yours. And a man too few. I lie down, hug, squeeze (the perfect fit of your back in my arms, the smell of your lips on the sweat of my neck). And even an orgasm confirms the hypocrisy of the flesh. I said goodbye to orgasms when I said goodbye to you. I've been to bed with so many women already and it's always your goodnight that puts me to sleep.

The drama of loving is creating only replicas.

Everything I love is you. One mouth, one skin, one sex. Everything I love is you. And there is no oxymoron more perfect than 'new love'. Your love alone is new. And there is no succession to a reign like that. Loving you is a fascist monarchy, a dictatorship within me. What comes after you only comes after you. Always after you. Every time after you. What comes after you only comes after me, and wherever I am, I am either alone waiting for you or I am alone with you. If love exists it is because you exist.

The drama of loving is loving you.

Suck one another: that is what a real God ought to say.

Our bodies are not for living; our bodies are for loving. And I must explore every vein to learn what blood you are made of.

'Use me up to what's impossible,' she asks, her samba hips along his obedient sex. 'Either you reach deep into the bone or you're still on the surface', and no fingers have ever learned more than that whole dictionary, those pages and pages of incomplete theories.

Consume one another: that is what a real God ought to say.

Our bodies are not for living; our bodies are for consummation. And I must explore every taste if I am to learn what pleasure you are made of.

'When I see that I'm going to make it, that's when I give up,' he explains, eyes lowered, hands on the threshold of her back. 'Either you're unreachable or you're too close', and the moment comes to discover everything again, the bed explored in the cleaver blade of an I Want.

Come with one another: that is what a real God ought to say.

Our bodies are not for living; our bodies are for flying.

'The best thing about touching you is feeling untouchable myself,' she explains, breathing laboured on the wet pillow, the whole roof and all the sky. 'I open your legs to raise your feet off the ground', and all the impossibilities rose up, all the divine mutinied.

They said goodbye in search of the perfect recollection: the final orgasm and absolute love. Anything better (hands detaching themselves finger by finger, a pain so deep that even tears cannot reach it) seemed impossible to them there.

('Whenever you open my legs I feel exposed.')

And it was.

The most dangerous thing of all is what's reasonable.

What is not good or bad – it's just pretty good, it's pretty bad. What neither excites you nor depresses you, what offers neither orgasms nor tears. What neither heats nor cools.

The most dangerous thing of all is what's reasonable.

And reason. Bastard reason. Ninety percent of people spend ninety percent of the time in search of what in ninety percent of cases is of no use whatsoever. Bastard reason. And then there's the 'I told you so', the 'I wouldn't have done it like that', the appalling 'that's what I said'. All because of the bastard reason. All because of the beast reason.

Only those who aren't afraid of not being reasonable can be bestial.

Those who know they can be wrong. Those who know that they're constantly making one cock-up after another. Not because they want to. Not because they're not trying. But just because they did, they took the risk, because they took that step forward when the beasts were all around them, shit-scared, telling them to stop here.

Better an idiot that fails than a genius that endures.

And I'm the guy who tries. The guy who wants things different to everything he sees. The guy who when he sees something cool doesn't criticise, resentfully, whoever did it – and who seeks, on the contrary, to do even better. I'm that arrogant guy who believes he can do better than everything he sees. And who does everything he can just for the sake of doing it. He might not succeed (and only he knows how it feels to be constantly over on this side, miles away from what you wish you'd done, from what you wish you'd produced). But he tries. He really does try. He tries without hesitation. And he subjects himself to the criticisms of the petty little beasts. Of those who spend their lives pointing the finger (and it's so easy to point the finger; anyone can point the finger; when you have nothing but a finger to point you point the finger in order to endure: to bear the weight of your inability to do). Of those who are always bloody reasonable because they never dare, not for a single moment, to do more than others have already done. Who are, and always will be, assistants. Eternal assistants. Guys and girls who will never lose their job – because they're sheltered behind those who show their face, who give their souls, their lives, for what they believe in.

Better an idiot getting high than a cowering genius.

Whenever anybody sees me replicating someone else's idea, they can shoot me between the eyes. When someone sees me doing only what others have already done, writing like others have already written, creating what others have already created, they can shoot me in the head. Because that's when I will be dead. Completely (and we all know it's possible to be only partially) dead. When someone sees me criticising somebody who's done differently, who's dared differently, who's invented differently, they can shoot me in the head. I'm here and I show my face. I'm Pedro Chagas Freitas and I fabricate ideas. I am buffeted by them. I'm Pedro Chagas Freitas and not a day goes by without my inventing something new. It might be a bit of text, the construction of a line, some radical use of a piece of punctuation. Or a children's game, a concept for a TV programme, a book that's so special it doesn't even have order. I'm Pedro Chagas Freitas and I'm an idiot: that's all there is to it.

Better an ostracised idiot than a domesticated genius.

And the chapels. And the half-dozen enlightened souls. Those who define what is good and what is bad with a blink of the eye. Those poor enlightened ones. The artists. Those poor artists. Let nobody dare, one day, to call me an artist – because I'm merely a professional perspirer. A guy who works like a dog to create what he once dreamed of creating. And create it he does. And it's not a lot. It's never a lot. There's always more to create. And when there's nothing left to create it's because it's time to switch off. The machines, the heart, the breathing. Stop it all. When there's nothing left to create there's nothing left to live. Kill me before that day comes. And write on the gravestone the following words, nice and clear: here's the idiot who just wanted to do what he wanted. And he succeeded.

All my fears fit in your lap.

And if God exists, He is the calm of your shoulders, the divine stillness that goes from your neck to your breast. And me, there, so small that I don't even measure up to my centimetres, and yet so big that even the sky wouldn't have enough space to keep me. We are creatures beyond the world, unique couples from a journey that even the end of our bodies will be unable to stop.

Even the worst of life is calmed when I am in your eyes.

There are bad people, mum. People who can't imagine what it means to endure inside this body, behind these bones, beneath the debris of an age yet to be discovered. There are people who don't know I'm a child who's scared like all children (a person scared like all people: grown-ups get scared, too, don't they, mum? – everybody gets scared, don't they, mum?), and yesterday an adult told me not to show up till I've grown up, and a child who was less of a child than me grabbed me by the hair and threw me to the ground, and the whole school watching and laughing, and the adult saying 'don't show up till you grow up' and the child saying 'take that, this'll teach you a lesson'.

Nobody knows how big a child is.

And it hurt so much, mum. The whole school laughing at my bleeding hair, at the words that just kept getting worse ('let's see if this son of a bitch doesn't learn once and for all not to be different from everybody else'), and at that moment I understood, I understood that stupidity is always the same age after all, that all men and all women act in the same way however much their bodies grow or stop growing; school is what they call the place I go to every day but it might just as well be called world – because that's where all society exists just as it does outside, in the obedient chorus of a tamed crowd.

Nobody knows what freedom is.

And then you arrived, mum. You and that look in your eye, your words ('I love you, my love; I love you and nobody's going to change that'), your lap (have I told you that even the devil can't get to your lap?), and it's as though my whole body rises up, my whole life is ready for another bad grown-up, for another bad child. You arrive and your eyes and your lap and tomorrow is a new day. Everything in life can be summarised in a belief that tomorrow is a new day.

If God exists His name is You.

What's the point of a floor if not to be trodden upon by you?

You were a child and your body wanted smiles, running races on the street (where the cars won't let you run now, you know the place?), playing hide-and-seek with your body the way you play it today with your soul; I was a child but obsessed with the idea that I was a grown-up, I didn't want to run races on the street or to play hide-and-seek, I just asked my body to grow, school to end and life to take me far away from there. If I liked common-places I couldn't like the place where you are.

What's the point of a body if not to transport yours?

We lived different lives and we were so close, there was no more than a wall between us, and also your mother (she was so beautiful, your mother) and mine (she was so beautiful, my mother), their eternal words ('better head inside, son, it's getting cold', 'better head inside, girl, it's getting dark'), the fear of the whole world collapsing down on to our backs; the first words I said to you were 'better wise up, kid' when you told me that one day you were going to be a movie star (you were in that grey dress your daughter has started wearing now, remember?), and then I turned my back on you and you stood there, I know you just stood there, watching me go, without even noticing your tears and your whole castle of dreams collapsing.

What's the point of memory if not to bring you back?

One day the road stopped being ours, I went off to marry (Joana, that scowling woman who lives by the butcher's, you know the one I mean?), you went off to university (I bet even then you already knew that you were a star without any need for the movies), and all time did was to separate us, separate us more and more, all roads carrying me far away from seeing you.

What's the point of opening my eyes if you're not standing right in front of me?

Even the street stopped with your steps all of a sudden, one after another, the office door opening and all my peace of mind closing. You came in, said 'excuse me', added 'I've come for the editor's position', and no word in me could be edited, revised, rewritten; you said you'd come for the editor's position and I understood you had come for the position of my owner.

What's the point of obeying if your orders don't exist?

I obeyed you, happily, for the happiest two years of my life, taking messages, bringing you coffees, trying to look at you so that you would understand how I wanted you, and after the happiest two years of my life you simply said 'better wise up, lad' when I told you that one day I wanted to wake up beside you. And you were right, just like I was right. I never got to wake up beside you just as you never got to be a movie star, but not even that made me give up on you nor did it make you give up on being a movie star. You went to Hollywood in search of a chance to shine and I went to Hollywood in search of you. One day one of us is going to wise up. I hope it's you.

What's the point of having a head if not to rest it on you?

(her on his lap)

'If I could choose, I would have been born in your arms.'

'...'

'So as not to waste time. So that I might understand, then and there, what the reason was for my being here.'

'All of us ought to be born in the arms of the person we're going to die with. Just a question of saving energy. To start out, right away, saving time.'

(his hand on her face, slowly discovering each wrinkle in the corners of her eyes)

'Every mother understands there are loves that are urgent.'

'Every one.'

'And that not finding the path until halfway along the path means half the path has already been lost.'

'Before you I was seeking; after you I seek still. But I have already found. I'm seeking more than I have found.'

'That's what loving is. Seeking more even after having been found.'

'At worst I'll just find you again.'

(a tight hug)

'Did you know that whenever I wake up I still look at you, I still touch you? To know that you are, to know that this exists.'

'And watching you breathe. I spend hours fighting back sleep in order to watch you breathe. I feel each movement of your chest as though I were feeling the space that life occupies within me. Your chest rises and I go with it, it falls and I go with it. And that's how I fall asleep, with the certainty of your breathing. With the certainty that I can sleep restfully.'

(tears on her cheeks, her head lost in his lap)

'We always wake up hand in hand. Had you noticed that?'

'It's as though even in our dreams we need to be together. I fall asleep and I take you with me, hand in hand, so that there is no path I take, even if it happens within my unconscious, that I take without you.'

'The other day I dreamed I was the happiest woman in the world. Then, when I woke up and saw you beside me, that was when I understood that after all I'd dreamed that I was the second happiest woman in the world.'

'If I could have chosen what I wanted to feel it would be less than what I actually feel.'

(the clothes are undressed; first his, then hers)

'And everything we say comes out of our souls. I speak to you and what I say comes from within, from the deepest part of me. If I had to lie to you I would have to tell you the truth.'

'We've never had one sole conversation. Everything we say stretches out. We speak the same conversation, however different the subject. When we speak, the subject is us. It could be biology, science or politics. When we speak, the subject is always us.'

(eyes on eyes, sweat, exchanged looks, excited hands)

'Love me as though we were endless.'

'There's no other choice: either you love as though it were the last time, and that's no kind of love at all, it's just covering fear up with pleasure, anxiety with moaning, the sound of silence with the sound of moaning; or you love as though it were endless time, and that's how love pacifies without ever stopping unsettling, like a strong current, swift but never hurried, never ceasing to unsettle.'

'Or desperate to just the right degree. Excessive to just the right degree.'

'It's necessary to feel too much without overdoing it.'

(the moment of one in the other)

'Love me as though you were talking to me with your body.'

(and the final moment)

'If I could choose, I would have been born in your arms.'

I don't know what I am but I know I'm your woman.

I don't believe in loves that do harm, despite being certain that all loves do harm. To love is to be certain that two birds in flight are better than one in the hand. Proverbs never know what love is.

I would change a life of orgasms for the orgasm of a lifetime.

There's an almost-happiness in each moment without you, and even the pleasure can happen without my coming with it. Cerebral people ask me for containment, they ask me for cancellation. But it's impossible to contain what makes us love. It's impossible to contain what makes us live. And if life exists it's so that it is like this for you, so that somebody, one day, can be like this for someone.

Only someone who never stops being completely her own can manage to be completely someone else's.

In you I am what I could never stop being, the woman who fled from what skin gives her, who never surrendered to the I don't care. If I do I do completely, if I want I surrender completely, if I need I bend completely. If I'm here to live a life I'm also here to yield. To know that I am no less just because I'm not a queen, and so that all kingdoms are governed from the inside.

Only someone who is able to be in shards can be herself entirely.

Only those who are pitiful stop halfway. I refuse to find myself in nothing. If I want to get there I'll cross to the other side, without pride but proud, trembling but without fear, and when they tell me I've been weak I'll reply with the contempt of someone who only accepts ecstasy when ecstasy is possible.

Strength consists in refusing sufficient satisfaction when there's a chance of having total satisfaction.

I don't know about the woman I am but I know about the woman I'm not. I'm not the woman who hides amid the cooking pots, the woman who is silent when it's time, who surrenders to the sham of security, to the supportive fraud of watching time pass. No. I'm not. I'm not a woman of *fados* and wailing, of fads and railing, of dreams that drag themselves round corners. No. I'm not. I'm not a woman of smiles when there's such a thing as laughter, of villages when there's the world. I'm not one millimetre less than I can be, and if one day I fall it's because I tried to jump and not because I chose instead to accept.

Better to be a *Titanic* that has sunk than a ship that never travels anywhere at all.

I don't know what I am but I know I'm yours.

When they asked me to show them my veins I held up a picture of you.

And everyone laughed and I didn't understand.

There's no science that can comprehend love.

Rip you out of me or slit my wrists?

And what's death but the moment when you realise that a vein has been amputated from your soul? Even if the body persists (bodies do sometimes persist, stubbornly, when all the souls have gone, when all the spaces are empty and all that's left is to close up the last lock; there are bodies that are stubborn, that don't understand that declaring someone dead doesn't depend on them, it never depends on them), even if there is the usual inspiring and the usual expiring, the seconds passing, one by one, slowly. I could even do without dreams if I had you beside me to make me dream.

All falling is useful if you can help me back up.

Just to feel that you exist for me, that you are there for me, and that there's no truth (I hear around the place that I can't depend on you like that, that no love can stand being loved like that) big enough to interfere in this invincible lie.

When I can't love you like this it's because I no longer love you.

When I don't feel the ground stop moving when you aren't there, when I don't feel my whole being embracing you when I look at you, when there's any imperfect moment to be yours.

Either it feels like everything or it's worthless.

Yesterday we went to the park together, old adolescents on swings, on merry-go-rounds, in the little toy cars where we learned to be children. And when I gave you my hand and looked at you among all those people I even wanted death to come more quickly. So that we could have a happy ending. So that we could end in the way that immortal things should end. Us and the smile (it's been so many years, your smiling at my efforts to make you laugh; and the unending tears as I told you it was for ever and you didn't believe it) that brought us together.

So death and that final marriage: let them come. And on our tombstone let them write two simple lines:

They died. And they lived happily ever after.

Any pen can start a war, and that's also what brings me peace,

when we went fishing you were happy, a fish bit the hook, you hugged me proudly, you said I love you in the middle of a kiss, then you looked it in the eye and obviously asked to throw it back in the water,

and I don't know why I'm wasting time writing what I remember about you, but probably it's just the best way of crying,

it's tears that save people,

it's not doctors or pills, and that's why I write, I'm looking for the word that takes me out of you, that's all it is and it seems so much,

only the condemned tell the truth,

others fear that something will end, that something will be lost, only someone who has lost their love is in a position to tell the truth, as I do on this page where I bring you back, how can we have been eternal if we're already over?,

a rope is the perfect representation of you, perfect for killing as well as saving,

my next aim is to divide up the silence, and incidentally also the yearning, you ought to know, trying to reject the intimacy of the void, to manage at least a few minutes of absolutely nothing, breathing has been a scarce commodity since you went away,

from the day I met you I had already loved you for ever,

we know how useless time is at such moments, twenty-four unending hours in my head, and the night comes and it's so big, I liked to find some noise that works for me, do you see?,

we need to deepen the escape, that's the thing,

to build better walls, hide the tears, call friends over to help you dig better, what costs the most is the memory of that skin, I could make an identikit sketch of your body with more detail than a photo of you, I assure you, I just need to shut my eyes and think of you, as I'm doing now,

if you want a failure, please teach me how to go wrong,

Who is it?,

Nothing is as coarse as your name,

Bárbara,

and I open the door to corruption,

Guilty, Your Honour,

but happy.

There's the urgency of courage in tears like those.

J. asks my forgiveness and says it will never happen again. She rolls herself up in the blanket, wipes her tears with the back of the sheet and spends the afternoon suffering. I say nothing, I do nothing – I just watch the time pass and the pain scatter.

No one knows what love is.

And things with no forgiveness, they're what kill. Someone who is beloved has no right to do what is unforgivable. Loving is too big to bear something so petty. 'Forget that you hate me and love me till the very end,' I hear, my chest wet on the inside, a whole hand squeezing my entrails.

I love you so much that I can't forgive you.

Out there, a bird teaches me happiness. It beats its wings and everything around it makes sense.

The sky only exists so that flying might be possible.

In here, beyond the silence, is the shout I want to give, the freedom that not even the throat can speak. And beneath the sheets J. is suffering, she is still suffering – the sound of her tears showing me that no aspect of what is eternal is painless. 'Whenever I remember your lips I forget what keeps me from you,' and it would be so easy to let myself go, that embrace once again, that faith once again, all those religions of life once again on the altar of two bodies. 'Cure me of not having you or kill me once and for all,' she says to me, all my muscles already in that embrace of hers even though it's still only my eyes that touch her.

It's through our eyes that all forgiveness happens.

There are no grounds for letting you in after the devastation you have left in your wake. All surveys refuse you, all inquests abhor you, all formulae declare that you are impossible. I know that if you return then all this pain might return some day. But I know if you do not return then all this pain will return every day.

I have no reasons for letting you inside but please do come in.

And all the 'Ah's are spoken now, all the 'I love you's are heard without a single word that can tell, me and our ghosts speaking the language of the incapable, walking through the sin of feeling as though we have no legs and this is the only way we can walk. 'Talk quietly so the world doesn't know that it is no match for us,' and we fall asleep like this, murmurings hidden within the sheets, waiting for nobody to know that we have gone back to being incomprehensible.

Nobody knows what it was that united us but it's our still being together that is inexplicable.

The most important thing in the world is vertigo.

And for there to be vertigo, we need there to be a precipice. I need to be there, next to the place where the fall happens, to be able to remain on my feet. All lives need vertigo. And it's in your hands that I find the thing that makes me fall and still I stay on my feet.

Every day I get up to the transgression of your precipice.

And I walk along the stones of the pavement just millimetres from the moment when there is a downfall awaiting me. Either I'm millimetres from the downfall or I don't think it tastes of anything. I need to feel that it can end, that it's always just about to end, that's what makes us people, what sustains us, the destitute of the skin, and if there weren't the danger of your pleasure I might as well die.

The most important thing in the world is knowing that one day you'll end.

And that is how I cling to the weight of the minutes without needing a set of scales, legs startled at each moment without you, waiting for you perhaps to be the final one, and while there's your life there's hope. One day you go and all this ends: you are all I need to get up for when the morning asks me to surrender. At the instant when I love you (the wrinkles of your hands, the sexual aggressiveness of your beard on me, the dialogue of two bodies in search for impossible words), every abyss knows how to open up. I know that I will die of you but I also know that without you there's nothing but dying left for me.

Every day I learn to be illiterate in you.

And I write only the silence, or the lines fill with something that has no order, and if there's chaos let it be that of our spilled sweat. Then you teach me, patiently and methodically, that I need to know a lot before I can be in a position to be oblivious to what binds us, and that all our embraces are an apprenticeship. Death follows immediately when there are no more embraces to learn, no more disordered lines to fill. I require your hands on me as though in hell, awaiting the final call of a consensual rage. I order you to keep me disordered for ever. And insist that the only command should be the one that obliges us to sin.

The most important thing in the world is what can, even if forbidden, be done.

How many knives are there in your no?

Like some fucking desperate woman here I still am, waiting for you to come over, waiting for you to say 'I love you', waiting for you to say 'I love you and I've always loved you and I'll love you for ever'. But the only thing that is for ever is what ends. It's over and it's for ever. For ever without the taste of your kiss again, for ever without the 'I'm coming' of your touch again. What never ends is loving you like this.

How many men will it take for me to forget your embrace?

I'm a desirable woman. I know it. I know that men look at me as they walk by, and I walk by and they look, and that my body will never be left alone, without the presence of other bodies to meet. But no other body cancels out yours, no smell keeps me from the memory of yours, no arms hold me with the strength of your embrace. The hardest thing for me is knowing you existed. And knowing that after wanting you like this all that's left to me is to be wanted.

All that's left for me is finding the someone who loves me most after I have lost the person I love.

Even your death would be good for me. Forgive my selfishness but sometimes I dream that you'll die and free me from the hoping. As long as you're alive I'll keep believing. However much I don't believe it, however much I may know that what I hoped existed does not exist. However much you don't want me I'll dream about you, in the most hidden nook of what I am, the most fetid corner of what I feel. Needing you like this makes me sick. Needing you like this makes me ashamed. And all it takes is a 'go on…' from you for all places to make sense.

I can let others make use of me but I am your inalienable property.

Whoever wants me needs to know it. Whoever wants me must be ready to lose me as I'm ready to win you. I'll belong to whoever wants me most right up until the moment when you want me, even if you only want me the tiniest little bit. Nothing is more unfair than loving like this. And yet nothing is more beautiful than loving like this. We would be perfect if you loved me just a third as much as I love you, if you desired me a fifth as much as I desire you. As it is we're just a couple-to-be, and me the stupid woman who offers herself to instability in the hope of the vision of what never ends.

How many times will I have to die to kill you from inside me?

If I hadn't been yours that night I would never have known what it is to be unhappy like this; but I also would never have known what it is to be happy to the tips of one's bones. You gave me, on that night when I bowed down in the face of happiness, the best night of my life and all the worst nights in my life that would come after you. I only regret not having loved you later, much later, right at the final submission. So that the ending would be like this. For ever like this. Me and you and the final night.

How many lives is such a night worth?

I do not write today,

     there's so much to do and here I am shut away,

     what is this life after all?,

     on TV a man who says he's prime minister talks and how very weak it is, a few others applaud, they exchange praise as though exchanging packages,

     so I give you this, you give me that,

     one hand dirties the other, not even proverbs can withstand filth, that's for sure,

     that must have been why God gave us the capacity for disgust, that's what I believe,

     then there's some football match, I love this small life for ninety minutes, it has in it a whole kind of dramatic comic quality, an excitement that if it doesn't make you laugh will make you cry, you can't get past excitement like this unscathed,

     if you don't love or hate the defeat or the victory then you're dead, that's what I'd say to my patients if I were a doctor after setting them to watch a game live for a few minutes,

     what we do when faced with what doesn't matter to us in the least is what defines us, surviving means being ready to give everything for what doesn't matter in the least,

     I would kill for a kiss from you, for example,

     and exaggerations do exist but this isn't one of them, I really would kill,

     you know that act by which someone prevents another person from being alive?, the truth is that I could even say I'd die for a kiss from you but that would be lying,

how could I benefit from a kiss from you if I were dead?,

that's the only reason I wouldn't die to go back to the inside of your lips,

last time I was so happy when I found your tongue,

and I go to the supermarket to look at the people,

there's an incredible resemblance between a supermarket and a book, inexplicable though that may seem,

all I need to write a novel is there, but I do not write today, let that be quite clear once again,

in the bread section there's a woman every poet would like to meet, whatever that may be,

when will I learn not to look at life in verse?,

maybe that's what a poet is,

or rather a poor wretch, depending on what fiction each of us is living,

and I'm even able to be normal when I want to be, a kilo of potatoes, a bag of pre-chopped salad,

you have to give people work seeing as you can't give them love, that's how you explain the existence of an economic system,

all that's left for me to do is waste a few moments talking to the neighbours, telling them about my life,

a writer isn't much into chit-chat only because he doesn't have much to tell, this occurs to me now and it's the truth,

it would be good to know about Senhor Gouveia's toothache, only yesterday I heard him complaining as he was coming up the stairs, the bad thing about a toothache is that it makes us rethink our whole lives,

if there were no pain there would be no poets, nor me,

it's already getting dark and I've done nothing, I've only lived and that doesn't feel like much, that's the great failure of whoever invented humans, anyway,

living is all that's left us and we're never satisfied, does that make any sense?,

sometime soon I'll lie down and that's it, I've produced nothing and probably that prime minister would have preferred if I'd never existed,

where have you ever seen a citizen who produces nothing more than being alive?,

if I were to write today it would be about your voice when you say I'm here and you really are, immediately I hug you with all the years we've already lived together, I ask you to speak to me of silence and we both go quiet, and that's how we end the day without insisting on any great happiness or any special commotion, simply content with the prospect of waking tomorrow and carrying on here, and maybe that's sad, it probably is, but it's also love,

or just poetry,

perhaps I love you, I have to tell you,

you're worth my whole life and you don't even help with the balance of trade or the deficit,

and the prime minister's just going to have to learn to deal with that.

Which was born first: life or you?

I ask myself daily how it is possible that we have reached this point, in the bed that's dishevelled by us, at the re-begun moment of all orgasms. I love you up to the limit of my body, and even then I still never tire of loving you desperately, as though your skin were a religion and there were no prayer with any other purpose than to ask for you.

I beseech you to devour me or else to abandon me.

When you feel there's something missing you will be sure that everything's missing, because I can never be filled by half a glass, because not even a nearly full glass can do away with how I need you. The only routine we share is our going all the way to the folly of what we have never experienced, inventing innocences that we have not yet lost, stages of evolution that no Man knows exist, and if some superior being does exist it will get depressed when it meets us.

How can anyone have created euphoria without knowing that you exist?

And it's when I remember your embrace that I measure how much a soul weighs. All souls are the subtraction of what we touch from what we feel. And the less the subtraction, the greater the addition. That's what I am: addicted to you and all the sums that our bodies never tire of calculating.

Since when does one plus one equal everything?

And what is the soul if not the formula that defeats all mathematics, the eternal equation that no science can comprehend? What is the soul but the thing with no body and yet which still causes movement? You sleep, the sheets tangled by all the adventures that just hours ago we had no idea were possible, the window closed so that no world understands that it's too small to compare to our life, and when you wake up I know that even the tears are coming to celebrate with us.

Only things that can make you cry make sense.

It will soon be time to go. I'll go to my house, you'll go to yours. That was the way we found to make ourselves uncommon, human treasures who spend their day wanting to live. We don't make promises, we don't make constant demands, we don't find a word or several that can define us, we don't believe in the capacity for fair justice for what no law could possibly contain, enclose. We want each other when one of us decides, we love each other when one of us needs to love. We know it isn't much for somebody with such desire. But what feels like so little is the only thing that keeps us alive.

Which dies first: not loving or loving too much?

The only illness is
having no passion.

There are people who find in this world a mere
place for passing through, who don't feel what
they see, don't touch what they find; there are people
who don't understand that whatever exists was created
for falling in love, for falling in love absolutely.

If there is no passion
why should there be life?

There are people
and then there is you.

You and the madness of wanting to devour what
surrounds you, you and this uncontrollable drive
for every second to be the last, for every moment
of life to need desperately to be worth the whole life.

If there isn't what you are
why should there be love?

And then I exist. The woman in love you taught
to fall in love. Before you there was no turn-on, there was
perhaps a slight thrill when something very
great happened to me. Before you I didn't know about

the beauty of fear, the unparalleled feeling of a heart in
someone's hands. Before you I didn't know that a heart is
either in someone's hands or dragging along the ground.
Before you
there was no you: you are enough to explain everything
that explains me.

If there were no possibility of embracing you
what is the point of arms?

My loving comes from your laugh, and from the pimples
on your skin, the way you gnaw on your nails, your
distractedness when you brazenly stick your finger
in your nose; my loving comes from how you wake me every day
in the middle of the night or the day to fill me with
pleasure or simply to say that you love me,
my falling in love comes from your being so fallible in all you do
and this, more than all the rest, shows me
that we are infallible in the love that we are.

I get up to life to fall in love and be in love:
that is what everybody, in the morning, ought to be obliged
to say and to feel. I get up to life to fall in love and be in love.
And even this getting up is my falling in love.

If there were no possibility of causing love in somebody
what would be the point of having skin?

Explaining what joins us is enough
to explain the meaning of life.

The only illness is
having no passion.

'You're the worst person in the world and I love you for ever.'

All declarations of love are incoherent. All loves are incoherent. There's a tacit agreement between the lover and the beloved: when you see this thing that we are starting to make any sense, shoot me in the head. A love needs to be thunderous – even if only because a bullet ends it.

Love makes so so many things but it never never makes sense.

Her words on that damn corner of the bed: 'I have every reason not to stay and that's why I'm staying.' He was incapable of loving. Which was why he limited himself to being a lover, to loving her for those possible minutes, to loving every moment of her body. Then, when the time came to love, he left. He didn't need to speak many words. Just a simple 'I love you until death but I will never love you for ever.' She knew none of it made sense, that what bound them defied all the laws of physics. How can something so fragile bear everything?

Love is so fragile that it can bear everything.

They would meet in the most varied places, always on an urgent mission. 'I need you before the sadness comes,' one of them would say. And all the places were such a short distance from somebody they needed so close. Each didn't know what the other did, or how old they were, or their favourite colour, or even what the hell they were called. He was her him, she was his her. 'In you I have all the pleasures of the world.' And all names would do within what they called each other. In all places they were happy. All places felt like so little – so that they might, one day, return to discover the rest, to try the rest.

Happiness is always leaving something behind to discover, something to try.

Consuming everything is a consummation. Consuming everything kills. 'You are my life and you will never be a part of my life,' she used to say, firmly, whenever the weakness of wanting more than that small everything appeared. 'We must be the extraworld, the extralife, that which is a part of nothing and therefore fills us everywhere.' That is how love is made eternal: placed to one side so as to be in the middle of everything, right on the fringes of what soothes, located pornographically right at the entrance to total contentment, 'If one day I want to love you every day it's because one day I've stopped loving you,' he explained, not knowing whether he believed what he was saying but certain that he had to believe what he was saying.

It's necessary to love entirely but only in pieces.

And scrupulously they would carry out a ritual whose existence they couldn't see, a routine that only somebody who loves couldn't see. They had no agreed times or set days. That was what left them rested, in the final stronghold of security. Even if, without ever noticing it, they met religiously every other day, almost always in the same place, at the same time. And they were, though they never knew it, the most tedious of couples. 'Only tedium can kill us,' she warned. And she called him over to the tedium of her lap.

Even what calms you is exciting when you love so excessively.

How many dreams can a body contain?

In order to see your skin I need to close my eyes, really close them, feel it the way you feel a moment of God, and wait for life to do the rest. The secret of happiness is understanding that there's so much to do before you wait for life to do the rest. You need to find everything that can be found and discover even those things that can't be discovered. And then, only then, wait for the moment when life shows you its worth. How much it's worth to us.

How many lives is your embrace worth?

You showed up as though you wanted nothing, you sat down beside me on the plane (please, miss, would you allow me to say you are beautiful?), and the plane hadn't yet taken off but I was already on cloud nine.

How did you discover within seconds that I was yours for ever?

No journey can be described through what other people see. Travelling is an internal process, however much the body may go from here to there, and however high that plane may have risen it was carrying me deep into my dreams, to the root of which all those who breathe ought to know how to breathe. Breathing is fundamental and also unnecessary.

Only what isn't breathed in full is felt fully.

How long have you been the owner of my heartbeat?

We married two days later (please allow me, girl, to tell you that you will be my wife; and only then I understood that there never was, there had never been in you, any kind of question; you were informing me what would become of me; no more; and no question could be put to us; if only we existed then nobody would have invented the question mark), and we refused to say that we would be together until death parted us. Who the fuck is death to want to part us anyway?

When you dream on the scale on which we've learned to dream, you must understand that if we're able to touch it that doesn't mean it stops being a dream. Our whole life they've told us (such a daft idea) to pinch ourselves to check we aren't dreaming, and it's exactly the opposite, the complete opposite. It's only when we're capable of pinching ourselves that the dream is actually happening.

Pinch me to check it's a dream.

And the priest is asking me, right now, if I want to love you in sickness and in health, in joy and in sorrow, and all I can say is no. No. Proudly no, just like twenty years ago no. I continue not to want to love you in health, not to want to love you in sickness. No. A thousand times no. I want to love you unconditionally. I want to love you: that is all that should be said in a wedding.

The problem with God is that He has never loved like this.

And the problem with weddings is that they have too many words.

My favourite demon:

I'm writing to you to say I do hope you go fuck yourself.

Anybody capable of loving in duplicate is not loving anyone. Anybody capable of dividing up his love doesn't deserve to have me multiply myself in his name.

Either you love each other totally or it's all crap.

You say that it's necessary to understand love in order to understand what you love. And I don't understand. What is loved, please note, isn't to be understood – this, most likely, is the biggest problem between us. You want me to understand what can only be felt and I want you to feel what you can only understand.

When you love with your head you aren't loving anything at all.

There's another woman in your path, another woman retrieving your arms. You ask me to understand, you ask me to see that it's necessary to be selfless to be able to love.

And I do hope you go fuck yourself.

I don't know why the word egoism exists if the word love exists already.

Loving is singular. Singular. Take note: singular. Sole. Just one. Just that one. Just what occupies everything without leaving the tiniest thread out, not the smallest little crumb in sight. I made you singular and you made me plural. That is what separates us. It's a question of grammar, even mathematics. But even love deserves to have every calculation made. And ultimately the result of me + you is me with nothing else. Me painfully and yet proudly with nothing else.

Better a solitary woman than a solitary fool.

I share you with no one. I share myself with no one. When I am I am completely, when I am I am myself completely, in my coming completely. And so many times I've said never to you, and then you came back and I came back. I don't think of myself as weak for still believing that you'll come back, that you'll come back one more time, with that look in your eyes that strips me from the world and gives me life. And when you come back you'll say 'come, there's no one but you'. And all I ask, all I've ever asked of you, is this: that there is only me. That it be only me. 'Come, there's no one but you', you'd say, and my whole body would open up to let you in, and the embrace would happen and all the suffering would make sense.

Loving is knowing that even suffering can make sense.

You haven't come back. You still haven't come back. And it does seem like this time that's it. You'll be sold to the other arms of the other women who accept you in parts. And here I am, in parts but whole, waiting for you to understand that what binds us is a privilege so great that it must demand exclusivity. If you don't come back, you mustn't worry about me. I'll keep on being that same old woman in love in the same old place, waiting for the same old man. Until someone arrives, slowly, someone who can teach me to deprogramme you from me, to dilute all I have of you within what sustains me. Until that time I will be yours and nobody will even have the right to look at me fully. And that's my final decision. But after my final decision comes yours. The decision is yours. Always yours.

Either you come now or I renounce you for ever.

PS I do hope you go fuck yourself.
And I love you.

I hope that your salvation comes from you: that is the first commandment of what keeps me alive.

They call it masochism but I call it survivalism. I live you to keep myself alive. Nothing recommends you, nothing advises you, and it's with the absolute certainty that you don't deserve me that I do everything to deserve you.

I'm so idiotic and so happy in your arms.

I liked knowing with my body what I know with my head, refusing with my skin what I refuse with my reason. But then comes our touch and even the masochism is worth it. Even the minutes of you in me are enough for all the hours of pain without you in me.

I'm so foolish and so yours when you kiss me.

And inside I'm comforted by being yours even if you will never be mine. I lie down into your arms, I awake into the heat of your pleasure, and knowing you aren't here but you could be here is enough to fill all of me there is to fill.

One day I will kill you within me but until that day I will die for you.

I'm really dying. I'm dying of desire, of will, of dreaming. Dreaming about a house of ours, with children of ours, with the world of ours, with the bedroom of ours. I'm dying for my whole life beside you like the whole life I have with you now even if you aren't here. All that's missing is your body for everything to be the way it is for ever. Better a masochist than a con artist. Anyone who doesn't accept he's needed will end up worn down. And then they enter that internal war of erasing

what no time can erase. Nothing but you to erase you in me.
I need you in order to stop needing you. You are too much in
me for me to be able to expel you. You are so in me that when
I kiss you I feel kissed.

I'm so ridiculous and so whole when you embrace me.

And now I go on, unafraid of being absurd (the absurd is
the only thing that makes sense, nothing can explain life but the
unexplainable), savouring each part of your absence. And that is
how I have you, so distant and so inside of me, like a landscape
you need only to look at to make it ours. You look at a river and
it's yours, just yours, at that exact moment. You absorb all that it
is, all that it gives you. You are all that it can be in you. Why can't
love be touched like a landscape? Why isn't just looking at you
enough to make you mine alone? I am only real when I dream
you where I am. Reality is what binds us when you do not exist
in me. All I need is me in order to have you completely. We are
experiencing a unilateral love, a two-person relationship in which
just one wanting is enough for both to be here. I love you without
needing permission. I love you beyond you. I love you without
needing you. I love you by illegal imposition. Whether you like it
or not you are the man of my life. How many lives do you need
to know that you are mine?

Only your orgasm can make me come.

Come.

Come now.

How many women do you need to know that it's me?

All love begins in secret.

She knew that she was wrong to go, just like that, not knowing why and fed up of knowing why, to meet him. They had never seen each other and already they loved each other. He didn't believe in love and all the same there he was, on that train where two souls were learning that there was a love for ever. When she got on she just kept walking. At least inside of him. He closed his laptop (it was still open but who was interested in it?), switched off his cell phone (it remained on but who was interested in it?), and devoted himself to watching her talk. That's just how it was: seeing her talk. Watching her be.

All love comes in through the eyes.

They spent the journey – the three most beautiful hours that any train has ever offered anyone – talking about absolutely nothing. They spent the journey loving each other without anyone being able to tell. There was no touch (just a hand of his, stealthy, trying to find out what her tall boots were hiding), but the two bodies felt more clinging and tangled and crushed and giddy than ever. Love needs to happen through the skin too.

All love needs skin.

She was afraid of staying for ever, there, inside his eyes; she was afraid that returning would be an impossibility. How could she return to the simple life after having learned to live? He just looked at all of her (her fringe, her large eyes, her irresistible shyness), and knew that the most that was left to him, now, was to surrender himself, although he had already surrendered long ago. It was the most immortal journey that any means of transport had ever known but the damned journey would never end again. There were two bodies in search of more.

All love is found in search of more.

They arrived. They arrived right away. Of course there was a car in the meantime, too, perhaps some hand or other touching some other hand. But only what was to come would occupy their memory. The whole universe awaited them in the simple room of a simple (and so small) apartment. And all the clothes were too many.

All love refuses clothes.

They loved each other for ever on the scale of that night. They went deep into the bones of pleasure, no sweat wasted. They don't know if it was hours or if it was only minutes; they know that from that moment onwards they would never understand life the same way again. They fell asleep, tired and hugging tight (their bodies slotted together as though they had been born to it: one to receive the other beneath the sheets; could the size of one body be defined as a function of the size of another?), and when they awoke they understood that they were waking for the first time.

All love wakes us for the first time.

From out there, through the window, came the sea that they hadn't even noticed was there, so close, so alert. They didn't know if they would love each other again like this but they knew that they would never stop loving each other. Life insisted, stubbornly, that they part just a few hours later. She returned, sad and happy, to the train where happiness had made history. He returned, sad and happy, to the bedroom where he had discovered he was alive. There was no certainty, nothing was certain. But the two of them shared the greatest of secrets, the most perpetual of life's mysteries. Only the two of them knew the taste of the sea.

All love holds the secret of life.

What's a brain for if not for suffering?

Grey days strewn around the house. The cats mew, hungry, and teach me that the only thing that matters is a plate full of food. And then living. There is a vast lesson to be learned each time a cat mews – but there's an even vaster lesson each time a cat lies down, totally unconcerned, and spends hours asleep, resting on a full stomach in the happiness of being sated. When will I be like that, sated in plenitude? When will I be capable of shutting my eyes, unconcerned, and simply sleeping with the incomparable happiness of a full stomach?

It would be the salvation of humanity to ask for lessons from those who don't think about the future and instead savour everything the present has to offer. No Man deserves to know that the future exists. It's knowing the future exists that prevents us from being, fully, in the place we are, in the time we are.

Either you are happy or you are unhappy.

We must understand that everything we are is fiction.

More and more people ask me for advice. They believe that what I write makes me someone special, capable of understanding what they do, what they feel, even what they write. I feel lost, with no idea what to do, with no idea what to say. And that is why I write. To write is to be lost and seek, with every line, a path. Or a simple sign that there might be a path, that there might be a hope. To write is to seek hope, every day, in what does not exist, in what is written to find out if it exists. I am not a writer, I've never been a writer, I don't want to be a writer. I'm just the guy who writes because he needs to write, because the days demand that he writes, because some urgency or other obliges him to write. I write like a biological necessity, and sometimes needing to write can cost you so much. It doesn't hurt but it costs you, it's a pain from the outside in, as if the letters were coming out through my skin, from inside my bones. And literature. What the hell is literature? I couldn't care less about literature. I don't want to write literature, I don't want the intellectuals on my side. When I've got a critic on my side it's because I've arrived nowhere. Everybody wants to revere the untouchable, to appreciate what is easy to appreciate, what everybody appreciates, read what everybody is reading because someone has defined what ought to be read. Either you invent everything all over again or all books will be the same. Anybody who is, wants to continue being: that's how you put an end to a dream. I don't want to do what the classics do, I don't want to replicate what so many have done already. I want to start from myself and end at myself. Just that: start from myself and end at myself, as far as possible in myself. I want to do what I fancy with the words that I fancy, face up to the critics and stab them in the chops that I'm writing and that I must keep on writing for ever. Even if it's garbage, even if it's a succession of pieces of shit that they, poor things, don't want to be literature. God save me from one day being a writer and saying that I've got a gift in me. The fuck I've got a gift. My sole gift is living, tirelessly, and making this life a race to who knows where. A race to who knows where: suddenly I see that this is what life is to me. I'm meant to die running, with the finishing line in sight, the wretched thing, always within sight and always so far away. And the artists. Better a thief than an artist. And is there any greater thief than an artist? What scum artists are. That festering race to whom God offered heaven and hell so that they might create something that messes with other people. I'll never be an artist. I'll never believe that there's anything in me greater than fear. I'm afraid of staying still, afraid of not moving whoever loves me, afraid of not questioning whatever concerns me, afraid of not laughing in the face of death. I'm so afraid of dying and that's why I live. Writing is the same: being afraid of dying. I write to avoid death and writing's also what kills me. I'm a poor little thing who doesn't have a place to drop dead but who insists desperately on finding places to keep moving about alive.

What matters is life, never letters.

'If you want to see me happy, give me chaos or nothing.'

There was within us, right from the start, a certainty that we lacked for nothing, that everything was ready to receive us, right the way up to complete happiness. But no happiness is predictable – and if there's something truly joyful in happiness it's that constant unpredictability, that sensation of a door to be opened with no idea of what lies behind it.

Life is almost worth it just for the opening of doors that hide we don't know what.

Everybody knew we had everything we needed to be happy and that was why we could only be unhappy. We had the perfect house, the perfect staff, the perfect cars, the perfect beauties, the perfect families. And later even the perfect children and the perfect educations that we gave them in such an exemplary fashion. We had everything and yet there was always something missing. And there's nothing more deadly than habit. Nothing is more damnable than the exemplary. Nothing is more destructive than the predictable. Knowing today what we're going to do tomorrow, knowing tomorrow what we're going to do the day after, knowing at all times what's going to happen at all times. We used to know, we always knew, what we were, who we were, and where we wanted to go. And that was why we ended up going no place.

No relationship can resist perfection.

Everything was adding up just right, the words were right, the looks were right, the decisions were right. We never argued about where to spend our holidays, what piece of furniture to buy for the living room, what name to give our children. We came to everything with the naturalness with which we had always approached each other: without a drop of conflict.

No story can be any good without a good conflict.

And the truth is, that's just how it was, without an argument, without a voice raised for one single word, without any criticisms at all, that was how we moved away from each other. You said 'you're perfect but I have to go,' I said 'you're perfect but I'm fed up,' and we exchanged one of our kisses (even our kisses had no conflict in them; and maybe that's what sustains a relationship: a kiss in conflict, a stolen kiss, a criminal kiss that goes into the mouth of someone who while not wanting it wants it more than anything) and then one of our hugs (as though we were hugging a ghost; we were careful with each other as though we were made of crystal and that was why we started breaking into pieces, inadequacy by inadequacy, surrender by surrender), and we understood in that instant that we were dying at just the right point, changing direction at exactly the right moment. Even in this we were perfect.

A separation between the couple of protagonists could even be a good ending to a story.

Now that I look at you, after such a long time, whenever you come to fetch the kids and you smile at me, I understand that we did what had to be done. Your looks are still to die for (your mouth like a landscape of paradise, your body with no trace of the passing years: you're so handsome that it's incomprehensible that you don't thrill me to the depths of my bones), and I continue to be the perfect woman all men want and from whom all men run away. And deep down we never stopped being anything and nor did we start being whatever it was when we separated. And in this way, in just this way, it becomes clear that a love does not really exist: when everything before it and after it remains unchanged.

We are too perfect to accept something as defective as love.

Playing with fire is the only thing that can heat you up.

Everything else is warmth, too slight to keep me alive. I need to know I might get burned for me to feel ready to take the risk. And if living isn't a risk you might as well be dead.

If there's no chance of going wrong, where's the use in going right?

The thing that gives me life is knowing that the worst could happen. Knowing that it could hurt, knowing that it could wound. Surviving unscathed is totally arid if I don't know that it can get me. I want you the way we want a precipice, the way we want to look out over a void, the way we want speed, adrenaline. You are the greatest risk I am prepared to take. And each day I risk a little more. It feels so good having you constantly on the edge of that blade.

Rather a minute on the edge of the blade than a whole life without a single fault.

What we are is so human. And that is love, that's the only thing that can be love: something so human that it can end, so human that it can wound, so human that it can make mistakes. We are made of the weight of mistakes, of the weight of the fallible. It's from cracks that we build our house, from tears that we build what protects us from water. We know that we lack so much to be perfect and that this is how we feel immaculate: each other's, and both inadequacies.

What we are unable to be is what makes us what we are.

And we try. We try so hard, my love. We try everything, everything. Really everything. We go right up to the end of what hurts if that's where we need to go to stop it hurting for ever, we go right up to the end of the dream if that's where we need to go to not stop dreaming. We risk all that we are on each day that we live. And that is the only way we know how to live.

All life must be called into question every day.

Everything we have must be in play as long as we're alive. Everything on the table. All in. Fearless but trembling with fear. All in. All our skin in the game, our whole soul, our whole bodies in everything we exchange, in everything we seek, in everything we decide. The two of us are here, entirely, whenever the two of us are here. All in. And from one moment to the next everything can change, everything can be lost. And until that time, that moment when, one day, we might happen to lose ourselves entirely, until that moment, it will make us greater even with nothing, even starting from zero, even with nothing but the loss to unite us.

Better to start from zero than to make life a simple number.

That is what we see around us. Couples and people and lives as though they were within a number. A circus number, an act they think is a theatre act. A depressing balancing number. And everybody is a trapeze artist, and everybody is looking for the naïve equilibrium that is only good for keeping going.

Kill me right now if the only thing you have for me is a continuing.

Continuing can go jump in a lake. Continuing can go fuck itself. I demand beginning. Beginning always. The first time. Every day beginning something. New game, all in. New game, all in. If one day I'm a trapeze artist it will only be in order to learn to fall better. To learn to suffer better, to learn to slip better, to learn to fail better. If one day I'm a trapeze artist it's also so as to love you better. Because loving you is being up on a trapeze or it is nothing.

Love me now at least: that is the only request I always make of you.

Conquer me at this moment, entrance me in this instant, promise that when you are here you're really here, that when you kiss you're in that kiss, that when you embrace you are that embrace, that when you hold me you hold me entirely. At least for now love me completely in the same way that at least for now I love you completely: this is the most ambitious declaration that anybody who loves can make.

A second of you is enough to love life for ever.

Today I write the poem of the common, the obscenity
ode, the bastard serenade. Today I send
the more or less to hell, and the politically
correct, even the relatively worthwhile. Today
I either smash the dishes or hope no one will hear my wishes.
    And
praying this way is what makes me yell today:

'Neither eight nor eighty' can frankly just go
fuck itself. 'Either eight or eighty', yes,
that's it. Either the most excessive all or the most
inconsequential nothing. Pity whoever needs
eyes to see. And loving you is so ill-advised
that I just want you in me everywhere.

Whoever doesn't take a risk on a step longer
than their leg is paralysed.

No body defines what it means to be
in movement. And there's no happiness at all
that doesn't begin with 'yes, I want to' or
alternatively a simple 'go fuck yourself
and come over here now.' And there will be some who criticise
my vocabulary, who call me vulgar, who
accuse me of being bad – but there's nothing stopping me from
the word that must be said, telling them to clear off,
give me a break, I'd rather have the filthy madness of the desperate.

If you aren't just a bit ill-bred
you might as well be dead.

And if danger exists for us to be alive, and
if being capable of shocking exists so we can
speak. Because life is obscene, because
to love is to try the unacceptable, because the
euphoria is what's left behind after the reasonable. And
I abhor what's impeccable, and I throw what's healthy
into the river, and I go in search of what's indescribable, of
the dementia of someone who wants only
to discover, of the extravagance of someone
who has never learned not to dream.

If I have to die let it be by falling, and
let me be the proof that it is possible to fly.

What could be more pretentious than believing in love?

Loving demands vanity, self-confidence and a decent dose of dementia. To rephrase that: loving requires an insane dose of dementia. Everything else will be added along the way – or subtracted. Anybody who believes in love believes that poetry exists and that there is a poem in each kiss given, in each embrace shared, in each body discovered à deux. Anybody who loves is Pessoa, Camões, Sophia, Neruda. Anybody who loves is either a poet or else they don't love at all.

Anybody who is not pretentious when they love, it's because they don't love, not really.

And being like this is so good. Writing with the bone of your fingers, going in search of the words beyond logic, into the insides of grammar. Nothing is badly written when it's written with love. Either it has absolute love or it's not poetry. Writing must be done without the obstacle of the why if the writing is to be love. We must refuse those poor souls who don't know it and who analyse a text of love just like they analyse any other text. But a text of love is not just any other text – for the simple and absolutely obvious reason that a text of love is not even a text: it is love. That alone. Whoever writes a text of love doesn't give a damn about literature.

What is literature when you love like this?

Anyone who writes a text of love puts himself so entirely in the letters that he can't imagine how they came out of him like that – but they could only have come out like that. And only someone who loves is obsessed with the idea of being a poet, the sweetest of obsessions, the most delicious of delusions. And he brings the verses together as though bringing bodies together, and kisses the words as though kissing mouths. Only someone who loves ends up looking ridiculous making poetry – because only someone who loves ends up looking ridiculous being poetry.

It's either mediocre literature or it's mediocre love.

And mediocre love can still be terrific – but it's not love. And that's why I write to you like this, my all, with the certainty that when the critics (those wretches, they don't know what they write) read me they'll see me as you see a writer, and not as the lucky devil who loves you and who limits himself to doing anything (even writing) so as to love you even more, to be able to show you the scale of what he feels for you, the size of what suffocates him. Pay no attention to them, my love. Pay no attention to those who when they see words see only a text.

I love you even beyond what is ridiculous.

I love you with mistakes in verb agreements, with words that don't even exist (how can something exist to describe us when we don't even exist yet?), with preposterous grammatical constructions; I love you with verbs in place of nouns, with adjectives in place of adverbs, with singulars in place of plurals. And that is why I can say heavenyou or foreveryou, or even youeternally. Because I really don't care about something that isn't knowing what this is, just this, which can tell you when you are in me.

When somebody starts telling you I write literature when I'm writing to you, leave me. I will have stopped loving you long before.

What are words made of
if not of the substance of which I love you?

Skins project the linguistics
of love, pronouns of pleasure in
the temptation of the verses, and when you lie
on me it's all the philosophy of life
that rises up, applauding, to hear
the absolute explanation of the orgasm.

What is it that makes up syntax
if not the study of the moment
when our two bodies
fit together?

Academics don't teach what
joins us, students don't learn
what the life in you makes me, and even
the lexicologist wouldn't know where to place us
in the dictionary nor would the dictionary know
if it had the space to define us. As I look at you
I invent the only language that
I understand, and when I hear your
'Ah' that's when I know that the alphabet
worth knowing is about to start.

What are phonetics made of

if not the analysis, scientific
and with the skin, of the untenable
noise of your sighs?

A tongue only exists so that
your kiss exists, because I deny
the need to speak when
I find such usefulness in
the existence of mouths, and more
dialogues always happen with the
size of silences than with
the dimensions of words. When
God comes to earth one day
He will see that you already exist, and
all religions will be useless.

What is faith made of
if not the unshakeable belief
that there is a superior being
located beneath you?

He arrived late for the most important moment of his life. That's something that can change a life. A minute earlier and everything would have been different. She would still have been there, impatient, her eyes on her watch, her hair, the sky – looking for some reason, any one would do, any reason to wait a little longer, to be able to say rationally that it would be worth the wait. The sun would have been shining, high up, implying, falsely, that it would never leave. And then he would arrive (sorry I'm late but the traffic), she'd start off by acting annoyed (I was actually just about to leave, you'd better not do this to me again), but then, bit by bit, with his words that are always light and cheerful (being fed up is pretty hard work, anyone truly lazy is always laughing because that's the only way to avoid getting involved with things that are hard to resolve), she'd end up as well as ever, in truth, she'd stop being (you're such a handsome bastard, you're so handsome that all I want to say is that I love you like a madwoman, that I just want to grab that neck of yours and pull you completely over to me, kiss all your skin, and you seem to have so much to give me, until there are no more lips to kiss. Even my lips burn from kissing you; you're so handsome that I cannot not forgive you for everything you do to me), they'd go to the usual café, to the pastry shop on the same old street, him just dying to tell her that he loved her as never before and had done for ever, her just dying to tell him that she still only believes in life because she still believes that he exists, but neither of them would say a word about what was going on inside them, they would continue with their trivial chit-chat (the government this, some club that, this film the other) until one of them, it makes no difference which because deep down it will be both, at the exact same moment and with the exact same intensity, doing it, would grab hold of the other with all the courage in the world, embracing them as though shrinking with pain, and they would suffocate deliciously in that pastry shop on the old street that once again was watching them loving each other like they have always loved each other except this time with their bodies doing what their souls have already been doing for a long time. And then would come the time with the sheets, perhaps in her bed (though you know every day since I met you I've prepared the sheets for us, every day I've woken up thinking that today would be the day and I've chosen my favourite sheets, ones I don't know if you'll like but which I'm sure you'll like, the sheets that smell of us even if you've never been here), the moment of heads lost, of stolen moans, of everything to which those who love each other have the right. They would end the night the next morning, tired and ready for more nights like this, at the most delicious breakfast that life has to offer. Some months later the moment would come for combining houses, this time at his (when I chose this house I was thinking of you, I thought it would be too big for me but perfect for us, and I chose the remote possibility of an us from the painful certainty of an I), and there they began their story. They would have children, a lad called Pedro like his father, a girl called Bárbara like her mother, and then they'd stick around, in the house where they would learn happiness and where every day they would teach their children, until the death of one (her first, because even in this he was a gentleman) parted them for one, two months – till the time when the other (him, who to her, for a change, was even late when it came to dying) went too. The children, those two, would cry at the loss, just as all such great losses are cried at, but they would be capable and have all the tools they need to walk on through life. One of them, one day, would fall in love with the most beautiful woman he'd ever had the good fortune to see. They would become friends and he would promise, before they lay down, that on the next day he would tell her how much he loved her. That's how it would be, were it not for the traffic. He arrived late for the most important moment of his life.

Standing at the button, heart racing and skin sweaty, L. was trembling. That button. She only had to press. Just once. It was enough to press down just once and everything would be set in motion. A simple touch and that was that. Whatever God wanted. But the problem with humans is that, almost always, they don't trust what God wants. They prefer to grab with both hands everything they can get hold of, trying to limit the damage, minimising it as much as possible. Humans created a God in whom they don't believe, in whom they believe only in despair, she thought, her finger resting on the button, her sweat getting ever thicker, her whole body unable to stop. She thought some more. She thought that her whole life she'd fought to have what she had never truly wanted. She had fought to have the house opposite the sea that she'd read in magazines and in books it was good to have, she'd fought to have the convertible car that films had taught her to value, she'd fought to find the job of other people's dreams and the career that now prevented her from dreaming. She had fought for the dreams of other people. Her parents' dreams, her friends', the dreams of all those around her. And she'd forgotten who she was, what she was, what she had aspired to. She'd forgotten the night when she'd fallen asleep, once when she was very small, hugging her teddy bear, and thought that all she aspired to in life was this: time, space and life to lie down in an embrace with whoever would protect her like that simple bear. That's another problem with humans, she thought now, her trembling finger on the button, they spend their lives not understanding what they're for, they spend their lives wanting to fill their lives, to occupy them with things to do, with intentions to fulfil. Humans spend their lives wallowing in futilities. Perhaps that's the best way not to feel the emptiness, she concluded later, her finger almost almost pressing down hard on the button. It's like a house filled with furniture. However much furniture an empty house has in it it's still empty, and the emptier the house is, the more furniture people try to put in it. To wipe out the emptiness, to bridge the nothing. To put an end to the silence. That's it, she said to herself, as though she had just described the secret to eternal happiness. People use things in order to muffle the silence. And there she remained, in silence, with her finger, now it's the index finger of her right hand, resting on the button that makes her tremble, on the button that will decide whether she's just another person, with no courage, no strength, with nothing but things for erasing the blank space of her days. I need to decide, she convinced herself. Now or never, she declared. But first she thought about the morbid perversity of comfort. That, comfort, is what kills humans the most. Wanting to be always well. Not great, not euphoric, merely well. And with a terrible fear of being unwell, of hurting. It's the constant flight from what hurts that harms humans the most, that removes them most from life, she thought. For the second time in her life after that night when she'd fallen asleep with the teddy bear, she came close to herself. And she pressed down, with no further hesitation, on the button. She only hoped, now, that he would hear the telephone ring.

They've met every day, at the same time, on the park bench. The third on the left as you come into the park from the south side. They've never spoken but they know everything about each other. He knows she's called Isabel, she's forty-five and has been divorced for about a year, since she, on the phone on the park bench, instructed her lawyer, with tears in her eyes, to go ahead with the proceedings whatever the cost. She knows he's called André, that he's forty-seven and that he's married to a woman he hasn't loved in more than twenty years, as he has written almost daily in his diary which she, not meaning to but not accidentally, managed to read out of the corner of her eye while he, on that bench, wrote with a frequency that was almost religious. Today, strangely, she has not yet arrived. He looks at his watch and confirms the delay, more than half an hour. Night is threatening to fall and still nothing. She doesn't appear. He looks, countless times, to the hands of the watch. Nothing. Then he looks around, as though seeking the cure for death. Nothing. Lost, desperate, he decides to go looking for her. He knows her full name, he knows which neighbourhood she lives in. It won't be hard to find her, he thinks, as he walks quickly through the streets of the city. The sweat pours down his face, a perfect photograph of the state of nerves that drive his steps. The minutes feel like days on that road that never ends. But lo and behold, he arrives. It's a peaceful street in a peaceful neighbourhood. The ideal place for a peaceful person, he says to himself, while at the same time looking around, in search of her face, of her legs, of her body, of her smile. How lovely her smile is, he recalls, and without his realising it's no longer sweat running down his face. He doesn't see her. But he doesn't give up. He goes house to house, trying to work out which is the house that deserves her. He had never needed any kind of question, any kind of word, to know everything about her. And nor would it be necessary now. He goes by one, two, three, four, five, six small but pleasant dwellings. And he reaches the seventh. The flowers, the garden, the tree, the dog barking at the gate, the swing where he imagines her in search of a possible heaven, even if just for a few seconds. She could only be here. He advances, without hesitating, only after having wiped away everything that insisted on running down his skin. He's less than a metre from the door, in brown wood, and he expects to be less than a metre from meeting her. He straightens his shirt one last time, centring it on his shoulders, and does what he needs to do. One second. Two seconds. Three seconds. Footsteps on the far side. He smiles, recognises the heels of her walk, and he knows he's in the right place. She opens the door and that smile. Next she embraces him, kisses him, takes him to the bedroom and loves him while he loves her with exactly the same intensity. Neither more nor less. They love each other in exactly the same way, and perhaps that's the only way to prove the existence of a love, that's what he realised, later, when without a single word just as it had always been without a single word, they say goodbye. Until the following day, when, at the agreed time, they meet on the park bench. The third on the left as you come into the park from the south side. By this point everything will be as it has always been, despite his having instructed his lawyer to begin, as quickly as possible, the divorce proceedings.

Life was over and yet there was still so much to live.

The story of a bearable end had been left by the wayside. I knew that I didn't love the man I'd chosen, and perhaps that's exactly why I'd chosen him: to show that there was a possibility of deciding my destiny beyond what destiny had decided for me. I wanted to play God when I chose him. And I prayed to Him for help.

But even God cannot silence a love. We lived in a state of all-out war for twenty years. Twenty years to figure out who was in command of whom. And the love, sickly and irrational like all loves, always in command of us inside. Everything we did was for love, to conquer love. That was how, each day, we would make ourselves be defeated. There were, of course, the usual escapes. A son, for starters. To hide the silences, to not have to put up with each other, to oblige ourselves, in front of him, to keep our mouths shut. And we started keeping our mouths shut. With us, it was love that fell silent too, like a wild animal that, bit by bit, with the triumph of age, starts allowing itself to be defeated, without realising that it's only when it's in motion that it can hunt.

There is always one child too many when a couple who don't love each other has a child.

We insisted. We insisted to each other. Forever at war but now in silence, stealthily, each with their own cool combat strategy. He stopped being my love – despite, as I now know cynically, still addressing me as the usual small and insignificant 'hon' – and started being just the target of all my internal movements. When is it that someone stops being our life and starts being what prevents us from living? Only stubbornness kept us together, such a great mule-headedness that held us close to absolutely nothing over more than two decades. Two decades. Fuck it. Twenty times three hundred and sixty-five days of my life lost like that, see who's the most resilient, see who didn't give way just for the pleasure of watching the other give way. I bet he dreamed, like I dreamed, about the day of liberation, about the day when he would arrive home and I'd say 'I'm fed up, let's just end this shit'. But the day never came. And the whole damn mess just grew. And our son increasingly realising that he was living with two different people in two different spheres and never with a couple. There were three houses in our house: mine, yours, and ours with him. And he, as smart as he's ever been, knew exactly how to act with one or the other of us. He did everything to make us find points of agreement, to end with a hug, however forced (or committed) they may be. I would have been capable, I swear, of putting up with it till the final days of my life. What bastard idiot prefers to surrender their whole life rather than surrendering once in their life?

It would have stayed just the same if you hadn't happened. I say happen because that's really what defines the moment when I saw you. You happened to me. And me happened. That's probably the best way to describe what you did to me: you made me happen. You made me understand once again that there was still space to try. From the beginning. Everything once again. You didn't need to say much. You said, 'Carlos, a pleasure,' and I heard 'Carlos, for ever'. And that's how it was, my love.

Until today.

The sun was shining and the wind was blowing and the world
continued as beautiful as only it could be, but
you weren't there and none of it mattered.

The worst thing in the world is a half-life, the cruel limbo
where the overwhelming majority of people
come to rest, sitting on a bed of things that are
reasonable. A reasonable job exists, a reasonable house,
reasonable feelings, even reasonable happiness, and it's only
later that you exist beyond all reasonableness.

The moon was full and the beach had sand
brighter than had ever existed before, but you
weren't there and none of it mattered.

A half-life consists of avoiding suffering as though
death itself were in it, giving up on going
in search of what might hurt and in doing so
giving up on going in search of what might delight. A
possible euphoria does exist, possible pleasure, possible days, and
it's only later that you exist beyond all possibilities.

The birds flew high and free, poems
continued to be the most blessed creations
of mankind, but you weren't there and none of it mattered.

I believed that being alive was no more than that, everything

I ever wanted in a moderate dose, in an adequate dose, life
served out in small portions. I smiled because smiling
was all I could manage, I was satisfied embracing whatever
crossed my path, I was convinced that this was
how my whole journey would go, and it's only later
I understood that you exist beyond all satisfactions.

The restaurant was wretched, the food an absolute
scandal, the weather out there was horrible, your
waiting-staff uniform was an attack on
good taste, but you were there and nothing else mattered.

The taste of your kiss was strange, as vast
as it was gloomy, and only then, after the first
touch of your lips on mine, did I understand that
there was a goodbye in the meeting of our mouths. It was
the whole construction of my half-life that was giving way
when faced with your overkissing. From us and from our
mouths there was a whole existence that seemed to be
performable, and we performed it all night long.

The bed was uncomfortable, the springs made
unbearable noises, your moans
were so piercing that they did away with my
ears, but you were still there and nothing else mattered.

'Half of me is you and the other half is sin.'

'How do you understand sin? How do you separate good sin from bad sin?'

'The pain. The pain separates the waters. The pain separates all waters.'

'What's painful is bad?'

'What's painful, yes. The rest isn't and nor is it. One must always choose what might be painful. Only what could perhaps hurt has a chance of perhaps making you love.'

'If it doesn't hurt it isn't love?'

'It if isn't capable of hurting it isn't love. Maybe it won't actually hurt. Maybe it'll never hurt. But it has that capacity, you know it has that capacity. Because it is down in your deepest layer, in your most profound dimension. Deep in your guts.'

'You love me all the way to your guts.'

'I love you until I find myself. You are my losing and my finding. I need you to lose myself and I need you to find myself. If I look around you and don't find you I'm lost, even if I'm somewhere familiar. If you're not around me it's because I'm not there.'

'Do you want to sin with me?'

'Every day. You are all the sin there is for the living. The good and the bad. But ultimately there's only one kind of sin: the kind that keeps us alive. Anyone who lives without sinning and dies without sinning has never really lived. He's just wandered through. Anyone who has never sinned is not a saint; he's a dead man. He was born dead. It's sin that creates changeability, irregularity. Life, despite being a regular cycle, must show some irregularities. They are the bends that give the road its charm. Always going in a straight line makes me sleepy.'

'If you're not transgressing, you're depressing.'

'If you're not transgressing, you're bad at tasting. I'm no good at rhyme. I'm no good at anything, really. I try hard to be good at loving you. That's the only talent I seek to have: loving you competently.'

'Competently. Such an ugly word for such a beautiful thing that binds us.'

'I don't like beautiful words. I believe we all have a limit to the amount of beauty we can spend over the course of our lives. I prefer to spend it on acts and not on words. Anyone who speaks beauty will later be left with nothing to make beauty. I prefer to be the poem, the novel, the literature. I don't want you to be my inspiration, I want you to be my titillation.'

'Another expression that's far from beautiful.'

'And yet effective.'

'You're right.'

'Come.'

'I'm coming.'

They discovered as they danced that the body of one didn't fit perfectly into the body of the other. That was enough for them, right then, to separate. He was fanatical about mathematical perfection and quite clear about what made him go far away: the dimensions between us are wrong. She heard him, understood that there wasn't much to be done when something was as impossible as that, and just said: there are some bodies that mathematics cannot measure. But she let him go, with no reaction, with no attempt to fight back. She believed that love was made of such moments, where you had to learn to lose, calmly, what it was no longer possible to win.

Yes, I do, he answered the priest. He had at last found the sought-after fit, after a ceaseless search, which included journeys to three different continents and a few seconds' dancing with thousands of women of every possible kind. But he was within reach of his great objective. That woman, who is now kissing him on the mouth as a celebration of a matrimony consummated, is mathematically perfect in her dimensions. Never before had any dance been so untouchably perfect. Their bodies as though composing, together, a second symphony to the strains of the first. Bodies like musical notes, he would conclude many times while dancing with her, understanding with some emotion that all the sacrifice had been worth it. You are the proof that mathematics is the complete science: it can even measure love, he told her, moments before they surrendered for the first time to the incomparable pleasure of the flesh.

It doesn't make sense, it doesn't make sense, he said over and over again, inconsolable, as he looked into his wife's eyes. You're the same size lying down and standing up, and I'm the same size lying down and standing up, and yet we seem to be lacking in closeness, there's too much space between us. I have your whole body on mine and you feel far away. It's as though bodies change size when they lie down. It doesn't make sense, it doesn't make sense, he went back, with the day already beginning and light coming in through the bedroom window, to repeating. And with a calculator in his hand, he got up from the bed.

The maths worked out just fine in the daylight. That was his first conclusion when he threw the thick, dense manuals into the living-room fireplace, the books he had used to guide him his whole life. Until today. Until the moment when, after loving the woman who one day the dance had shown could not be perfect for him, he understood that there was an irreparable defect to science, a glaring inadequacy as regards the capacity for measuring what is loved. Mathematics doesn't understand the difference between a love lying down and a love standing up; it's as though it measured only what bodies show and didn't consider that, in some cases, what measures two bodies is not the actual size of the two bodies but the distance that they allow to be created between them; it's in scarcity that you measure love: the less space there is separating them, the greater size the bodies attain, he now wrote, aware that he was just a few moments from starting a historic revolution, a new current of thought, who knows maybe even a new discipline that henceforth would be studied in schools and universities across the world. But, strangely, he gave up on all this right away. The woman he loved was still there, watching him, over on that side. She was asking him, desperately, for one more embrace. And he went.

Love me until you stop knowing yourself.

That was how you started to enter me. Suddenly, without our ever having seen each other, your words like bullets in the middle of the local library: fuck me until you stop knowing who you are. And me silent on the inside, even if on the outside I couldn't prevent a smile and a few opportune words made up on the spot (how the hell is one supposed to know what the opportune words are for an opportunity that has never existed before?): I like the way you kid around, I said. But you weren't kidding around. Ten minutes later you were on top of me with your clothes already torn off you and myself already torn off me. We had confirmation: I no longer knew who I was and I was completely unprepared for this.

If you abandon me I'll run away.

That was your threat when, fed up with your eccentricities (one day I arrived home and you were showing the peculiarities of the colour of your left nipple to my best friend, another day you decided to cut my finger with a kitchen knife to find out what my blood tasted like, another day you threw yourself out of the living-room window to be sure that your wings were only on the inside), I was standing at the door with my bags in my hand. And you insisted: if you walk out of that door you can count on it that you'll never see me again. I didn't believe you. And I thought I was right when, less than a month later, I was already back home, our home, aching with longing for your love that prevented me from knowing who I was. But you were correct and you were right once again: the person with me now was no longer you. You, more than me, had run away that day. And it had been my fault.

Either you go back to being crazy or I'll go crazy.

Those were the words with which I asked you to be you. Desperately you. I could no longer bear the dementia of your being this normal person that you, these past months, had been. You always kept the house nice and tidy, the perfect housewife, an attentive and affectionate wife (we made love like grown-ups and stopped fucking like lunatics) and your greatest madness in this period was to try, one day, not putting sugar in the milk you drank at breakfast. You were too sane and this was making me crazy.

He's a son-of-a-bitch genius and that's why I adore him.

Those were the words you said to me when, for the nth time, we were summoned to school to put out a fire started by our boy. This time (after previously having, for example, managed to get the Judicial Police to surround the school believing there was a kidnapping with hostages; or, on another occasion, having convinced hundreds of students to paint the façade of the school a new colour thinking it was a direct request from the School Board), he had, in one hour, done his own test and that of five of his friends. The six of them got top marks but, who knows how, somebody spotted the mess. You were proud of him while I, back at home, said to him harshly: I'm ashamed of this behaviour of yours; that's not how my son acts. And you, you might not believe me but I saw it, smiled.

My name's Filipa but I don't know who I am.

That was how his girlfriend introduced herself when she came over for dinner. And she added: I'm from Barreiro but I don't know where that is. I was simultaneously sorry for her and envious.

'We only join lips so that a single mute shout is heard in the world.'

That was the poetic version of what he said to her. Then there was the other one. The one that hurts. The one that destroys. The one that tramples. This one:

'I love you; now go.'

Without warning, after so long together, he asked her to leave. For good. He didn't make any claims. He didn't give any explanations. He just told her to go, his expression sombre, without a smile, without a grimace. Go, he said. And she, laden down with suitcases and tears, went.

'Promise me that you will never question me in order to be able to love me.'

Those were his only words when she was already on the other side of the door. She promised. She asked nothing, however much she wanted to know what had happened, where she had lost what had always kept them together. She didn't see him for years. She met a new husband, thought she was in love with him, had the children she'd always wanted and everyone, even her, was sure that she was a happy woman. When if not now?

'Yes; yes, please.'

That was her answer when, from the other end of the line, someone asked her if she would accept a reverse-charge call. She shivered. She didn't know why but she knew it was him. It was. And he had news to tell her.

'I love you too much not to tell you the truth.'

That was his explanation after having revealed that he was, this whole time, being treated for some serious illness (whose name he refused to speak because he believed that what he said would, in this case, come to pass). I need all my strength to feel that I'm not disappointed at the scale of us, he added. She started out by refusing his explanation, then she told him to stop talking, and finally, without hesitating, she hung up without a word.

'I love you too much for you to be able to love me.'

Those were her words, months later and without a smile, before making a proposition that he accepted at once. The searches for the two bodies, following the accident that involved both their cars, lasted several weeks, and to this day there are people who swear they've seen them, many years later, swimming, together and happy, in a lost lake in a distant land. But everybody thinks that's too far-fetched to be true.

I was all ready to receive my happiness,
and you never came.

I loved you long before loving you. We were what
lovers were and we didn't even need
bodies for this, because what we said
satisfied us, and whenever life happened it was
to each other that we needed to speak. If there's one thing
I fear in the world, it's your end. I spend hours feeling
indestructible, certain that nothing can
touch me, that nothing can hurt me enough to
make me pull back, and then you show up. You and your image
as far as the eye can see, your eyes when you look at me, your
mouth when you speak to me, and it's then I understand
I am finite, a poor human, and I burst out crying in
search of the telephone and a word from you to
convince me you still exist. It's in the possibility
of your ending that I find humility.

It was the most beautiful day ever on earth where I was,
and you never came.

I don't know where the world ends but I know that
life ends in the depths of your lips. I had the
words ready to tell you that more than anything
what we needed was to do with our bodies what
all the rest of us had done already. Then I would tell you that

since I'd looked at you I already knew what your kiss tasted of
and that it was time for our mouths to know it too. Then
I would slowly undress your tongue without your
noticing that around us not even clocks dared to shift
so as not to disturb the movement of the earth. Finally
you'd say that it was predictable that we'd end up like that,
just to prove that of all the completely
unpredictable things love is the most predictable
of all. That's where the words of that day and that night
would end, or of that night and that day, and out there we no
        longer
knew if it was light or dark, sunny or raining, as
it's surely true that eyes have many abilities
(kissing, hugging, touching, licking, sucking, grabbing,
        squeezing)
when you're in love but seeing isn't one of them.

For the first time in my life I cleaned the dust behind the
furniture at my house,
and you never came.

There could be no possible explanation for your not being here
        and
I still believed that you would be coming perfectly on
time so long as you did come. I tried calling you but
you didn't answer; I tried crying for you but even the tears
didn't come, and when the body makes decisions
by default it's because it knows perfectly well what
it's doing. That was what rested me. I decided to lie down
a little and sleep. Sleeping is always the best way

of waiting for you, since if there's any moment
when I get close to you it's when I am
allowed to dream. When I awoke you weren't there and
I felt like shouting. Fortunately I didn't do it because
I might have woken you. You were asleep, I later understood,
on the next-door bed, having arrived late
the night before and found me with
my eyes already closed. Now it was my turn
to lie down without a word and wait for
you to wake, or wait for you to fall asleep, because
deep down all I care about is that you stay. You
had arrived so late that you might as well not
have come, but it's just as well you did.

My will ached to squeeze you and talk to you,
but you had come already.

When you wake up I promise that we will fall asleep
every day
together for ever.

He was a man like any other, which was why, at this precise moment, he was crying. The whole house silent, still, listening to him suffer. Quiet, he's about to hurt.

She was a woman like any other, which was why, at this precise moment, she was dreaming. The whole beach silent, still, listening to her flying. Quiet, she's about to jump.

The meeting happened at the most unexpected hour of all – which, now we think about it, could be any hour because any hour would be the most unexpected of all for someone who never, ever would have imagined that this meeting might one day happen. He was, as he was for much of his day, crying. She was, as she was for much of her day, dreaming. But on the outside he was the man who cleaned the swimming pool in her beach house and she was the rich woman married to the rich man who had a house by the beach. They'd already seen each other over and over again before that moment when they looked at each other. The whole swimming pool silent, still, listening to them feel. Quiet, they're about to try.

Close to you I lose myself. Her words in his ear. Him smiling, and yet still crying more than ever. I'm sorry but I only like small things and what I'm feeling is too big for me even to acknowledge it as a possibility. His words for her to hear. I'd be grateful, miss, if you wouldn't approach me like that again. And her turning her back. But only for a moment. Then she turns again, kisses him, he kisses her back. You get better at that every time. Anyone who didn't know you might almost believe it. Her words between licked lips. Your fool of a husband still thinks I'm a perfect little saint. And she laughs, and he laughs, and there they are, the two of them together by the pool, discovering the extent of their bodies. All the walls silent, still, listening to them lie. Quiet, they're about to be justiced.

This man's pistol, the barrel pressed against another man's head, is a pistol like any other. One can suppose, therefore, that it is capable of killing. This would, at least, seem to be the fear of the woman who, hands on her head, watches the spectacle that is subsequently played out. Please don't do this to him. That's what she asks. The man with the pistol agrees. She approaches them both and, within just a few seconds, takes the pistol out of the hand of one and fires at the other, who falls, instantly and with a crash, on to the floor. That's how you should have done it. I was fed up of watching you waste time. Just fire and that's that, fuck it. He lowers his head and agrees. And there they were, the three of them, naked bodies, embracing and smiling in the middle of the swimming pool. A few metres away, and all around, there are many people in white overalls and many other people without white overalls but with strange movements (one has been walking in circles for several minutes, another has been looking at the sky and shakes his head vigorously for even more minutes, another is simulating a speech on world peace in a very loud voice and nobody pays him any attention). The whole cinema auditorium silent, still, listening to them perform. Quiet, it's about to end.

Knowing that you were
is what stops me
being.

Your voice on waking: come, love me. And me loving you
without thinking of the time, my watch stretched out on
the bedside table, fed up of knowing that even
he, time, would have to wait till you were
ready to let me go. And later.

How am I to invent someone to replace you
if you're still here?

Later you went and left nothing behind, and that was
your way of remaining intact. And if I'm still able to get up
for life it's because I'm still hoping that you'll come, tears
in your eyes, asking my forgiveness for having gone, for
having dared to eradicate from me what made me want.

The only thing I want
and have always wanted
is that you want me.

In our bedroom there's a museum waiting for you. Your
shoes abandoned in the same place where you
left them: every day I clean them religiously
the way every day you used to clean them religiously. Your

side of the bed unoccupied – and woe betide anyone who
    dares enter
what belongs to you. When you return you'll find it all the
    same,
ready to receive you. It will be a different way of absolving you.

What you did to me is unforgivable,
but that you did not come here for me to forgive you,
there's no forgiveness for that.
It might be late – and it is. But between waiting a whole lifetime
for you to come and fearing a whole lifetime that you'll leave
I prefer the second option.

Better your hand in my hand
than two other hands
without love.
I will wait for you however much you convince me to the
contrary. And
the best men in the world might show up, the most
perfect creatures in the universe, and still it will be enough
to know that your defects want mine again
for ever to be yours for ever again.

Please come back and bring your imperfections.
That's enough
to make me happy.

The priest has already given the order to close the coffin, and I never told you I loved you.

The worst thing about words is the feeling of those that remained unsaid, the irreparable weight of what never existed and what nonetheless will never stop existing: they will never let me exist. I had your whole life to tell you what I saw in you and I failed. I gave you company, friendship, I offered so much to you, and I never believed that one day you would leave without warning. So naïve. I should have known that everything you did was without warning. Why should it be different at the hour of your death?

I have an empty apartment I dreamed would be for us, and I never told you I loved you.

We were bodiless accomplices, we met every day to offer each other whatever life we had to offer, you used to laugh so much and I wanted you so much, did you ever know that when I fell asleep it was the image of your happiness I was thinking of? I imagine you, even wherever you are now, scattering happiness, and what brings me rest is the certainty that your death will be happy ever after. Did you ever know how much I needed you?

Your desk is being sorted out by your parents, and I never told you I loved you.

We were almost perfect lovers, an almost perfect couple, almost perfect happiness. There were days when our bodies wanted it, days when our bodies forced it. On those days we embraced, my hands around you, yours around me, a complete embrace to prove the only thing we needed was courage. It would have been enough for me to tell you what I never stopped telling you, what every day I practised telling you, so that this weight that will now be mine would have been diluted in sweat. Will you forgive me for loving you for ever in silence?

Your parents are reading the letters we wrote, and I never told you I loved you.

Even my hands fell silent when they needed to speak of the scale of what I felt for you. So often we were able to say those things that hurt, like when I told you it was shameful the way you were running away from a job just because you didn't like one of your colleagues, and you stayed, you listened to me and decided to stay; or when you told me that I was being idiotically selfish by not agreeing to go with my siblings to Disney World when this would make them happier than a dream, and I decided to go, I listened to you and decided to go. So often we were able to write to each other all there was to write, and we never said, I never told you, the only words that whether written or spoken needed to be said, so that there should be nothing left over from what we were, so that there should be nothing now left over from what we have been. If I'd told you that I loved you for ever would you have driven more slowly that night?

Your parents are showing me a scribble of yours in which you said that I am the man of your life but you never told me that you loved me, and I never told you that I loved you.

How could we have been so stupid and so happy?

The country burns. Everywhere there are people in pain and scorched earth. There is Hell in the air. And it's when Hell arrives that it's important to have a little Heaven to escape to. A space of absolute non-life to make it possible to live. It's at these moments, when all that the world can offer is pain, that the melancholy arrives, sneaky, waiting for a wounded defence so that it can wound again. That's when art arrives, heroically, to save the honour of the moment.

There must always be a book to read to save our lives.

Or otherwise a musical note, a bit of genius to show us that life's worth it, that the world deserves to go on. If it weren't for a perfect line of poetry or a note that changes our lives, what would life be for? What's the point of the world if not to shelter art within it? And all that we are is people and all that we need is people. It's when the melancholy arrives that we understand it's people who save us from the abyss. The people who write what we want to feel, the people who create the music that makes us keep going, the people who draw the picture that makes us believe. People. When the abyss comes close, that's when people are there to grab hold of us and to allow our salvation. It's not the planet that needs protecting; it's the people. They must be protected to the utmost, showing them that they are the reason for life. The country burns and ironically it's just millimetres away from utter misery when other people save themselves from utter misery. Sometimes it's necessary for things to recede for the world to grow.

And the bastard politicians and their calculations. How

can you think in the plural if you don't respect the singular? The problem with politicians is the angle from which they view the world. They look at the world the way God looks at it and then they sin from a lack of power. Because they're watching us from above while they're down below. Only by treading the earth can you understand how to walk. And they abandon the all for the individual, forgetting that it's of the individual that the all is made. One stone out of place is enough for somebody to trip. It's so simple to live when you think with art inside you. Governing as though writing a poem: that's what I'm proposing. Governing as though composing a piece of music: that's what I'm proposing. Make each decision the most beautiful one in the world. And carry it through. It's when the melancholy arrives that the individual runs the risk of leaving.

Today I'm inclined to give up but at the same time I'm inclined to live for ever. Because there will always be a poem to discover or a melody to explore. A poem is all it takes for being alive to make sense. And an embrace. Oh God, an embrace. Art and embrace: a definition of happiness.

The country burns and there are men and women saving men and women from the utter misery: that's a more than adequate reason to be worthy of the privilege of being alive.

For each bastard who rises up there must always be two or three heroes to make him bend.

I've unlearned from life so many of the things that life gave me.

I've unlearned how to love the future – because what's left of it for me is this soul that is so ready to keep going and this body that is so ready to stretch. What's the point of there being an after me if I won't be here to live through it?

I've unlearned how to discover what drives younger people, what forces them to be what they are, what they need constantly to be. I don't know why there is such a thing as envy, as ambition, the sum total of banknotes kept in a safe. I don't know why there's such a thing as health if all it's good for is earning money. What's the point of youth if we don't know what the point of youth is?

I've unlearned how to understand the people contained in this world. There are people who expend their lives on the lives of others, on the happiness of others while martyring their own, people who don't grab hold of the so-much that they have and prefer to reach for the so-much that they will never have. There are people who waste themselves on life. What's the point of having your whole life ahead of you if everything we do makes it turn its back on us?

I've unlearned how to disdain the moment – because I've already got so few moments left to disdain. The images come and they stay, they stay around here, as though they knew that each of them might be the last, the one I take with me to who knows where but to somewhere that certainly is not here. How many smiles do I have left to see? How many embraces do I have left to hold? How many euphorias do I have left to feel?

I've unlearned how to devour time as it rushes past. Now I consume life in mouthfuls, each piece in its proper place. There is an assigned place for each moment, the right space for each precise feeling. I no longer want any of what is fragmentary – and that's how I feel whole. What's the point of having everything at once if there's still an afterwards to fill?

I've unlearned how to waste pleasure. Happiness is about avoiding gulping life down in one go, but rather having just a little taste here, a little taste there, setting the bar way up high but never touching the sky. Above the sky there's nothing but death, and there's still so much I want to rise to before reaching the absurd summit of the end. How many orgasms are there in each life?

I've unlearned from life so many of the things that life gave me.

But what I've never unlearned was the size of your skin, the illogical eternity of liking you like this. I did the sums yesterday and there have been more than thirty thousand days when we've fallen asleep and woken up together, in the bed where I'm now writing to you and from where I hope to go to you again. Thirty thousand days watching you sleep, knowing the cold or the heat of your body, understanding what was hurting you inside, loving each new wrinkle that appeared. Thirty thousand days of me and you, of this house that one day we said would be ours (what will become of a house that knows us so well when we are no longer here to occupy it?), of the difficulties and the yearnings, of our children running down the hall, of the longing of knowing that we were always going to end up as just us. Thirty thousand days in which everything changed and nothing changed us, of your tears that were so beautiful and so sad, of the few times that life forced us to be parted (and one evening far from you was enough for neither home nor life to be the same). Thirty thousand days, my adorable grouchy old lady. Me and you and the world, and all the old people we once met have already been taken by old age. We are still here, thirty thousand days later, together as ever. Together for ever. Thirty thousand days in which I have unlearned so many things, my love. Except loving you.

There is no longer sun nor your naked body, and the beach where I'm lying is an empty space.

You came alone, your steps resolved to speak to me of life. I knew that you were coming for the goodbye, for the moment that would make all pains seem small. Why do you have to leave for somewhere where I am not? Why is there the possibility of a life of yours that doesn't include my whole life? You came alone, and in your aloneness when you arrived there was the certainty that you wanted to be alone when you left. How many embraces would you need to know that you are mine?

The light is no longer the same, nor does the sea seem to follow its course, and the beach where I'm lying is an empty space.

You said we needed to carry out the last kiss, to construct the final moment; you said also that it was in our hands to manage to avoid the impossible, the absurd separation that neither you nor I wanted. And you left it to our lips to say the rest. I'm the most beautiful woman in the world when I know you love me, the most sensual body in the world when I know you want me. The hot sand had never seen anything like this. Your body with no clothes and my body soulless even though with all my soul, as we seek to avoid the dissolution of what will bind us for ever. All the kisses rose up and all the hands met. Why does something so eternal have to end?

Already the moon doesn't look so full nor does the water look so infinite, and the beach where I'm lying is an empty space.

The problem with everything that exists is one day having to stop existing. The certainty of a future ended in an orgasm. We looked at each other for several minutes, the still beach watching us suffer. Once again you were the first to speak. You said 'I wish we were possible' and I heard you. You said 'promise me you love me unconditionally' and I heard you. You said 'if you say nothing in the next thirty seconds I'm leaving for good'. Then you looked at your watch and counted along and I heard you. I wanted to say I'd give my life for you not to go, that eternity only exists so that there's enough time to contain all the time I need you for. But I just heard you. You said 'time's up' and I heard. You said 'I love you until I have no skin' and I heard you. You said 'goodbye' and I heard you. Why the hell did you demand words when everything in me was saying everything in you?

The night is already less calm and the wind seems so human, and the beach where I'm lying is an empty space.

Far from anything that is land, I am trying, here, to return to the lap of your memories. I know I was one sentence away from being happy. I imagine you might return one night, repenting or in a moment of revelation. But I quickly stop imagining.

The water is no longer as cold and nor do the waves seem so large, and the beach where I'm lying is an empty space.

I needed to find the start of life,
and the greatest charm of your smile was its being mine.

I used to tell you that God inhabits the flesh of
the poem, that the words I wrote
were so far from deserving you, then
I'd grab you hard and show you that even
love knows how important the body is.

I needed to find the end of the kiss,
and the greatest dream that could exist was your being real.

We met on the corner of orgasm, after
the sweat and the whole discovery of pleasure, and
people knew that when we were united the whole
building needed to know it, and I'll bet that when
you came you were the diva whom everybody applauded.

I needed to find the science of ecstasy,
and the greatest human genius is having
observed the existence of happiness.

We lived in an amusement park, we recast
the definition of each room, and the kitchen was there
for loving, and sometimes also for cooking, the living room
was there for loving, and sometimes also for living in, the
    bedroom

was there for loving, and sometimes also for sleeping; everything
that was there for us was there for loving however much it might
also have some other purpose.

I needed to find the logic of the embrace,
and the greatest trick in the world is having invented unity.

At the end of the day I would tell you the inside of what
I had loved in you as I loved you, describe to you each
sensation you offered me, you closed
your eyes and tried to feel what was happening within
me, then it was your turn to tell me how
you moved, in what and when we were ourselves again
we no longer knew if the sensation that thrilled us was ours or
the other's, and we understood that skin
and bone do not exist to separate us
but merely to protect us.

I needed to find the perfect words to say to you,
and regrettably the best result
I could find was 'I love you'.

I feel trapped in our home, and
woe betide you if you let me go out.

Summer ends and the world restarts. The streets fill with people in a hurry, thinking about the best way to spend their lives to allow them to earn. At this point I like to understand what drives people, what's going on in their eyes, what forces them never to give up. I sit at bus stops, in hospital waiting rooms, in cafés more or less full of people, on park benches where lives that are over come together to celebrate the end of the road with a little less pain. And it's true what happens. A man has just hugged a woman. I don't know his age nor her age, because their hug only allows a diffuse shadow to be seen. It's as though they'd managed to disappear into each other, and if that isn't the best way of loving then I don't know anything at all. Later a curious child is looking for something behind the plants in the park. He knows he isn't supposed to, but he does. He moves aside a plant, then a flower, glancing out of the corner of his eye hoping to spare himself from being caught. And he manages it. It's a ball, a small one but the whole planet to that kid, which makes him happy. And there's a whole philosophy infused within a boy who, though he knows it's forbidden, looks for an insignificant ball that is worth everything to him, behind the untouchable flowers in a park. Children are the best life teachers that God has ever created, I believe they even come after adults, they are the evolution of what adults are. If there were a just order in the world that's what would happen: we would be adults first and then children, starting out by fearing everything that moves because we're adults and adults are afraid of everything ending because they know that everything ends, and then we'd end up fearless, with no terrors, looking for whatever we fancy wherever we fancy. And if that isn't the best way of living then I don't know anything at all. Further up, a couple is arguing about money. All over the world, at this moment, there are couples arguing about money, couples killing each other over money. She seems to be apologising, he seems to be insisting on the uselessness of the purchase. Then she replies, she talks about I don't know what which cost I don't know how much, and that's when I decide to stop paying attention, because I understand that the best aphorism of the day has already come out of it, when the woman said that there's I don't know what which cost I don't know how much. The notes are I don't know what which are worth I don't know how much. And if that isn't the best way to define money then I don't know anything at all. Night seems to fall and the street, after the worn-out employees and the worn-out people in worn-out jobs, starts to strip itself of anxiety, of agony, the cars are already thinning out, the horns lying down now until the morning of a new day, and all humanity seems to exist again. Men and women are no longer seeking destinations, and walk the pavement, savouring the pavement, through the park, savouring the park. When the day ends and the rushing stops, only the humans are still in the outside part of the world. The rest remain, at home now, in front of their television sets, in the wild search for some manoeuvre that will allow them not to give up. A goal on the football pitch, a kiss on the TV soap, even a death on a cult show. As for me, when humanity returns to the streets, it just keeps providing me with exactly what I'm always looking for. Your hand loving mine, your gaze, here and there, looking for me in search of validation, your head sometimes resting on my shoulder, and the words that never needed any rush to make them immortal: I love you.

Whenever I talk I use the first-person plural. It's my way of having you with me, as though it were possible to use words to define what words define. An inversion of the natural order of the whole process of life: first you say what you see, then you see what you say you've seen. And whenever I see myself I see you with me.

'It cannot be. It hurts too much.'

'You're going.'

'I've got to go. I've got to run away. It hurts too much to bear.'

'What can I do?'

'Love me. Keep loving me. That is all I ask of you.'

'Forget about bodies. Forget about touch.'

'Remember bodies. Remember touch. Believe in the possibility of sometimes everything not even needing everything. Believe in the possibility of just a part perfectly fulfilling the role of the whole.'

'I'll be amputated from myself if you go. Tearing you away from me is tearing me away from me. You go and you take me with you. How can I live completely if I don't even have myself?'

'Think of it the other way round. Think about how if by going I take you with me, then you're still with me just like you really want to be. If by going I take you with me, then we will be together for ever. Isn't that what you want so badly?'

'Yes. Thank you for making me happy.'

'I'm going now.'

'Go. Be happy for ever.'

You went. Whether happy, I don't know. But you went. And now I understand it was the words, it's always the words, you and that peerless capacity you have for convincing me of the impossible. You abandoned me and I thanked you. And I was left without you thinking I was with you. And the worst of it is that despite everything you feel like my wife to me even if I have no idea whose wife you are. I imagine you wherever you are carrying me with you, I imagine me wandering in Paris, arm in arm with the most beautiful woman in the city; I imagine you in your village, your whole family at the table, and you saying that we're happy, the two of us, in this way we have of never being more than always together, then I imagine your mother saying to you once again 'wise up, girl', and you replying once again 'there goes my mother always wishing me the worst', and finally your father would appear, pacifying as ever, hugging you both and saying secretively so as not to hurt you too much 'I'm so envious and so sorry for my little girl', and there we'd be, the four of us, me in you and you in your parents, hugging in an impossible embrace that feels to me like everything; I imagine you everywhere in all the world because I know you're crazy enough to go everywhere in all the world, but I know you're not crazy enough not to take me with you wherever you go. Not least because, as you know, that isn't up to you.

When people ask my name, I answer 'we're Pedro.'

Today I found the Facebook profile of someone who died yesterday,

oh God, the pain,

what is this whole technology crap after all?, a person dies and is still around just the same, as though he were alive, we're exactly the same and we no longer even exist,

we're not even a forgetting, if we are strict about it,

mister lawyer died yesterday and today his profile is intact, his health perfect and the same friends as ever, I'd bet it'll be months before they even discover he's died, some ironies are so sad they shouldn't even be called ironies,

nobody touches our most intimate hand,

I can't bear much of what I feel, I obsessively put myself on the far side,

and his children, and his wife, and his life?, fuck it's so unbearable having death,

life is a long erasing,

each day we disappear a little, and we take a bit of those who love us, if heaven exists it will have a whole lot of my mother, probably her smile, the way the world opens up when she looks at me, a whole lot of my dad, I'd bet it would be his strange sensitivity, his unbearable egotism, a whole lot of the woman I love, no doubt her skin on mine when I wake up, her perfect lips inside mine, a whole lot of my sister, of my niece, if there isn't a bit of each of them then heaven doesn't exist, that's for sure,

what I cannot be undoes my mouth like a gag,

the problem is the possibility, the existence of options, everything for the sake of making an attempt, the feelings, orgasms, connections, affection, and then the ending of them all,

ending is an insurmountable bullying,

the end massacres me daily, I know it's stupid, I ought to think about what I've got and not about what I cannot have, but in truth if I do think it's because I believe, let me be struck down by lightning if I'm not going to live for ever,

we accumulate events like we accumulate trash so as to have something that isn't ourselves to throw away,

mister lawyer,

may he rest in peace, but mostly in commotion, since not having a body is already enough for it to be a drought, right?,

it was his birthday recently, you don't have to go far down his wall to see it, before that he'd been in the Dominican Republic, even in the Congo, he seemed happy with his wife, everything impeccable and he died,

how do you clean death off the internet?,

programmers need to be taught emotions, and so do I right now, every day so I don't forget,

what would his final litigation have been?,

make it a poem, make it defy continuity, that's what a lawyer ought to devote himself to while he's alive, proving with no possibility of appeal that no man deserves to end, or at least that he should be aware of this, have you ever seen an animal depressed because it's going to die?,

either immortality or ignorance,

when I die create several Facebook profiles for me, and maintain me bit by bit, or otherwise not at all,

LOL.

I'm writing to you today about the important ifs of life. Hold on to them, and then, when at any moment you feel alarmed, grab hold of them again. You'll find you never want for anything again. I promise.

If you love with complete security, give up on loving, because, you should know, when you love with complete security you're not loving in the slightest.

If you weren't afraid of saying you love, of how you felt when you were exposing the vastest part of yourself, give up on loving, because, you should know, it's only what makes us afraid that's worth our being afraid to lose it.

If you didn't go to sleep every night with an inexplicable desire to wake back up just to be in the arms of the person with whom you've fallen asleep, give up on loving, because, you should know, it's only what makes us fall asleep happy while still wanting to wake up happy that is real love.

If you don't wake up every day with an inexplicable desire to go back to sleep just so you can fall asleep peacefully beside the person you love, give up on loving, because, you should know, it's only what makes us wake up happy while still wanting to fall asleep happy that is real love.

If you aren't lost whenever you are without the person you love, even if it's a few simple seconds, give up on loving, because, you should know, if you love you're only in the right place when you're in the same place as the person you love.

If you aren't stupidly happy just to see the person you

love happy, give up on loving, because, you should know, happiness when you love only exists as a pair, and when one of the two is happy without the other being happy it's because both are unhappy as long as they aren't both happy.

If you can't imagine yourself growing into a little old lady alongside the little old man who is the person you love and if this isn't an image that shivers you with happiness from the tips of your toes to the end of your hair, give up on loving, because, you should know, when you don't understand that growing old is cool because it offers you the possibility of loving the person you love until the end of your days then probably you don't really love at all.

If as you read all these words I have written for you, you don't fancy coming with me round behind the science building and embracing me more tightly than you've ever embraced anyone before, give up on loving, because, you should know, I decided a long while back, when I saw you walk into psychology class for the first time, that you were love, and if there weren't you then it had better be just me. After all, better to spend my life just dreaming of being yours than spend my life just pretending to be someone else's.

With infinite love,

Pedro, from 10J (the kid who sits next to you in Portuguese class)

It's pain that tightens the knots. The rest tightens little bows, at most.

It's necessary to go deep into what already exists, to be able to bear what is yet to come. There's always another layer of pain to experience – and only someone solid in every layer right down to this one can bear the impact of what will come then.

Living with the reverse of pain means not putting up with the reverses of life.

Abhorring pain without ever stopping facing up to it as something natural: that's the secret to healthy survival.

Pain happens. There's nothing to be done. Pain happens. And it's unpredictable. Nobody can predict pain – at least not the way pain can hurt. Being ready for pain means knowing all its steps, measuring its every movement. And attacking it without ever stopping accepting it.

To deny the existence of pain is to deny the existence of life.

What binds us is what has hurt us. Nothing particularly serious. But what binds us is what has hurt us. We found ourselves to be capable, when the pain arrives, of joining together without yielding to the easy temptation of each suffering just for himself. Loving isn't every man for himself; loving is everyone for one another. We save ourselves whenever there are tears to be shed. We don't acquiesce, we don't accept, resigned. But we save ourselves. If you hurt I'll do it, I'll take on a part of your hurt, share a part of me that does not hurt.

And that's how we regain our balance. You with half of what doesn't hurt in me and me with half of what hurts in you. You suffer half of what you could suffer and I suffer half of what you could suffer. I don't even think about the equation I'm solving. I think only that I'm extracting half of your pain. And that's enough for the half of the pain that hurts in me, for even that, to be happy. And then the opposite happens. When I'm hurting, you come and share out what wants to kill me. And so we go on, we two, at the mercy of the tide, but always trying, all the time, to reverse the rushing of the waves.

A relationship without pain is not a relationship; it's a performance.

There's so little to savour beyond what puts us here, unique while still being so alike. We are made of the weight of the desire to live. We look at life the way a child looks at a toy. We want to know what it does, what it's worth, how much fun it can offer us. And we have fun. Sometimes, of course, the toy does hurt us. A wheel comes away and needs to be replaced, the leg of a doll pops out and she needs to go to the doll hospital. That's when we become the most responsible adults in the world. We accept the defects and go in search of solutions for them. We love each other like children mad about toys and we save ourselves like superhero adults. We are half irresponsibility and half saviours of the planet. It's our way of saying that we are loved.

I love you irrationally. And with all good reason.

Use deodorant.
Say at least all the swear words you feel like saying.
Clean your teeth.
Do something that scares you.
Tell jokes.
Don't choose what's easy just because you think it'll be easy.
Don't eat with your mouth open.
Don't do what's difficult just because you think it'll be difficult.
Love without looking at whom.
Eat chocolates.
Love only when you feel somebody.
Kiss with your tongue.
Dream about something impossible.
Be proud of every wrinkle.
Experiment with new sexual positions.
Laugh at yourself.
Dream about something possible.
Laugh at others.
Imagine your worst enemy sitting on the lavatory.
Laugh at everything.
Never think you're playing too much.
Cry.
Skip rope.
Take someone you love to a motel.
Throw yourself in the sea whenever you can.
Love the sun.
Hug.

Love the rain.

Forgive whoever you love.

Love the wind.

Forgive whoever you don't love.

Have a bath every day.

Never give up on an orgasm.

Share.

Help.

Look.

Make a point of touching with your skin.

Smile at whoever wishes you well.

Hug tight.

Smile at whoever wishes you harm.

Don't be afraid of giving up.

Be unique.

Don't be afraid of not giving up.

Respect the majority.

Be happy with everything you're scared of.

Crap on the majority.

Give all that you have to all those you love.

Go the opposite way just because you feel like it.

Use moisturiser.

Do what you really want to do.

Marry for love.

Laugh for ever.

Live for love.

Be a risk-taker.

Be a rule-breaker.

Be pornographic.

Get addicted to adrenaline.

Go on.

Keep moving.

Wash your sex regularly.

Do all of the above in the name of pleasure.

Love regularly with your sex.

Insist on being alive.

Come regularly.

Keep on with this list.

Every day.

All the time.

Right now.

The skin was there to persuade me you existed, and when
I touched you I also found proof of the existence of God.
Missing you exists to show me how small death is, because
after losing you only the certainty of extinction gives me rest,
    and nothing
hurts more than looking at life and not finding you there.

I used to like defining immortality as if it weren't
your presence in my mortality, I spend the day
attempting alternative plans, manoeuvres for entertaining my
pain, and at night when I lie down I swear I try to avoid
your smell of everything on the empty sheets.

Life cannot happen if you've stopped happening to me, nothing
    happens
but the breathing, the obligation, the steps I don't even need
to want to be able to take, because even bad things
stopped having a *raison d'être* because I couldn't
digest them beside you, and there's nobody to tell I love you
    like a
madman if you weren't here for me to love you like a madman.

The greatest madness is your being my sanity, needing
you to not fall into the dysfunctional me, into
the inability to bear what with you was mere life.

The secret of love is transforming it into mere life, making it

greater life, and even an ordinary day is unforgettable
when it's done with you.

Either you come back to me or I'll kill myself for ever, not
with weapons, but with poison or sterile suicides, just
like this, each day, living our death,
slowly, as though all the meaning of life
were going from me to you.

If you come back
bring me with you.

How many lives are there in your life?

'When I die trample me to death,' you used to say, that smile hidden behind your lips, you rascal, whenever anyone said to you that one day they'd have to go, the way everybody has to go. 'Being alive consists of not dying,' you'd add, 'and actually I've been doing pretty well on this task of being immortal,' and your whole gaze would bring me that detachment that I never knew how to have and you never knew how not to. Why is it that death only kills those who don't fear it?

I spend my life trying to forget you and that's why I remember you constantly.

Your place untouched on the sofa, your scent spread everywhere, so long afterwards (you've already been gone a year and you still haven't said anything?) all over the house. You're the person to whom I comment on the news (there's a government now that's even worse than the last one, did you know that? People are fed up but they don't show that they're fed up, they just wander on, talking but not moving), you're the person with whom I watch those TV series that so often, into the early hours, we used to share. Me in my place and you in yours, the way it had to be. I swear when I close my eyes I can feel your hands in my hair (your skin; nobody ends up with skin like that when they're dead), and all the tears make sense after having loved so powerfully.

I devote my life to your death the way I used to devote it to your life.

And I'm not unhappy, my love. Disabuse yourself of that, I'm still the same old woman, your woman, with the same old imperfections and the same old desire to see you happy. I know you no longer have a body, I know we no longer have our touch, but every day I still get up and go to bed in order to see you. Before you went I used to open my eyes and see you; now I close my eyes and see you. And maybe that's what dying is, maybe dying is no more than an uncontrollable desire to spend more time with your eyes closed than with your eyes open.

I fall asleep to find you and I am happy.

The doctors are concerned, they talk to me about grieving, my family (your children are beautiful; Carlos has gone to college to do engineering, like his dad; Joana is the best student in the class and she's already started dating – he seems like a good lad; and everyone loves you all the way up to death; and everyone loves you in death) ask me to detach myself from you, to abandon this house where we are happy and seek out other houses, other bodies, other lives. Poor wretches, they don't know what they're talking about. They don't know that when you love the way we love death isn't much, it's a longer journey, that's all. You're waiting for me at the house that will be our last just as I devote this house to you until the last.

There's always a ridiculous happiness when I remember you.

'When I die don't forget to go in search of what you never found because of me,' you said, your white deathbed, the doctors with tears in their eyes (only you could make doctors cry, you and that sense of humour you had to your last breath; and that smile behind your lips, so naughty, so lovely it hurts), 'and please, no fucking crying at the funeral; build a bonfire around the coffin and dance till sunrise', you asked, the whole bedroom (it was number 23 on that floor of the building where my ground fell away beneath me) with insides wounded, and I no longer know whether you said anything else before your eyes closed far from me. The best tribute we paid you was to get the best DJ in the country to your funeral rave. There was dancing, happiness and pain, so much pain beneath the music, and no sound could silence your goodbye.

How many songs do I need to hear to stop hearing you in me?

Now it's just the two of us again. I am living you in search of forgetting and that's how all of time is scarce and at the same time useless. When you want me to go I know you'll call me. Until then I'll close my eyes whenever I want you. Like now, right now, I want you.

See you soon.

One day, perhaps, I might want to be free, but today I'd rather be yours. To wake up clinging to your skin as though there could be no alternative, kissing each of your lips like a wished-for punishment. To remain imprisoned in this little corner of freedom that we call bed sheets.

One day, perhaps, I might want to be perfect, but today I'd rather be fallible. Failing when you ask me to touch you without being precise or when you demand that I hug you without squeezing you to tears. And subsisting, inadequate, in the all-powerful moment of loving you.

One day, perhaps, I might want to be normal, but today I'd rather be strange. Trying out fear the way you try on a pair of shoes, walking down roads nobody wanted to tar, and knowing that if people look at me with amazement it's only, quite simply, because I am amazing. And in this way insisting, stubborn and happy, on the possibility of inventing impossibles that are as yet untried.

One day, perhaps, I might want to be a judge, but today I'd rather be the person being judged. Doing things that somebody might criticise, things that might never even be appreciated, or simply things that serve no purpose and which I do just because. And being illogically happy, being so giddy that all I need is to create to make me feel up to being alive.

One day, perhaps, I might want to be immortal, but today I'd rather be finite. Believing in the scarcity of life, in the limited world of the skin, even in the counting by sighs of the time when I've really known how to be alive. And remaining entire at the gates of death, wretched and euphoric, every day, always just about to die and always stupidly alive.

One day, perhaps, I might want to be independent, but today I'd rather be belonging. Belonging in your lap so that I have existence, at the moment when you look at me for me to exist as a look-at-able object, or to accept once and for all that it's inside your body that I discover the existence of mine. And knowing that while for other people there's a God, for me there's you to make my faith in God endure.

One day, perhaps, I might want to end this piece of writing, but today I'd rather leave it as it is, incomplete and candid, waiting for you or someone (or simply life) to come along and find the concluding paragraph, the one that makes everyone go Aaah. And that's how I go, without connecting the words, to your open body once again.

One day, perhaps. But not today.

The people I love.

The people I love have defects, their feet might even smell, they believe in eternal life, and they know that heaven is the moment when we learn to love. They don't hesitate to try when the easiest thing would be to say 'I don't know' and 'I can't', they aren't afraid of criticism whenever they're exposing themselves by doing whatever they want to do. And they carry on, proudly, failing like lunatics and forever lunatics when they stop failing.

The people I love.

The people I love have wrinkles on their faces even if they're children, a skin which daily teaches them that we have to keep moving forward before we are left behind, and an unshakeable desire to change the world with every gesture they make. They don't shirk their responsibilities as human beings, still less do they deny ageing as one of the constants of being alive, they suffer like the soulless because deep down that's the greatest proof that they have souls. And they insist, impudently, on a road to stable perdition that takes them to meet their unbalanced happinesses.

The people I love.

The people I love are hard to understand, sometimes they talk about strange things, have unattainable desires and worst of all they go off to try and get them satisfied. They don't waste time speaking ill of people who have done, they don't waste energy searching for the inadequacies of people who have tried. And they continue, frivolously, developing their own theories of existence, their own manuals in every speciality that the speciality in being alive contains within it.

The people I love.

The people I love spend their lives goofing around, telling anyone whoever requires them to wear a tie on their souls to get lost, who are fans of the repeated pornography of undressing dreams and acting on them, and if anyone asks them for a hand they have no problem giving their whole arm if they can. They don't turn down pleasures, they don't say 'no' to an orgasm, they don't believe in a faith that castrates and in all the gods that sell hardship. And they throw themselves, almost always head first, towards a wish for everything for the first time, life for the first time, and day, and night, and all the evenings that never come late.

The people I love.

The people I love aren't the best people in the world. But they are people.

And that's enough for me to be able to love them.

The poet sat down, took a deep breath and wrote:

'An Infinite Sentence for an Infinite Love

One day we spent the day defining what was
surrounding us, we started with what was closest
and saw that happiness, if you think about it,
consists of looking at what doesn't cause pain, and
that's how we spent that evening of that day
when we spent the day defining looking at each other, without
a word, because we all know and we all
knew too that all ends begin in
words, said or yet to say, and all we wanted
was for none of that, me looking at you or you at me
for us both to be looking at happiness
after we'd defined it, to end, and the truth is
it didn't end: I continued to be happy looking at you,
you continued to be happy looking at me, I'd bet
that you told me I was beautiful and I'm sure
I told you you were beautiful, without a word
I also told you that we would need to stretch time
so that the whole of life left to us was a good beginning
for all the minutes I wanted to love you, then
we decided to go in search of new definitions and
the words returned, you said it would be good to define fear, and
before we knew it the two of us were embracing,
saying to each other that fear was the ending of

what we were, and we had to cling tight not to
let it get away, and like that, without realising, we were already
    defining
an embrace, that thing that, deep down, is no more than the
way in which humans, being so impotent, find to maintain
the illusion that this way they can stop the person they like
    most
from getting away; and while we embraced we were already
thinking that there was so much more to define, the sea or the
wind, for example, you started saying that the sea
is what when you look at me seems so small and I
said that the only function of the wind was to push your
voice towards me, then I also said that I didn't believe
in the blue of the sea since I'd seen your eyes and you said
that sometimes you're afraid of the wind because there are
    words it
might carry away from you which you so want to hear; that
    was when I said
I love you and even the wind didn't stop me, you said love me
    and
tell me so always even if it's over the noise of every wind, and
    suddenly
your hug was tighter once again, and happiness
was once again better defined, and the only definition
left was the greatest one of all; I started, fearful, and
I stated with conviction that love is what suspends
life, you agreed and added that perfect love
is what suspends life throughout a whole life,
and I still wanted to specify that in some contexts
people say that love and life can be perfect

synonyms but I disagreed firmly, because
it's quite clear that life isn't nor ever would be
a match for the size of love; it was
at this point that you gave up on the hug and preferred
a whole body, and the only definition we touched upon again
that day and that night was of moaning, which we left,
polite as we are, for all the neighbours who
had the patience to listen to our pleasure

And thus, without any full stop at all as there needs to be, ends
the infinite poem'

The poet wrote, before lying down, alone, and spending the
night crying as he listened to the pleasure of the neighbours
upstairs.

He believed he ought to have two women: one for loving and one for company.

'There's no way to combine the two sides of what I want: if on the one hand I want peace, on the other I want war. The woman I love unsettles me; the woman I have for company soothes me,' he used to say, whenever he was asked the reason for such a strange way of looking at his feelings. 'I'm a two-girl man only,' he'd conclude, and smile, as he tenderly kissed the woman he had for company, and then, heatedly and passionately, the woman he loved.

One day, one of them, the woman he loved, died suddenly. In distress, after a few minutes he quit the company of her relatives and their unbearable weeping and, unable to shake his desperation, he sought solace from the woman he had for company. He arrived at the house, said the usual 'honey, I'm home' but didn't hear the usual 'I'm in here, love'. He searched the house countless times. Then he searched the city countless times, and the hospitals, the homes of their friends. He phoned everywhere. Until at last he went to the police. He gave her name and then finally someone said they knew exactly where she was, without volunteering any further details. Barely breathing, he wrote down the place and went on there, anxious for a hug that might give at least one of his sides some peace. Until he arrived, onto the threshold of total distress.

'Thank goodness you came back,' cried the distraught mother of the woman he loved, dressed in black and tears, when she saw him approaching from a distance. 'We didn't know where you'd gone, you left without telling anyone,' she added. And she rested her head on his defeated lap.

He seemed like a normal man but he was a man without love. Though he doesn't seem like it, a man without love is no man at all.

'Do you dance?'

The woman, who he had never seen before, was looking him straight in the eye, staring fixedly at every movement of his mouth as though expecting to hear the secret to eternal life.

'Sorry, I just haven't got a knack for dancing.'

His expected answer, whenever there was the possibility of something that might hurt him. 'If you can't conquer it, get yourself involved in it' was his maxim when it came to fear. But that woman was fearless. Or if not, she didn't give a damn about him.

'Not having a knack for something is, for me, the best possible reason to carry out that something, countless times. It's only then that doing something gives you that real rush: when we don't know much, or really anything, about how we're supposed to do it. And we just test it out, experimenting, running risks and inventing new paths. Doing something you haven't the vaguest idea how to do, that's probably the most exciting thing in the world. After love, of course.'

All this without a smile, without the slightest sense that she was joking: that woman didn't joke when on duty. And her duty was well defined.

'Do you dance?'

In silence, feeling as though he were being observed in an

ultrasound of emotions, the man tried to run away. The man always tried to run away. (Man always tries to run away.)

'I really haven't got the knack, like I said. And besides, I don't like it. At all. I really don't like it at all.'

Plan B is under way. The strangest thing about fear is the way it forces us, in order to avoid doing something we're scared to do, to do something we're even more scared to do. Running away is an act of disguised courage. But if you're going to be afraid, let it be a sensual fear, a sexual fear. A fear with an orgasm inside it.

'Not liking something is the second strongest reason for doing that something. When we don't like something, the problem isn't with the something; the problem's with us, that we can't extract from the something in question whatever it has to offer us. We need to turn that something around, look at it from every possible angle. And then we always find reasons to do, and enjoy doing, that something. Sometimes we have to do it first and only afterwards understand why we've done it.'

The woman insisted. The woman was one of those unusual people who don't give up until she's won. That, deep down, is the only possible argument for giving up on winning.

'Do you dance?'

Finally he danced. Around them people didn't even register him or her. They were just another couple, just another love winning the battle. Just the world winning the battle. It's courage, perhaps more than dreams (dreams imagine; courage is), that make the world leap and move forward.

'Do you dance, miss?'

He asked strangely, on the most special day of his life,

in the middle of another of the times when the two of them went out dancing. And she understood that, this time, it was an invitation to stop. She stopped. And said yes.

Till death would them part.

'I'd like to forget the name of the sheets when I have you, the space unoccupied on the bed when you aren't with me, but time passes and it may be too late.'

These were the first words she wrote to make him come back. But they didn't last long. She looked at them, felt they were too poetic to tell the truth, which was so primitive, about what she felt. She deleted them. And started again.

'I've got a stomach ache from not having you. There's a hole that doesn't get better in the centre of what I feel. Come back to my lap or I don't even know why I want this body at all.'

That was her second attempt. It seemed much better, she thought, the right words in the right place. But then she read it again. She saw that it was perhaps too visceral, that it was perhaps too physical. She wanted something more balanced – and yet still able to show him the imbalance of not having him. She needed something that connected the physical lack to the total lack. Without beautiful words, without exaggerated metaphors, without surrendering to the temptation of the clichés you can read in any cheap paperback. She needed to be unique. And she tried again.

'You are the best way of living. I could say to you I want you for everything that you are. But I'd be lying. I want you because of everything that I am with you. I want you because of what I am. Because I feel I am, in you, the person I want to be. You are my best way of living. I want you out of egotism. That's it. I want you out of egotism. I hope you want me for the same reason.'

Now that was it. She read it through. She adored it. That was it, that was exactly what she wanted to say: honesty needed, at this point, to be the right approach. There was no use for complex ideas, poems that were beautiful but empty. Only sincerity, the purest sincerity, might be able to make him come back. Before sending the text to print, on a dry white page, she read it once again. She liked it even more. She had achieved the perfect text for such an imperfect moment as this. She had her finger on the 'print' button, ready to press it, when she understood that, after all, she still hadn't found what she wanted. He had just arrived, he looked at her and opened his arms to her. She looked back at him and didn't even need to speak.

That text stayed where it was, still, the excitable cursor watching them love.

The neighbour opposite always insists on vacuuming her house when I'm loving you, I hear each speck being sucked up as my desire for you breathes me in, and if there's something coming through the light it's your eyes and your kiss.

There's so much fear in the room when you leave, I lie down, all wrapped up, waiting for you to come, the windows bringing me life that just keeps on going, as though it were possible to keep on going without you, people looking at me, lying down and all wrapped up, and they feel sorry for the old man who's just waiting for somebody to take him away to nevermore.

The neighbour opposite does her vacuuming, I don't know how long I've been seeing her like this, every day, the usual time, not too early in the morning nor too late, or maybe it's just not too early in the morning nor too late within me, and whenever it is that she vacuums I'm loving you.

Like now, as I look into the cracks in the ceiling, I'll deal with them one day, I promise, for something that I don't know quite what it is, maybe a deeper hole, or a different-coloured stain, all around there's a darkness I can't bear, your smell visible each time I try to open my eyes.

I need your smell more than I need life, and I never told you, coward that I am, that there's a courage within me that depends on you, because there's something telling me that you're the justification for everything, and that even killing for you wouldn't be a sin. And that damned vacuum cleaner, when are you coming back?, it doesn't stop and doesn't let me stop, probably there isn't even a vacuum cleaner or a neighbour, it's just me in search of you, and you already know, have I told you this?, that whenever the neighbour does her vacuuming I'm loving you.

Yesterday I saw you doing the washing-up and I thought about God, or about some other thing that's just as big, I thought there's a declaration of love whenever I look at you, and that we've discovered that life doesn't pass by when we convince ourselves of its end. Then I stopped thinking and went over to you, ran my hand down your back, your smile as I discovered you, and you helped me to love you while I helped you to put the dishes in the machine. What kind of god would let something like this end, would allow there to be something as small as our two bodies sustaining things as large as our desires for ever?

The neighbour vacuums and we love each other, and if there's something coming through the flesh it's your eyes and your kisses, and whenever the neighbour vacuums, have I told you this?, I'm loving you.

The day puts me to sleep beneath its eyes, and your hands are the skin that God has chosen for touching the world; there is no place more divine than your kiss, and when I want to fly I lie down at your feet.

I ask you not to go, to stay just so I can stay, to remain on your side of the bed, and me on mine, both of us feeling time running on, and you can even fall asleep, you can read the women's magazine with the red carpets and those men with abs that nobody has, or just look at the ceiling and think about you; I'll stay here, looking at you so I know that I exist, thinking about how much I love you and how much I have your body within mine. Knowing that there is the curve of your back for finding the curve of life, my eyes watching your sweat running down, understanding the possibility of eternity.

Immortality is an orgasm with you.

You moan until the world is ending inside my ears, my whole body comes when you're about to, and the truth of the universe is the cramped physics of the space between us. You hold me tight for ever until the ends of my bones, until flesh is impossible and there surely must be something more to explain our existence.

All I know is that I'm more than a body when you come to me to hold me tight.

When I embrace you even the poem bends, too small in its poetry for the intangible that unites us, people don't believe something like this happens and that's what saves us from excommunication. Then you go, you ask to leave, as life also exists and the bills need paying, and I finally understand that the problem with all this is that nobody understands what's important in life.

The cleaning woman arrives and finds me pen in hand, writing you these words and some others, stretched out on my side of the bed, waiting for you once again, and in silence she goes on cleaning whatever there is to clean, she already knows not to clean the marks from your feet on the kitchen floor (your feet all over the house are so beautiful), still less the already smoked cigarettes you've left in the ashtray, and I keep writing I don't know what, which I'm only writing to free myself from you for a few moments, I don't know where the words go but I suspect they don't know much about me either, and many minutes or hours later, with so many words already between us, the door opens, the cleaning woman is no longer here, there's no evidence in the kitchen that when I was writing to you I fed my body to stay alive, because it's only alive that I can love you, and your smile. All these words, a day's work, and your smile. Why write when your smile exists at the end of the day? I feel like tearing everything up, all the sheets of paper and all the hours I spent without you, and search for the perfect verse inside of which I can see you when at the end of the day there's the door and you and your smile. The only reason there are still people who read me is because there are still people who don't know you. I'm so small for the scale of you, my love.

When I embrace you again I will have a new text to give you, I promise you every day. Until you arrive and nothing is up to scratch, and the great artist, listen carefully now, the great artist is just a man who always falls short of whatever he loves.

He was able to resist anything except the irresistible. He was, deep down, just like all men and all women: he could bear even the unbearable.

That was when she arrived. Quiet little words, small steps, skin as though untouchable. She asked for a coffee and he knew that he was lost. Then she said 'thanks' and didn't even realise that he, within his 'yes, ma'am', had already surrendered to her eyes, her shyness, the fatal inevitability of loving her as though there were no other possibility.

He was capable of avoiding love as long as he didn't love. He was, deep down, just like all men and all women: he loved even the detestable.

That day, he walked with her almost the whole day long. She didn't know it, but she walked with him to every table he served, with every 'yes, ma'am' he said. When he left work, as he took off the jersey from the café where he'd worked for more than twenty years, he saw her face in his mind once again, and her gestures, her voice right in his ear even though she was more than a metre away. He tried to tell what her mouth tasted of, her skin like silk, the moment when their lips met. That was how he fell asleep, kissing her, and woke like this, holding her to protect her from the world.

He was capable of being courageous so long as he didn't feel fear. He was, deep down, just like all men and all women: he feared even what could make him happy.

It was on the third day but it could have been on any day. She arrived, he filled his chest with courage and said as much as he could about her beauty. He waited, his heart raging, just a few seconds. She said 'thank you very much' and asked for the usual coffee in the usual way. She continued, then, reading the newspaper and making notes on a small pad she brought with her every day. He went to fetch the coffee but he had already been dead for a few seconds. He stood still, watching her, to prove to himself that he was able to bear even death. Then she said 'have a good day, take care' and headed off towards the exit as she always did, he replied what he always replied, but she added a strange 'happy reading' when she was already outside the door.

He was capable of living for ever so long as he was mortal. He was, deep down, just like all men and all women: he lived off even what could kill him.

'If you're here tomorrow I guarantee you'll have to love me for ever' was what was written on the piece of paper she'd left on the table. That night he slept in the café, under the counter, just in case the alarm clock got up to its old tricks again. And she arrived.

There's something godlike in the way you love me, mother.

People are not as great as you. People cry, people suffer, people go through life in search of a better way to live. But you love me, mother. You love me like this, unconditionally, and it's as though when you love me you don't even exist. You're just there, seeing me exist, and that's how you discover and teach me that life consists of watching somebody you love living.

There's something impossible in the way you love me, mother.

The possible would demand that you stop when it hurts you, that you stop when the world, the bastard world, obliges you to invent new ways to give me everything I need. The possible would tell you that, no, a single person, as small and as big as you, cannot bear the weight of two lives. And yet there you still are, as strong as only you are, as impossible as only you are, smiling when you see me with my exercise book in hand saying I'm the best pupil in the class. Of course it's good to be a good pupil, but my greatest pride is being the son of the most impossible mother in the world.

There's something brilliant in the way you love me, mother.

People don't invent time the way you do, people can't understand what equation allows you to be always wherever you need to be, people arrive late, people fail to meet their responsibilities, people sometimes forget what they have to do, people can't make just half of what they need to live on be enough for them to live wanting for nothing. And you manage the miracle of the loaves and the bodies, you're in exactly the right place where I need you at the exact time when I need you with the exact words I need, talking to me about how important it is to believe that we know everything even if it's important to believe that we know nothing, and I hear you and I understand that the secret of your existence is knowing that only love can defeat mathematics, and that there's no number that is a match for when you hug me.

There's something of all of me in the way you love me, mother.

And when they ask me how old my mother is I'll just say for ever.

And your smell spread all over the bed.

The socks you wore to go out at night, folded to perfection as though you had discovered in them some complex mathematical theory, the high-heeled shoes lined up by colour, the dresses arranged by size, the floor and the scratches from your heavy steps when you were in a hurry and life was waiting for you.

And the kitchen in disorder, the plates piled up, an unbearable stench of a lack of you all over the house.

I'm the most fragile man in the world when I don't have you, I wander around these pieces of furniture in search of a reason to talk, I sit on the sofa not knowing where to go, and the truth about life is that your arms don't exist and I have nowhere to lie down.

How am I supposed to believe in God if even your body is not eternal?

What's left is the space of memory which is ours alone: when you were angry and still didn't stop being beautiful, when you cried and still didn't stop being beautiful, when you said that your whole body hurt all over and still didn't stop being beautiful, when you died and still didn't stop being beautiful.

Loving is the person you love never stopping being beautiful, you told me, I don't know if it was one or two hours before letting yourself go, and I came home with your death and dedicated the following days to loving you. I visited your cell phone, your emails, the loose sheets of paper you'd written here and there, the messages we'd exchanged to keep us together. I didn't find a single character flaw in you, a single inconsistency. You were the healthiest woman in the world and perhaps that was why you'd died. So that life can continue to be unbalanced, so that the world can be made up of people who fail the way you'd never been capable of failing.

You're too perfect to deserve anything as fallible as a body. No body was a match for you and it was necessary to put an end to you before your perfection put an end to whatever it is that keeps the world in balance.

Your large photo on the living-room dresser, the way you smiled whenever you didn't know what to do. You're so beautiful, my love.

And now there's too much time left for a life without you. The days don't pass, the words don't come. They are sad people who think a writer lives off his pain. If I'd lived off my pain I would have written more than these poor lines since you left. If I'd lived off my pain I'd be alive for ever.

Your toothbrush beside mine. What could be more of a bastard than needing you like this?

The worst thing about life is needing to sleep. Eyes close and there you are, eyes open and there you are. There are pills that force me to stop. But then there's the dreaming and everything in it that you make me and everything that you are. What kind of cruelty is it making me wake up somewhere where you are not? The worst thing about life is needing to wake up.

People feel sorry for me, they look at me as though looking at a dead man, and in those moments I envy you; you're dead and no one can see you, and I still need to walk, need to eat, need to say 'good morning' to somebody who brings me nothing – because they don't bring me you. Next time promise that when you go you'll take me with you. It doesn't even need to be anything romantic, anything dramatic. You just need to do what you've always done: go and take me, that's all.

And your smell spread all over the bed. Maybe that's why I stay alive. Or in whatever state this is that I'm in.

I write to you every day to try to remember you again. So the words reconstruct you, so the poem gives you life. I write every day to try to remember you again. And they all end with a final shout, which all the neighbours know now and ignore. This one too.

He'd decided it wouldn't go on beyond that night. Life was hurting too much to go on and he had to put an end to it as soon as possible.

On the table were the various possibilities for a happy end: the pills that, he'd read on the internet, in just a few minutes, if taken in excessive quantities, would fulfil their task without too much pain; the revolver belonging to his late father, God preserve him, already loaded and ready to do its duty, just point it at the right place, something he'd already studied in some detail in an old school textbook; a dish full of his favourite food, which was no more than a dish filled with deadly poison, a mixture he'd learned years back during a strange conversation with a doctor friend, which included rat poison and even a bit of balsamic vinegar; and finally a generously proportioned pillow, which he had bought one day for reading in bed but which might, now, be perfect for saying his goodbyes to the world in silence. Besides all these possibilities, there were a few others too, which weren't on the table but were still on the table: the window was open, and a leap from the fourteenth floor certainly would not result in anything less than death; and the bathtub was full, so a drowning couldn't be completely out of the question.

All he had to do now was choose. And, of course, write the farewell note that, as he'd seen in the movies, it would be good to write. In it he wouldn't blame anyone concretely – just this life, that bitch of a life that had taken from him his job, his wife and, with her, his children who he hadn't seen for months.

He'd write that he wasn't even going to bear a grudge about anything, against anyone, but he just felt he'd reached the point when he should find a different path and try new things. Death, then, seemed to him the right experience for this stage of his life.

As he wrote, he thought about who would be the first person to read those words. Maybe the ambulance man, Senhor Gouveia, such a sweet man, who'd been so tireless at the time of his mother's passing away. Even knowing that there was nothing to be done, he'd still rushed her to the local hospital, putting her so carefully on to the stretcher and treating her, in the final minutes of her life, like a real princess. Yes, it would probably be Senhor Gouveia. And he'd probably look at the dead body and think it was a waste, that life is so big and so beautiful and that nobody should be able to put an end to it without just cause. And the only just cause for dying, he'd say as he said so often, is not being able to stay alive.

Then, he thought as he kept on writing, Senhor Gouveia would call Carla. She'd come over with that sleepy look on her face, that skin that was still baby-soft, and she would read, the tears unfairly making her more beautiful, what he had written. She would understand his words perfectly, and his reasons, and then she would hug Senhor Gouveia, who would just repeat countless times: let it go, child, you're not to blame.

The children's turn would come next. António, the eldest, would be so disappointed. Doubtless he'd think it was a lie, how could his superdad, who was never afraid of anything, do a thing like this? Joana, the little one, wouldn't even really understand what was going on. She'd ask why daddy's lying so still, or she wouldn't ask anything at all because no one would let her see him again. She would never see him again and she'd end up forgetting him for good. Her mother, all the same, would speak as well as she could about him, since in this regard Carla (who is, oh fuck it, so, so beautiful) was exemplary: she would never stop sticking to the story that their father, their coward father who'd given up on living, was the greatest hero in the world.

The note was, at last, written. It was time to decide where to put it, and this could only be decided if another decision were taken first. Deciding how and where you're going to die is a privilege, it is, he thought; but he also thought he'd never imagined it could be so complicated. He should have just come up with one possibility and followed it through, he concluded, while remembering the many times he'd accompanied Carla (who is, oh fuck it, so beautiful; she's really so beautiful) on a shopping trip and, after three or four hours, come out of the shop empty-handed because she, liking everything, couldn't buy anything. Dying – he concluded now while simultaneously stroking the pistol, the pillow, the plate full of food – was a complication.

The food. It was decided. He sat down calmly, tucked a napkin into his collar, like a bib, as he'd learned from his father (any man who is a real man doesn't get his suit dirty, son), and, with knife and fork in hand, began to die. I'm going to have a well-seasoned death, he even had time to make an ironic aside to himself, before putting the first piece of food in his mouth and being interrupted by the ping of his cell phone. They won't even let you die in peace, he joked, but still he couldn't resist his curiosity and got up to go to fetch the little device he'd put on the kitchen counter. Curiosity, sarcastically, is one of the few things stronger than death, he theorised, as though wanting, in his last minutes of life, to leave some kind of philosophical thesis to those remaining behind. He picked up his cell phone and read, a smile on his lips, the name of the sender. Carla. It was a simple message: 'Guess what! It's nearly morning!'

Nobody believes in the words of the skin, there are
fears, steps running away, the impossible
shame, and the only certain words are those of the body.

On the nights of our sheets, the silence
was overvalued, I understood the word
through your eyes, and you understood that everything
there was to be said had to be touched.

Loving is easier than speaking, watching the
grammatical movements of pleasure, hearing the
absurd and irresistible discourse of orgasm.
We loved each other through words without needing
to speak, because when you moved an arm
all linguistics moved with you,
all syntax was in motion, the lexicon
changed within our bliss, and
however much silence we heard, never
was our life so far from keeping quiet.

It was at the moment when we needed to speak
that the unwelcome silence arrived. I started
telling you of your beauty, of the unstoppable scale
of our moments, you replied that only
poetry would speak what we were doing, but the
problem with words is their being finite, there are always
more people than adjectives, more people

than adverbs, and being dependent on a sound
means accepting right away that one day silence will be for
        ever.

Whose idea was it to invent verses
when we already had pleasure?

Now we're alone with the words, you
where my eyes don't see and me isolated
in my need to write to be able to feel you
beneath the letters. All love exists
but it keeps quiet so long as we unlearn
the moment of silence. Perhaps one day I will be able
to find you again in the gloom of the empty night,
in the harmonious construction of a noisy
absence. Until then I'll keep looking at you in the
small photograph you left on the living-room table, in this so
        happy
silence. It's the only way I have of hearing you.

Whose idea was it to invent text
when we already had love?

Fuck it, but I love you so much. I want you so much, need you so much. Fuck it, but it's so good to love you like this, as though I were short of breath when I'm lacking in you and even shorter of breath when I've got you.

Today I want to forget all the beautiful words, gentle words, and be savage and tough and strong the way my feelings for you are savage and tough and strong. Today I don't want poetry – apart from the poetry of wanting you like a madman, desiring you like life. Today I love you in big words, in bad words: fuck it, I do love you so much, my love.

And your body, your bastard body, your damnable body. I seek it out like an insatiable addict, as though there were no world beyond your skin. And the truth, the bastard truth, is that there isn't. There's the curve of your shoulders, the empty space of your lap when I'm not in you, the gluttonous mouth of your smile. And your legs opening to me as though all needs were concentrated in the need for you, as though pleasure owned the world. And it does.

I want everything else to go to hell if you're in my arms. It's the cruellest of sentences, may other people forgive me, may even God forgive me and His sin too, may the politically correct forgive me and those poor little things left behind along the way. May all people forgive me but all I want is the certainty of your body and the truth of your soul. That's enough for me to have the certainty and truth of myself, of this me that only you have brought, of this me that only exists with you. This me that wants only life, the purest of lives: to love until the end of the day, to love every day, to love until night comes and to love until morning returns. To love you so that I lack for nothing. The end of the world appeals to me with you. And you're enough for me to lack for nothing. It's enough that you come over, with that princess-like demon-like step, that look in your eye that says 'protect me with affection but never stop fucking me hard', and you tell me to give you tenderness without drawing out your sweat, to give you complicity without drawing out your moans, to give you communion without being afraid of devouring you, down to the very last drop, on the floor. It's enough for me that you come and that you come, that you want me and need me. It's enough for me that you should be this sort of everything, this sort of absolute mistress of what I am and feel, of what I feel and think. It's enough for me that you are.

Today I need to tell you that only small loves can survive on small words. On a simple 'I love you', on a sweet 'you're so pretty'. Only small loves can survive on small words. Ours is too big even to survive on words like other words, on words that already exist, on words that somebody once put, so often had they been used, into a dictionary. No. Ours demands new and big words, like 'Iloveyoulikefuckohmygod' or 'Iloveyoutothedepthsofmybonesfuckit', and so many others that every day and every night, in bed, on the sofa, on the street and so many other places where we've loved each other (and we've loved each other everywhere, thank God), we've been inventing to say to each other. It's our way of making ourselves in words. And we're not at all healthy, not at all advisable, not at all balanced. We want total belonging or we want total absence. It might be impractical to sustain this strength, this arousal, this intensity, this 'itsnowornever', this 'eitheryougivemeeverythingoryougetoutofhere' for ever. Deep down, you know and I know that we can easily be impossible. But what fucking use is what's possible?

Pretty soon you're going to love me, I know it,

after the beer, and the game's almost done, but I start busying myself with tidying up the kitchen, there's some washing-up to do, clothes to wash too, sweeping the floor just real quick, starching your shirts and that's it, I think about the hug you'll give me, I'm so happy when you hug me, did you know that?, the way your body protects mine,

it won't be long before you're mine, there are lots of ways of loving and that is yours, I need to understand that.

Pretty soon you're going to love me, I know it,

after the dinner with the friends from work, you're the most valued employee of all, that doesn't surprise me, it's natural that they should want you present at everything, you even tried not to go, to find some excuse or other, I did see that, but it didn't work out, they insist on your being there and when you come back that's when it'll be, I'm so happy when you touch me, did you know that?, you've got to come quickly so that I lack for nothing,

it won't be long before you're mine, there are lots of ways of loving and that is yours, I need to understand that.

Pretty soon you're going to love me, I know it,

after waking up, you promised me that on the weekend you would be mine, it's four in the afternoon and you still haven't woken up, you've been so tired these days, the firm concluding a big order and you feeling totally swamped, right?, but you won't be long waking up, I'm sure of it, I like cleaning the sleep from your eyes, you see, making you look so handsome for me, I miss the depth of your arms, the inside of your mouth, I'm so happy when you kiss me, did you know that?, just a few more short minutes and you'll be here, I can't bear it, I'll admit,

it won't be long before you're mine, there are lots of ways of loving and that is yours, I need to understand that.

Pretty soon you're going to love me, I know it,

after that orgasm, you were so distant when you wanted me, you grabbed me far away and I wanted you so close, you barely looked me in the eyes, you've been really tired, your life's not easy, of course, but when the need is over then the love will come, you'll hold me tight in that way you have of saving me from the world, I'm so happy when you hold me that way, did you know that?, you'll say to me I love you down to my bones which you haven't said for such a long time, and everything will go back to making sense in this sweaty bed, I'm sure of it,

it won't be long before you're mine, there are lots of ways of loving and that is yours, I need to understand that.

Pretty soon you're going to love me, I know it,

after the frustration, these things pass, I have no doubt, you feel I've been an absent husband, and I have, you want everything to be different, that's all, today I sent you flowers and a kiss in the mail, I wrote you ten or twenty messages, maybe about fifty, I mean, you didn't reply and you don't need to reply, you're totally in the right but this rebellion will pass, you'll come back home, to our home, remember?, I don't even recognise it since you haven't been there, I'm so happy when you're at home, did you know that?, another day or two and you'll come back, definitely,

it won't be long before you're mine, there are lots of ways of loving and that is yours, I need to understand that.

Pretty soon you're going to love me, I know it,

after signing this, you're insisting I do it and I understand why, your sadness demands it and I respect that, I'm not going to give up, I'm going to continue with the notes, the messages, the flowers, today I demanded that my boss give me a regular schedule, I want to arrive home in good time to love you, you just need to come back, please, I'm going to sign this so that you understand that the most important thing for me is your happiness, I'm so happy when you're happy, did you know that?, and mostly so that you look at me like the person you love once again, do you promise?, it's signed, here you go, you're a free woman now, free to love me again, go any time you want because I'll be waiting for you in the same old bed, I've put new sheets on it and I've been sleeping on the sofa, they're going to have their debut with you, whatever it takes,

it won't be long before you're mine, there are lots of ways of loving and that is yours, I need to understand that.

'I don't know where I'm going, but I'm going with you.'

Her, sitting on the bed, floral-print pyjamas, the sweat of a night of pleasure running down her back.

From afar, the morning.

'Freedom is a blind whore, who opens herself up to me the way hell opens itself up to death.'

Him, still lying down, his body with no clothes on and the sheets covering only his legs and the start of his stomach.

Next door the neighbour is scrubbing her floor.

'I need to free myself from your body. Whenever I think of pleasure I think about the touch of your skin. Whenever I smell orgasm I smell the wild taste of your sex. Whenever I want to be happy I imagine you in me. I can't bear myself without you. I can't handle myself without you. I need to free myself from your body. To go far away, to where you aren't. And hope you don't come. Hope that the start of everything is in the body.'

Her, already standing up, in front of the bathroom mirror, eyes damp with sweat and maybe the beginnings of tears.

In the living room, clothes scattered on the sofa.

'And what's the point of health if we don't have pleasure? Why do I need me if there aren't orgasms?'

Him, grabbing her from behind, the mirror starting to steam up.

    In the bedroom the empty bed.

'I needed much more than your arms, much more than your skin. I needed much more than you if all you can give me is this. The inadequacy of all this. I needed much more.'

Her, turning towards him, lips reaching out and the image in the mirror of two excited mouths.

    On the window the rain beating.

'Why are you thinking about more if this is worth everything?'

Him, his arms wrapped right around her, his whole body ready to love.

    Next door the neighbour is doing her washing-up.

'To be a whore, then your whore.'

Her, the bed occupied, sweat on her back again.

    And then him.

'To be incomplete, then worth everything.'

And finally love.

    And finally love. All lives should start like this.

You ask my advice, now that I'm going, now that this bed holds someone more dead than alive, and I think there are so many things I can say to you, I could say so many beautiful words, to inspire you; I could even quote you a poem from Pessoa or Rilke, a thought from some famous philosopher or other; I could tell you how important it is to make the most of every second, or something about the magic of knowing we love; I could be the most cultured old man in the world but I prefer to tell you just to look. So simple, just that. Look.

Look. Always look. Look a lot. Look with eyes that touch, with eyes that feel, with eyes that embrace, that love, with eyes, even, that hate. But look. Never stop looking. It's through the eyes that life happens. Even if you've got them closed, even if they cannot see. It's through the eyes that life happens.

Look at the empty space between a dream and reality. Fill it. Try to fill it with everything you are. There are great difficulties to overcome, moments when you'd rather not look. Those are the moments when you have to look even more, those are the moments you have to open your eyes even wider. To see what you can do in order to see something different. The secret of success is seeing well. Realising who you've got in front of you, who you've got beside you, who you've got behind you. You need to see well if you are to choose well, to decide well. Even if it hurts, even if it comes at a cost, even if you'd rather not look. Look. Always look.

Look at what you've got. And you've got so much. You've always got so much. Look at who loves you. Look at who wishes you well, who seeks out your happiness. And look at the crowded street, thousands of people you can vanquish. Grab what you can. Nothing less than grabbing should do, never give less than everything, never set about any task if you don't mean to devour it, consume it, lick it, taste it without leaving a single piece intact. Look with eyes that live. Look with eyes that want, that kidnap, with eyes, even, that steal. Steal the world that is your due and even more than that steal the world that isn't. Look at everything you can, everything you know. The happiest people are those who see best, those who see first and fastest – and above all those who see from the right place. Everything has a correct place from which to be seen. Find yours. All looks have a place that is happiest. Look from just the right angle. You might even get tired, you might weaken because weakening is human. But never stop looking.

I'm taking from life what I've looked at. And when I close my eyes it's what I've looked at that keeps me busy, that keeps me entertained when the pain hurts more and more and death approaches. I think about your grandmother that afternoon when I first touched her hand. And I look. Her hand, small and lovely like she was, and then the slight smile when my body, not deliberately and yet wanting to, brushed hers. All that's left to me of life is what I've looked at. The vision of your mother on my lap, then you, your brother. I carry whoever I love with me inside the things I've looked at. Even the spaces. The neighbourhood esplanade where I've so often read the newspaper (I carry the newspapers with me, the printed letters, the most powerful headlines – I still sometimes look at the news about the old fire in Chiado, did you know that?), the park bench where I was the devastating domino champion, supreme lord of *sueca* (God help you if you aren't a great card player yourself, our family tradition needs to be upheld), and the holidays far away, the sea, the sand and the horizon as far as the eye can see. What I have looked at is what I take with me. I take with me what I was able to look at. And that's why, that's the only reason why, I want you here, now that the moment for one last look is arriving. Let me look at you hard, hold you, consume you inside my look. Let me look at you for ever, will you?

The woman sits down on the bed, back against the wall, opens her laptop and writes, while wiping away, as best she can, the tears that fall on the keyboard.

'I'm not a half-a-glass kind of woman. If it's not full, I don't want it. If it's not full, it isn't even a glass. I'd rather not drink at all than drink only what's possible. To hell with what's possible. What's possible is too easy to get me excited.

This is just to say that you lost me on the day you left. I know exactly how it was, I feel exactly the way I felt. One minute you were there and the next minute you weren't. Black magic, perhaps. You talked to me about life, that's how it had to be, that people, sometimes, need to make decisions. And you decided to leave.

There are people who say it had to be, that the most difficult decisions are the most important ones, that you've got to choose, often, between the terrible and the unbearable. You chose the terrible and left me with the unbearable. But the good thing about the unbearable is that it's already clear from the very start. It is not borne. Full stop.

Unlike what's terrible, what's unbearable does not leave you with any hope. You know that you cannot bear it, that there is no way to bear it. And you see other paths. The unbearable is more human than the terrible, I know that now, as I write you these words knowing you are miles from here and will never come back. I can't bear the image of what we were, your smile when I told you one of my jokes no one else found funny, the way you made me laugh when you tried cooking like the great TV chefs do it, and of course, the way your skin seemed to be discovering mine. I can't bear what we were and that's enough to make me ready for what I want to be.

One day you'll understand that loving at a distance only happens when you don't love. When you love, even the distance of a kiss is too far. You wanted to test us, to put us to the proof. You made promises of eternal love and then what remained of you was so very little.

You remained of you.

It was hard for me, at first, to understand how life could exist if you did not. I would wake up, each day, searching for your body, searching for your lap, searching for your hand, and I'd end up like that, all night and all day, searching for you in all the places we were happy. Nothing is more painful than happiness that won't come back, happiness you've lost which, whenever you recall it, afflicts you on the same scale that it made you happy.

But it does pass.

The best thing about life is that everything does pass. The searching passed, the hurting passed. And this is what remained. Me and this. Me and a bottomless hole in the centre of life.

And the courage has arrived. This very day, right now, at this very moment. I'm going far away from distance for ever.

If we need to be far apart, never let the body be left out.

From your past one,
Me'

The woman stands up, gets dressed, walks over to the study next door to the bedroom, picks up the sheet of paper she has just printed, puts it down on the bed, on the place where she has just been sitting, and leaves, no more than a minute before the man, opening his eyes, realises that he's alone in bed and there's a piece of paper beside him.

Melancholy is the philosophy of the body, the moment when I find myself entirely in order to reflect. I sit myself down within what I think and I start to challenge, one idea at a time, what it is that makes me alive. Melancholy is necessary for happiness to make sense, it's important to understand each moment of distance for any presence to happen.

My cat's eyes taught me life.

There are days, like today, when happiness consists of being like this, melancholy, understanding the reason for life. Writing a few words, like this, looking at the world that resists me and persists: the lady at the traffic lights, her eyes downcast, waiting for the green light to appear so she can escape from herself once again; the child who, indifferent to the rain, keeps kicking a ball against a wall where he imagines glory and a packed stadium cheering; the college student thinking about tomorrow's exam while dithering about calling the girl he likes to ask her out; and me, reflected in this windowpane, waiting for this melancholic happiness to leave me.

There's such a big space between what I see in myself and what I am.

Falling short hurts so much. I'd like to have been brilliant, to make these lines the screenplay for humanity, all the women and men saying my words as though speaking the laws of the world, and yet all I can manage are loose, empty ideas, when faced with the appearance of the flesh. In the beginning was the skin; that's what God would say, if He only had a body. It's in my skin that I live, and there that I find all the paths for whatever there is in me. The problem with the soul is that it needs substance, and ultimately suffering is the most physical act one can experience.

The old lady with her daughter choosing a place to die.

The incomparable abyss of pleasure, the memory of what I was, the mute sadness of never again returning to the first time. The greatest cruelty in life is having just one first time, just that one appearance of the discovery, one moment you don't know and the next you are; the greatest cruelty in life is allowing just one first time for one first kiss, one first time for a first chocolate; the greatest cruelty in life is that nothing more than this exists, a man or a woman and their proof, their paltry limitation. The greatest cruelty in life is being just one.

The baby crying as though it already knows it's going to have to grow up.

These are the days when I forget to go on, and I prefer just to stand and watch what's left of me keep moving. There's a dogmatic construction in what I see, because the only thing that exists is what is sieved through me, because the only thing that exists is what exists in me. I think about the deepest place of intimacy, I shut myself off with no way back, but then I sit down at the table, the whole family together to live and eat, and I know I've got to smile and find out about the others, invent new happinesses for the new melancholies, and believe in the possibility of going on. The one certainty is that it's going to hurt.

When the pain comes it's good if it finds me jumping about around here.

I want to know how to survive the moment of your not being here, she asked him, the door already open and his steps. I want to know how to survive the moment of your not being here, she repeated, and he kept going, and the door open and his steps. Nothing happened apart from the end of everything. That was what she thought, alone, stretched out on the floor as in the past she'd stretched out towards him, an insane and unscrupulous rug. Love requires going past any scruples, beyond all ethics, behind every honesty, she wrote, hours later, on the wounded keys of a computer he had agreed to leave behind. She doesn't remember having written what she wrote next, her hands on their own, abandoned to the precision of a touch, addicted to the need to possess him even if it's only for the moment of a finger on a key. The size of your arms not even God can remember, because it's only by squeezing the inside of what I feel that you can know how to measure an embrace. The tears, fragile as all tears are, and an empty bedroom and an empty woman and the letters on the keys and the keys wounded. How do I learn not to love, endless questions in the endless words, her and the doubts of someone who has suddenly lost any doubt. How do I learn not to need, how do I learn not to have you in what makes me live, how do I learn to seek salvation when you are not here to save me. With no question marks, with no questioning, because life-changing questions never require answers, because life-changing questions are never quite questions, just the easiest way to learn how to answer. I'd like to understand what makes you not be here, and the wandering neck, in search of his body, him coming in through the door, him coming in through the mouth, him coming in through the whole body. But there is no him, there never really has, perhaps, been a him at all. There's the bedroom like the house, immobile as they watched a woman passing by, a bedroom and a house with no love inside, rather than there were a bedroom and a house with no love inside, as though a bedroom and a house were not, more than spaces for living in, actually spaces for loving in. The sudden hope for a telephone ringing, him at the other end, 'sorry', her at this end, 'I love you and there can be no excuse', him on that end, 'I need myself again to be ready to love you again', her at this end, 'if you take more than twenty minutes to come back you'll never have me, I guarantee it', and her knowing it's a lie, that if she'd only been able to tell the truth she'd have said 'you have my whole life to come back, I guarantee it', and him on the other end, 'I need to understand myself in you to be able to love you', and her without a word, the phone discon-nected, the computer keys once again, and the questions once again, the answers once again, the tears once again. The cats lying there oblivious to the fact that the world has just ended. I want to love you without needing to love you, she wrote, and she thought these were the last words, so that she could invent a new body, a new person, she thought she wouldn't need another word, that line would be enough, that sentence, for the justice of solitude to be pronounced; but there was another moment when everything would change, later she would call it, euphemistically, life, and the truth was it was more than this, probably the moment when everything that exists is concentrated in what is existing. There was an ocean, as great as the distance between those ten, fifteen minutes, separating them, until the door opened, he came in, and even the cats understood that no more words, at least not made up from letters, would need to be written. The cursor, in the middle of the screen, continued to blink, she embraced it as though embracing survival, and she survived. It was only later, a day or more later, that the final line was written. Nobody, she wouldn't allow it, got the chance to read it, at least not until the moment when, more than fifty years later, the computer was found amid the debris of a dead woman. It was he, who wanted to die too so he might go with her, who found it. They say he stopped breathing at the exact moment when he finished reading it, but perhaps that's an exaggeration. Everybody knows she never needed any words to stop his breathing.

Love is good for many things but never for receiving.

Loving is a happiness – but loving is also a calamity. But what's the point of the world if there are no calamities?

Today I loved you with everything I had, just as I always love you with everything I have. I gave you all the sex, all the sweat, all the tears, all the veins all throbbing, all the kisses inside all the lips, all my life in seconds, in minutes, all the meaning of life stretched out on a bed. I passed through your body as though passing through eternity – and if there is anything eternal in life it's only pleasure, the immortal moment of an orgasm, the interminable second of euphoria.

The irony of life is that it lasts just long enough to be eternal.

And there, only there, is where love comes in. Love is the lying bastard who persuades us that something that's a part of life, even if life is finite, can be infinite. The bastard who persuades us that despite being a part of something that will end and that has to end it will never end in us. Love does not exist – which is why, the only reason why, it's the realest thing we can have in our lives.

Love is good for many things but never for living.

Love kills. It kills violently. It kills with all its might. It kills every day. And it's only in these deaths, in these small deaths, that the importance of life is to be found. It's in these small deaths, and only in these small deaths, that life happens. Today you killed me more than once and I could spend my whole life being murdered like this by you.

Love is a delight – but love is also a disgrace. But what's the point of the world if there are no disgraces?

Touch my skin and I'll know that I'm alive, my hands seek your body in search of the salvation of your bones, the continuity of your heat. There is no code of ethics between us, we screw however we can, whenever we can, in whatever way we can, each of us in search of his own absolute pleasure, his own piece of tangible immortality. There is a pitiless battle for orgasm, one person's body the support for the other's, the needs and impulses and thrills as owners of all our movements. We don't think about each other, not even for a moment, when we choose the way we are going to love. We don't want to know about the other's pleasure when we are made happy within our own pleasures. We couldn't care less about the other's orgasm, and we don't give a damn what the other wants and desires. We want ourselves, in ourselves, fully whole, giving what we have to ourselves. We are the most selfish lovers in the world, the most deplorable sexual partners on the planet. We fuck ourselves in our own name. And this is how, the only way, we share ourselves absolutely.

There are those who call us self-centred, sons of bitches, selfish. They call us happy.

Love is many things but it is never politically correct.

If you need proof that words lie it's that 'stealing' is such a bad word and yet can be so lovely, like when someone like you comes into my body and takes away my soul, and you know it was stealing, no less than that, and if I could I'd like to be stolen like this by you every day,

One day I'm going to write a dictionary of ugly words you have transformed into poems,

Like 'kidnap', for example, an awful thing, everyone knows, except me, since that day you came to fetch me at work and said to me 'come on I can't bear it any longer', and I said 'I can't', and you said 'you can, you can', and the truth was I really could, everything is always possible when we want it completely, and off the two of us went, me kidnapped by you, we went into the back of your car parked on a dirty dead-end street in the neighbourhood, and that was where I realised that places are also like words, you never know what they are or what they are worth until you know how you're going to have them, how you're going to experience them, and that lost alley in the centre of town, smelly and almost uninhabitable, managed to be, on that afternoon you made the word 'kidnap' a work of art, the most beautiful destination in the world, and if you'd asked me to choose one of the most dazzling places on the planet I would have chosen that one, because the most beautiful places in the world, you taught me on that day and on so many other days like it, are just those places in the world that are the happiest,

One day I'm going to write a grammar of glaring mistakes you have transformed into rules,

Like my absence with the long pauses when I write of you, or to you, or about you, I want to breathe more, longer breaths, use full stops, and I can't do it, and all that comes out are commas, short pauses, like these, just these, a half-breathing, an almost-breathing, maybe because thinking of you takes my breath away and stops me breathing properly, maybe because I don't want full stops, I'll allow nothing that means distance between us, and then I want to make transitions some other way than by using 'and', and this happens, I want to believe, because there is always me and you, but no word can separate us, only an 'and', an 'and' that joins, that brings us together even in the words, and maybe this is the right time to end this text, or at least this paragraph, perhaps a full stop really will come at just the right moment, a strong phrase and a full stop and everything will be perfect, nicely rounded, closed off, literarily perfect, and the critic will say, 'yes, sir, we have a poet here, or a writer', and my readers would like it but they wouldn't say, as they do say, that this text is boring, repetitive and unmelodious, but if you want to know I couldn't care less about the critic or my readers, I'm writing to you and when I write to you I won't accept that there should be a full stop, not in this text nor in any text that writes us, and that's why I'm going to leave this one like this, hanging there with an 'and' to end it, so everyone will know that this is how all writing of love, of real love, ought to end, without a full stop and with an 'and' at the end, I just ask you never to forget that I love you and that if I'm writing it's to write to you, and if there's a moment when I have to choose between writing well and writing you well I'll always prefer to write you well, love you well, hold you tight in paragraphs and punctuation marks, invent stylistic resources that deserve you, love you beyond every letter, and

Eternity is knowing that you exist, opening my eyes while you're sleeping, or otherwise falling asleep while you watch me, and then living for ever.

I couldn't care less about being eternal, I confess, because eternity is a lot of work when you aren't mortal. It really is good to know that I'm going to die and you will happen. I'm sure that the great advantage of life is the very fact of it ending, being finite, for the time of a breath or an orgasm to be worth it. Wanting to make life eternal is wanting to put an end to life, removing its value, reducing it to just another one of those eternal, uninteresting things the world has in it.

Why should I care if a stone is eternal if it never stops being a stone?

The rarity of life is what delights me about life, the certainty that it's so small, so fragile, almost nothing, and if someone told me that I was going to die for ever I'd kill myself right now.

Love me as though we were to end: that's what I ask you, for us to be eternal.

That's how I immortalise myself in the smallness of life. I fall in love with what fascinates me, I surrender myself to what makes me fall in love, I'm complete in what I surrender myself to. I don't think about the possibility of for ever, I don't even yearn for the perfect moment to be stretched out in time, because as luck would have it I've learned that the perfect moment, when it's stretched out, becomes a stretched-out moment and not a perfect moment. The value of valuable things is in their continuity, in their inability to be infinite, and it's only in that way that they make themselves infinite.

What is immortality if not the moment when something unforgettable ends?

When you hold me tight in the centre of your arms, I'm certain that we are corrupt, there are too many eternities in the moment of our bodies, as though God had offered us extra lives, mistaken lives, and the most interesting thing about life is how we want at all costs to remain alive when the eternal is what kills us.

Kill me every day for as long as you live: that's the request I make of you so that you keep me alive.

I'd like to survive the same way the world seems to survive around me. People tired of living ask their doctor to prolong their lives, people who have never lived still won't give up on living, as though life could be measured in numbers or hours, as if such a person aged ninety had more life than me. I know I've already lived as much as I was supposed to live, and if there were any justice I'd die right now and make way for younger people, for those who might have long dozens of years of life but never live. The most perverse thing about science is the belief that life is scientific, that a few machines and a few medications can define the meaning of anything at all. And then there's the security, the strange obsession with wanting to know everything when what creates the magic in everything is the not knowing, not even nearly, everything. I like blank spaces, explanations not yet given, phenomena not yet understood.

If I ever discover the reason you make me come like this I bet I'll never come like this again.

I don't want you to live for ever and nor do I want our love to be eternal. I want us to end one day and never to happen again.

Now come over here and please fuck me to eternity.

He used to get up whenever he felt like it, normally about ten or eleven o'clock, because of a neighbourhood that, on some days more than others, tended to be quite bustling first thing in the morning. Then, with all the calm in the world, he would get dressed, always those same white clothes he loved wearing whenever he didn't have to go out, comfortable and able to let him move around freely, he'd have his breakfast, sometimes alone and other times with company, and he'd devote the rest of his morning to dreaming.

So he would sit there staring at a stain on the wall, or out of the window, for a long time – never less than an hour or two. During this time, he would travel the world, and his memories, imagining what he might, one day, do with his life. He had already, as you might expect, made many plans, and he was absolutely certain that he would make them a reality.

Next, when his dreaming was interrupted by his stomach, and often by the ceaseless noise that his neighbours kept making, it was time for lunch. He ate well, he liked to savour what he was given, and he believed that happiness was also in this ability always to savour, in the best possible way, what he was given.

In the afternoon, he liked playing outside, in the large green garden he was lucky enough to have – and so great was his enjoyment that he didn't even remember to have his afternoon snack. Sometimes he pretended to be a soldier and imagined himself conquering new lands with his powerful army, other times he pretended to be a football ace who with his incomparable dribbling and personal technique managed to dupe any defence. Whatever the game he played, he always ended the afternoon, as night was beginning to take over the sky, feeling tired – but above all, always lucky and always a winner.

It was then time, now more hungrily because playing works up more of an appetite than dreaming, to eat again. He would devour whatever there was to devour, exchange any possible words with whomever, and off he went, happier and more reassured than ever, off to his bedroom, where every night, without exception, he would receive a call at around eleven p.m.

It was his brother, who worked locked away in an office, from eight in the morning till noon and from one to seven or eight or nine or more, six days a week and sometimes also on Sundays, and who had had him committed there, more than ten years ago now, believing that he was the crazy one in the family.

She stretched out on the bed, shut her eyes, and focused on crying. There was so much to cry for. The loss of her eldest son, the unbearable noise of the metal crushed against the wall; the redundancy, after forty years devoted to the local shoe store; the immense sadness of not loving the man life had chosen for her to marry. So much to cry for and only a bed for company. She turned over again, her eyes still closed, and with her head on the pillow she tried to cry even more, even more deeply. She felt all her flesh contracting within her, the feeling of a world drawing to an end, the end turning a corner. And she slept.

She arrived home earlier than usual, perhaps because she felt there was some reason or other for arriving home earlier than usual. Along the way, as usual, she cried behind her dark glasses, the memory of her eldest son always falling into her arms. How do you survive the loss of a child?, she has asked herself every day, with no answer, since the day he left. Sometimes she thought she had to bear it, that life had to go on, and that if it had happened then it had to have a lesson to teach; other times, however, she just wanted to give up on that bus she entered daily so that the noise would prevent her memories, and on that life that seemed to have nothing but suffering in store for her. But on that day she arrived home earlier than usual. She walked past the sofa, where there was nobody, past the bedroom of her eldest son, which had been untouched since he left, the word Ricardo stuck to the wall in the poster she'd given him for his tenth birthday, past the empty kitchen, and finally to her bedroom, where she could hear a strange silence.

Being alone had its advantages, he thought, sitting in the usual café, as he leafed through the usual newspaper at the usual table. It allowed him to choose the time he wanted to do the things he wanted, to fill the blank spaces with whatever he fancied, find the best solutions to the problems that arose. Being alone is the best way of being at peace, he concluded, and got up, said his usual greeting to Senhor Gouveia, the final see-you-tomorrow and the habitual goodbye. He already didn't believe in life very much and he suspected the feeling would be mutual. To tell the truth, it had already stolen from him everything he loved and left him there, a surplus bit of trash waiting to be collected up by time. Right up until her eyes.

Life is the moment when people. Just that. Not another word. Life is the moment when people, he said to her, wrapped in her arms, his old body as if new. There is always a person for each miracle, she replied, her hand on his unexpectedly excited member. There is always an extra body for each life, she added, her old body as if new. They loved each other, there, he doesn't even completely remember how he ended up there, as if there were no past, as if there were no future. They loved each other there at that exact moment of life. She was called Carla and had loved him for ever. He was called Luís but lately he didn't call himself anything – he just yelled and wept. They met in a café which hadn't been made for people to meet each other, a café made for solitude to have some space. They were both just a few years from ending, death getting ever closer. They decided, in the middle of the bed where their bodies were young again, to love each other until the end and not weep for the other's death. When I die I want you to live for ever, to find more people to keep you alive, he asked her. She nodded, an embrace with no distance, her skin bristling as though it were not old. Then mouths came together, lips seeking out eternity. And they found it.

It was unintentional, but then everything worthwhile in life is unintentional. You were in the corner of the room when my father was taken off to be buried. And suddenly an inexplicable desire to smile. My father – God keep him, and how much I loved him, how much, so much that even today every second of distance hurts – going for ever beneath the earth and then your eyes. An absurd desire to smile. You weren't even especially attractive, a man like any other among so many men like any others. The priest saying goodbye in the name of God to my father and your furtive eyes on mine. All places are good for loving, I remember thinking that on that day, understanding that even the funeral of someone you love can be the most romantic moment in a life. There wasn't, on that day, any kind of advance made. But nor was there any kind of retreat, which for somebody who loves is always a good start. It was my father who introduced us after his death and it would have to be my father to bring us together again. It was seven days later, at the customary mass with the customary tears – and how I cried that day, as if it were only then, a week later, that I'd understood that, yes, my father had gone and he wasn't coming back. The most ironic thing about loss is that it can happen gradually and sometimes with a delay of days or months. I was crying over the end of life when your eyes in the second row. How did you learn to look like that?, I asked you with mine, I don't even know if I even managed to bear the smile that I was smiling inside. You looked at me and you seemed to be asking

my forgiveness for looking at me like this when everything in
me was hurting me everywhere. All tears are small when you
lose a father, you know that? You did know that, of course,
which was why at the end of the mass, at the door of the
church, you plucked up the courage to come and say what
nobody else, on that day, ever said to me. You began with the
trivial 'my condolences', and I thought you were just another
guy and that your eyes didn't exist after all, but then you said
'congratulations' and my legs went weak. You saw my baffled
silence, you said it again, 'congratulations', and just added
'for that look in your eyes', before touching my shoulder
gently with your hand and turning your back. I swear I saw
my whole life going with you into that small white car where
I couldn't imagine how someone your size could possibly fit
in. I knew then that everything in me could die but what I
had seen in you would never die. Later there were so many
people between us, we did a thousand and one dumb things,
travelled a thousand and one roads, until, more than five
years after the first time, you arrived at the door to my house,
I was already a married woman and the mother of two kids,
and you said, as if it were the most natural thing in the world,
'hello, I'm Pedro and I'm the man of your dreams', and you
handed me a piece of paper which just said 'Write something
on here if you'd like me to leave right away' and I thought
about writing something but my hands stopped, my husband
in the living room asking who it was and me, there, standing
in front of you, with a piece of paper on which I had to write
something if I didn't want you to be the man of my life. I
never wrote a word for you, at least not until today, as I write
these letters with you lying beside me the way you're always

beside me when I'm working, and when I ask myself whether there was anything left to be said between us I always answer yes, there were words I never had the courage to say or to write. And it's just as well.

'A coffee and an everlasting love, please,' he said, the look in her eyes like life. All around there were all the tables and all the people at the tables, the hot, acidic smell of caffeine, the vagabond sun coming in at the big, dirty-paned windows. The need for more words was erased when the silence remained, for a second or two, to say what there was to be said. Of course they both smiled, of course she didn't bring him love that was everlasting but she did bring him love that was possible, hidden in the paper of one of the sachets of sugar. He didn't want to read it right away, he wanted to act strong and he withstood, he drank (slowly, he thought, but actually it only took ten or twenty seconds) the coffee while considering various possibilities about what might be written there, and of all the possibilities the one he chose would always be the simplest of all, something like 'I get off at midnight' would be enough for him.

'I get off at midnight,' he said again, repeating it over and over, the note in his hand (which was firm, he thought, but actually was trembling so hard that the employee wasn't able to take hold of it at first) and his breathing lost somewhere between fear and hope. 'See you tomorrow, then,' he said as he left (normally, he thought, but actually nobody in that café heard a word he said, such was the speed at which he said it), his hurrying steps and the small sugar sachet which was so big that it filled his entire body. He wanted everything to be perfect when he read it, he wanted to read it somewhere that deserved it, so that he would never forget that moment, and he was already imagining himself many years later, sitting by the fire, telling his grandchildren how he'd met their grandma, their adventures, with a simple sachet of sugar taking one of the leading roles; then he thought about how the story would be passed down from generation to generation, how four or five hundred years from now, when maybe sugar wouldn't even exist any more, people would still know the story of that sachet that made a whole family possible. 'I get off at midnight,' he said one more time, as though asking whoever's in charge of the world to do as he pleased.

'The sea is always a good place for loving,' he thought, already seated on the sand, two or three metres between him and the water that came in and went out. The piece of paper crumpled in his hand, the cold sweat and aching arms, his whole organism begging for mercy. He summoned up the courage, opened his hand, the sun was already setting behind the sea (he thought it couldn't be more perfect, as a tear fell without his noticing on to the sand), and he gradually unfolded the piece of paper, some grains still alive and making themselves felt. He looked once, he looked twice, he raised the palm of his hand to wipe away his tears, he looked again. Half an hour later, the night and the moon and the cold sea, he looked once again and everything was still just the same. There wasn't a single word written there, nothing, really nothing at all, just the make of the sugar, the company that made it and the ingredients, perhaps in tiny letters the expiry date, and he was sure he had the wrong sachet, and that there just had to be another lost in the trash somewhere with everything there was to be read. The moon seemed dark when, his eyes on the ground and the weight of all his illusions on his back, he left the beach, a homeless man looking at him sympathetically with a little pat on the back. He saw his whole family disappear, the grandchildren in front of the fire, the myth over so many generations of the sachet of sugar and the message that created life. None of this, he was sure, without tears now but with his eyes sagging, was going to happen. There was no note to be read. But she would be getting off at midnight all the same.

The rain started falling on the wet ground
and that's why I love you.

There is of course your smile, the way
you cut the fish when we sit down
at the table, the effort in your eyes
not to cry when I kiss you,
and that's why I love you.

Your skin tastes of what keeps me alive,
and that's why I love you.

You wake up in a bad mood, you don't
use words or open your eyes completely, as though
asking the light not to drag you out of what I know
is a dream in which we love each other for
ever, you turn the other way, waiting for
my body to hold yours once again, you shrink down
completely so as to hold me in you,
and that's why I love you.

We go out and people do exist even if
neither you nor I see them any more than
necessary so that we can love in secret,
we know that everything we kiss is à deux and
nobody can see it however many men or women
see us hugging and kissing in the supermarket

queue or when we're waiting for the popcorn
before sharing in the cinema, with your badly behaved feet
on the seat in front and your hands
so often seeking the underneath of bodies
in the adolescent darkness of the late-night screening,
and that's why I love you.

When I want to smile I remember
that you exist and I'm always smiling,
and that's why I love you.

Amid so many people I immediately had to find the only
woman in the world who like me has no interest in travelling,
and that's why I love you.

We spend our lives moving from place to place because
it has to be, we know that we have to work and
things like that for us to love each other
without thinking about getting something in return,
we get to know the cities where we take our
love, the beds we show the market value
of sweat, we go in search of a stop someplace
where we can love in peace and understand
that if we are together
then we are loving each other in peace,
and that's why I love you.

The first time I saw you I promised myself
that I was not going to love you,
and that's why I love you.

We went to bed without noticing the time, the day already
existing or about to exist, we laughed a lot
in bed, you say something interesting, I
say something of no interest, our
laughter alone would be enough for us to be
together, but there's also the way we reach
orgasm, which consists of the difficult task of
loving each other, you love me and I love you and that's how
we strangely reach orgasm,
and that's why I love you.

I'm absolutely certain that staying with you is
the stupidest decision of my life,
and that's why I love you.

The depth of her moans could be heard all over the building, or maybe it was just inside my ears that it could be heard all over the building. When did you learn to love me like that?

He got up after orgasm, barefoot on the cold bedroom floor, he went over to the kitchen, had a bite of something, and thought the most important thing in life is the moment when, every day, you are reborn. Through the window he saw the boats on the sea, he imagined all the possibilities that a world can contain, people and more people living their lives under the gaze of other people and still more people, he thought that it might be selfishness on his part to be concerned only with his own business, but when he was really going to think about this properly she appeared, with not a single piece of clothing to cover her body.

As of today I'll never love you again, that was more or less how I told you I was yours for ever. The silent house smiled, you were left with the certainty that there was no room for anything but us, and we loved each other without our bodies knowing. The only thing I'm certain of is that your skin does not exist, nor your smell, nor even your touch – they are unrealities that bind me to life, sensitive memories that prevent me from dying.

It's feeling you that keeps me alive and that is going to kill me, she said again, ten times after the first time she'd said it, at some other orgasm in some other bed. No orgasm is ever repeated but they all transform us, and those words in her voice stopped all breathing. When had she learned to lie like that?

Lunch had been in the cheapest restaurant in the neighbourhood, her and her eyes, and he who was there by chance thought that being a millionaire meant loving eyes like those. That was how it all began, they both knew that. But nothing lasts for ever, especially not what is eternal.

I like to wander the streets with you, giving you my hand and showing you you're mine, knowing that I have the happiness of your company for a few minutes, everybody, I'm sure of it, believing that if you love me there must be something special about me. And of course there's the money, all the things I give you, but even that request you just made of me to go with you to the bank doesn't persuade me that you want me for any more than I am myself. When did you learn to deceive me like that?

She said 'here' and he signed, then she said 'and here' and he signed, two or three of the bank's employees smiling on the outside and shaking their heads on the inside, a feeling like in a casino when somebody hands over the very clothes they're wearing just to be able to keep playing. There was the goodbye, 'it's been a pleasure,' he said, and he shook the hand of the bank manager, who for the first time wasn't disgusted to be shaking the hand of a poor vagrant without a cent deposited there. On their way out the woman at the reception desk looked at them with pity, smiled the most natural smile she could manage at that moment, the door opened and they left, both on their feet but him, despite being so big, fitting perfectly in her two divine hands. As they left they gave each other their first kiss without money getting in their way. When had she learned to free him like that?

I have nothing but this house in which we live, you kept everything of mine and I'm happy. Yesterday when you arrived you said there was one more hungry child I'd allowed to grow up and that the world was a happier place now. I was happy, of course, for the child and for the world, but if you want to know the truth I don't give a damn about the child or about the world, I just want to know about your body and about your being here. The great usefulness of money is helping you to love me, and if you want to know I'm not sure that wasn't actually why it was invented. When did you learn to teach me like that?

There's a crack of light coming into the bed,
and the greatest injustice in life is your existing and being
    mortal.

In the small hours when we discover pleasure, the
sheets stick to our bodies, hands searching
desperately for skin, until all the happiness shrinks
to be able to understand us. You teach me to find the
place between your legs, the space where all
orgasms meet, then there is a whole texture
to be found, the wise wrinkles around your eyes,
the soft touch of all the curves of your breast, until
absolute truth asserts itself. All of you pulls me
inside you and all of me pushes me
into the heat of your belly. And heaven happens.

There is a fine line of sweat joining the head of the bed to its
    foot,
and the greatest injustice in life is your existing and being
    mortal.

The morning arrives with its illogical light, the certainty that
night has gone and it's important to keep going. Each time
I love you I find the perfect death. We get up,
our lazy souls not knowing what to do with
life out there, the secret desire for the world
not to exist. And then you disappear, minutes later,

and you show me the emptiness of all things. Everything that
is useful to you exists only to be useful to you. When the
        morning falls and you
aren't there, the whole house goes quiet waiting to hear you,
        I walk
the hallways like a vagrant of myself, and a mere
'I'll be back tomorrow' from you is enough for all the furniture
        and all
the beds to make sense once again. Either I'm with you
or I'm alone, I always think when you aren't there, and I end up
getting tangled up in myself and in tears in the space
on the bed that belongs to you, defeated by
the possibility of there being a final embrace, one day,
to surrender, by the cruel existence of life in you.
Why must you be human if I love you so much?

There's a door opening slowly, the cat already knows it's the
        whole world coming,
and the greatest injustice in life is your existing and being
        mortal.

You were the most beautiful woman in the world and the worst thing of all was that the world had already realised it. The whole hall stopping dead at the sight of your arrival, that long dress, those things you told me were called sequins or whatever the hell they are, and your bare ankles, only them, supporting the weight of a whole God. And all those stares, everybody, women and men, all of them in love with your steps, one after another, your head raised high and your smile. When you smiled, that day I went into a party arm in arm with you for the first time, with photographers and cameras and the two of us as alone as if sitting on a sofa together, everybody stopped to watch you go by, and my body next to yours was invisible just as I always imagined love should be, as I always asked you for love to be. All I wanted was to be the person who accompanied you, to get the chance to see your smile when you smiled, and to be certain that you were only smiling like that because you had me there. What other meaning could life have besides making you smile?

Men, so many men, around your body, trying to find some flaw, some gap, some pathway to what united us. You looked at me all night long and asked me to forgive you for there being so many people wanting you like that, and I knew how much it hurt, how tight it squeezed, but then I remembered that you only existed like this, so big and so unbearably beautiful, because we existed. Loving you is a privilege, I know, I didn't need any of that crowd wanting you so completely to know it; and when you tell me you feel like the most blessed woman in the world because we exist like this I'm sure it's true – it's true I'm just another guy like any other guy, I don't create characters, I'm don't get invited to elegant parties, I don't give interviews and I'm not hounded by photographers, I don't have people worshipping me, but I have all the love in the world in me and that's enough for me to want for nothing. What other meaning could life have besides our wanting for nothing?

That night you taught me the meaning of myself, you said, between one forced nod and another whenever the world asked you for a reaction, when you thought about going to bed you would say my name, you didn't talk about sex or about being tired, you talked about this, the simple act of one body grabbing hold of another and saying 'go to sleep' and the other goes, the two of them bound by those words that are so sincere, 'go to sleep', you'd say, and I'd go, and it could be the other way around, I'd say 'go to sleep' and you'd come, and off the two of us would go, arm in arm, or one resting on the other's shoulder, or the other in the arms of one, to the untouchable space of under the sheets, where all life is summarised into the essential: either love or nothing. That night what was essential about life was no different. After the photographs and all the requests, after all the smiles (have I told you that each time you smile my life gets at least ten or twenty minutes longer?), and all the autographs, the two of us would return to the most secret place in what we are, the most primitive existence of two creatures. And I do still remember, as though it were yesterday (and the truth is it's always at just this moment that I remember in this way), the words I said to you when you looked me in the eye and without a word asked me for the perfect embrace. 'I consume you while they covet you,' I whispered, your open laugh and urgent lips. That night, as on so many other nights when we slept together, we didn't sleep at all. Happily that's what the morning is for. That's where we are, right now. I'm going to stop writing to let you sleep a little more, that's what I'm going to do. What other meaning could life have besides a morning with you beneath the sheets?

At least we still have football, said the old man at the bus stop, his eyes heavy from all the life he had behind him, and me standing there, not knowing what to say, and I felt like telling him I had no interest at all in football and all that crap, if Naná, the babe from apartment 10B, the one who I'm sure should be the woman of my life, wants nothing to do with me, or even if my mother, in her uniquely annoying way, won't let me go to the end-of-year party at the high-school bar. At least we still have football but fuck, old-timer, what'll become of me if I can't have Naná or go to the party where the whole crew is going to be?

And the bus stopped suddenly. And what I saw next I'd never seen before in my whole life – and it's been more than seven decades on this godforsaken earth. Two adolescents, who can't have been more than thirteen or fourteen, got on, their tongues locked together in their mouths, tangled up together as though there were no tomorrow and as though there were nobody else there. He was doing his best to get his hand in between her tight clothes and her skin and she was rubbing against him as though expecting the genie of the lamp himself to appear. They're shameless, the youth of today, that's what they are. And they went on like that the whole journey, they didn't even need to talk very much, I just learned that her name was Naná, what the hell kind of a name is that?, and him Carlos, I can't even tell you how I know that, only God would know if he wasn't too ashamed, because their mouths were too busy to be bothering themselves with words. This country is completely done for, that's for sure, and I've always said so. At least we still have football, at least we still have football.

If you knew how much I love you, my little genius. If you knew that if I'm going on like this it's because I want to provoke you, look into your eyes surrounded by all these people and see whether you want me, whether you need me, whether you seek me out the way I seek you out whenever I think about what's going to become of me. And now that you look at me, in this bus full of people, and you tell me without a word that you'd like to be Carlos, that you'd like to be the body that is feeling mine, I know it's worth it. All of this is worth it, all this effort, because love demands sacrifice and I'm ready to test out any bodies necessary till I find the perfect soul. I'm a modern romantic, who gives herself to many in order to belong to only one, and I'm for it if my mother finds out but it does have to be like this. I love you, my little genius, I love you the way they say love ought to be, and I only hope that one day you get the courage you've never had and come to me and tell me that you want me to be yours for ever; I hope you come with that beautiful head of yours, and invent all the words for all these feelings, and then the whole school is going to stop still in order to watch us love. The whole school stopped still watching us love, when will you come to me and give me that moment?

And then I went, the old man was saying, some children sitting opposite him round about five or six, their mouths open, listening to his story. I got right up next to her, even though I knew she was going out with the captain of the college football team, and this is what I said to her: if any words, in my life, are left unsaid, let those words not be I love you. I love you. The grandchildren looked at one another, one of them even wiped away a tear, and the other asked: and then what, grandad, then what? Then the old man didn't say another word, he got up, opened a drawer, and took out an old photograph, which showed a young couple embracing by the door to a university. Then there was this, the old man explained at last, showing them the photo as though displaying a cure for death, then there was the life you must know existed, me and her and the family, me and her and football, me and her and movies. Then there was me and her, the old man emphasised, maybe that thing moistening his face now was a tear, and with total serenity the eyes of the children getting mistier and mistier, he just said those words which still hurt today when I think of them: I didn't even still have football, not without her.

I like it so much, I like all of it, when this happens, the TV turned on and suddenly you looking at me and loving me, the touch of my knee between your legs, the untenable weight of your body on mine, the TV goes on, with the movies and the series and even the football, and they also help us to be happy, but when the time comes for one body on the other, or one pair of eyes looking into the other, or just the time for waiting for a pain to pass, a hug to help bear what hurts, when the time comes for us nothing that makes us happy is enough to make us happy, what we need is us absolutely, you give yourself up absolutely to the task of making this fucking life immense, truly immense, you know?; and forgive me, there's always a moment within that moment when I remember my old man and his story, and I tell him that, yes, always, at least we still have football, grandad. And everything else that, oh, is so fucking good.

Tell her I love her, please. First of all tell her I love her. That I ache in the darkest insides of my tears, and that her things scattered around the house teach me that the only thing you can do when you love is forgive. Tell her that if I'm here so far away it's because I need time to feel I need her, like a starving man who decides to spend one more day without eating so that his food will taste even better. Tell her I love her, please. And that when I close my eyes I can still see the other man with her, their naked bodies and our house with him inside it. Tell her that when I shut my eyes I still can't bear the weight of how much it hurts, that imagining her being somebody else's in the place where we were sacredly ourselves makes me crazy, and that if there's something unbearable it's having to bear what she did to me in order to be able to take her back. Tell her that what she did isn't something you do but I'd rather have the betrayer I love than some faithful woman I could never possibly love. Tell her I love her and that I'm stupid enough to want her back. Tell her also that love is an idiotic, illogical thing, without the least bit of coherence. That I wake every day with her in my eyes, that when I meet the future she is always there. Tell her I love her, please. And that forgiving her is unforgivable. That the way she treats me and has always treated me goes beyond all limits, that I'm not her little lapdog but if she wants I actually could be her little barking man. That she has never valued me as I deserved, never told me like I told her that life only exists so that she exists, never brought me breakfast in bed, never stroked my hair while I lay with my head in her lap, never even hugged me when there was something stressing me. Tell her she shouldn't begin to imagine she deserves me but that I want to be hers for ever. That everything that is to be recommended doesn't recommend her, that continuing my life beside someone who I don't even know if she loves me makes no sense. That when I look at the toothbrush she used to use, and which I've brought with me, God knows why, I just think about breaking it into pieces to see whether I can be rid of her, to see if I can break her in me, to see if I can liberate myself from this prison of liking her so much, of wanting her quite so much, of being such a slave to somebody who probably doesn't want me even as a slave. Tell her I even miss her ill temper, her furious tears whenever she didn't get her own way, the almost childish, or childish, way she sulked for hours just because they didn't have her favourite chocolate at the supermarket. Tell her I still wake up in the middle of the night to pull the blanket over her, that I still try to find her beside me in order to get to sleep, that the cold of the bed without her has no words to define it let alone blankets to warm it up. Tell her I'm hers for ever. That there must be so many lives in us, so many men and so many women, and that it will still be her, always her, the most inexhaustible her, the most untrustworthy her, the wife of me. That if I had to choose somewhere to die I would choose the depths of her arms. Tell her I love her, please. First of all tell her I love her. And tell her too that I'm not coming back.

First I was happy, then I became adult,

here's hoping old age comes to rescue me, a bit of uncon-sciousness and it's easier to get by,

what wounds is the obsessive presence of the brain,

only fiction is eternal, only what doesn't exist, what happens within what I feel, a kiss, of course, the touch of your hand, a word from you in my ear, or simply the scent of the wind,

only an old man or a child can recognise the scent of the wind, isn't that right?,

there's an indisputable relationship between a naked body and happiness, pleasure almost always happens without any clothes, for what that's worth, an undressed person is more seldom unhappy,

the uncertain weight of regrets suffocates me,

and I've done so many things I shouldn't have done and sometimes I regret them, other times I'm proud of them, I don't know how something that was so good could be so bad, there's an inexcusable inconsistency in whoever created all this,

how long since I've had a complete day?,

something is missing from my hours and I don't know if I can bear it, I must confess, I urgently need a life, or a skin,

happiness is loving like a tourist, and never belonging anywhere,

seen from outside even war is beautiful, do we need another reason to abhor the judgement of our eyes?,

to die is not an immovable verb,

age doesn't stop moving but it's life that kills, the days that are unending and too short, people with their own lives set up in ours, there is no such thing as egoism, only survival,

only an idiot would separate flesh and soul, like God, for example,

old age is a sad resurrection, it teaches us to live and then it kills us, the fascism of the body hurts till I'm tired of it, I have to tell you,

the unfinished time hurts me, the enormous party I can't get into, I'd like to go back to the beginning of the whole bewilderment, start everything over,

and cry better,

but I don't want to cry, I can declare that much,

it's not death that is an intransigence, it's the final body, the deceitful edge, the beginning and the end of chaos, only what's cuttable with a knife is perishable, not me,

it's not death that's an intransigence, but it is intransigent to die,

while I'm alive.

'You are, despite your not realising it yet, the woman of my life.'

'I am, despite your not realising it yet, a man.'

It's one of those things about life: sometimes it ends. Mine ended, at that moment. It went. And yet, strangely, it let me remain behind. Abandoned by two women in the last five years, I am now, disastrously, in love with a third who is, in fact, a man. Deep down, it's just my subconscious being faithful to a promise I made myself when Joana left me: that I'd never fall in love with another woman.

'You do have a feminine side.'

'Yes, it's the left. The one with the make-up on.'

'You are, despite being a beautiful man, a beautiful woman.'

'Fine, fine, I'll let you fuck me. Your room or mine?'

It's one of those things about seduction: sometimes it works out. This, without the slightest doubt (not least because he's the first I've tried to win over), is the easiest man of my life. I need to decide: my room, even if it's only been mine a few hours (since I arrived at the hotel), is already too much mine to be shared with anybody. Least of all a man. I do, I confess, have certain prejudices against homosexuals.

'You have the biggest penis of any woman I've ever met.'

'...'

'But for now, do please move it over to one side, OK?'

'...'

'Much obliged.'

It's one of those things about heterosexuality: sometimes it's reversed. The biggest problem (small though it is) of sex with a woman with a penis is the member itself – which does, evidently, lead to a logistical problem, of placement – of getting things to fit. Fortunately ever since I was a kid I've got used to living with things being lacking; and so encountering things in excess is pretty easy.

'I'm Rúben.'

'Pleasure.'

'No. I'm satisfied for now. But thanks.'

The strangest thing about our impossible loves is that they sometimes happen.

She chose, after much consideration, the really tight blue skirt, to wear at the most important moment of her life. She put on her make-up with the care of somebody assembling an atomic bomb, each line in its place, she chose the tall boots so as to feel more protected, as though having her skin covered would protect her from the world, then finally looked fearfully at herself in the mirror, gave the best smile she could manage, her lips trembling and a tightening in her eyes, huge anxiety governing her body.

'Forgive me,' she practised in front of the mirror what there was to be said, 'forgive me for having once believed that there could be life without there being you,' confidently, sure of herself, 'I want you for ever and I'm sure that won't feel like much,' and she went out into the street, her suit impeccable, her shoes impeccable, her love impeccable, and reality, only reality, stained by a mistake she wanted to correct now.

They met at the café from before, the table empty as they'd hoped. He arrived first, his rehearsed words well memorised in his head, the gestures, even the gestures, thought through right up to the tiniest detail. Until she arrived, her steps as though treading over people, the tight blue skirt and all the men looking. He said what he had to say, she heard what she had to hear. They both wanted to embrace right then and there before the world ended. But neither one took the risk. He waited for her to say, 'yes, I forgive you', she waited for him to say 'I'm sorry I'm going to embrace you all over even if you don't want me to'. And the right time for the right moment was lost.

At home, she took off her blue skirt and her tall boots and surrendered, her body lay down on the bed as though suddenly drained of blood. He remained in the café a few more minutes, just to say goodbye to what he had been unable to do, before returning slowly to the empty room, her smell and her clothes, if he were a courageous man he'd have had the cowardice to give up on life.

They married and they were almost-happy ever after. Not to each other, of course. She found a perfect man and he found a perfect woman. Time passed, and along the way, they gradually unlearned how they had once run, what had once made them run and jump – but never walk. Children came, new challenges, wrinkles, grandchildren, the skin giving in and all of time becoming increasingly rare episodes of passion. They died far apart, as far as geography would allow, with even the unbearable size of a sea separating them. It happened that, oddly, both of their gravestones contained the same mistake, 'an unforgivable typo', according to their respective husband and wife: the date of death given was more than thirty years earlier, and nobody was ever able to understand why. And the inscription, immediately below the date, had no mistake in it at all.

'It isn't stopping that is dying, it's going away.'

She is naked and all the cells of her skin rise up with the passing of his tongue. The sound of a boat leaving, a woman with short steps and high heels, and now his tongue slips between her legs, maybe the sound of airless breathing from one of them. The bed like an altar and the wordless devotion of both bodies that bend to a greater faith. She twists slightly, shifts slightly to the right, the tongue finding a new angle, he continues along the track of what she's seeking, the two of them united in the search for a soul that is hidden amid the sheets (I hear the voice of God when you touch me like that). His hand moving up her belly, sweat and fingers, in the distance the barking of a dog, her hand on his head, her fingers in his hair, aggressive and soft, as though they wanted to lead him, and the bedroom just standing there watching them win.

Use me completely so that you can love me everywhere.

That was her desperate request. They were in the most expensive hotel in the city, nothing could be heard now but the disquiet and the hurried breathing, and outside there was all life and nothing that mattered. He didn't answer right away, he looked at her, he thought he could tell her just how much he liked her, the profound inability to imagine himself beyond her; he thought, too, that he could tell her that he was lost, that his whole life had been squandered from the moment he'd met her, and that the only ability he retained was to love her; then he thought he would never be able to give her what she needed, the cars, the houses, let alone the travel, because if he was ruined because of her then he couldn't because of her go back to what he used to be; finally he thought about the irony of the whole thing, how perfect and how stupid his life without her would be. He didn't know if he hated her but he knew he loved her. He was perfectly hers. Perfectly hers, in so far as a crazy wretch of a man can be perfect. He could have said so many things to her, everything that occurred to him, everything that made him think he was minutes away from losing her for ever if he told her that he loved her for ever. He could also have told her so many important things, so many definite things, but it was enough for her to take hold of him and pull him into her for him to understand that only the silence was urgent.

They made use of two bodies to make use of life.

It was their best man who wrote and read, his hands already tremulous with age, everybody dressed in black to say goodbye to two old folks who had given up on everything in life except orgasm. The photo on the tombstone didn't show the face of one or the other of them, just the sweaty bed sheets and the two of them, as always, her naked and all the cells of her skin rising up with the passing of his tongue.

If she had boarded that train, on a cold March day and the station packed with people, perhaps her life would have been different. Perhaps he would have been waiting for her, in the last row in the last seat in the last carriage as always, his eyes open in search of a risk he did not yet know. Later, certainly, she would have made her way down the aisle as though making her way down a road to her destination, with him getting closer with each step. And then the look, the train pulling out and an unhurried look, him looking at her as though undressing her completely, her looking at him as though there were nothing left to be done.

There'd be nothing left to do and that was why they wouldn't waste any time doing it. The train would be full, so many people and so many lives and not one would get between them, about three hours' journey and the whole counting of time for them would restart with the rest of the time they had left for themselves. They would talk about everything, him serious and excited, her shy and excited, but in reality they would only ever talk about love. About theirs, of course, born without anybody realising it, just like all loves are born without anybody, least of all those who love, realising it. They would come to know a lot about each other, she would learn what he created, words that were meaningless when he was in her gaze (not a single vein was still, all wanting the moment of the skin); he would learn her fears (he wanted to protect her, with all his bones, from what hurt, to ask her to come into his arms and breathe), even a bit about her past and what she had left behind.

They would certainly understand that all defeats have a meaning and that everything they'd lost had brought them there. It would be the shortest journey in both their lives and they would never travel so far again. There wouldn't be, not until near the end, any daring advances, nor any attempts beyond eyes giving pleasure. Until, and later he wouldn't be able to explain how, she wouldn't be able to explain how, the hand happened. He would love her with his hand inside her tall boot, to this day he can define her touch precisely, the moment when he discovered a piece of her skin and believed he had discovered the secret of the existence of faith. She would blush a bit but she'd let him continue, she'd understand then and there how love really can consist of blushing a bit but allowing to continue. The hand would remain, it would keep remaining, the final stop and two people focused, their whole minds, on the few centimetres in which the hand of one was inside the tall boot of the other.

Nobody would notice it, the train rolling along as though everything were just as normal, but the world itself would be changing there, irremediably, without any God able to prevent it. Because the moment of the kiss would arrive, you do always arrive at the first moment of the kiss. It was nothing like in the movies, there would be no racing about, there would be no huge embraces, still less any well-rehearsed movements, just him with the courage deep down to take the risk of a kiss on the threshold of everything, and her not knowing how to refuse what she didn't believe was refusable. Absolute love really can be a shy kiss in the last seat of the last carriage of a train that unwittingly changes the meaning of the world.

Then the journey would end and by now there was nothing that could prevent them from beginning the fateful journey. There would, of course, be bed and orgasm, but none of that would be complete without what long after – by which time she believed, sceptically, that all great adventures could only go wrong in the end (reality can only punish perfection severely, and that might actually be logical, poetic justice to rebalance the world) – they would both euphemistically call love for want of a more befitting word with which, twenty-four hours a day (really twenty-four, because twenty-two or twenty-three would be an inexplicable waste of something so ludicrous that it couldn't possibly exist), they would have to live.

If she had boarded that train, perhaps she would be, today, by his side, on a bed where one day, for the first time, reading a text exactly like this one, which he had written seconds before kissing her on the shoulder, running his hand over her lips and telling her that if he could go back he would do everything exactly the same, her, him and the train where the world changed, and the inadequate I love you, at last.

'I love you.'

'Just this morning I made two new girlfriends.'

No one knows his name but everybody knows his words, the grown-ups are afraid of him just like they're afraid of anything strange, the children adore him and say he's got a 'tired head', and there's nothing more fascinating than the sensitivity of children, no one but they can understand, in just a moment without even thinking about it, that that head has already done what it needs to do and is now in rest mode, lost so as not to have to meet what it has left behind.

'One day I'll change the whole world with just a few words.'

And in the streets of Cascais, the bay stretching as far as the eye can see, there he goes, from here to there and there to here, nobody knowing whether to laugh or cry and those steps and those words of the madman who just has, so say the kids, a tired head. What could madness be but the precise moment when a head gets too tired?

'You're such a beautiful girl I can't tell you.'

The girl laughs, she really is beautiful, aged maybe thirty, no more than that, she smiles and keeps walking, she doesn't look at him, she doesn't have the nerve to look at him, he keeps looking at her but he doesn't follow her, he's already made two girlfriends today and he doesn't seem terribly bothered about making another, whatever happens happens, he's got to take another walk around the town, for more people (so many tourists and the magic of a madman at every tourist spot just to liven up the crowd) to hide from him, mad men frighten people more than bad ones, the sun starting to set way off in the distance, at the end of the sea, and the tired head is not discouraged, he keeps tiring out his body so as to balance things out at his centre.

'The whole world depends on just a couple of words from me.'

A man standing beside him, probably English from his pronounced accent, looks at him and wants to give him a banknote, he refuses it without needing to refuse, he doesn't need charity, only words, he continues on his way among the people, the daylight fading, the height of winter and the cold, a tired head returning home, a day won, one more, before returning to the cardboard box round the back of the barbecue place in the centre of town, a warm goodnight to his neighbours, a quick stop by the trash can, just so he doesn't starve to death, and the restful sleep of a warrior who has tired of fighting.

'You still exist.'

She woke him as she has woken him so many times before, in the house hundreds of kilometres away which one day he abandoned, nobody ever knew why, she ran her hand over his face, she didn't say a word, he opened his eyes, never had a cardboard bed seemed so cosy to him, he didn't want to believe what he was seeing, he rubbed his eyes again, and again, and understood that, yes, it was her, he squeezed her in his arms, her white clean skin in his dirty black T-shirt, and he said again, much quieter now, maybe nobody heard it but her, that one day he was going to change the world with just a few words.

'I love you.'

And he did.

She had waited her whole life for the love of her life and it took someone dying for him to appear. He was dressed in black, the way all deaths are dressed, and it wasn't till four or five months later that she saw him smile. He was a man who had lost his wife, the cemetery was full, and there she was, not knowing what to do with what she felt about someone she had never seen but already loved.

'The stupidest thing about love is being so stupid that you don't even need to get to know the person you love,' she wrote that night on some page or other of some notebook or other. She felt like an adolescent and all she wanted was to deal in an adult way with what was coursing through her veins. But how do you become adult when faced with love? How do you make a person in love into an adult if love consists, largely, in taking us back to childhood, to that moment when everything is for the first time again? These were two of the questions that she didn't write but she might have written, were it not for the strange fact of, rather than being afraid of what was happening, having begun to be afraid of what was not happening.

'Nobody waits their whole life for something that's not worth a whole life,' she wrote later, and what followed this was very simple: a phone call here, a phone call there, and within a few minutes she was more peaceful despite (or maybe even because of) being much more unquiet. Knowing where he lived was, at that moment, the perfect victory, the possible victory, there was the pain of him and the impossibility of someone who had just lost the person they love starting to love again on the same scale. Anybody who has waited a whole life can wait two, she thought, though this is pure speculation because she wrote nothing. All we know is that she lay down, with a smile on her lips and a piece of paper with some letters and an address in her right hand, and fell asleep, as though she were in love already.

'When you fall asleep as though you're in love already, that's when love really begins', and the morning arrived, he was still at the address she had, she was still lost with desire for it to be right now. It wasn't. She would have to wait for that first moment, but still there could be intermediary moments: 'moments of aloneness à deux', as she would later call them. She would love him without his knowledge, is there any more infallible love than this? She would follow him, calmly, wherever she needed to follow him, get to know him so as to love him better. She would love him in silence, is there any less noisy love than this?

'If one day you look at me, I promise I'll look back at you,' that was the declaration of love that she still had left and to which she'd promised to be faithful: she wouldn't enter his life if he, however or for whatever reason, didn't enter hers. There was even a moment when all the promises stopped counting. She followed him on to the bridge in the centre of the city, she didn't understand what could be taking him there, stepping weakly with doubtless a few tears falling on the ground, and she watched him looking down there, all of life or all of death just one step away. That was when she realised that the thing she insisted on watching was about to happen, she didn't ask permission and she looked. He looked at her, he looked at her deeply, and she surely would have been the last image he saw in his life.

'It was when you made me come down off that bridge, that was when I realised I was being born once again,' he would write, one day, on a post-it that he would stick on the fridge of the house they shared, a two-bedroom that was small but so big that neither of them needed more than a little bedroom and sofa to have everything they wanted.

'I waited my whole life for a death like this,' she didn't write, and nor did he. They said it, without anyone else hearing, in each other's ear, and all the moans gave up on waiting.

Love.

Brushing your teeth next to whomever you love.

Fondling their ass brazenly.

Eating chocolates until you're bored of them.

Spending the night talking nonsense.

Always kissing with your tongue.

Spending the day talking nonsense.

Telling your boss to go to hell.

Spending your life talking nonsense.

Leaving declarations of love around the house.

Making your father happy.

Lazing around regularly.

Making your mother happy.

Throwing the alarm clock against the wall occasionally.

Making whoever you can happy.

Sleeping fifteen or twenty hours in a row.

Sticking your hand out of the car window.

Painting your hair blue or yellow.

Sticking your head out of the car window.

Singing in the bath for the whole building to hear.

Licking yoghurt tops.

Running on the beach like a lunatic.

Failing like an idiot just because you tried.

Practising oral sex frequently.

Trying like an idiot just because you want to.

Changing the décor in the whole house in a single day.

Dancing when you're happy.

Spending hours just taking care of yourself.

Dancing when you're sad.

Saying nice things about a person you love.

Sticking your finger in your nose in secret.

Saying nice things about a person you don't love.

Dancing while you're alive.

Keeping unconfessable secrets.

Trying unlikely sexual positions.

Telling unconfessable secrets.

Masturbating without shame.

Having unconfessable secrets.

Seeing how fast your car will go.

Saying what can't be said.

Crapping assiduously on social conventions.

Dreaming about what can't happen.

Orgasming whenever you can.

Scratching backs and having your own back scratched.

Moaning whenever you can.

Spending several hours telling jokes.

Falling asleep all twisted up on the sofa.

Spending several hours listening to jokes.

Laughing madly.

Getting an outlandish hairdo just because you fancy a change.

Laughing at everything and nothing.

Crying indiscriminately, left and right.

Rolling around in the sand when you're all wet.

Crying because that's also your right.

Cuddling your cat or your dog.

Telling austerity to go fuck itself.

Kissing tirelessly.

Not taking yourself remotely seriously.

Getting rid of whoever annoys you.

Playing some instrument or other.

Forgiving anybody human.

Giving up on what doesn't work for you.

Fighting for the right to silliness.

Writing a book.

Prioritising pleasure.

Reading a book.

Never giving up on whomever you love.

Learning wildly.

Spooning whomever you love.

Teaching wildly.

Getting out of breath at least once a day.

Being born at least one time more than you die.

Living wildly.

Yourself.

He was a good man but he loved two women.

One was his tranquil woman, his peace woman, his sharing woman, his complicity woman. Whenever he needed a shoulder, there she was, arms open with a whole embrace for him to rest whatever was hurting him. She wasn't particularly sensual, she wasn't particularly attractive, but she had a beauty he found beneath her face that was tired from the everyday, the family, the house, two children and a whole life on her shoulders. He loved her in total peace, in sweet tranquillity, without any shivers, it's true, but also without any bit of violent hurt. She was the perfect woman for living with – and he knew that he couldn't survive without her, he wouldn't be able to bear what so often assailed him. She was the insurmountable barrier, the last redoubt of what he was able to bear. It was in her that he learned survival, it was in her that he learned not to give up. He loved her because it was the best way of loving himself as a person, someone as good as her could only love somebody equally lovable, which he didn't always feel. He loved her out of selfishness, it's true, but he did whatever he could to make her happy, he was romantic and affectionate, he surprised her with gifts and if there was anything she wanted he went gladly to the ends of the earth to be able to give it to her. She was the woman of his life even if there was another woman in his life.

The other woman was his hard-on woman, his volcano woman, his adrenaline woman, his pleasure woman. Just one look from her was enough for the whole world to tremble, for every hair to stand on end, for all his skin to come alive as it brushed past her skin. She wasn't level-headed or prudent or well trained or tame. She was a wild animal whom he loved as a wild animal, and if she were ever to calm down he could certainly stop loving her. There was no possible peace, by her side, no feasible quiet: it was orgasm or nothing. She didn't believe in the existence of grey and saw the possibility of pleasure as the only true proof of the existence of God. 'You either fuck me now or you could lose me for ever,' she'd say to him fearlessly whenever she sensed any kind of hesitation when it was time to go in search of the greatest moaning in the world. She was profoundly superficial, maybe that was the best way to describe her; she had an unshakeable faith that there was nothing more profound than the right to a perfect now, and if she ever discovered that there was nothing new left to feel she'd probably kill herself in frustration. She was addicted to first times and that was why whenever they met they had to start out as total strangers who come to know each other slowly. She was the woman of his life even if there was another woman in his life.

The problem of loving two women is the danger that one day, owing to an awkward coincidence, they will meet. Which is what has just happened. He was with the tranquil woman, apron on and food nearly ready in the oven, when the hard-on woman showed up. She didn't ask for permission and she asked ('you either fuck me now or you could lose me for ever'), then and there, for total pleasure. That was what happened. The other woman, poor thing, disappeared instantly, in the time it took for an apron to be taken off and dropped on the floor. The advantage of loving two women is the danger that one day, owing to a delightful coincidence, they will meet in just one.

'The crazy thing about life is the body, you know?'

In front of him a woman with tears wired into place, a forced smile, feeling as though at any moment he might leave, the usual man, the usual life, and now if she could she'd want to have all the arguments over again, and once again that way he had of sometimes not giving her his full attention, anything to get him out of that bed which like all the beds in the hospital smells of something very close to the smell of death. What does it smell like, the thing we smell when we're beside someone we're going to watch die?

'Promise me you'll be happy with the first man to make you happy?'

There might even be tears, and now there are, she can't bear it and she really cries, but there's also the certainty of a future, he asks her to continue after him, because love can be, often, understanding that the other side can survive beyond ours.

'Why don't you get up and come play with me, daddy?'

The child arrived, she wasn't meant to have arrived but she did, she doesn't yet know what's happening there but she knows that her father is there not moving, as if he were just some lazy guy who just didn't want to get up, and what is death or closeness to death if not a laziness that never passes?

'Daddy can't just now.'

No father should have to say that he can't, 'can't' is impossible for a father, 'can't' is impossible for a mother, all fathers and all mothers should know that they contain super-powers, and that if there's one thing they can't do it's say that they can't do whatever it is. The proof of this will follow shortly.

'You see, daddy, you can!'

He can after all, it took a few minutes but it happened, the father, impelled by his whole life and all the strength in his arms, one arm on the woman he married and the other on the woman he saw being born, he raised himself up, he's standing, the tubes coming out of his body don't even seem to exist, it's just him and those he loves, and he's standing, and the women's eyes as usual, in love with what he is, complete love appearing completely, never will a few simple tubes prevent a complete love, there's a man who loves two women and two women who love a man, that's all, only this, all around everything is perfect when inside us there is a space that's occupied, totally occupied, by those we love within us.

'Go on, let's take a walk, daddy!'

If we wanted to look at what's happening from a negative viewpoint we might say this is the last walk in this man's life, supported by two people, one on either side, one small and one big, and the tubes go with him, a trolley with saline too, and they're small steps, on squalid, thin legs that hurt, making each centimetre a victory, making each advance a hero, but there's to be none of that, no last walk, just three people who love one another taking a walk, three people no body could separate, he might walk more slowly but it's still him, he might be thin and wasted but it's still him, and when you love each other no body puts an end to love, what do incapable legs matter alongside someone who loves like that?

'Look over there, daddy, it's our house.'

And there the three of them go, eyes in the window, and way out there in the distance, lost amid so many houses, is a house where the three of them arrive now, they imagine themselves there again, the girl playing and jumping in the garden, the woman and her husband watching her from the doorway, they smile and hug, it was worth it, one of them would say, I love you, and I love her, the other would say, then he will teach them the rules of some game or other, the three of them playing in a garden where all their memories would remain, and there they would remain, whatever happened, within the space reserved for those people who can't imagine themselves unless they're imagining themselves beside other such people.

'I'll be back tomorrow so you can take me for another walk, OK, daddy?'

Yes, she'll be back tomorrow, she'll always be back, even if one day the bed is empty and daddy's had to take a walk somewhere else, somewhere she won't be able to see him, tomorrow the child will be back and one day when she's a grown-up she won't stop coming back, to the house where she took her father, the house where her father took her, to show him that nothing you touch with your skin stays on your skin, and what is being alive if not being capable of bringing feelings to others?

'Whenever you come back I'll be here.'
And he is.

When I get up I like to lie back down beside you, and wait for the moment when sleep returns, understand the unstoppable scale of the absurdity of being alive, and fall asleep back to you.

I love you emotionally, and with total reason.

I prefer the early hours because they are what wake me for you while you sleep, and when I touch you and you open up to me I don't know whether there will be life enough for us to love each other entirely.

I'd need to explain the beginning of the world to explain the beginning of us.

Today you are far away and the sound of the cars isn't the same, the empty window without your body in silhouette in the middle of the outside light, my father's words without your look, and your ears seem like a sign that nothing exists but what passes through you.

I don't need you until death, I need you until life.

Night falls and my missing you rises still further, I left you a few hours ago and I lost years of my life, I've already forgotten what existed before you, and if you want to know the truth even my hands hurt from old age as I write you these words.

I only fear silence when I don't have you unspeaking beside me.

It's so incomprehensible how much I love you, as though the only things that happen are those that happen to you, the people beside you, the lights, the TV turned on, so many people I love but who are not my place in the world.

Tell your parents please that they invented God.

Through these words I'm trying to get closer to your skin, probably all pieces of work are borne of this violent desire to curtail distances, to bring bodies closer together through words, and when they tell me I'm a genius, they will know they're talking about you.

The secret of literature is abdicating language.

Nobody loves while thinking about words, words are used for loving and not the other way around, and I luv you are always the most correct words in the world – because nothing, least of all some insignificant spelling code, can make a luv like this wrong.

Only if you're getting love wrong are you getting writing wrong.

'What are you drawing?'

'God.'

'But nobody knows what God looks like?'

'Then wait a few moments and you'll find out.'

That was how I met Zambé, the kid I'm going to be telling you about today. A mischievous kid, beautiful head, his whole life in his eyes when he looked at me, in that schoolroom, and when he made me believe that the only things that didn't exist were those that couldn't be imagined. From Zambé I learned to be a child and I reckon there can be no more valuable learning than that.

'What do you want to be when you're big?'

'Small again.'

And he was. He really was. Just a few months ago, when I ran into him again, there he was, the same look in his eye, the same desire to discover everything for the first time, he was carrying a child and I understood he'd only become a father so as to have an excuse not to grow up.

'So what are you up to?'

'Inventing.'

'What have you invented today?'

'A new way of hugging.'

He taught me that hug immediately, with the whole street stopping dead to laugh at us, some expressions of derision, Zambé and me leaping up and down in a kind of hug that nobody understood but which feels damn good. After all, what we take away from life is what nobody understands but which feels damn good.

'What are you doing?'
'Teaching my son to read.'
'But he's two.'
'Yes, but there's still time.'
'And does he know his alphabet already?'
'Who needs their alphabet to know how to read?'

And there he was, that illogical smile like you can only find on people in books, a two-year-old child in his arms in the middle of the park where everyone is thinking about bills, about crises, about insignificant things like survival, having forgotten that the most important thing was happening and it was called life, and now the sun is shining brightly high in the sky. After all, what we take away from life is it happening and the sun shining brightly high in the sky.

'What are you giving him for Christmas?'
'I was thinking of giving him a kiss.'

With all the seriousness in the world, Zambé was playing, maybe that's the secret of children's happiness, can there be anything more serious for a child than playing?

'I'd like to attend my funeral.'
'Why?'
'It would prove I was still alive.'

Zambé was, if you'll excuse the pleonasm, a philosophical child.

'You're afraid of dying.'
'No.'
'Why?'
'When it comes I know it won't take me alive.'

And it didn't.

It's unbearable wanting you this much but it's impossible not to want you this much.

And it consumes everything when my need is so urgent, when it becomes clear that all struggles are possible except the one that goes against my liking you. All dreams don't seem like much when I don't dream you within them.

What is happiness if not what happens to us when we are together?

I want an embrace as much as I want to not want an embrace.

And I embrace you. With all the desperation of a woman needed, a mere addict to staying with you, and it's as sad to need to be so yours as it is overwhelming to be deep in the marrow of your arms.

We lack for so much, and yet an embrace is enough for us to have everything.

All power is undone in kisses.

'I want to fall asleep in the immortality of your lips,' I say to you, and your smile tells me that you don't give a damn about the words, and your open mouth seeking to ruin me tells me you only want me for what I give you.

But what is love if not being addicted to what our beloved gives us?

Only those who need the unadvisable deserve to live.

What nobody believes exists is what makes our existence worthwhile, and the reality is a succession of tediums until you find what takes off your shoes and makes you comfortable. When they ask me to define life I'll say 'fools', and you and I both know that only folly can prove that happiness exists.

Two fools in flight are better than one on the ground.

All around there are regular loves, loves that stabilise, loves that turn solid with each day of conceding. But between us there is no conceding. Between us there is an unfettered battle that does, very often, involve frontal collisions. And more often than not, these happen without any clothes to cover our body.

The good part of being at war with you is knowing that even when I lose we end up winning.

Because the two of us are in different trenches but we're still on the same side. You want to love me in your way, I want to love you in mine. But we both want this love to continue.

And what is life if not fighting every day for love to continue?

They're so stupid, people who aren't stupid.

And they don't understand that even routine can be exciting, that every day exists for the unpredictable to happen, for something to leave us with our heart in our hands. And they sustain. They keep their desires for later, their fantasies for another time, their rebellions for never. And that's how they keep putting off waiting for the day of prearranged happiness, the moment of scheduled liberation. But happiness can be anything except it can't be pre-planned. If happiness is pre-planned, it's going to be bland, it ought to be canned. Because only what takes our breath away swells our breast, and coming up with new ways to love you is my daily tribute to you.

Naïveté is why I get up every morning. And ninety percent of happiness is naïveté and the other ten is ignorance.

Better to have innocence every day than to feel guilty for ever.

The day I left you, it was you who didn't want to stay.

All things considered the world is simple, at least the world that matters:

there is your smile and life, and right here we can easily understand what a pleonasm is, and most of all how much wastage of words there is around.

The perfect dictionary would have your photograph on the cover and all the pages inside blank, and then the language would be born again, your face alone would just occupy the beginning of the tongue, all the historians would talk about the revolution of your body, and by the final page I would have torn out all the others already so that nobody would discover that it's with forced words that I've been winning you over.

The day I left you, I wanted you to stay to see me coming back, did you know that's how poets love?, I imagined you'd be waiting for me in the lingerie from our first night, the cheeky smile of your half-open legs, lips painted just to have a serious impact on me, I would play hard to get, you know how it is, a serious look here, a sharp word there, maybe even a tear I'd practised in front of the domestic appliances store before coming back, you'd ask me please to forgive you for something, I swear, at this point I have no idea what it could be, I just wanted the bed sheets pulled over us and your cold body on mine for us to invent the perfect heat.

When I returned to forgive you, you hadn't yet forgiven me, the house standing empty with everything in it, the place where I would forgive you only had the blanket and the dead sofa where I was sure you would have to forgive me for I don't know what it was you'd done (what the hell had you done to make you ask my forgiveness?), I looked for you everywhere to forgive you, and gradually I realised you'd gone because I left you in order to be able to love you more strongly, go figure these poets and their little obsessions.

All things considered, poetry is simple, at least the poetry that matters:

there is your love and the poem, and right here we can easily understand what a pleonasm is, and most of all how much wastage of words there is around.

I wanted to pull the string to stop you from bursting, to understand that you still loved me beyond pride, to make you feel insecure so as to feel secure myself, and when I lay down you weren't there and it was me and the poem, all the lies that literature created just shattered right there, but what is all this crap about the artist being solitary when I spend my days trying to write a work of art and only end up writing to you?

The day I left you, it was you who didn't want to stay, and now (I swear I'm ready to come back and you're forgiven):

do you? do you want to now?

They assured me I'd never be able to walk again, and I accepted it after my fashion,

so my grandfather once told me as he ran alongside me in the park, me as a boy and him pulling me along,

They assured me that I'd never again be able to have children, and I accepted it after my fashion,

and a year later my father would be born, and then I started to understand that accepting doesn't mean giving up, you have to keep going after the acceptance,

It offends me that they should want to choose for me, that's all,

a hero after all is merely a man who's more wilful than others, more short-tempered than others, more unbearable than others, if there's such a thing as bearable heroes then in fact heroes don't exist at all,

You're only a person when you know how to get away with it without saying a word,

that was how I learned to write, with him beside me and his words, a man from the countryside teaching me the importance of language, a phrase here, another there, earlier he'd lent me his grown-up boots and I became a person around the farm, it wasn't big but it could hold my entire dream, and the livestock, and me and my grown-up boots,

We need to learn early on how to be in big people's shoes,

milking the cattle, working the soil, travelling by train, my grandfather was a ticket inspector and he was the best ticket inspector in the world,

Even when I'm urinating I make a point of being the best,
and I didn't even know what urinating was,

why the hell don't they teach a five-year-old boy what urinating is?,

his hand on my back, so much life in those fingers, each skin has a thousand books to write,

Take this pen and do with it as you please, even if it's making money,

and I became a writer just to try out your gift and your words, a Parker pen with smudged ink that I still keep religiously,

And I don't believe in God but I have faith that He exists,

but I need your harsh voice to calm me down, your coarse way of loving me,

And I don't need your grandmother at all, except to stay alive,

the most profound declaration of love I've ever heard, nothing I read after you comes close to the look in your eye when you were telling the truth, and only the truth,

What stays on the surface makes me sick,

what do you mean sick, grandad, you were probably just born in the wrong century, who knows?, you wanted to go deep into the bones of humanity and they just gave you skin instead,

Humility annoys me, it's arrogance that changes the world,

and all those mealy mouthed words, the do you reckon it's possible?, the let's see if I can, the sorry if I'm going too far, without arrogance nothing can happen in the world but mediocrity,

We need to take a risk, to be the best of all, and of all time, or nothing,

and I'll keep trying, grandad, I'll try and I'm so arrogant it actually hurts, you know?, I'm sure nobody does it better than me and I still won't stop, just to create a greater distance, so it's impossible that somebody one day, and there's always somebody one day, isn't there?, would know how to breathe where I am,

I live to dismantle obstacles,

and there's me asking you what dismantling is, to teach words is to teach the world, what's the point of a hug if you don't even know what it is?,

I see the solution in the unknown, never the problem,

if it already exists it's not for me, if it exists it doesn't feel like much, inventing things is the least we can do to give thanks for our existence, are we here to make a difference or to make up the numbers after all?,

They assured me I was going to die of this, and I accepted it after my fashion, but just in case tell your grandmother I love her like a whole field ready for sowing,

and I told her.

You tell me to take the rubbish out with you, and life is so beautiful.

I promised never to like anyone the way I like you and still I don't feel inconsistent, or maybe I do but the most beautiful thing in the world is actually inconsistency, doing now what you couldn't have done earlier, all reason is overrated, since if what makes us happy rarely has any reasonable cause then why should we place reason above all things?

We hug good and tight, leaning on the wall next to the bottle bank, and life is so beautiful.

We've got the whole world against us when we love like this, before you I believed in the possibility of happiness not existing, it was just a childish fable you get told about from an early age, and writers were these diabolical creatures who had created something that could only make us suffer, and loving for ever only existed in the movies, two people in love running towards each other in the middle of the hot sands of a beach, but then you showed up at my cake shop, it's not really mine but it's as if it was because whatever I love is only mine, you smiled fearfully and asked for an orange cupcake, I don't know how, not least because I'm not one for gags or anything like that, but I said no, it wasn't a cupcake, still less was it orange because I don't even like politics, and you, and I still completely melt when I remember it, I swear, you laughed a lot, until you had to cover your mouth with your hand, you were so embarrassed about your laugh, and right there, at that moment, I believed in all the writers in the world, so the bastards had invented what did already exist after all, and probably that's the main function of art (what do I know about art?, but here goes anyway): inventing what already exists is the greatest kind of creation.

An old man is bringing over his rubbish and walks past us shaking his head, and life is so beautiful.

I like it when your tongue finds mine, that's what life should be like, whatever licked the most would be the richest, perhaps it already is, perhaps it is and it's just that nobody's realised it, perhaps wealth is licking whatever life gives us, a yoghurt top, the tongue of whomever we love, even the tongue of someone we don't love but who we want out of nothing but passion, I have no idea, I've never had any idea about these things, I just know that when you lick my tongue with yours I forget who I am and I know myself to be profoundly me, probably that's what love is, love can only be this: what makes us not know who we are and what makes us know ourselves to be profoundly ourselves at the same time.

We climbed the stairs together because the lift is too quick for all the desire we have, and life is so beautiful.

Then we made a date, you said you'd arrive at six and it was five thirty and you were never going to arrive, me drenched with rain, there was still half an hour to go but I couldn't run the risk of not arriving in time, it was four in the afternoon and I was already as happy as though it was six, but in any case it was five thirty and I was in the rain and when you arrived you asked me why I didn't have an umbrella and I asked you what for?, you laughed (I'd exchange my whole life for a second's laugh from you) and you didn't understand that I wasn't even joking, I was standing there drenched and I hadn't even remembered my fucking umbrella because I was just waiting for you to come and I'd been happy since the morning (or before that, I can't guarantee it wasn't earlier still), then you asked why I hadn't taken shelter by the door to the café or the shop, and I asked you again what for?, and this time you laughed less, and when you laugh less the world stops and I need to do something to correct it (isn't that what love is, us doing everything we can to correct a laugh that's less than a laugh from someone we love?), I then grabbed you in my arms, God only knows how I was able to do that but I did it, and there the two of us went, without an umbrella (you dropped yours on the ground and left it there, hopefully someone who wasn't in love found a use for it), going down the road to the restaurant in the certainty that we were going down the road to for ever.

You tickle me when we get home and I twist myself around completely until I've stretched out like a madman on the cold floor, and life is so beautiful.

I was so suspicious of writers and now I'm writing to you as though I was one myself, I hope you aren't thinking about grammar and things like that when you read this, just think that there must be someone who won't believe me when they read me, but then there will be some cake shop or other, and another you for that someone, and then all literature will start to make sense.

You fall asleep on my shoulders and I cry as I look at you, and life is so beautiful.

'Love me as though you'd only just now discovered me.'

On the last night of the year what I fancy is what I've fancied every night of the year: your body with mine, there may not even be an orgasm but I'm happy all the same, and life, really slowly, passing by with your skin on mine.

'Teach me to grow old happy.'

I'm a woman of simple tastes, I wouldn't say I insist on the best, I merely say that I either have the best or I have nothing.

'Promise you'll completely forget about time when you touch me.'

And he promised. It was nearly midnight, the world of that country was trembling with anticipation, there were fireworks almost exploding in the air, a new year is always a good reason to celebrate, and the touch happened.

'Everything happens for a reason, my foot! Everything that really happens is what has no reason at all.'

They weren't, they aren't, perhaps they never will be, a couple like any other, they don't believe in living together, they don't believe in marriage, they don't even believe in children or family. They probably aren't even a couple, if we're going to be strict about it. They believe in the moment of love, as they decided to call it. They love each other as though they were loving life, they consume each other desperately, invent new parts of the skin to taste. Then, each goes back to their house and they devote themselves to loving each other without their bodies having anything to do with it at all.

'I don't know what I love more, your skin or the memory of it.'

They believed above all in a maxim they'd created between them, according to which they mustn't leave any kind of happiness untried. That was why, despite neither of them ever having done it before, they each allowed the other to be free to do whatever they wished to do with whomever they wished to do it.

'We've got to try whatever we fancy.'

That night, as the passing of another day was being celebrated, they returned to the usual ritual. She held him tight, asked him never to let go of her again, he held her and asked her never to let go of him again, they remained like that a few minutes, changing position as they held each other, until she asked him never to let her go again and she let him go, and then he asked her never to let him go again and he let her go. They walked silently out on to the street, where each of them continued on their way and where, once parted, they felt that theirs was the true connection, which allowed them to retain just the best memory of what was loved, just the best moment. They felt, then, fully consummated.

'Please love me with defects.'

Or not. Or it was nothing like that at all. Or she understood that what they loved was one species of love, and she didn't like species of anything at all.

'Either I beget a species or I'm a species of person.'

And he received her in his apartment to which she'd never been before because they'd decided always to meet on neutral territory (why would we bring to a space that's already occupied something we're going to occupy entirely?), and she said, 'I want you even if you're weak, even if you have problems, even if sometimes you annoy me or hurt me, even if we have to suffer like dogs to stay together,' and he opened his arms to her, he said to her, 'I never expected you to love me the way I love you, I've been missing you ever since I've had you, the memories are so good but to tell the truth I prefer the original to the copy.'

'Today I feel like living with you for ever.'

The biggest decisions are those we make without thinking, and today I feel like having you as mine without anybody else touching you, today I feel like being your wife and not allowing you even the least temptation, call me selfish if you want but what you can't accuse me of is leaving happiness untried.

'How many years do you need to know that it's for ever?'

He wasn't sad at being just one woman's all of a sudden, since he'd always been so even when there had been no need, they embraced and this time they decided not even to celebrate the new year any more, there were decisions to be made, a house to choose, all the things that every couple has to do to begin a life together.

'I never thought being normal would be so extraordinary.'

They married and were themselves ever after: all children's stories should end like that. Theirs, however, is a story of adults. But that doesn't mean it isn't childish.

They married and were themselves ever after.

The only thing they could be sure about was that they loved each other, and yet they believed they had everything.

They were young and they didn't know what they were doing, they didn't study what they were supposed to and they didn't learn what they could have; then they became grown-ups and they continued not to know what they were doing and as old people it was exactly the same, maybe it really was just inherent in humans to do what they didn't know how to do, and perhaps that's what they call apprenticeship, I dunno. They believed that love was enough to make life happen, but they forgot there was a living to earn. All of which is to say that she absolutely loved reading but they had no money to buy books; and he didn't love reading – maybe because he didn't even know how to read.

The truth is that love strangely united a woman addicted to reading and a man who didn't know how to read or write, and if that isn't a bad start to any novel then there's no such thing as a bad start to a novel.

And so he picked up work wherever he could, he was pretty skilled with his hands, and she worked as a cook in a restaurant, what she brought home at the end of the month was enough to eat but never to read. Of course there were libraries and things like that, but the closest (they lived in isolation and far from their parents: his had emigrated and hers had forced her to choose between them and the illiterate man she loved, and it's plain to see what choice she made) was many kilometres away and getting the bus there meant leaving work early, which she never, or almost never, managed to do. She worked every day, even Sundays, and only on holidays, when she was able to take holidays, could she feed her addiction and read four or five big classics in a week and be all set to survive the rest of the year.

But there was love, and if there's one thing love doesn't do it's make you give up.

So what happened then was the following: he, without her knowledge, stopped being illiterate, nobody can quite understand how, they say a client of his had lent him some books of his youngest son's who was in the fourth grade, and that he, without her noticing or something like that, managed to understand of his own accord how you connect one letter to another and another to another, and then came the words and finally came the pieces of writing. It was, undoubtedly, a laudable effort for him to have made in the name of love, most probably he was doing it so as to be able to read with her, or simply to be able to share with her those few things she did manage to read, since love is sharing and also friendship; or alternatively he just wanted her to love him even more, to want him even more, that way they'd be able to talk about what they'd managed to read, since what makes love secure is, all things considered, the ability to keep chatting about things.

So we have a man who learned to read and write for love, and that alone would already make a great love story.

But there was more, the man didn't love just any old love and nor was he just any old man, he knew exactly what he wanted when he learned to read and write, which was why nothing could be left undone, and when somebody loves they can even tolerate their own unhappiness but never the unhappiness of the person they love. There was an immense pain inside the woman because she didn't have books to read and she needed books to read (people who saw it happen say she used to read the restaurant menu countless times the moment she arrived just to see if she might find, somewhere in it, any piece of literature that might nourish her), and there was a man who now knew how to write ready to fix it, and so if he already knew how to write then why shouldn't it be him who gives his wife what she so needs?

All great books are written for love, and the first thing he wrote was very far from being a great book but if it wasn't a great book at least that wasn't the reason.

The phrases were constructed basically, the words he used were very rudimentary, the binding was done by hand with thin string and pieces of cardboard he cut out of milk cartons, it was of doubtful taste to say the least, but the truth was that when she received that book (here, read it, it's yours, I hope you like it) from his hands, she needed only to read a line, not even that, to be sure that she was starting to read the most impressive piece of work in all of the world's literature.

When she finished reading, she looked at him with gratitude and wanted to kiss him down to the depths of his bones, but he would only accept one quick kiss and a tough review, and that was what she gave him mercilessly.

There was no time to lose, he jotted down all her criticisms and set to work, all his free time was devoted to this, to his book, and without realising it (and you never realise it when it's the real thing, when it's from the soul) he had become no longer just some odd-job man, some handyman, he was now, yes, a writer, because someone who spends his life writing is a writer and that is all.

The second book was done, it was already quite different, it had the same ugly jacket and the same coarse binding, but what makes a book is the way it talks not the way it's dressed, in that regard books are like people, that's just the way it goes.

By the end of the last line she was crying, he wanted to know why, but she couldn't speak, she just gave him a kiss with her whole life in it and asked him for a bit of time to breathe.

'I've read the best book of my life' was what she said a few minutes later, and he smiled, thinking she was patronising him, and asked her for the tough review he needed. This time she chose to say nothing, he was sad at first but eventually accepted it, and he kept writing, of course, that's the way, keeping on writing, it's what a writer knows how to do, that's just the way it goes.

There was once a couple with everything to suggest they

would go wrong, but there was love and all things considered that's all it takes to go right.

So she understood it was her turn to play dumb, for there are some secrets in love that are proofs of love, and she handed the book (the best one of my life, definitely the best one of my life, and I've read so many and such good ones, it's the best one of my life and I'm not just saying that because it's by the man of my life) to the owner of the restaurant where she worked, the restaurant owner read it and wept and loved it, and gave it to a friend who was a friend of a friend of an important publisher and when, more than three years later, someone knocked on the door of the poor house of the poor couple, the sound you could hear was not the boom-boom on the door, it was the boom-boom of two hearts that, without realising it, had managed to survive entirely on an entire love, can there be any greater sustenance than that?

It was a high-ranking representative of a high-ranking publisher with a high-ranking contract for him to sign, he read it proudly (I know how to read and I can read contracts when they're put in front of me), such an unusual picture to see a writer as happy as a child because he knows how to read, and he signed it at once, he had this strange insistence on trusting people, not without first asking for a small addendum (yes, an addendum, that really is what it's called, and I know that's really what it's called), the proud writer demanded that the publisher guarantee him a daily delivery, to his home, of at least four books, because however hard he tried his writing pace could never keep up with the reading pace of the woman he loved.

And so it was that every day, in the late afternoon, a van from the publishers would stop at the door of their house and drop off four books, sometimes more, and that was how they'd spend their evenings, her reading and him watching her reading, and the whole world and all their effort now made sense for ever.

Of course his book was a resounding success, of course all his books from then on were resounding successes, of course she gave up the restaurant, at least the kitchen of the restaurant (she would later become a business partner of the man who had also helped her man to become his favourite published writer), of course they stopped living in that poor house, but it's also of course the case that the evenings never stopped being like that, her happily reading and him happily watching her reading, and everyone, deep down, comes to this, some people reading happily and other people watching them reading happily, hence there are books so that life can survive.

The only thing they could be sure about was that they loved each other, and yet they believed they had everything.

And they did.

He was a good man, but he hated skin. He was repulsed by touch, sickened by warmth. He loved at a distance, in safety. Or, as he insisted on explaining, 'the way you love a landscape'.

She was a good woman, but she was addicted to skin. She felt a compulsive need for touch, an uncontrollable urge for warmth. She loved through contact, through muscle. Or, as she insisted on explaining, 'the way you love a food'.

One day they met, at some party or other of some friend or other. She said her name and wanted to move close to him for a polite kiss, he said his name and stepped two metres back. All the same, through some impulse which they would both, later, call love, they kept talking. She told him about her family, about her dreams, about her fears, while she advanced, bit by bit, towards him; he told her about his profession, about his plans, about his passions, while he retreated, bit by bit, towards the wall. They did at least two complete circuits of the whole room, a good-sized room of at least fifty or sixty square metres, like this: him retreating from her advances.

Until they decided to talk about their differences.

He explained his theory, that people are beings of soul and not of touch, hence the greatest pleasure is to feel the immaterial, to savour the intangible. Or, as he said over and over again, 'touching with our eyes'.

She explained her theory, that people are beings of veins and not of spirits, hence the greatest pleasure is to nourish what can be felt, to devour the corporeal. Or, as she said over and over again, 'looking with our skin'.

They left the party together, though separated by two or three metres, and got into the same taxi, albeit quite apart. Then he allowed her to touch him for a second, maybe two, and she allowed him only to look at her for a second, maybe two. Next they lay down together, as they would lie down together from then on, each in their own bed in the same house. They lived – and happily, according to all those who knew them – like this. One of their closest friends would describe, one day, how they loved each other in stages: now he'd allow himself to be anaesthetised so that she could touch him for a while, now she would stay still so that he could just look at her for a while. There was never any evidence that this had happened. But it's certainly true that all those who were with them both at the moment when he died heard the last words he spoke to her: 'I want your embrace,' he said to her, to general amazement. And he closed his eyes. 'Now that he can no longer love in his own way, he wants to love in mine,' she said, seconds before following in his footsteps. And they went on, happy for ever, to love each other in just one way.

The doorman told me he saw you going past, you were in your blue school skirt and you were running, I bet you were singing that song of Ralph's or whatever his name is, it's unbearable but if you hear it I've got to hear it, and if you like it I've got to hear it, maybe one day you'll get good taste and start listening to Adele or something,

in any case if you went past the doorman at that time then you must be about to arrive, you'll just stop by Gaby's café to meet up with Joana and Andreia then you'll come,

and I've already taken a seat in the corner desk, all the way back here, waiting for you to come, I hope you sit in the usual place, after all I missed my lunch so as to be here, to be able to say hi to you when you arrive, and so that we can then read the texts together in our Portuguese class, I pretended to forget my book and I know the teacher will tell me I'll never get anywhere with that kind of attitude and he'll tell me about the future and blah blah blah but what matters is that it will get me closer to you, I'm sure of it, you'll be right next to me and we'll read boring old Camões together,

there might even be some cool line or other and I'll read it while I'm looking at you, maybe you'll understand that I'm telling you what I feel and you'll laugh, God willing, and even if God doesn't want it I do.

You really are wearing your blue school skirt and don't hold it against me but I looked at your legs, and as I'd hoped you came over to sit next to me and it wasn't only because you like coming back here and this was the only free place because I'd been occupying it until you arrived with my big football backpack, so if you liked footballers, well, then you'd find out I'm an ace and that I'm the best player in the whole class, but instead you like that Ralph guy even if he can't sing and he's ugly, yes I know I've got to respect you, I've read it so many times that love means respecting the other person and I never learn, sorry,

now you're singing quietly to yourself while the class discusses some line or other, and your voice is so lovely that I could spend my whole life listening to all Ralph's songs so long as you were the one singing them, the amazing thing is I'm singing with you, no one but you could get me to sing this crap that feels so good,

the worst part of it is that the teacher has already spotted us and he's coming over, stand your ground and I'll protect you, I tell the teacher it was me and he gives me an earful, he asks if it was only me and if it wasn't also you and I don't hesitate before saying that, no, you have good taste and you'd never sing anything like that, and the class laughs and you're laughing too, oh God it's so good making you laugh,

the teacher has gone now and you touched my arm with your hand, I swear my skin came alive and my breathing stopped, and in a few minutes the class is discussing some other line and you're singing another of Ralph's songs completely unironically and I laugh all over to hear you sing and I sing with you, some guy my dad likes to listen to says that you don't love someone if you aren't listening to the same song and if he's right then you'll be mine for ever however hard it is, oh boy won't you be, and here comes the teacher, you grab me hard and ask me to help you, and Crazy Joe is laughing because he already knows we'll be out on our ear, he's right and off we go, me and you and disciplinary proceedings and yet I'm still the happiest man in the world, I love you so much and one day you're going to know it, I promise,

so now give me your hand and let's go, the two of us, to Tó's bar to buy chewy candies and think about what we're going to tell our parents to explain that I love you.

You asked me to write you something happy, maybe the secret to the perfect opening of your smile, or the way you cross your legs as though you didn't know that you are the end of the world and the beginning of me.

In any case you asked me to write you something happy and what occurred to me was to tell you that there's a seagull living on the tips of my fingers, I don't know what that could mean but it's what I feel and it's so beautiful and it flies, and deep down that's what binds us, something that you and I don't know but which we feel and which is so beautiful and which flies.

I could also tell you about the silence that connects us, you lying beside me, I write, while inside the cats are stretched out on the sofa in the sun, above us and below us there are neighbours doing things that make noise, doing the washing-up, tidying the house, talking to one another and watching series on TV, but as it happens we are in this bedroom, the light off, just me and my words to you, the bed in chaos, the blanket pulled right up to your neck, your delicious need to lay your skin against mine for you to be able to sleep, a total absence of words, and now you've come over to me once again, what proof of happiness could be greater?

I know we're going to die one day and that hurts, you know?, I know we're going to rot away, too, our skin, these bodies that are now touching, will become flaccid, I might even become more grouchy and you more stubborn, just imagine, and what's left when people stop having their worth determined by their skin and by their bodies is what defines people, some become unbearable and ugly, because everything they had is disappearing, and then there are others, who continue beyond what they've lost, they gain new lives just as this one ends, they stop having their skin and their dreams, but they become so lovely, such depth in their eyes, with such stories to tell, speaking the wisdom of someone who has lived long and believes they still have long to live, the loveliest thing about beauty is that it's not only to be found in what the eyes can see.

I'd have liked us to have been two old adolescents, I think you should know that, I'd like to wake up next to you every morning and look at you for several long minutes just to know that you were there and you were breathing, beside me as you are always beside me, then immediately we would bring our worn old skins against each other's, I'd kiss you gently, feel that your lips still exist, say the deepest I love you that anyone could ever say, and fall back asleep right through the morning, our bodies folded over by time and by our desire to seek each other out to bear it,

and in the afternoon we'd go out for a walk, find out what the city has to show us that's new, talk to people who love us, our children, grandchildren, probably even great-grandchildren, understand that every day we're young in our existence, and finally return home, is there any word more beautiful than that?, our home, the dinner we'd make for the two of us, me peeling the potatoes and the carrots, cooking the rice just the way you like it and how I learned to do it just because you like it, you seasoning it the way only you know how, we could even have our dinner by candlelight, two old people in love and a romantic dinner,

then there would be the sofa, a film about beautiful young people who love each other, just so that we can imagine back again to when we met, our whole lives ahead of us, and then finally bed, me and you and our whole lives beneath the sheets, me snuggling the blanket right up to your neck, our cold feet warming up together, and if death comes let it come there, when I'm with you, and I think it was worth going on for so many years to construct a moment like this.

You asked me to write you something happy and I remembered us, is there any greater happiness than that?

'The shame of the world is that there are numbers.'

That was the way he found to tell her that he felt super-fluous inside that bed, and what's most ironic of all is that the whole thing was a number.

'Whoever invented numbers didn't know how to love.'

She was more concerned about counting orgasms than hearing words, and she went on with the discovery of the two bodies that were beside her, a lot of people would call her a slut if they knew what she liked, but those people didn't know that you often need quantity to silence the quality of what makes us hurt, better to fill your life with noise than for ever to hear the unbearable void of a hole in the middle of your veins.

'There's nothing like nourishing the body to silence the soul.'

After a few minutes, and between one skin and the other, she lay back a bit and showed what she was thinking, she presented her theory, according to which it's essential to give the flesh what it wants so that the soul, even if only for a few seconds, forgets that it exists.

'I would like to be what prevents you from needing more.'

Love me entirely even if it's only out of pity, that was more or less what he meant by that, he'd spent his whole life trying to be her life, he waited for time to pass, for chaos to order itself, and the most he'd managed to be was what he is being now: a body, a number in that complex sum in which two men plus one woman add up to one frustration.

'I'd so like not to see you as a body but please shut up and move on to round three.'

The numbers continued, her body was satisfied, her soul was threatening to emerge, she knew that when she arrived home the silence would return, she'd sit in front of the TV and everything she saw would bring him back, then she'd put on the music they both listened to when they got married, she'd feel the hope and the happiness that she would never feel again, life adding up at last, and she'd end up spending a sleepless night loving him without even knowing where he is.

'If I have to suffer let me at least get some pleasure out of it.'

She lost her shame when she lost her love, is there anything you don't lose when you lose your love?, and they know what they are: two bodies, two evasions, two nameless material objects. They're there to block out the sun as best they can, to share what hurts, to entertain what's left of a woman who one day loved and then never stopped loving, the worst thing about life might well be love, and the best thing about life, too.

'I don't know your name but take me with you.'

She was desperate and she wasn't afraid to show it, he accepted it, even just a bit is better than nothing, and off the two of them went, the other man stayed, he didn't want anything to do with anything except pleasure, most likely the secret of happiness is being able to isolate pleasure, make it the owner of a single space to which even love doesn't have access.

'Let's build a love that's exemplary.'

She heard the promise he made and believed it, she believed that she would at last have what she deserved, a house, somebody romantic, travel, even children, everything well balanced and completely correct, could there be anything more senseless than looking for sense in what you love?

'Let me teach you a love that's good for you.'

And she let him, she continued seeing the other man every day, which didn't do her any good but which made her whole, he saw inside her eyes, inside her actions, inside what was good and inside what was bad, but bit by bit he started to grow smaller: 'less numerous', as she liked to put it, and the very least someone we love can be is numerous.

'The most I have to give you is one or two minutes of hope.'

They were at her wedding, everything adding up very

nicely, and the other man arrived, shabby-looking, his clothes dirty and yet still him, he said what he had to say, what he had to offer, she heard him and smiled, she had to choose between a whole life of good and two or three minutes of for ever. She chose, as she always did when it was time for a decision, mathematics.

'The shame of the world is that there are numbers.'

And love, too.

'I will leave you when I find a reason to be with you.'

The direction of life is moving upwards or it doesn't have one at all, she went on, this time she just thought it, but inside the idea kept on going, he didn't hear it, nobody would ever love anybody if all our ideas were spoken aloud, he scratched his chin and looked out of the window, the sky as naked as he was, the stars empty and a sense that the world is probably about to end.

'I want to love you but all I can manage is to despair of you.'

The abyss of love is the freedom that it takes from us, the certainty that there's a rope around our neck that we cannot master, he went on, he didn't say it but he thought it, their shared history inside his head, an accident caused like in the movies, her picking up her books from the floor, him helping her, and then after that even the high school gave up on parting them, then came university, their dreams, their professions, and suddenly the reason for things appearing, as though reaching a state where it's necessary to understand where love came from?

'It's impossible for what brought us together to exist, and that's why we're together.'

Each person has within themselves a foreign land, she

understood that love was ninety-nine percent discovery and one percent pleasure, or the opposite as you approach the abyss of orgasm, but what she didn't acknowledge was that there existed an affection interrupting the veins, still less a tenderness to calm the breathing, either she felt everything trembling or she was stopped still, and stopping isn't dying: it's worse.

'Sometimes I like stopping still with you just to look at what we are.'

Opposites compact and no scientist has ever understood love, the stars go on, a stray cat rummages in the trash in search of one more day of life, he lights a cigarette, his lips tremble and squeeze the filter as though squeezing fear, tomorrow the day will return, and in the silence he tries to find the importance of the words, what can you do when you've loved too much?

'Today all I want from your mouth is a kiss.'

Neither did the windows close nor the words continue, he yielded as he always did, she only had to hesitate for him to comply, to dictate to somebody is to be loved by somebody, and she didn't want to dictate or be dictated to, she just believed in the perfect state of what is unexplored, she preferred what was left unsaid, to retain the hope that what's not in view is better than what there is to be seen, and when the bodies were tired out she fell silent and moved away, many people would think it coldness but to her it was love, she used what was perfect to save herself from tears: and she cried.

'Tomorrow I swear I'll want you for love but today I want you for survival.'

Those were his last words in the early hours of that morning,
          and all those others that came after.

the worst part of all isn't even the crying, it's not that at all, crying makes you suffer but it also calms, what hurts dissolves into water and everyone knows that, you have to wet the thing that cuts so that the cutting hurts less, and

the worst part of all isn't even the crying, I say again, I know you're asleep and you can't hear me, I preferred to stay awake to try and understand how your eyelids close, the round shape of your eyes when you sleep deeply, and touch your skin lightly and thank the good fortune of this bed and us, your legs on mine, so heavy that they hurt and I bear it, better the pain of your weight than your absence weighing me down, resting my head on your arm and your shoulder, hearing you breathe, and finally breathing, and

the worst part of all isn't even the crying, I don't know if I've mentioned this already, when I wake up I seek you out with my arms, perhaps even before I wake up, my body asleep and already homeless, as though it wanted to guarantee its survival even before being born, you're sleeping and you don't know it but I love you with my body too, a muscular love, you might call it that, and when you went to sleep and straight after said three or four times 'I love you, Carla', I understood that love's like that and that's why we love, so that not even sleep will stop us loving, and in this we are the same, we love even while we're asleep, and it's so beautiful having such a great love, and the worst part of all isn't even the crying, this is the last time I'm going to tell you, I promise, because the worst part of all isn't even the crying, it's that there's nobody to see our tears, the world in a state of collapse and everything around us as though it were happening, the worst part of all, I'm actually going to tell you one more time, isn't even the crying, it's crying alone, our tears and nobody with them, homeless tears, and

the worst part of all is nobody being there to see your tears,

and my name not being Carla, of course.

'I need one euro to go on not needing any money.'

There's a strange peace in a person who doesn't have a roof over his head, the tramp who asks me for a euro smiles without my being able to understand why, he has nothing and he smiles and I who have so much find it hard to believe, maybe he's here because he wants to be, he doesn't look like a junkie, he looks good and he's happy, but nobody gives charity to someone who looks good and is happy, charity is only given to those who need it and someone looking good doesn't need it, that's the law of appearances, ninety percent of the world is appearances and the other ten looks bad.

'I used to be a lawyer then I grew up.'

What must the price of freedom be, probably the price of a house, a career, when I imagine this happy wretch in a suit and tie standing in front of a judge it doesn't stop me feeling sorry for him, what's the use of money if not to obstruct, I don't know if I should give him a euro or my whole life, my clothes, my car, all that I am, what is this preposterous temptation?

'The problem with money is that it's not made of chocolate.'

He sits down next to me, me and the tramp next to the

car I'd left in his park, and the two of us look up at the size of the sky, there are more stars than yesterday, and without even realising it I'm understanding the value of money, or at least of chocolate money, he offers me a five-euro note that's nice and sweet, and in a moment I stop understanding why the piece of paper I have in my pocket is worth more than this piece of chocolate, his hand patting me indulgently on the back, which of the two is a poor wretch, the one who works to have pieces of paper in his pocket or the other who spends his life with pieces of chocolate in his mouth?

'I stopped believing in science when they told me I had to die.'

And off he goes, he apologises for having to go but the perfect wave is just about to arrive, he picks up a piece of wood that's leaning on the wall and he doesn't even say goodbye, the perfect wave is just about to arrive, and there I stay, an important meeting ahead of me, dozens of ties and professional gentlemen, schedules and salaries, I go into the office building and I still have time to see him in the distance, the perfect wave hasn't yet arrived but he doesn't need it to be able to feel it, the science of life is feeling above all what doesn't exist, and when I arrive late to the meeting I just say that I've been looking for myself.

'Would you give me just a moment and I'll be back never again.'

And they did.

'If one day I'm not here, look for my words.'

The basis of humanity is syntax, he added, it was in the word that he saw the beginning of the world, whenever he met someone he didn't want to know who they were, what they were like, what they had, he wanted only to understand what they said, the perfect woman was one who used the perfect words, and however inadequate all the rest was, words were enough for all the rest to happen, and then she arrived and said

'In you I see the beginning of the world.'

At a different time it would have been the ideal subject for an ideal debate, he would say with the full force of his convictions that it wasn't him but the word where everything began, then he'd give examples of great poems that changed the geography of the world, then he'd open one or two books and read two or three lines and within moments whoever heard him would understand that, yes, it had to be yes, hearing those lines changes the whole world, and finally there was an embrace and the certainty of having managed to convert more people, and the only thing we'd need would be the word, always the word, without words we are animals, he'd repeat again and again till nobody could forget it, but now she spoke and he didn't reply, he was looking at her and hoping she'd talk more, even the silence before a word beginning is a kind of word, he would have said were he not silent and unable to stop being silent, what back alleyway does language come from?

'The basis of humanity is your skin.'

When she approached she had already touched him all over, but hands count too of course, especially when they grab hold of a body, pull it towards her, there was also the mouth, hers on his, the tongue, the woman consuming him and him without a word and all the same everything making sense, what the hell is this that says everything and doesn't even need to speak?

'Tell me now or disappear for ever.'

There are moments when people have to be spoken, he knows this before anybody else, more than anybody else, but he doesn't say it, he wants to say it but he doesn't, he just looks at her, standing there in front of him, their bodies asking for the right word, the right phrase, and nothing, nothing comes out of his mouth apart from a desire to kiss, to press his mouth against hers, she's far away, more than a metre away and still waiting for his words, this man who is a specialist in silent words, all her veins unable to understand the syntax.

'If one day I'm not here, look for my words.'

That was what she said before leaving, it was in the word that she saw the beginning of the world, and when she met someone she didn't want to know who they were, what they were like, what they had, she wanted only to understand what they said, the perfect man was one who used the perfect words, and however inadequate all the rest was, words were enough for all the rest to happen, and then he arrived and said.

'When I see you with open eyes you can absolutely kill me as I'll be dead already.'

And you made me that promise, yes, you'd kill me, people might even be interesting but they do have the problem that they exist, I'm interested in what does not exist, and that's where you come in, the least possible person in the world, there's no way of explaining you and hence the reason for everything I'm looking for.

'I spend the whole day in search of you when I have you by my side.'

That was what he was always telling her, the two of them arm in arm and him explaining to her that he wasn't interested in anything that you could see with your eyes, then he introduced her to a theory according to which it's only with your eyes closed that you could see what mattered, he even offered a few examples, orgasm, adrenaline, even fear, everything worthwhile you couldn't see with open eyes, when you can see there's a non-life, a half-baked little life, and he took her everywhere except home just so as to avoid the end of what kept him alive.

'Your body is always for the first time.'

Today they are in a motel which is not to be recommended

but yet to be discovered, he only loves her as if she were new, his eyes closed and him on her, the legs, between the legs, the mouth, inside the mouth, sometimes he opens his eyes just to see where he is but it's when he closes them that he finds himself, and she doesn't know what she's seeing, looking at him with all her eyes, with all herself, her sweaty body telling her she exists.

'Close me in your eyes so you can love me.'

She believed in love at first sight, she asked him every day to look at her with his eyes open, to love her with his eyes open, they had opposite ways of loving and that was how they managed to love each other, until one day he understood that he was wrong, that she deserved to be looked at, no one knows how many years it took for this to happen, but it did, he found her so many years later, after so many years of loving her and finally he looked at her.

'I was blind when I didn't want to see you.'

That was what he said, but suddenly he felt a knife being plunged into the middle of his chest, a physical knife, at least it hurt like a physical knife, the pain spreading right across his body, an empty pain, a pain that didn't hurt except through a lack of something, a pain that resembled the loss of a finger, perhaps a whole hand, him looking at her and being sure that he loved her but at the same time being sure he'd seen too much, seen what he should not have, all the illusions on the sharpened blade of a knife inside him.

'Loving is the inability to open your eyes.'

I wanted to be inadequate, I wanted to try and see you and not be able to, my eyes always closed, but now I saw too much and now you exist, and if there's anything that is not loved it's what exists, if it exists it can be explained, there's a science to support its existence, its shape, everything it is, if there's a science to explain it then it can no longer be what I love, either it can be loved or it can be explained, you can't love what science comprehends, I see you so much and not even like that can I love you.

'I love you completely and it feels like so little.'

This is what he'd say before saying goodbye to her, there was a promise to be kept, and she would never fail to keep her promise, he would definitely understand, it was only the police who wouldn't.

Staying still is intolerable. Not changing. Bearing-up. Surviving. Remaining. Even if there's not very much, even if there's not enough. Keeping everything the way it is just to avoid running the risk of its getting worse. Not forgiving, not acquiring, is intolerable. It's just criticising, just pointing, just attacking. And not creating, not remaking, not imagining. Not believing is intolerable. What isn't marvellous is intolerable, what isn't delicious, what isn't fantastic, monumental, blessed, miraculous, astonishing. Waking up to the day only to refuse the day, that's intolerable, or not wanting the day, not fancying the day, not thinking about the thousand and one ways of making it unforgettable. Leaving it be. Not moving, not wanting the wound if it's through the wound that you come to the cure. Being cautious, forewarned. Everything that isn't exaggerated is intolerable, that isn't disproportionate, that doesn't seem prohibitive. If it doesn't seem prohibitive it's unbearable. I don't want it. I won't allow it. I won't allow myself. Repetition is intolerable. Today as an exact replica of yesterday and as an exact replica of tomorrow. The same things, the same words, the same actions, the same movements. Always identical. Always the same. Going on for the sake of going on, that's intolerable, continuing for the sake of continuing, living for the sake of living. What's normal is intolerable, what's regular. What never killed anyone but also never changed anyone's life. What doesn't mess with your guts. The text that doesn't stir you up, the decision that doesn't transform you, the kiss that doesn't make you tingle, the sex that doesn't make you moan, cry out, leap. Not being in love, that's intolerable. With a woman, with a man, with a cat, with a dog, with a smell, with a sun, with a job, with a house, with a skin, with a taste, with a dream, with a job, with a path, with a desire, with a sin. In love. Like a lunatic. In love. Recklessly, frantically. Unceasingly. In love. With all your veins in search of passion, with all your body in search of pleasure. What isn't extraordinary, that's what's intolerable. And extraordinary things don't demand extraordinary actions. Extraordinary things only ask for easy moments. As ordinary as cuddling a blanket, sharing a dessert, having a dip in the sea, stealing oranges from the neighbour's tree, spending the afternoon telling jokes, listening to your parents' stories, going to the park with your kids, sharing a table with your friends. Extraordinary things demand nothing extraordinary of you. And that's precisely why they're extraordinary. Like extraordinary people. Oh, those extraordinary people. I'm addicted to extraordinary people. To those who manage incredible feats. Like making me happy, for example. My wife is extraordinary. So beautiful I can't even tell you. And she loves me. How she loves me. How she wants me. How I want her. And she's more extraordinary every day. Pity on me if she weren't. And the hardest thing is sustaining passion. Avoiding the intolerable. The intolerable replicating, the intolerable keeping going, the intolerable bearing-up. The intolerable gerund. Carrying on living is the same as carrying on dying. What's normal is intolerable. I demand the extraordinary. And all those I love are extraordinary. Oh God, I'm such a happy man. So happy. Even when I cry, even when I hurt, even when it's tough, even when everything I am, everything I need, seems so little. I'm so happy. It's such an extraordinary feeling, so extraordinary to want like this, to exist like this. Until the ends of your guts, to the depths of your bones. Not suffering, not struggling, they're intolerable. What isn't too much. And only what isn't too much is a mistake. Making no mistakes, that's intolerable, I'm sure about that. But the most intolerable thing is not to love. I love you excessively, I'm sorry. But the really intolerable thing, I may have mentioned this to you already, is not to love.

What I have been hurts me so nearly,

legs opening slowly to death, you know?,

the worst thing is the body that life's got to put up with, we're made of junk and we just have to bear it, it's in the small gestures that old age happens, when I have to bend myself over to pick a piece of paper up from the floor, when I have to go down the stairs and my knees ache, when even my arms as I write show me that I will end,

when I was twenty I had forty years till I'd turn sixty and now that I'm sixty I was twenty just a month or two ago, at most,

time happens to our whole selves, and the worst thing of all is that we remember perfectly what we used to be able to do, it's so appalling,

all memories have the precision of a target,

when I was a child, old people were the strangest creatures, the most distant figures, absurdly mysterious, I was as far away from them as I am now from myself, in truth, but I need a body to live, that's the biggest injustice of all,

have you seen what we'd be capable of if we had no need of flesh, skin and bones?,

it isn't what must be that has great strength, it's what can no longer be,

only an idiot can have invented photography,

what possible happiness could come from pictures of what has already died in us?,

once upon a time it's already in the past, the best way for an old man to suffer is to believe in what doesn't exist within him, like the poor guy who lives opposite, a month in the hospital because he wanted to compete on a fucking bicycle, if he'd just been able to swap bodies the old man would have won, I'm sure,

swapping bodies would be enough for us to keep going, it seems simple enough for a God who's invented all this, doesn't it?,

an old man is a library, and how wretched mine is, I just wanted to learn and I have to content myself with teaching,

the lucky thing is that death kills but orgasm does too,

go on, that's it, come,

and still I don't stop being here,

if there's one thing I'm grateful for it's pleasure, anybody who doesn't believe in miracles has never come like this,

listen to the old guy and learn.

You've left at last and I can try out freedom, watch football all day long, stay out with my friends till late, drink as many beers as I'm in the mood for, go beyond the limits that your presence imposed on me, try visiting all those websites that Heitor from the office told me about, life exists and it's so good.

You've left at last and the space of the house is mine alone, I don't even need to tidy it up much, I stretch out on the sofa and time just passes, occasionally a woman will visit, pleasure really is so simple after all, nothing to tie me down, I'm a free man and I have to make the most of it, life exists and it's so good.

You've left at last and I'd been missing me, looking at myself noiselessly, thinking about the meaning of the world, realising what I am and what I want, devoting myself to discovering where I begin and where I end, understanding the importance of mistakes, building a new Me, and above all smiling, life exists and it's so good.

You've left at last and today you didn't answer the phone to me, maybe you're at the parents' meeting, but you could have answered as it was important, I wanted to tell you that I'm well and I send you my regards, thank you for not being here and making me happy, I'll try again soon, life exists and it's so good.

You've left at last and I enjoyed having dinner with you yesterday, your hands gently touching mine as we reached for the glass at the same time, some coincidences are worth it, and your hair so big, so free, you said something about a bit of paper we both have to sign, I didn't hear you and just looked at you, the inside of your eyes is so beautiful, but I have another woman I met in the library and I'm happy without you, life exists and it's so good.

You've left at last and soon I'll be going to fetch you at home, I've bought a suit at a shop in the mall, this cologne is the one you gave me for my birthday two years ago, I'm picturing you in the green dress that brings out your eyes, the restaurant's already booked, me and you in front of the sea, or next to the sea, whatever, it'll be you there and your hair loose, we'll definitely talk about our lives and about what we've done, I don't care, to tell the truth, I'll have two hours or more of being able to look at you, and who knows, maybe after that we could take a walk in the park, share an ice cream for two perhaps, life exists and it's so good.

I'm seduced by the existence of one day after another, my father's wrinkled hands on mine, my mother's open smile since the very beginning. I'm seduced by hearing the grocery man's stories, my grandfather's frank confessions, my older cousin's jokes. I'm seduced by the absurd dissatisfaction of being alive, the unbearable cost of temptation, the colour of the sun on the city's stone. And the woman who sells chestnuts on the street, the teacher who teaches as though he were teaching life, the mystery of cats, the dog's happy tail when his owner arrives. I'm seduced by the child with a desire for everywhere in his eyes, the hot taste of tea, the intimacy of a love letter hidden in the drawer, even the haughty way a bird takes flight. I'm seduced by the modesty of geniuses, the way the sea consumes the sand, the deafening silence of complicity, one friend in the arms of another, the solitary tears of an ecstasy. I'm seduced by the constant questioning of the adolescent, the fundamentals of pleasure, the desire to live for ever beneath the sheets. And the noise of the rain on the glass when we're loving, hands warming on a boiling hot mug, the steam in my face freeing me from hurt. And I'm seduced by getting up to face the day, believing in the existence of people, reading on the balcony on summer nights, writing the perfect line of poetry, closing my eyes and managing to dream. I'm seduced by sharing a newspaper on a train, inventing a past for someone I don't know, offering a banknote to a homeless person. I'm seduced by so many things, so many things, but nothing seduces me like the movement of your legs when they open to me, the small moan only I can hear when you kiss me, the almost second in which you ask me wordlessly for pleasure, the perfect geometry of your clothes strewn around the floor of the house, the complex algorithm of the sum of our skins. I'm seduced by so many things, so many things, but nothing seduces me like knowing that so many things have seduced me since I met you, and that you still seduce me just the same. I'm seduced, and I obeyed.

'It ended because it took up too much space.'

She explained to him why she had to go, she schematised motives (you're reckless, you don't want the same life I want), she elaborated conclusions (it's not going to work, you're too big in me for the small space you want us to occupy in you), but the truth is that he had already left long before and she was still there just talking to herself, giving up on somebody who doesn't love us is less painful than being abandoned, however much it may be exactly the same thing, words have always been the best way to suffer.

'Silence me with your body, please.'

Ever since she had lost him (where are you if you aren't looking for me?), she'd been trying new diversions, alternative skins, alternative smells, finding salvation in perdition, and however many men she had (who are you and what are you doing inside my body?) he was always the one she fell asleep with, she retrieved the sheets she kept in the cupboard, laid them down on the sofa, rolled herself up in them and imagined the door opening and her whole life coming back in, the impotent tears, she knew she ought to bear it, that she ought to survive, but nobody survives a love, at least not alive.

'One day I woke up and you were gone.'

What happens when a love goes?, you fall asleep with it and then the day comes, and the light, you look next to you and it no longer is, and when I looked at you that morning and you looked back at me and I saw that, no, there was a hole in the centre of my chest, you were the most beautiful woman in the world but I no longer loved you, and there's no greater reason than not loving the person we wake up with, one day it ends as it began, and I began loving you without knowing how, me and you and our first kiss, our first bed, me waking up beside you, the feeling of for ever, there's always a bed and a waking up to decide who loves.

'Lie on me and make me wake up.'

He allowed himself to be seduced and she returned to the house, to the bed, he wanted to understand if it was still happening, if love explained itself, and they lay down, and she was happy once again, so happy once again, and they loved each other, bodies and nostalgia, moans, orgasms, and finally sleep, sleep arrived and when they looked up they would understand what there was uniting them, there's always a bed and a waking up to decide who loves.

'Uncertainty is enough for me to be able to love you.'

There was no exact conclusion, the morning arrived, he looked at her and didn't see her as the for-ever woman and he didn't stop seeing her as the for-ever woman, he looked at her and wanted to embrace her, to give her a kiss where her face began, then he said something to her that made her cry, she just said stop talking and do it, within a few minutes their sexes were in charge, the bed sweaty, him compliant and faced with the impossibility of an explanation, love really can be what makes us have no certainties, or it's nothing of that at all, but being with her counted for everything, that much is true.

'One day I wake up and I don't know if I love you, and that's how we love.'

She couldn't forgive him for loving her like this.

One day he asked her to stop being perfect, she replied with an utterly perfect yes, she grimaced and he said 'lovely', then she stripped naked, her whole body, all her flaws, she drew his attention to the stretch marks on the backs of her legs, a scar in the middle of her stomach, begged him to look closely, and by the time she realised what was happening he was already crying, his eyes and his perverseness in believing that even what aesthetics condemns is admirable, love is blind and it really opens our eyes.

After the storm comes the orgasm.

They embraced with all their lives in their arms, it's not clear how tightly they held each other but certainly when they detached themselves, more than half an hour later, there were deep marks on each one's back and skin, they had to return to their jobs, routine constraining the eternal, she talked to him about the scale of her fear, of the brief interval between courage and madness, he preferred to expound on the brief interval between death and routine, all of it in seconds and the aching of the clock, there's a moment when you have to choose between losing yourself in life and a life lost.

They still had madness to keep them sane.

They wasted hours discussing the uselessness of loving and when they finished they'd changed their lives, she said that love hurt, erased, lit up, wept, created, destroyed, constructed, fell ill, leapt, moaned, suspected, was left over, laughed, tore, cut, stuck, sewed, touched, fled, freed, tied, looked, hid, and he added that besides this love also killed, lied, seduced, taught, led, possessed, discovered, dominated, thrilled, infected, controlled, rejoiced, feared, and all that was why it was no use at all.

They gained a deep understanding of the stupidity of loving and only then did they love.

There was no news report that they had returned to their jobs, nobody ever understood how it was they lived and what they subsisted on, they knew only that they were always together, and that when someone asked them, more than forty years later, what they did, they just replied 'we love', and the person who asked realised the absurd silliness of what they'd just asked.

Fairy tales don't exist, the fairy tells us.

'Go on, I'll pay you with a smile.'

That was what the woman said, the man and a tube going in his nose, another two or three stuck into his veins, his arm hurt with so many cures that needed performing, all around the smell of slumped people, the white dirty walls, illnesses smell of something indecipherable, perhaps there's some way of dying that doesn't need that smell.

'Don't look at me like that or I'll jump you, you bastard.'

And he smiled, he knew she wouldn't, she couldn't, sex had stopped, like his whole body had stopped, ever since this had started, his wife sitting there, and his wife so very beautiful, and her smile, if life had ever given him one good thing it was that smile, her eyes wide whenever she looked at him, the certainty that he was loved as though he were the only man in the world, and the illness interrupting this love, where have you ever seen a body that wanted to stop something like this?

'If God exists He is not between us.'

This time it was her who smiled, or even laughed, at his words, she missed having him beside her on the bed, yes, his tight body, his strong arms, all his fear squeezed inside his chest, yes, she missed having him beside her on the bed, but she missed his words even more, the way he made her laugh at nothing and everything, always ready with some corny jokes, the way he was so clumsy at home and needed her for everything, love is more than anything needing someone for everything.

'Go on, I'll pay you with a smile.'

She insisted, he finally agreed, he struggled to his feet, the blue smock revealing half of his thin body, she put his arm around her waist, gave his ass a furtive squeeze and he laughed quietly, she took him to a big, spacious room, with daylight coming in, and the two of them like boyfriend and girlfriend, then she gave him a gentle, very gentle kiss, on the left side of his face, she felt the wrinkles and the harsh skin and it tasted to her of love, he raised his hand and took hers, all his strength going into that movement, into the moment when their hands joined, a passing nurse wiping away her tears, maybe a death in the next bed, and he and she savoured that smile, her opening hers up completely, him happy to be smiling with her, the tubes and blood invisible, the two of them with their eyes closed, so much health, all memories heal and kill in equal measures.

'Don't tell anyone, but that smock turns me on.'

She could have cried but she was laughing, with him back in bed now, visiting hours over, a desire to stay there and never leave, to die here, with him, him smiling goodbye, him saying 'I know what it is you want', he's good at kidding around when things get this serious, maybe it'll be different tomorrow, maybe tomorrow the nurse will say he can go, that everything's fine, that this crappy illness has backed off, maybe tomorrow, not today as she's already gone, maybe tomorrow, there are moments when just having a tomorrow is enough.

'Go on, I'll pay you with a smile.'

And he smiled,
and went.

I've just met you and that proves the non-existence of the past.

And she arrived late (I'm so sorry, the traffic, the traffic), she sat down hurriedly at the table and waited for his question, recorder in his hand (I see the precise world in your eyes, I don't know what that means but I see the precise world in your eyes), she smiled (yes, that's a passage from my book, just as well you've read it, good that somebody's read it, did you like it?) then blushed slightly, her eyes wandered over to the wall of the café, then up to the ceiling, finally to the waitress who came over with a tray in her hand (hello, what's it to be?), and he (her kiss and then death) asked for a piece of toast and a glass of milk, wanting to cry and wanting a hug, how many hugs does each person owe the world?

I don't find any beauty at all in your face, and you're so beautiful.

He said yes (your best ever, I read it three times in one night, seriously, I'm not exaggerating), his hands were trembling and he wanted to touch, even if only lightly, hers, she wanted to say something intelligent which was why she had to keep quiet, she waited for a question, that was why she was here, to be asked, she didn't have to wait long (how many men have you written into the man you loved?), it wasn't quite what she'd been expecting, it wasn't what she'd been expecting at all but strangely she had the answer on the tip of her tongue (only you), her hand pulled on his, the earth stopped spinning, but it was just a joke (yes, I do like the title, it was one of the things that most fascinated me about the book), she let go of his hand and smiled, how many truths does a person owe the world?

It must be unbearable living with you, do you want to marry me?

And the worst thing was he really did say that, this time it wasn't a quote, at least not one she remembered, she wanted to smile but couldn't do it, she wanted to remain serious but couldn't do it, she wanted to stay still but couldn't do it, she wanted not to get up and hug him but couldn't do it, and he couldn't do anything, least of all not cry when he had her in his arms, least of all not tell her that he loved her even though he didn't know her, least of all not tell her he was sure that she was nothing that she wrote and that was why he loved her, she just said yes, she'd marry him, once, as many times as she needed to, every day if necessary, they walked out of the café and didn't even pay or take the recorder, they ran far away to be able to be close, the café owner standing there with the recorder in his hand, the waitress not knowing who to give the bill to, the sun high in the sky, an old lady sitting in her garden and a smile, how many people does a person owe the world?

I don't believe in God but I believe in you, oh yes, I do.

Life exists at the moment when you change, you're either inconsistent or you're dead, and being at night the same as I was by day is a waste of a day.

'Hi, I'm Jaime and I haven't changed for forty-eight hours.'

Applause in the hall, everybody's afraid of addiction, the most disloyal servitude of all.

'You're just the same and you've managed to change everything in me.'

People need people. To bear things, to escape, to grow, to live. But also to die.

'My Jaime.'

Possession excites. Having excites. The woman who is now sticking her tongue into Jaime's mouth has. And excites. Jaime should know.

Borderline cases are able to cross the borderline. Any border, actually. There was, when he woke up to face the day, a man content with his reality, breathing peacefully, confident that all life boils down to being at peace. And there is, now, as he lies down for the night, a man who can barely breathe. And who, for this reason, is more alive than ever: breathing better than ever. All life boils down to being at peace, and for this very reason disquieted.

'Hi, I'm Jaime and I'm addicted to you.'

Meetings that change the world require, on average, only two people. The one who loves. And the one who is loved. And then it stops: the one who loves becomes loved; the one who is loved starts to love. People are afraid of addiction, and it's only when they're addicted that they manage to let go of it.

'I heard about a guy who managed to free himself of his addiction and now I'm going to his funeral.'

Complicity relates to accomplices. An extreme complicity is all you need to die. And also to live.

'I have an infallible memory but I no longer remember why.'

Happiness doesn't belong to those who live better. Happiness belongs to those who forget better (remember this always).

'Hi, I'm Jaime and I no longer know my name.'

You're the best person I have in me.

I love you and it's the fault of the person who loves me so much but it isn't you, the cruelty of the world is that there are so many people and only you are you, and I can't forgive God for having created millions of possibilities, millions of arms and embraces, and then so many lips, and none of them gives me what you give me, the cruelty of love is that it takes away from us the possibility of another love, how many lives would I need to find you again?

I want you for what you are – but even more for what you make me be.

And feel, above all what you make me feel, I watch you as you sleep, the way you move, your skin in search of mine, and I believe that's the only way I am, the thing that concerns itself with the way you lie, with the smell of your skin, with the so-small space that the two of us together occupy in the bed, there might even be sex, of course, but the space where we are is the space where the best thing that I know happens, loving like this might not even be healthy but it does me so much good.

I wake up with you like somebody who wakes up to heaven.

It doesn't matter what the day's going to be like, what the

hell I'm going to have to put up with, what I'm going to have to do to make life happen again, there are so many things to hurt us, so many tears we know we cannot defeat, but it doesn't matter what's coming down the track if at the end of it all there's the night and you, our bed, stretching my body out and hearing you breathe, that's enough, so many heavens and your moment stopped within me, the best of days is the day that brings you.

May my mother forgive me but it was you who gave me life.

You might think they're just words, so easy to say, how many poets have lied about love before now?, and there's so much bullshit for each useful phrase, but the truth is that what happened to me is simple, there was a being to love and then there was a being who was loved, and it's when you love that life happens, if I ruled the world that would be the only place a registry would happen, we'd have a card with our date of birth, 'born 30 January 2014', we'd choose our name with the person we loved, whoever came up with the idea of saying that it's when our body is born that we become people didn't know anything about love, nobody exists until they love, before you I was just a path towards me, an almost me, a kind of me, I loved you for myself to happen.

If they want to know where I am, let them search for you, and then look by your side.

Words are also good for loving.

We talk enough for so much to be left unsaid, you arrive tired, your work, the company, friends, football, bills, you let everything pass through the spaces you don't fill, and when I hug you and ask you how your day's been you say your regular Just The Usual, not one detail, not one story, where did those days go when you used to tell me everything?, where's the euphoria from when nothing existed between life and words?, if you just said I Love You that'd be enough and everything in me would be calmed, three little words, you didn't even need to say any more than that, to do any more, what's the distance between a word and poetry?, you could stay just as you are, the sofa, the TV and your eyes lost, just a few words and I'd be yours for ever, love needs everything, even including a bit of grammar.

One day I'll leave you to be able to love you again.

At dinner we are two different worlds, we exchange phrases the way you might exchange a dish, we're on the surface of something that's increasingly deep, there was so much to find but neither of us has the courage to look, open up the cracks, tear them down to the bones, rip the flesh off this intolerable peace that is tolerating us, and understand what remains of us, what is left over from what we once knew we were, and it could be me, I could be the one to tell you I can no longer bear it, I no longer want it, it hurts too much, but the truth is I'm a coward and I'd rather invent love in your embrace, invent an orgasm in your cold need, invent an I Love You in your empty Fuck Me, I could be a brave woman and lose you so as to be in a position to win you again, but I'm afraid of your discovering that you can lose me and still be alive, there's always at least one coward when there are two unhappinesses.

Today I will seduce you or I'll kill you in me.

I've changed the furniture so as to seek you better, maybe the geography of a house will bring you back, then I bought a new outfit, with a tight skirt, even a little make-up, your favourite food in the oven, you come in and I smile at you, I kiss you with my tongue and you find it strange, I ask you for a hug, I so miss being hugged tight by you, my love, you surrender your arms, even a bit of your back and your torso, but you're so far away that not even the dream can see you, how many parts are you divided into to keep yourself whole?, I fancy giving up right now but I insist, loving until the very last also means trying until the very last, I hitch up my skirt a little and ask you for pleasure, you need to know how to be a whore to know how to love entirely, and when you came it was time to go.

When I'm ready to live without you, then you can come and fetch me.

That was what she said, with her suitcases and not

another word, there were a lot of tears to cry outside, she wanted something from a storybook, the romance, the white horse, the bent-backed kisses, even the prince if at all possible, he didn't realise how he had failed her, he'd always done what showed up in books, being faithful, being respectful, taking care of the bills and being a good head of the family, and what separates a couple is often the wrong literature.

All unhappinesses should be for love, and all happinesses too.

I'm proud of the time when I cry, of seeing the human dimension in the look in a dog's eye, of caressing hands with my mother's wrinkles, of the filled-up space of a hug with someone I love, and there is nothing about pain that prevents me from believing in love.

Courage is the heroic side of love, and it's an idiot too.

And so today I said to him I wanted him stretched out in my arms, I talked to him about my life being occupied by his, I told him all the stories about when I used to wander the streets hoping to see him, I'd leave home in the morning, nice and early, I was just a teenager and I didn't even have any classes, but off I went, going out nice and early, I'd get into the packed rush-hour bus and had no interest in books or anything else, I walked the streets looking for him, I knew what time his father dropped him off by the park, I knew he would then go for breakfast with his mates at Cunha's patisserie, I'd just be there watching him without taking any initiative at all and without even feeling unhappy, we had our whole lives to love each other and maybe if I'd made a move then it would have been too early, and there is nothing about time that prevents me from making it stop.

I waited twenty years to ask you to marry me, and later also to tell you my name.

And when you looked at me and didn't find my request strange nor my words, I realised that all this time we'd been in the process of forming this minute, I was braver, I'm almost forty already and though you wouldn't know it my body is no longer what it was, I'm afraid it's age that will prevent you from fancying it, I don't want to risk anything more and that's why I took the risk, you didn't react badly, a smile, an 'I'm already married but thanks', not bad, I have to admit, there are eternal loves that start off much worse than that, you should know, I respect your chances for happiness too much, I'm not going to insist on loving you and like that I will love you, you'll be happy and you owe it to me even if you'll never know it, and nothing about your not being happy with me prevents me from feeling important in your happiness.

I'm so happy in your happiness, and in the happiness of whoever is making you happy, too.

And one day the wind is blowing your way, like now, when I left, the sky overcast and everything prepared for another absence of you, and suddenly your hand on my shoulder, a simple smile, how am I to explain to the world that the beginning of the dream is what keeps us alive?, your words as though they were the invention of life, and nothing about being the happiest woman in the world when you kiss me prevents me from feeling unhappy with each second that you aren't kissing me.

Love me for ever but most importantly of all love me always, and also right now.

I'm proud of the occurrence of us, and nothing in the occurrence of a future prevents me being reckless.

Pleasure is the first of arguments, and the last too.

'Today we're going to stop being rational and we're going to be Men',

explained the woman, and she slowly started undressing, words are useful for undressing, and even more so for loving.

'Something is useful to me is the most damnable expression I know, nobody can accept anything, nobody can condemn themselves to what is useful to them. The only thing useful to me is the certainty that I love you, and little more than that',

the naked skin of one was already hidden under the naked skin of the other, and the reason for all things consists, give or take a little, of orgasm.

'There are people who satisfy themselves with an explanation of impossibility. There are people for whom it's enough to understand that it can't be this, or simply why it must be that. There are people who don't want to interpret what could be and prefer to realise what has to be. I don't, in this bed, see any of those people. And it's hard for me to understand, but it's so good',

perhaps they were coming to some agreement now, at least on the matter of the uselessness of sheets and the pleasant way they fell on the floor there seemed to be consensus, as well as on the question of the bed's interesting capacity to support the occurrence of pleasure, only what has been created to support love ought to exist, even people.

'The world is divided into two kinds of people: those who understand life, and those who are happy. Only what's absurd creates change, and if life isn't change then it might well also be the case that philosophy doesn't exist, at least not one that makes sense of me. It's so easy to do what has to be, and then carelessly forget what only might possibly be. It's so easy to make reason explain things, and not understand that the reason we exist is in the simple possibility of losing it entirely, free will is the way God found for saying orgasm',

they could choose, after the crazy moment of their bodies surrendering, to balance out their futures, her finding a space for him in her routine, making him her husband, giving him a corner of her sacred bed, he could dedicate himself to her every day, set himself up as the head of the family, the house, with food and clean clothes, they might even believe it'd be possible to maintain that happy impatience for years on end, but that, as everyone knows, would be completely impossible, and that was just why they did it.

'Being in you twenty-four hours a day might be unsustainable, I know, but not being in you is unbearable, I'm sure',

when they awoke they were still by each other's side, neither one of them understood it, and that was why they went back to sleep in peace, whoever you want to share your sleeping with is the person with whom you ought to share your life, however unromantic that might be, and yet it's actually not.

'Less shaving, more loving.'

Your hands are on me and I obey, of course, I put down the blade, I even cut myself on the chin but what does that matter?, I feel like saying I love your mouth and everything that comes with it but I don't get the time, there's so much to feel and only one body to ensure it, and preserving a love is delivering it from evil, amen.

I do truly love you but I have a secret I can't tell you, because there are always words I can't say to you, gestures I can't make, there are things that have to be kept far away from in between us, and preserving a love is delivering it from evil, amen.

I do truly love you but I have a secret I can't tell you, it isn't the secret of how your lips open to mine, nor even how important your skin is for preserving the balance in my nature, least of all of the moment when you look inside me and I'd like to believe in God and only then in you, and preserving a love is delivering it from evil, amen.

I do truly love you but I have a secret I can't tell you, I could say I want to forget you all the time, tear you out of me and never see you again, that would already be too painful to be said but it's not that, not least because after wanting to forget you what I want is to remember you for ever, keep you in the inexplicable moment of my memory, fall asleep with the recollection of you in my lap, or of your pleasure when we go into the night without death impeding us, I want to forget you all the time, like I said, and then I want to remember you for ever, and preserving a love is delivering it from evil, amen.

I do truly love you but I have a secret I can't tell you, not because I don't want to but because you know it already, that's the only possible explanation, we agreed ten o'clock and you never showed up, and I just stood here restlessly waiting for you and you didn't come, I'm sure you already knew what I had to tell you and never told you, it hurts me so much to say that to you, you know?, I can bear a whole life's hurting so long as it isn't yours, just imagine how much space your tears occupy in me, the scale of your hurt in what makes me hurt, and now you don't come and it's as though I weren't here, the street is here but I'm standing still, nothing happens when you're not here, just me and a secret I didn't tell you for fear it would hurt, and maybe now it's hurting you and I'm not there, loving is also being prepared to share what hurts, and preserving a love is delivering it from evil, amen.

I do truly love you but I have a secret I can't tell you, for no particular reason, just because it's no longer a secret at all and it's already too late to tell it to you, I have an insuperable desert on your side of the bed, how many silences can missing somebody bear?, preserving a love isn't delivering it from evil after all, it's rather understanding its evil and accepting it as good, amen.

You're the most beautiful woman in the world but you don't love me,

you walk past me and you don't even register, a forced hello while you're thinking about something or other you don't tell me, you probably don't even know my name, I'm just that big, bumbling guy from work, and just a little while back I told Joana that one day I'll get tired of being yours,

but not now as I love you so.

You're the most beautiful woman in the world but I do find it hard to believe,

and I hope you like this restaurant, I spent hours thinking about what to do, I looked online for the best reviews, imagined which place you'd want to preserve as a memory of me and you for ever for the first time, fortunately Joana suggested this place to me and here we are, it seems perfect to me, but to me just having you here and knowing my name would be enough for nothing to be wrong, you know that, any minute now I promise I'll summon up the courage to kiss you,

but not now as I love you so.

You're the most beautiful woman in the world but this weather absolutely won't do,

as I wanted to look at you better and hide you inside my eyes without needing an umbrella, you chose the most beautiful dress in the world, Joana had already told me there could be no more beautiful bride than you, but to tell the truth any dress would have worked for me, and the church so full,

where did we have so many friends hidden away?,

the priest looks at us and he knows we've found God, and He must be jealous up there, what matters is that it's not long now before you'll be my wife and I'm crying now just thinking about it, I'm sorry, I'm so happy I can't cope, just give me a few minutes to be strong again,

but not now as I love you so.

You're the most beautiful woman in the world but I don't know if I can bear a house like this,

so much space taken up and an intolerable desert, I wanted to believe in the existence of us, to fight for what we could still be, but when you appear you don't bring me with you, there's a strange feeling when I hug you,

what the hell am I missing to feel the whole of you?,

Joana says it'll pass and we're not too late for happiness for ever, maybe tomorrow I'll just give up on the whole thing,

but not now as I love you so.

You're the most beautiful woman in the world but if you want to know the truth I don't love you,

Joana isn't dazzling at the altar and I'm up here forgotten with you,

how do you tell somebody that we've got lost along the way?,

it's the same priest who married us, what the hell has happened to my life, so many people, so much fear, how do you interrupt a wedding ceremony with a proposal?,

one day, I promise, I'll stop doing something like this for love,

but not now as I've wasted so much already.

Why do I write, anyway?,

the doubts every day, the tired eyes and still the urgency of a phrase, I write to ask, no more than that, or to seek out, there are so many things that hurt and nothing to explain, God's cowardice above all,

who are these people who're ruling the world?,

so many stains on the wall and not one to cover me up, I'd really like a childhood just so as not to know how you reach clear-sightedness,

bring me a bit of unconsciousness and I'll prove it right now.

Of course I believe in the genius of mankind, but with him comes everything that wounds, no invention is inoffensive, not even a poem is inoffensive, and when I write I know there's also the danger of a tear shed, a sheer blade perhaps, deep inside whoever reads me,

such a dark day today, a car horn in the distance, my mother in bed, the foolish desire to alter the world, do you think if I squeeze my eyes shut it'll change?,

this text is already too long and I just wanted to write that I don't know why I write, and I'm afraid that when somebody knows why they write they're not writing at all, I'll probably be meagre but never a bureaucrat of letters, a writer can even not write but what he can't do is not feel, there are so many geniuses who have forgotten to be ingenious,

and I like my wife so much and now I feel like crying,

and I'm really afraid a genius is whoever cries best,
bring me a bit of inconsistency and I'll prove it right now.

How stupid it is to live several lives, one is unbearable enough, somebody at a presentation asks me for an autograph and calls me blessed, oh, the magic of ignorance, nobody can imagine what it is to write, and nor can I, and that's why I write,

for how many lives must there be sufferings in the world?,

and I'm so lost this morning, I woke up with my fingers hurting, the index finger discovered the first few words and the rest is what you can see, I don't know where this is going but it's already reached my depths,

what is this water that's coming out of my eyes?,

there must be a character being born, and it hurts so much knowing I'm going to kill her,

my God, so many deaths in a writer's hand, when I'm big I want to have just one life, to be born, and grow, and die,

anybody who needs fingers to write is a one-handed writer, it just occurred to me,

and I could write a whole poem about this but my wife has woken up, there's always a kiss to calm an artist, fortunately I'm not an artist and I have the right to several of them and a lot of hugs, too,

see you soon,

bring me a bit of humour and I'll prove it right now.

Obscenity is suffering,

it's what can be heard in the back row of the bus, seventy-five seated places, thirty-two standing, more than a hundred people in there and so many empty spaces, one man and another man and a strange conversation in the row in front, it's not normal finding words like that at eight on a Monday morning, life stops us thinking about it, the great benefit of living is that it prevents us from looking, nobody thinks about the meaning of life when they're busy fighting to stay alive,

Either obscenity or death,

the same man in the same row, the same bus, she can't see his face but she's suddenly taken with his hair, how strange life is when you can love someone without knowing what they look like, maybe that's exactly how it is, maybe that's how it has to be, loving always happens without knowing what someone looks like, when you love and you know what they look like right away it can be so good but it's not love, pleasure perhaps, but not love, loving is this, one man talking to another and we only know his hair and we already love him like crazy, you love the words first and only then comes the person, in the beginning was the word, and only afterwards came the slave,

Hypocrisy is what's obscene,

the journey is coming to an end and it cannot come to an end, the man is talking to the other man, what's obscene is wanting him so much already and not knowing how, it doesn't matter why when the big question is how, she could find out what he's called, maybe ask someone who knows him, it's a big city but someone's got to know him, right?, then just by chance she could sit down next to him and that man, or opposite, these seats that force people to face each other have to be good for something, and out of nothing, who knows, she could set out her theory about obscenity, it would begin quite simply,

Obscenity is loving you,

then she would go red as a tomato, the skin can't lie, we all know that, he'd look at her and with any luck he'd go red too and a few minutes later they'd already be on the patio of some café, or, God forgive me for the thought, in some bedroom, it would feel so obscene and still the words wouldn't be lacking,

Obscenity is not to be fucking,

it was a punch and a kiss at the same time, and what the hell is the use of something that isn't a punch and a kiss at the same time?, the journey ended and he finished those words, she woke up, she was still a long way from her usual stop, the store had to be open at ten as usual, what do we do when there's nothing decisive to influence our decision?, she could lose her job but she mustn't lose out on the moment, that was what she thought and she made a mental note, she had just conceived her life philosophy, her new life philosophy, I can lose my job but I mustn't lose out on the moment, she said again, once, twice, him just there in front, just two or three steps ahead, she's already seen a bit of his profile, an elongated nose, perfect, and the deep, dark look in his eyes, how many looks like that do we need before we go blind once and for all?,

I can lose my job but I mustn't lose out on the moment,

and this time he heard her, she said it out loud and he

heard her, he turned, smiled, approached her, only if you've never loved can you claim that time never stops,

I was afraid you wouldn't come,

and neither of them called it a kiss even if their lips did meet and their tongues and all that, they always called it 'that', they never explained why, possibly because they never found a better name, or just because the opposite of 'this' is 'that' and if love isn't what takes us out of this to that then it's quite possibly no use at all,

Obscenity is not to be fucking,

and they were prudish for at least that whole night long.

He eats a crust of hard bread, and he's happy,

the kid on the street, and he cares for nothing,

in happy people there's a condescending morality, a kind of satisfied detachment,

the small, thin hands, the smiling look in the eyes, he walks as though jumping, or even as though flying, it makes you want to hug him and run away at the same time, how many bad things can an angel do?,

he's very cold, and he's happy,

my bones hurt, one day I'll snap on the inside, I swear it, the damn boy has a thin jersey on and he doesn't stop smiling, his eyes looking all around him, wide open, every second there's a new discovery, when did I lose my capacity for discovering, for fuck's sake?,

and I'm still so addicted to completely crazy things,

one mad idea is to take the boy with me, give him everything he's lacking, a school too, why not?, but then I look at him more carefully and I understand that it's on the street that he feels at home, how many people can a free person run from?,

he's so alone, and he's happy,

he stops in front of a grown-up in a suit and tie and holds out his hand,

an unfortunate wretch isn't someone who doesn't find, an unfortunate wretch is someone who has nothing to look for,

he tells him about his poor family, about his poor life, his poor destiny, immediately strikes a wretched pose, I'd almost swear he really was crying,

the ghetto is where theatre was born, I'm sure of it,

the face with black smudges, not long ago I saw him dirtying it on purpose, and within a few seconds he has one or two coins in his hand, he doesn't even say goodbye and races off, how many coins are enough to make you a millionaire?,

he's such a liar, and he's happy,

no idea where he's going, still less where he came from,

what has happened to his life?,

and me here following him, a morning devoted to learning who he might be,

I'd like to understand what makes me go but as long as I don't understand I'll just keep going,

and I see now that he knows I'm following him, how could he not have noticed if I'm sure he even knows the meaning of life, the little brat?, he looks sidelong at me regularly and I can almost make out his mischievous smile, hidden on some filthy corner or other, when because of some oil on the road I fall flat on my face and smash my nose against the tarmac, somebody helps me, I struggle to my feet,

whenever we need to get up we finally see we're just these bloody old people, I learn,

and there in the distance, at the top of the avenue, there he is, looking at me and smiling at me, a little victor toasting the big man he's defeated, and then running really far away, my inadequacy preventing me from going with him, how many falls does a hero need?,

he's so cruel, and he's happy,

it's hard for me to get home, it's hard on my legs of

course, it's hard on my back, it's even hard on my feet, but what's hardest is not knowing about him,

I've an insatiable appetite for intolerable stories,

I sit in the rocking chair and write these words, write this column to try and find him, might he read after all?, I imagine him under his favourite bridge, newspaper in hand, my photo at the top of the page,

look at the old guy I humiliated the other day,

and finally he lies down with his little head on the page,

you're going to be my pillow today, old man,

and I don't understand these tears I cry for him, if I'm the old man with just a house, how many homeless people exist in the city's buildings?,

and I envy him so much, and I'm happy.

We is,

a mistake in verb agreement, spoken by a northerner with a Matosinhos accent,

can you love an accent?,

a singular combined with a plural, a construction that's impossible and yet perfect, her hands on my face, then her big eyes, the inside of her veins and I melt completely,

what's the point of all that grammar crap if getting it wrong feels so good?,

we is,

she doesn't believe in bad people, she doesn't believe in forgiving, she believes in going all the way with what you attempt,

happiness exists or death, she tells me countless times,

yesterday she showed up here dressed as a mermaid, would you believe it, she could hardly walk and she was laughing so hard, she's crazy and I can only stay sane with her, I don't know what to write to show her how things ought to be, one day I'll invent the theatre of the insane, or the play of the true, or a novel of people who're nuts, something to pay tribute to her, whatever, in the meantime I'll devote myself to loving her and I really fear I might never get past this stage,

people are strange, did you know?,

she asks me, she's already covering me with kisses, she's already taken off my trousers and she's already looking for the beginning of the orgasm, but not even this prevents her from explaining the rationality of her choices, even philosophy can give you pleasure, at least mine can,

I'm only prepared to cherish a person I love, you see,

and I say yes, she laughs out loud, she touches me gently with her tongue on my skin, she finds another virgin centimetre and I shiver, there's an immensity of shivers and only one life, for the years we live we have too much body to explore, dammit,

I'm only prepared to respect a person I love, you see,

living is simple after all, I've spent my days looking for complex supports and life is so simple after all, people complicate things and they are strange, that's what I think for a second or two, no more than that, there's a kind of electric current feeding my brain, I swear I wouldn't know where she's touched me but I'm alive, thinking is such a big drought when you could be doing,

people love without looking at themselves, you see,

it makes sense, when her mouth takes hold of mine I find nothing that doesn't make sense, to tell the truth, but it makes sense, I was saying, that way I'm able to complete my reasoning, I'll try, it makes sense because people are strange and when they love they don't love themselves, I'd so like to write a whole thesis on the need to not be completely in somebody else's hands but she's on top of me and I don't have time,

we is,

and in spite of it all I'm the one who's in charge of myself, who does she think is?, I'm the one who dictates things for myself, let me make that absolutely clear, I know it's me and I'm always going to do whatever I want and only what I want,

so long as it's what she wants too.

So many people in a bad way with a steering wheel in their hands, dear God,

there's a kind of obscene sharing that happens when you stop at a red light, the whole city in half a dozen cars, the inside of people's eyes, the taxi driver who tells me the story of his mother, poor woman, may she rest in peace, next to a middle-aged woman, or maybe younger but she looks middle-aged or even older than that,

faces are strange things, aren't they?,

every face is born with the faculty to lie prodigiously, that's enough to tell us what we're here for, why we were born, if we weren't meant to lie we'd be simply incapable of doing so, like flying, for example,

the worst people are those who fly the least, I'm quite sure of that,

the taxi driver is still telling me about his mother, the middle-aged woman looks out into infinity, occasionally scratches her blonde hair, turns the radio up, I'd like to hear what she can hear so as to know more about what she's feeling, I need to know about people, guess them, have an integrated sense of their states of mind,

who was it who invented sadness, does anyone know?,

on the other side a boy, ten or eleven years old, he's drawing on the glass with his fingers, he's misted it up with his own breath and now he's writing letters beneath his drawings,

childhood is the start of happiness, and the end too,

when I was small I used to hide away to watch the world,

now I just need some traffic lights, a few moments a day and I'm ready to write, all the characters in my book are people who exist even if I invent them,

a writer's a guy who manages to invent what already exists, that's just how it is,

the taxi driver's mother is a good person, she wanted him to study,

I want you to be a doctor, my son,

but people are evasive and they make unexpected choices, and then there's love, of course, some woman or other changed this man's life, it's not clear whether it was for the better,

who knows what might have been but I could never love like this, that's for sure,

he loves her so much and my sadness, the kid keeps on drawing and writing, he doesn't even notice I'm watching him, naïveté is too lovely to survive long, the middle-aged woman can no longer stand it and she cries, she doesn't know I can see her and she lets herself go, she must have a husband at home, children, a kitchen that needs tidying,

there's a difficult relationship between a kitchen that needs tidying and the dreams of a lifetime, who can say why,

I could have been a doctor but I'm happy, the taxi driver's words are the most brilliant life philosophy I've ever heard,

I could have been a doctor but I'm happy,

and I give him a banknote and tell him to keep the change, I look at the kid for a second or two, and at the woman, I say goodbye, I race out of the taxi and go in search of you, you're a bad influence and you're going to stop me writing,

but to hell with it,

how it's taken me this long to realise I have no idea, but I'm still in time, let's hope you understand, the most important thing is that I love you and I've already complied,

I could be a writer but you make me happy,

how does that sound to you?

'Fuck me like a dog but never like a poet.'

and I look at you inside those words, I could spend my whole life writing about the way your body mingles with your words, and maybe that's actually what I'm doing,

loving gently is insulting, even obscene, a kind of pretence, perhaps,

'Poetry is cool but I've never come in verse, I have to admit.'

your hands and the diabolical extension of my sex,

it was animals who discovered pleasure, the beginning of humanity happened at the beginning of pleasure, only an evolved being can understand an orgasm, let alone how to reach one,

a house without orgasms is a third-world house, or fourth-,

'Go on, come, screw me, it's not poetry but it could well be art.'

and I obey you as best I can, and I can do everything, literature that's finished in the way I hold you tight,

the rough blood is the whole poem, the blind mystery of all salvation,

it's through your veins, not through your nose or mouth, that your body breathes,

'Take my breath away at once to show me the miracle of all inspiration.'

loving you is an epiphany, a second of happiness that never passes, there are some extraordinary words and 'I'm yours' is one of them, even if it's two, your mouth with those words to explain the existence of God, and mostly of my own,

'No book has ever given me an orgasm like that, go and tell that to the Nobel people and tell them I sent you, OK?'

for a few moments I didn't know whether to laugh or cry,

is the best book the one that turns you on the most?, a couple of seconds would have been enough to answer but she was one or two seconds away from coming,

and I with her,

being a poet is also being smarter, and coming better than men, choosing who you kiss,

and I chose, I did,

'In a second or two you condense the entire meaning of life in me: so take that, Sun Tzu, and tell Confucius he can take it too.'

or 'yes!',

'I've said. But mainly I've come.'

if you weren't tragic you'd be comic,

and I laugh all the same.

'Man, have you thought how fucking lucky we are to have tomorrow? You can see how it goes? We're here, today, the two of us. And tomorrow can exist. Tomorrow really can exist. Being here, just today, just for now, just for this moment and for all these moments of today, man, that's already some amazing shit. But having tomorrow, even having the possibility of a tomorrow, that's truly unbelievable. Unbelievable. Isn't it? Imagine you just landed here on earth without knowing anything. And you start living. And you start feeling everything there is to feel (and there's so much to feel, isn't there? The smell of the trees, the flash of birds flying, how do they do that, I mean how? And then, oh man, the people; the people are something, truly something...it's like they're impossible. People seem impossible. So complex and so unique. There isn't one who's like another, not even a bit alike. All different. And their touch, and their eyes. Truly something. Their eyes are just inexplicable, right?)... So then you show up here, like I was saying, and imagine, really just imagine, try to imagine, you don't know anything till you get here. You arrive here as an adult, you land here as an adult and you've come from somewhere, you don't know where, and you were you don't know what, but you definitely weren't human, you didn't live all that as a human, and you arrive here and you see all this and you start to feel all this. And it all starts coming into your veins, flowing in your blood. And it makes you want to cry. Don't fuck with me, man. Don't fuck with me, there's no other possibility; if you landed here amid

all this and started feeling all this at once coming into you for
the first time, man, you'd really have to cry. It's too big. It's
too intense. It's too impossible, you know what I mean? It's
like this shit didn't exist. Living the way we do, with all these
possibilities (you can run, jump, shout, touch, taste, smell,
hear...and love, man. Loving is the bomb, seriously. Loving
really is impossible. Imagine you arrive here and immediately
realise that you love, that you have this unbelievable capacity
to love. What must that whole love thing be like to someone
who arrives here all of a sudden? Oh man, it'd be to die for. It'd
be something that'd make you want to stick around, feeling
that. There are so many possibilities, so many things available
to you just by being. You need only be. And these things are
there, these sensations are there)... And I think I've got myself
lost again, haven't I? Oh yes! I was telling you that with all
these possibilities to experience it's like none of it really exists.
It's like we're in some imaginary space. And that's the magic
of all this. The magic is exactly that: hell, nothing exists.
None of this exists if you don't exist. At least for you. This is
all yours. This only is because you are. If you aren't then this
thing doesn't exist, it disappears, kaput, finito, game over, get
it? But I think I'm already talking too much and maybe you
haven't yet understood what I've been trying to say from the
start. Let me start at the beginning. So...the basic thing I'm
trying to tell you is this: tomorrow there'll be a new day. Do
you understand the greatness of that? This shit is so big and
so overwhelming even for only one day, even if only for a few
minutes. If you were here, dropped down here from out of
nowhere, for only two or three minutes, you'd already leave
saying it was the best experience you'd ever had, the most

son-of-a-bitch amazing experience you've ever had. Man, one minute would be enough. And that would be that: you'd be vanquished, overwhelmed. A minute would be enough and you'd be happy for ever. But man, no. Hell, no. You'll have, and with any luck you'll have many times over, a tomorrow. Tomorrow you'll wake up (and even sleeping is awesome, even sleeping is an extreme experience, a little kid's death, entering a different zone, living different lives to yours; fuck it, it's just too good! Too good. But I'm not even going there because otherwise I'll never leave)... Tomorrow you'll wake up and you'll have the possibility of everything all over again. You can feel the same and you will feel the same, and you can even feel more. Even more, do you see? More new things. More things for the first time. You can kiss like never before, eat what you've never eaten before, see what you've never seen, say and hear what you've never before said or heard, do what you've never done. Man, it's incredible. It's a miracle. It's a fucking miracle. Inconceivable. Tomorrow you can wake up and change everything or keep everything the same. You wake up with all this within your grasp. The whole world, this whole vastness, over again. Seems impossible, doesn't it? And you still have the fucking nerve to cry so much, to complain so much, to beat yourself up so much. Better to see sense. And don't try my patience. Get away from here, go on, try being impossible. Just one more time. And then another. Go on. Be impossible. Until it really is impossible for you to do it.'

When I die I want the whole family alive beside me, tasting whisky for the first time,

and a quick cigarette just to see what it's like, by the way,

I believe in death the same way I believe in life, if I'm here and I exist for some reason then perhaps one day I'll have to stop being for the same reason,

then I'll get everyone together and we'll go to the movies, the whole family all in one cinema, I'll rent out an entire one in some shopping mall or other and we'll all be there watching the big screen,

I want a dumb romantic comedy, one of those movies with no substance at all, just so we can laugh with one another, just so we can fool around with one another,

it could be *Notting Hill*, for example, but if anybody would like to suggest something worse I wouldn't mind at all,

and João would also have to come along with one or two other friends, all the ones I've got, I've never been the type to make friends easily, and even my friends don't know everything I am and do, may God protect them from that and protect me even more,

death will be arriving at around that time, more or less halfway through the movie, but a cheerful death, a little-girl death,

and I've already imagined her and everything, in a schoolgirl's skirt, toy sunglasses, those brightly coloured ones,

they could be Hello Kitty, am I allowed to advertise in a story like this?, a nice, happy child waiting for me in a park in the city, it might even be raining, that wouldn't bother me,

death will be a happy child waiting for me in a park and that's such a lovely way to die, isn't it?,

and I'll want my cats there too, of course, has anyone ever seen kittens in a cinema?, everybody stroking them, treating them as equals,

and the cats, since I had come there to die, would allow the people to treat them as equals, they're very humble and they like me, they don't mind coming here for a few moments, they're such darlings,

when the plot of the movie is at its height, with the couple being parted, everything seeming like it has no possible resolution and everybody fed up with knowing that it's bound to end well, I'll already be switching off completely, I'd like to start with my eyes, to be able to devote myself entirely to feeling,

you can feel better with your eyes closed, haven't you ever felt that?,

nothing that matters in life happens when you have your eyes open, orgasms, dreams,

death must surely be a good thing, if it mostly consists of closing your eyes for ever that can't be bad, right?,

and I wouldn't want to make a big speech, and definitely not to suffer,

suffering is a son of a bitch, I hope when I die that I'll be able to explain it better, there's got to be a reason that's beyond me why pain exists, and it's probably a really cool reason and I'll laugh myself silly when I discover it, if only,

so I'll just thank everyone, not bothering them too much

since by now the movie would be nearly over, and me with it, ask them never to forget a happy ending, of course, but a happy middle even more so,

it's the road that defines us, never the destination, everyone ends up at death, see?,

then I'll stop hearing, and I'll be left with the smells, the recollections, my mother's words when she kissed me, my father's voice when he hugged me, the car horns honking, the wonder of the breeze at the window,

you ought to know you have all this, are you happy or aren't you?,

at these moments the highly anticipated end will be arriving, the family so moved, by the film and not by me because I won't allow it,

because I'm only dying and that's no sadness when I'm dying the way I want to die,

the last bit of me that I want to go is my hand, just one would be enough, the right or the left, either way,

I play table tennis equally well with both hands, I can also die equally well with one or the other, no doubt about that,

an ambidextrous death, that's pretty fancy, isn't it?,

we'll be complete, you and I, inside my hand, I'll be able to feel that very first time, on the train, Porto to Lisbon so quickly, me inside your tall boots,

you still have them, don't you?, please tell them I love them,

and I could even end there but I won't be able to resist running my hand over your whole body, understanding every one of your wrinkles, until finally,

the main characters in the movie are already racing

towards each other and it looks like they aren't going to make it in time, can that be right?,

your hand calming my fear,

however much death might be a happy girl playing in the park, it does make me afraid, you do understand that, don't you?,

and at last I stop being,

they lived happily ever after,

and I love you,

and I you.

Pedro Chagas Freitas is a Portuguese writer, journalist, editor and professional public speaker who has published more than twenty works. He studied linguistics and teaches creative writing.

Daniel Hahn is a writer, editor and translator with fifty-something books to his name. His translations (from Portuguese, Spanish and French) include fiction and non-fiction for children and adults, from Europe, Africa and the Americas. His work has won him the Independent Foreign Fiction Prize, the Blue Peter Book Award and the International Dublin Literary Award, among others, and been shortlisted for the Man Booker International Prize and the *LA Times* Book Prize.

Oneworld, Many Voices

Bringing you exceptional writing
from around the world

The Unit by Ninni Holmqvist (Swedish)
Translated by Marlaine Delargy

Twice Born by Margaret Mazzantini (Italian)
Translated by Ann Gagliardi

Things We Left Unsaid by Zoya Pirzad (Persian)
Translated by Franklin Lewis

The Space Between Us by Zoya Pirzad (Persian)
Translated by Amy Motlagh

The Hen Who Dreamed She Could Fly by Sun-mi Hwang
(Korean) Translated by Chi-Young Kim

The Hilltop by Assaf Gavron (Hebrew)
Translated by Steven Cohen

Morning Sea by Margaret Mazzantini (Italian)
Translated by Ann Gagliardi

A Perfect Crime by A Yi (Chinese)
Translated by Anna Holmwood

The Meursault Investigation by Kamel Daoud (French)
Translated by John Cullen

Minus Me by Ingelin Røssland (YA) (Norwegian)
Translated by Deborah Dawkin

Laurus by Eugene Vodolazkin (Russian)
Translated by Lisa C. Hayden

Masha Regina by Vadim Levental (Russian)
Translated by Lisa C. Hayden

French Concession by Xiao Bai (Chinese)
Translated by Chenxin Jiang

The Sky Over Lima by Juan Gómez Bárcena (Spanish)
Translated by Andrea Rosenberg

A Very Special Year by Thomas Montasser (German)
Translated by Jamie Bulloch

Umami by Laia Jufresa (Spanish)
Translated by Sophie Hughes

The Hermit by Thomas Rydahl (Danish)
Translated by K.E. Semmel

The Peculiar Life of a Lonely Postman by Denis Thériault
(French) Translated by Liedewy Hawke

Three Envelopes by Nir Hezroni (Hebrew)
Translated by Steven Cohen

Fever Dream by Samanta Schweblin (Spanish)
Translated by Megan McDowell

The Postman's Fiancée by Denis Thériault (French)
Translated by John Cullen

The Invisible Life of Euridice Gusmao by Martha Batalha
(Brazilian Portuguese) Translated by Eric M. B. Becker

The Temptation to Be Happy by Lorenzo Marone
(Italian) Translated by Shaun Whiteside

Sweet Bean Paste by Durian Sukegawa (Japanese)
Translated by Alison Watts

They Know Not What They Do by Jussi Valtonen (Finnish)
Translated by Kristian London

The Tiger and the Acrobat by Susanna Tamaro (Italian)
Translated by Nicoleugenia Prezzavento and Vicki Satlow

The Woman at 1,000 Degrees by Hallgrímur Helgason
(Icelandic) Translated by Brian FitzGibbon

Frankenstein in Baghdad by Ahmed Saadawi (Arabic)
Translated by Jonathan Wright

Back Up by Paul Colize (French)
Translated by Louise Rogers Lalaurie

Damnation by Peter Beck (German)
Translated by Jamie Bulloch

Oneiron by Laura Lindstedt (Finnish)
Translated by Owen Witesman

The Boy Who Belonged to the Sea by Denis Thériault
(French) Translated by Liedewy Hawke

The Baghdad Clock by Shahad Al Rawi (Arabic)
Translated by Luke Leafgren

The Aviator by Eugene Vodolazkin (Russian)
Translated by Lisa C. Hayden

Lala by Jacek Dehnel (Polish)
Translated by Antonia Lloyd-Jones

Bogotá 39: New Voices from Latin America
(Spanish and Portuguese) Short story anthology

Last Instructions by Nir Hezroni (Hebrew)
Translated by Steven Cohen

The Day I Found You by Pedro Chagas Freitas (Portuguese)
Translated by Daniel Hahn

Solovyov and Larionov by Eugene Vodolazkin (Russian)
Translated by Lisa C. Hayden

In/Half by Jasmin B. Frelih (Slovenian)
Translated by Jason Blake